LINDA LAEL MILLER

The LEGACY

Books by Linda Lael Miller

The Legacy
Taming Charlotte
Yankee Wife
Daniel's Bride
Caroline and the Raider
Emma and the Outlaw
Lily and the Major
My Darling Melissa
Angelfire
Moonfire
Wanton Angel
Lauralee
Memory's Embrace
Corbin's Fancy
Willow
Banner O'Brien
Desire and Destiny
Fletcher's Woman

Published by POCKET BOOKS

LINDA LAEL MILLER

The LEGACY

POCKET STAR BOOKS

New York   London   Toronto   Sydney   Tokyo   Singapore

An *Original* Publication of POCKET BOOKS

A Pocket Star Book published by
POCKET BOOKS, a division of Simon & Schuster Inc.
1230 Avenue of the Americas, New York, NY 10020

Copyright © 1994 by Linda Lael Miller

ISBN: 0-671-79792-1

Cover art by Mitzura Salgian

Printed in the U.S.A.

For my lovely Aussie friend
and kindred spirit,
Jennifer Gibbs,
with much, much love

LINDA LAEL MILLER

The LEGACY

1

Ian Yarbro was in no mood for a party.

Dingoes had brought down four of his best sheep just since Monday.

Water holes all over the property were coming up dry.

And worst of all, Jacy Tiernan, damn her, was back from America.

The first two plights were sorry ones, all right, but a man had to expect a fair portion of grief if he undertook to raise sheep in South Australia. That last bit, though, *that* was something personal, an individualized curse from God.

With a resounding sigh Ian leaned back against the south wall of the shearing shed, a mug of beer in one sore, lacerated hand, and scowled. Every muscle in his body throbbed, for he'd shorn more squirming woollies than any man on his crew in the days just past, and he felt as though he could sleep for a month, should the opportunity arise. That wasn't going to happen, of course, not with all he had to do around the place.

Ian took another sip from his beer, which had lost its

1

appeal while he pondered his troubles, and surveyed the rustic festivities.

The music of the fiddles and mouth harps seemed to loop and swirl like invisible ribbon in the warm summer twilight. Shearers and roustabouts alike clomped round and round the long wooden floor of the shed, some dancing with women, some with each other. The night air was weighted with heat, since it was January, speckled with dust and bits of wool fiber and rife with the smells of sweat and brewer's yeast, cheap cologne and cigarette smoke.

And Jacy was back.

Ian muttered a curse. It had been bad enough, this past day or so, knowing Jacy was living right next door at Corroboree Springs, but at least she'd had the good grace to keep her distance. Until about five minutes before, that is, when she'd walked into the celebration with her father.

Ian could have ignored her completely, and would have, if it hadn't meant slighting Jake. Jacy's father was one of the best mates Ian had ever had, and he was just out of hospital as it was. Collie Kilbride had flown the pair of them, Jake and his daughter, up from Adelaide in his vintage plane the day before yesterday. If he was going to live with himself, Ian reasoned sourly, he'd have to go over to Jake and shake his hand and tell him it was good to see him up and about again. No need for so much as a glance in Jacy's direction, as far as he could see, but if an acknowledgment was required, he'd just nod at her in the most civil fashion he could manage.

Frowning, he pushed away from the wall, tossed what remained of his beer through the open doorway of the shed, and handed the mug off to Alice Wigget as he passed her. Wending his way between the spinning couples was like moving through the gears of some enormous machine.

The colored light from the paper lanterns dangling from the rafters played in Jacy's fair hair, which just reached her shoulders and curled riotously around her face. She'd put on a bit of weight since he'd seen her last, as well. Too bad, Ian thought uncharitably, that it had all settled nicely into just the right places.

Drawing nearer still, Ian saw that Jacy's blue-green eyes were luminous with affection as she gazed up at her father's face. She was good at *looking* as if she gave a damn, but where had she been for all those years, while Jake's luck was getting worse and worse by the day? Where had she been when her dad's health had started failing?

Ian was seething by the time he reached them. He felt a muscle twitch in his cheek, set his jaw in an effort to control the response, then thrust out his hand to Jake.

"It's about time you got back and started tending your property, instead of leaving the whole place for your mates to look after," he said, half barking the words. Even though he tried hard, he couldn't force a smile to his mouth.

Jake, always good-natured and full of the devil, had no such problem. He beamed as he pumped Ian's hand, but his grasp was not the knuckle-crusher it had once been, and he was thin to the point of emaciation. There were deep shadows under Jake's pale blue eyes, and his face had a skeletal look about it.

"Well, then," Tiernan teased, "let's see what you've made of the job before you go complaining too loudly, Ian Yarbro. I've just been back for these two days, and for all I know, you've 'helped' me straight into the poorhouse."

Ian was painfully conscious of Jacy's nearness; he felt her gaze on him, caught the muted, musky scent of her perfume. And, God help him, he remembered too damned much about how things had been between them, once upon a time.

"Hello, Ian," she said. He felt her voice, too—soft and smoky, evoking all kinds of sensory reactions.

She was going to force him to acknowledge her. He should have known it wouldn't be enough for her, just coming there and stirring up all those old memories again.

He forced himself to look down into her upturned face and instantly regretted the decision. Jacy was twenty-eight

3

now, as he was, and far more beautiful than she'd been at eighteen. He saw a flicker of some tentative, hopeful emotion in her eyes.

"Hello," he replied, and the word came out sounding gravelly and rusted, as though he hadn't used it in a long time. Jake and the shearers and the roustabouts and their women seemed to fade into a pounding void, and there was only Jacy. Ian hated knowing she could still affect him that way, and he hated her, too, for ripping open all the old wounds inside him.

The dancers pounded and thumped around them, shaking the weathered floorboards, and Ian had an unsteady feeling, as though he might tumble, headlong and helpless, into the depths of Jacy Tiernan's eyes. He didn't notice that the music had stopped until it started again, louder than before, and strangely shrill.

Jake put one hand on Jacy's back and one on Ian's, then pushed them toward each other with a gentle but effective thrust. "I think I'll sit this one out," he shouted, to be heard over the din, and then he stumped away through the crowd.

By no wish of his own Ian found himself holding his first love in his arms. He swallowed hard, battling a schoolboy urge to bolt, and began to shuffle awkwardly back and forth, staring over the top of her head. Jacy moved with him, and they were both out of step with the music.

Nothing new in that.

"Is it really so terrible," she asked, in the familiar Yankee accent that had haunted his memories for a decade, "dancing with me?"

"Don't," he warned. The word was part warning, part plea.

Ian felt exasperation move through Jacy's body like a current, though he was barely touching her.

"Will you just lighten up?" she hissed, standing on tiptoe to speak into his ear. "You're not the only one who's uncomfortable, you know!"

Ian's emotions were complex, and he couldn't begin to sort them out. That nettled him, for he was a logical man, and he hated chaos, especially within himself. He wanted to shake Jacy Tiernan for all she'd put him through, but he also wanted to make love to her. He was furious that she'd come back, but at one and the same time he felt like scrambling onto the roof and shouting out the news of her return.

He clasped her forearm—it was bare and smooth, since she was wearing a sleeveless cotton sundress—and half dragged her to the door and down the wooden ramp to the ground. The farmyard was filled with cars and trucks, and the homestead was a long, low shadow some distance away.

"What are you doing here?" he demanded in an outraged whisper.

Jacy raised her chin and put her hands on her hips. Her pale yellow dress seemed to shimmer in the rich light of the moon and stars, and her eyes sparked with silver fire. "That depends on what you mean by 'here,' " she retorted just as furiously. "If you mean why am I here at this damn party, then the answer is, because my father wanted to come and see all his friends and neighbors, and I came along to make sure he didn't overdo and land himself back in the hospital. If, on the other hand, you meant why am I in Australia, well, that should be obvious. My dad had a heart attack, and I'm here to look after him."

Ian was fairly choking on the tangle of things he felt; he might have turned and put a fist through the rickety wall of the shed if his hands hadn't already been swollen and cut from all the times he'd caught his own flesh in the clippers while shearing sheep. "Ten years you stayed away," he said instead. *"Ten years.* Do you think he didn't need you in all that time?" Do you think I didn't need you? he thought.

Her eyes brimmed with tears, and because Ian wasn't expecting that, he was wounded by the sight.

"Damn it, Ian," she said, "there's no need to make this

so difficult! I'm here, and I plan to stay for an indefinite period of time. If you can't accept the fact, fine, just stay out of my way, and I'll stay out of yours. When we have the misfortune to run into each other, let's try to be civil, shall we? For Jake's sake, if nothing else.''

Ian couldn't speak. He was reeling from her announcement that she wouldn't be leaving the area anytime soon. Only one thing would make him crazier than her absence, and that was having her live at Corroboree Springs day in and day out.

Naturally, she couldn't leave well enough alone and keep her mouth shut. Oh, no. That would never have done.

"Well?" she prompted with a sort of nasty sweetness.

Ian shoved a hand through his dark hair. With all the business of mustering and shearing the sheep, then dipping them in disinfectant to prevent infection in the inevitable scrapes and cuts and to keep the blowflies away, he'd let it grow too long, and it felt shaggy between his fingers.

"You should have stayed in America," he said stubbornly. "Jake has mates here. We'd have been glad to look after him, with no help from you."

She dried her eyes with the heel of one palm, smearing the stuff she wore on her lashes, and then tossed her head. "God, Ian, you can be *such* a bastard. Would it kill you to be polite, at least?"

"Would it have killed *you* to say good-bye before you left?" he snapped, regretting the words even as they tumbled from his mouth. "Even 'go to hell' or 'drop dead' would have been better than just leaving the way you did."

"So now it was all my fault!" she flared, making less of an effort to keep her voice down that time. "Has it escaped you that Elaine Bennett came up to us in front of the movie house in Yolanda and announced that she was carrying your baby?" She threw out her hands for emphasis. "But maybe you *did* forget. After all, you certainly never got around to mentioning that you'd been sleeping with her while we were going together!"

6

Ian tilted his head back and glared up at the stars. He didn't know why he bothered to tell her, since she'd never believe him, but the truth was all he had to offer. There had been many occasions in Ian's life when a lie would have been convenient, but he'd never gotten the knack of it. When he tried, he stuttered and his neck turned a dull red, so he'd long since given it up.

"Elaine and I were all through before I ever touched you, Jacy." He made himself meet her eyes and saw there the incredulity he'd feared all along. "And somewhere deep inside yourself, you know it. You knew it then. You just needed something to throw between us, some excuse to run away, because you were scared to death of what you were feeling!"

Jacy retreated a step and hugged herself as if a chill had struck her, even though it was nearly ten-thirty and still hot enough to smother a camel. "Okay, so I was scared," she murmured testily, but with less conviction than before. "I was only eighteen."

"So was I," Ian responded brusquely, giving no ground whatsoever. "And I was just as frightened as you were. But what I felt for you was real, and so was the hell I went through when you walked out on me."

It was all he could trust himself to say. He turned to walk away toward the long, one-story cement homestead he shared with his nine-year-old son, Chris, intending to wait out the party there. Chances were, no one would miss him.

She clasped his arm, and Ian stopped cold, bracing himself, refusing to turn and face her. "I'm sorry, Ian," she said. "Please believe that."

He wrenched free. It wasn't good enough, after the way he'd suffered. "Do us both a favor," he said, still refusing to look at her. "Go back to America and stay there." With that he strode off toward the dark and empty house, where the light and music of the party wouldn't reach, and it was like walking into his own soul.

* * *

7

Jacy stood watching as Ian disappeared into the shadows, trembling a little, flinching when she heard a door slam in the distance. She hadn't expected their first meeting in ten years to be easy—not after the way things had ended for them—but she hadn't anticipated anything so wrenching and difficult as this, either.

She needed time to compose herself, not wanting her dad and the friends, neighbors, and workers jammed into Ian's shearing shed to see how shaken she was, so she sat down on a crate in the shadows, drew a deep breath, and folded her arms. Some of the things Ian had said stuck in her spirit the way briars and nettles stuck in the sheeps' wool and the callused fingers of the shearers—especially that bit about her being afraid of the love she'd felt for him. It had been as vast and deep as an ocean, that youthful adulation, full of treacherous beauty and alive with mysterious currents. She'd thought, sometimes, that the great waves would encompass her one day, and she'd drown.

Jacy sighed, looking up at the summer moon, mentally tracing its gray ridges and valleys of cold light. Another of Ian's accusations had struck its mark, too; she'd neglected her dad, keeping her distance those ten long years when she'd known how much her visits meant to him. It had been hard staying away, because she and Jake had always been kindred souls, but she simply hadn't been ready to face Ian.

She still wasn't, she supposed, though she hadn't had much choice in the matter.

"Jacy-me-girl?"

Startled by her father's voice, gentle as it was, Jacy jumped a little and turned her head quickly.

Jake was standing at the base of the ramp, leaning on the cane he'd been using since he left the hospital. His heart attack had left him weakened and gaunt, and Jacy still hadn't gotten used to the change in him. He'd been so strong as a younger man, as vital and tireless as Ian, though always more good-natured.

"It didn't go well, then?" he asked in the lilting accent she loved.

Jacy blushed, knowing Jake had had hopes of his own for the evening. He had been a second father to Ian, since the elder Yarbros had passed on within a few years of each other, when Ian was still very young. Jake had never made a secret of his belief that Jacy and Ian belonged together.

"It couldn't have been worse," she said with a sigh and a rueful, shaky smile. "Except if he'd drawn a gun and shot me, that is."

Jake made his way to the crate with a slow awkwardness that was painful to see, then took a seat beside his daughter. "Give him time," he counseled. "Ian's a hardheaded sort, you know."

"I hadn't noticed," Jacy mocked, but she moved a little closer to her dad and let her head rest against his thin shoulder.

Jake patted her hand. "Once he works it all through, he'll come 'round."

Jacy stiffened. "I don't want him to 'come around,' Dad. Not in the way you mean, at least."

The glow of the moon only highlighted the amused skepticism in Jake's face. "Is that so? Then I'll confess to wondering why a simple shearing shed would be filled to the rafters with blue lightning from the moment the two of you spotted one another. There was so much electricity flying about in there that I'd have been afraid to step in a puddle of spilled beer."

Jacy couldn't help smiling at his description of the tension that had coiled between her and Ian earlier in the evening. She slipped her arm around Jake and said, "I've missed you a whole lot."

"Don't be changing the subject," he replied, his accent thicker than ever. It happened whenever he was being mischievous or having trouble controlling his emotions. "This is a small community, and you and Ian won't be able to avoid each other forever. You'll need to settle things."

9

She linked her fingers with her dad's and squeezed. Jake had a point; Ian's property bordered their own, and if that wasn't enough, they were bound to meet in nearby Yolanda, in the post office and the shops. Or in Willoughby, the slightly larger town fifty kilometers to the northeast, where homesteaders and townspeople alike went to see the doctor, purchase supplies, and attend to various other errands that couldn't be taken care of in Yolanda.

"Are you sure you wouldn't like to come back to the States with me, just until you're feeling strong again?" she ventured, though she knew as she spoke what the answer would be. Jake had nothing against America—he'd married a Yank, after all—but he'd often said he was no more suited to the place than a kangaroo was to Manhattan.

He simply arched an eyebrow.

"All right," Jacy burst out. "Then we'll go up to Cairns again, like we did when I was twelve. We could collect seashells and lie out in the sun and eat those wonderful giant avocados." She still had some of the colorful shells she'd gathered back then, displayed on a shelf in her room at the homestead. To her the shells symbolized eternity and the extravagant, careless continuity of life. "We could leave tomorrow. What do you say?"

"I say that you're trying to run away again." Jake paused, still gripping her hand, to study the spectacular display of stars, their majesty undimmed by the lights of any city. When he looked at her again, the expression in his eyes was sad and gentle. "You've done enough of that in your young life, Jacy. It's time to stop now, and face matters head on."

She averted her eyes, afraid of all that was in her heart, good and bad, noble and ignoble, terrified that all those mixed-up emotions would spill over and disgrace her if she let down her guard for so much as a moment. There was no point in denying her father's words anyway, because he was right—Jacy's unspoken credo had always been *She who loves and runs away, lives to love another day.*

10

Only she had never loved again. Not before Ian, and certainly not after.

"What do I do now?" she asked in a soft voice.

"Nothing much," Jake replied easily. Tenderly. "Just stand still for a time, Jacy-me-girl. That's all. Just hold your ground and see what comes toward you."

She laughed, but the sound resembled a sob. "What if it's a freight train?"

Jake chuckled, slipped an arm around her shoulders, and gave her a brief hug. "See that you don't stand on the railroad tracks, love. Now let's take ourselves home, shall we? I'm tuckered."

Jacy was relieved to be leaving Ian's place. At the same time she was worried about Jake's physical condition. "You're all right, aren't you?" she asked, peering at him anxiously. "We could drive over to Willoughby and see the doctor, just to be on the safe side—"

"And rouse the poor bloke from his bed?" Jake spoke amicably, as he almost always did, but Jacy knew the suggestion had annoyed him because he shook off her hand when she tried to help him stand. "Get a grip on yourself, sheila. I can't go waltzing off to the doctor every time I feel a bit worn down, now can I?"

Wisely, Jacy said nothing. She just walked along at Jake's side, and when they reached his dusty old truck she got behind the wheel and left him to hoist himself into the vehicle on his own.

Jacy rose early the next morning, even before Jake was up. It was her third day back, but she was still greedy for the sights and sounds and smells of the place. She loved the house, with its green lawn and sheltering pepper trees and the old-fashioned roses Grandmother Matty had planted at one end of the veranda. Loved the shed, although there were no horses there now, and the paddocks, though there were no sheep. As little time as she had spent there, the homestead and the land surrounding it were dear

11

to her in a way her mother and stepfather's luxurious townhouse in Manhattan had never been.

She lingered on the veranda for a while, watching the sunlight sparkle and dance on the surface of the spring-fed pond a little distance away, in the midst of a copse of thirsty trees. From there the water flowed away through the paddock in a wide stream, eventually forming the border between the Tiernan land and Merimbula, the huge cattle station to the south.

Standing still, she heard her mother's voice in her mind. "You're an Aussie through and through," Regina had often said, always adding a long sigh for effect. "It's in your blood, that hot, lonely, harsh place, and for that, my darling, I offer you my sincerest apologies."

Jacy smiled. She'd spent most of her life in America, but there was an element of truth in her mother's words. She *was* an Aussie, in so many ways.

Some of her pleasure faded. Despite her Australian heritage, Ian and not a few other people would always view her as an outsider. It would be naïve to believe her former lover was the only one who thought she'd failed Jake by staying away all those years; in the bush, where everyday life was a challenge, abandoning someone was just about the worst thing a person could do. A betrayal of one was a betrayal of all, and the homesteaders around Yolanda had long, long memories where such matters were concerned.

She turned reluctantly and went back into the cool shelter of the house.

Jake was still sleeping, apparently, so she returned to her own room and pulled Grandmother Matty's handmade quilt off the bed. The coverlet hadn't been washed in a long time, and it had a musty smell to it.

In the homestead's primitive kitchen Jacy heated water on the gas-powered stove, making as little noise as possible. Then she rinsed out the quilt in the kitchen sink, wrung it gently, and carried it out to the clothesline in back of the house. When it was drying in the warm morning sun she

12

brewed a cup of tea and sat on the back step to drink it, watching with delight as a mob of kangaroos sprang across the paddock separating her father's property from Ian's.

She was exhausted, and not just from the hasty trip across the international date line, after she'd learned about Jake's heart attack, and the long vigil at the hospital in Adelaide that had followed. There were troubles waiting back in the States, snarls to untangle, things that, true to form, she'd run away from.

The way she'd run away from Ian.

"Ian." She spoke the name softly, but aloud, and it hurt more than she would ever have expected. Memories overtook her like a bushfire; tears stung her eyes, a sob escaped her, and finally she knew it was futile to try to hold back her grief any longer. She wept in earnest.

When the personal storm was over Jacy sniffled, tilted her head back, and closed her puffy eyes. Scenes from that awful time ten years before played on the screen of her mind in Technicolor and stereo.

She made herself walk through the memories, facing them one by one. Having done that, she reasoned, she might be able to look Ian in the eye the next time they met without losing her dignity.

Jacy saw in her thoughts a smaller and wilder version of her sophisticated twenty-eight-year-old self, a sunburned waif in blue jeans. Her dark blond hair had been short then, and she'd ridden all over the property, and some parts of those adjoining it, on her aging white mare, Biscuit. She'd been free as a gypsy in those days, knowing nothing of heartache. Even her parents' divorce hadn't truly touched her, for she'd been too young to remember leaving the homestead with her mother, and she'd made the long trip Down Under often throughout her childhood to stay with Jake.

Ian, like Jacy, had been just eighteen the year the world turned upside down, but more man than boy even then.

He'd already begun taking over the responsibilities of running the property he'd inherited from his father.

Jacy had fallen in love with Ian at a spring party much like the one the night before, after the shearing had been done and the wool baled and sent off to Adelaide in semis to be sold. Miracle of miracles, he had felt the same way about her, or said he did, at least, and in secret places on her father's property and his own he had taught her to glory in her womanhood. He had introduced her to the most excruciatingly sweet pleasures, and, in fact, no man had touched her so intimately since.

They'd planned to marry, over Jacy's mother's frantic long-distance protests. Regina Tiernan Walsh was strong and smart, but she'd entered into a rash marriage in a foreign land herself once, and subsequently her bridegroom, Australia, and her own disillusionment had combined forces to break her heart. Not surprisingly, Regina had been terrified that the same fate awaited her daughter.

In the end, though, it had been Elaine Bennett, daughter of the American manager of Merimbula Station, who had brought Jacy's dreams down with a soul-shattering crash. She'd come up to Jacy and Ian outside the theater in Yolanda, looked Ian straight in the eye, and told him she was going to have his baby.

Even after a decade Jacy could still feel the terrible shock of that moment and the helpless, fiery rage that had followed. Ian had not denied the accusation; neither had he troubled himself to explain or apologize. He'd simply expected Jacy to understand.

A distant bleating sound jolted Jacy from her musings, and she rose slowly from her seat on the step. Way off she saw a sea of recently shorn sheep approaching, kicking up the dry red dust as they came.

Jacy's heart rose immediately to her throat and lodged there, impassable. The sheep were Ian's—she had no doubt of that—on their way to the springs to drink.

For a few moments she nursed her scant hope that someone else would be driving the flock, or mob, as the locals called it—one of Ian's two or three hired men, maybe. Even before Ian himself came into view, however, mounted on that enormous liver-colored stallion Jake had written her about, she knew she couldn't be so lucky.

She wasn't ready, she thought frantically.

Not so soon.

The baaing and bleating of the sheep grew until the racket filled Jacy's skull and stomach, and she watched the mob divide like water coursing around a stone. Two lean dogs kept the odd-looking beasts moving when they would have stopped to nibble the grass in the yard, and great clouds of red dust billowed in the hot, still air, covering the freshly washed quilt with grit.

Jacy just stood there on the back step like a felon on the scaffold, waiting for the noose to tighten around her neck. Her clothes—jeans and a white T-shirt—felt all wrong, her hair probably looked like hell, and she hadn't bothered to put on makeup. She'd never felt less prepared for anything.

She figured she'd be really upset about the quilt once her thoughts calmed down, but at the moment she was too distracted.

In the dazzling light of a summer day it was plain that Ian's features had hardened with maturity. His violet gaze seemed to slice through her spirit, cutting cleanly, leaving no jagged edges.

Her knees went weak, and she sagged onto the step. Jet lag, she insisted to herself, though it had been more than three weeks since she'd landed in Adelaide.

Ian was wearing perfectly ordinary clothes—a battered stockman's hat; a blue cambric workshirt, the front of which was stained with sweat; jeans and boots—and yet the sight of him stole Jacy's breath away.

"How's Jake this morning?" he asked, shouting to be heard over the last of the sheep and swinging down from the saddle. There was nothing cordial in the question; she could see by his expression that things hadn't changed since the night before.

"See for yourself," she replied, amazed that the words had gotten past her constricted throat. Her heart was pounding like a ceremonial drumbeat, and she feared she might be sick to her stomach.

Ian tethered the horse to a rusted hitching post, resettled his hat, and crossed the yard to stand facing her. "See for myself I will," he answered in that low, rumbling voice that had once urged her to passion and then consoled her afterward, when she'd feared that all the scattered pieces of her soul would never find their way back to her. "If you'll just get out of my way."

Jacy looked straight into those impossibly blue eyes, and her heart shattered all over again. She rose and turned her back on Ian, praying he wouldn't guess how shaken she was.

"Dad was sleeping before your sheep came tramping through here like a herd of buffalo," she said in a moderately acidic tone. She could feel him behind her, though of course they weren't touching, feel the heat and hardness of him in the small of her back, the space between her shoulder blades and her nape, the tender flesh of her thighs and the insides of her knees. "I don't suppose you noticed what those creatures did to my clean quilt."

They entered the kitchen.

"I don't suppose I did," Ian said, utterly without remorse.

"I'll tell Jake you're here."

"Thanks for that much, anyway," Ian grumbled. In an involuntary backward glance Jacy saw him hang his hat on a peg beside the door and shove splayed fingers through his hair.

Suddenly the old anger crashed through all her carefully constructed defenses, swamping her, and it took every ounce of Jacy's self-control to keep her voice calm and even. "What did you expect, Ian? That I'd welcome you with open arms? That I'd thank you for teaching me that love has fangs?''

Ian's jawline hardened, but before he could speak, Jake appeared in the inside doorway, leaning on his cane.

"Hello, mate," he said. "I wondered when you'd get 'round to paying an old man a visit."

Ian's laugh was a low burst of sound, only too well remembered by Jacy and somehow excluding her. "You think I've got nothing better to do than eat biscuits and sip tea with the likes of you, Jake Tiernan?"

Jacy hurried outside before her father could suggest that she put the kettle on. She'd eat a bale of raw wool before she'd make tea and fetch cookies for Ian Yarbro. If he wanted refreshments, he could damn well serve himself.

2

STANDING OUTSIDE, HEARING JAKE AND IAN TALKING IN the kitchen, Jacy was restless and not a little resentful. The dust had settled, but the sheep were almost as loud as before, since they were just across the yard and down the slope in front of the house, at the springs.

Ignoring the quilt, which would have to be laundered again, Jacy turned her attention to Ian's massive horse, its flesh glimmering with sweat, and felt a stab of pity for the creature. She brought an old bucket from the shed, which was practically falling down from neglect, and filled it from an outdoor faucet.

She was just setting the pail on the ground so the stallion could drink when Ian's voice lashed her from behind like some invisible whip.

"Get away from that horse. *Now.*"

The words had a cold, brutal edge, and they sliced deeply into Jacy's pride. She flushed, stunned and angered by this new emotional blow, and stepped aside. "I was only giving him water," she said when she found her voice again.

Ian came toward her, grasped her hard by the shoulders, and half dragged, half thrust her away. "Damn it," he hissed, through his teeth, "that's a brumby, and he's all but wild. Last week he kicked in a man's ribs!"

Jacy gave the hem of her T-shirt a sharp tug and tossed her head once to let Ian know she wasn't daunted by him *or* his damned wild stallion. Furthermore, she resented the implication that she was a witless greenhorn bungling into danger. She'd been around horses all her life.

"He seems tame enough to me," she said, giving the animal a cool once-over before glaring directly into Ian's narrowed eyes.

A tiny muscle in Ian's jaw clamped visibly. Then, in a sudden, furious motion, he tore off his hat and threw it hard at the ground. Jacy jumped, startled, and the stallion danced and nickered nervously, pulling at the reins that tethered him to the hitching post.

Jacy had recovered by the time Ian bent, with a muttered curse, to pick up his hat. He slapped it once against his thigh, making the dust fly, then wrenched it onto his head again.

"No wonder that thing looks like it's been stepped on by every elephant, giraffe, and pony in the circus," she said with a sweetness calculated to irritate. "You ought to learn to manage your temper, Mr. Yarbro. For the sake of your wardrobe, if nothing else."

With that Jacy turned and walked toward the house. She could feel Ian seething behind her, there in the dooryard, but she didn't look back. As she passed Jake, who had made his way to the bottom step, she saw just the ghost of a grin touch her father's mouth.

The sight cooled her temper a little, giving her new hope that Jake would soon be his old, mischievous self again. She was still profoundly shaken, though not because of any near-miss, real or imagined, with the brumby. Jacy's nerves were bristling because Ian had touched her.

She heard her dad stump into the kitchen with his cane,

19

but she didn't look at him. "We'll have something cool for lunch," she said, wrenching open the refrigerator door to peer inside. The rush of chilly air was heavenly, for she was drenched with perspiration, being unaccustomed to the heat.

There were still some casseroles and salads in the fridge; word of Jake's return from Adelaide had spread fast, and several of his friends had come by with food the first day he was home.

"Never mind lunch," Jake said quietly. "It's plain to see that the last thing you want right now is a meal, Jacy-girl, and I'll feed myself when I get hungry."

Jacy only nodded without meeting his eyes and hurried into the sanctuary of her room. There she stripped off her jeans and T-shirt and put on a cotton robe. After that she crossed the hall to the bathroom and took a cool shower, keeping it short because water was so very precious in the bush.

When she came out of her room some twenty minutes later her hair was still wet, though neatly combed, and she was wearing white shorts, a tank top, and sandals.

Jake was seated at the table by then, reading the weekly paper that was published up in Willoughby. He made a *tsk*ing sound at something he'd taken note of and shook his head.

"What's so fascinating?" Jacy asked, opening the fridge again. Now that she'd had time to cool down, literally and figuratively, she was hungry. She chose a creamy fruit salad over a beef and noodle casserole because she didn't want to use the propane stove while it was still so hot. There was no electricity at Corroboree Springs, and whatever wasn't powered by gas ran off a generator.

"Another of Ian's letters got into the paper, that's all."

Oh, sure, Jacy thought sourly. It had to be something about *him*. Weren't there any other topics of conversation?

"Ian makes a habit of writing to the editor?" she asked

airily, to prove she had her emotions under control. Which, of course, she didn't.

Jake nodded, and again, in a sidelong glance, Jacy caught a glimpse of his old smile. "Ian thinks there're too many foreigners coming to Australia these days. He doesn't take to those people who run Merimbula—says they ought to go back to the States and leave us alone."

Jacy couldn't help the immediate association she made. Ian had certainly "taken to" one person on Merimbula—Elaine Bennett. He'd liked her well enough, in fact, to father her child.

She slammed the teakettle onto the burner with unnecessary force. "Ian's a bigot," she said irritably.

"Is he, now?" Jake asked in a distracted way that meant he was reading the paper again and not paying any attention at all to what she was saying. "I'll have a bite to eat after all, if you wouldn't mind dishing it up."

They didn't speak again until the plates were on the table and Jacy was sitting down across from him.

"I'd better drive into Yolanda for supplies," she announced. "We've about finished off the stuff your neighbors brought by. Want to go along for the ride?"

Jake shook his head. "Believe I'll rest instead," he said. He ate hungrily, "You might get some meat pies while you're there. Couldn't get one to save my life while I was in hospital."

Cheered by her father's good appetite, Jacy ate her lunch and put the leftovers back into the old refrigerator, which chugged and rattled once in genial acknowledgment. Then, humming softly, she began washing the dishes.

"Jacy?"

The earnestness in her father's voice made her turn from her task and look at him with concern.

"It means the world to me that you came back," he said. "Thank you."

Tears of love sprang to her eyes—she'd done more crying in recent days than she had since Paul's death—but she

21

knew it was good for her. "Nothing could have kept me away," she replied.

Jake made an effort at a smile, scraped back his chair, and labored off into the other room. Moments later Jacy heard the familiar, comforting creak of the rocking chair.

Before setting out for Yolanda, Jacy applied sunscreen to her nose and cheeks and ferreted an old straw hat out of one of the closets. For good measure she put on a long-sleeved cotton shirt.

The dirt track leading into town was hardly better than the rough sheep trails crisscrossing her father's property and Ian's. The summer heat was enervating, and dust rolled in through the open windows, half choking Jacy.

A lot of good it had done her to take a shower and wash her hair, she thought ruefully when the town finally came into sight.

Yolanda was an odd assortment of shacks, houses, and shopfronts tumbled across the stark terrain in no particular order. There was one grocery shop, one patrol station, a school, a pub called the Dog and Goose, and a post office. The picture theater was closed down, probably for lack of funds, and the single church looked weathered and small against the vast landscape that sprawled beyond its rickety picket fence.

After one turn around the town for old times' sake Jacy pulled up in front of the grocery, tossed her old straw hat onto the passenger seat, and went in.

The inside of the shop was like something from the fifties. The large white coolers roared with the effort of keeping milk and eggs and frozen dinners cold—Yolanda, unlike the outlying regions, had electricity—and the Coca-Cola sign over the counter would have brought a fortune at an antiques sale back in the States. The floors were bare wood, worn smooth by decades of passing feet, and the cash register was scrolled with brass.

Darlis Shifflet was sweeping the floor, her dishwater blond hair straggling from a loose bun at the back of her neck. She wore an old cobbler's apron over her faded cotton dress and a large plastic pin with her first name printed on it.

She offered a tentative smile. "Jacy Tiernan?" she asked.

Jacy nodded and smiled back. "Hello, Darlis." She didn't ask the usual question because she could guess how Darlis was—still married to Redley Shifflet, no doubt, still getting beaten every Saturday night, and still making excuses for her husband. The sad thing was that Darlis's predicament wasn't all that uncommon, either in the U.S. or in Australia; she was trapped by her own lack of self-esteem.

Her husband, Redley, was what Jake called a no-gooder, and just the thought of him made Jacy fighting mad. To men like that, women and children were property, not human beings, and deserving of whatever punishment their lords and masters chose to mete out.

Still, if Darlis wouldn't help herself, there was nothing anyone else could do. Jacy pushed the problem to the back of her mind and concentrated on her shopping list. She opened one of the coolers and took out milk, a non-dairy concoction for Jake's coffee, some butter and eggs.

Darlis wheeled over one of the two carts in the store— a rusted one with a squeaky wheel. "How's Jake doing?"

"Better," Jacy said, though she wasn't sure that was the whole truth. She glanced around, but apparently she was the only customer in the store just then.

"You tell him Darlis and Redley say g'day," Darlis said.

Jacy ached for the woman. "I will," she said gently, and she pushed the cart into the aisle where cereal and pasta were displayed.

As she was loading her purchases into the truck a small crowd gathered. Revelers came out of the Dog and Goose, cue sticks in hand, to ask after Jake's well-being, and old Mrs. Dinter even left the post office to wave and offer her good wishes.

When Jacy arrived at Corroboree Springs the sun was

finally relenting a little, and an almost indiscernible breeze was ruffling the leaves of the pepper trees Matty had planted fifty years before. She pulled around to the back of the house so she wouldn't have to carry the groceries so far and was startled to find the yard full of old trucks and cars, along with the odd horse and one rusty motor scooter.

She smiled as she got out of the truck and walked around to the other side to reach for the first box of groceries. More of Jake's "mates" had come to offer an official welcome home.

Jacy set the box on the kitchen table and went back for another, pleased by the sounds of laughter and talk from the front room and at the same time hoping Jake wouldn't be too worn out by all the excitement. She was turning toward the house again, her arms full, when she collided with Ian.

He'd showered and changed clothes since she'd seen him before, and his dark hair was still damp. Without a word he took the box from her and carried it inside.

Jacy followed with the last of the grocery order and felt a wicked and very inappropriate thrill when she saw that Ian was still in the kitchen. He was leaning against the refrigerator, his arms folded, regarding Jacy with a slight frown.

His presence seemed to fill the whole room, not just the space he occupied physically, and his eyes were troubled.

"I've got some beer," Jacy said awkwardly, unable to bear the silence any longer. If only they could pretend that nothing had happened between them and start over without all the emotional baggage. "I don't think it's very cold, but—"

In the living room someone made a raucous joke, and an explosion of laughter followed.

"Never mind the beer," Ian said. "How long are you planning to stay at Corroboree Springs?"

She'd already told him the night before that she meant

to stay awhile. Evidently he was hoping she'd changed her mind, or that he'd heard her wrong the first time.

So much for the idea of live and let live.

"I bought a one-way ticket," she replied in a mild but defiant tone. "Why don't you write a letter to the editor and complain about me? Maybe you can get me run out of the country on a rail."

Ian glared at her, opened his mouth to say something, then snapped it closed again.

Jacy was ridiculously pleased to see that she'd stymied him, momentarily at least, but she was also deflated. It was painful feeling so unwelcome in the very place that always tugged at her heart when she was away.

On the theory of quitting while she was ahead Jacy turned her back on Ian and rummaged through the boxes and bags until she found the beer. Then she opened one for herself.

Only when she'd poured the brew into a glass and taken several sips did she bother to look and see that he was still in the kitchen, glowering at her as though he hoped the very heat of his gaze would incinerate her.

"Was there something else?" she asked with acid politeness.

Ian was leaning against the fridge. He narrowed his eyes as if he thought Jacy were an infuriating puzzle with no solution forthcoming. "Jake's been getting along well enough without you these ten years," he said at last. "You're not needed here. You'll only cause more trouble."

Jacy's fingers tightened around her glass, and she raised her chin a little. "You don't get to tell me what to do, Ian," she said, making an effort to keep her voice down so she wouldn't spoil her father's party. "Whether I go or stay is my decision, and Jake's. So why don't you just go off and tend to your own business, along with your sheep?"

Having blurted out this speech, Jacy found that her energy was depleted. She sagged back against the edge of

25

the sink, needing its support, wondering why the simplest encounter with Ian Yarbro had to be an athletic experience.

Ian didn't trouble himself to respond to her taunt—not verbally, at least. Instead of speaking he pushed away from the fridge, crossed the space between them in a few unhurried strides, and leaned in close, trapping Jacy against the sink. His hands were braced on either side of her, and the muscles in his arms seemed hard as concrete. His breath touched her face, smelling of mint, and the soap-and-fresh-air scent of his skin was better than any cologne could have been.

For the longest time they just stood there staring at each other. Finally, though, Ian broke the silence.

"It seems we always get off on the wrong foot, you and I," he said in a voice just above a whisper. She felt the words, soft against her mouth, and they made her lips tingle. The sensation moved quickly through the rest of her system, pulsing in all the wrong places, as if her heartbeat had multiplied. "Why is that?"

You know damn well why, Jacy thought, but she couldn't quite manage to speak out loud. She'd used up her nerve before. Now it seemed that all she could do was tremble.

Ian bent his head and brushed Jacy's mouth with his own. Then his strong hands closed on her waist, and he kissed her in earnest, tracing the seam between her lips with his tongue, coaxing them to part for him.

This is insane! Jacy thought wildly. The man broke your heart! Somehow, though, she didn't try to push him away. Indeed, she returned Ian's kiss in the old way, and in that moment she lost touch with reality. They might have been kids again, making love in the sweet soft grass that grew around Corroboree Springs.

He raised his hands slowly to her breasts, brushed her nipples with the callused pads of his thumbs. Even through the fabric of her blouse and the thin lace of her bra she felt the peaks harden and reach for him.

26

And all the while the kiss went on, fiery, eternal, forbidden.

Jacy's mind was bedazzled; her most primitive instincts had taken over; her body wanted Ian's conquering and was preparing itself for it.

Ian took a breath, turned his head, and took Jacy's mouth again with a fevered desperation to match her own. He released her throbbing breasts to cup her bottom in both hands and press her hard against him.

She moaned, so ferocious was her need. She'd thought she'd mastered it during the years away, but now she knew the dangerous desire had been there all along, just beneath the surface of consciousness, waiting.

It was the worst, and the best, moment for Jake to come in.

He cleared his throat, and they bolted apart, both embarrassed and disoriented. Jacy's heart pounded against her breastbone like a bird beating its wings in a frantic effort to fly away, and she knew her face was crimson.

"Sorry," Jake lied good-naturedly, going to the bag that contained the beer and extracting a bottle.

Only then did Jacy realize that his party had broken up. Behind the house car doors were slamming and engines were starting. Thank heaven the celebrants had left via the front door, she thought.

She felt ruffled and hot, like a teenager caught rolling about with a boyfriend in the backseat of an old Chevy. She moved away from Ian without looking at him, but she could still feel him pressed against her. In fact, she feared she would bear the imprint of him on her skin for the rest of her life.

Ian gave a ragged sigh—no doubt he was relieved that fate had rescued him from the clutches of the dreaded foreigner—then murmured something to Jake and left.

Jacy burst into tears and fled into her bedroom as if she were eighteen again and the cracks and fissures Ian had put in her heart were brand-new.

*   *   *

27

Inside his late-model truck Ian knotted one hand into a fist and slammed it against the steering wheel. What the hell had he been thinking of, closing in on Jacy like that, kissing her, practically making love to her in her father's kitchen? Losing her had nearly killed him once before. Hadn't he learned from that?

The plain fact was that Jacy Tiernan wasn't cut out to live in Australia. She was pampered and rich, like her mother before her, and when things got hard, as they always did in the bush, she would get on an airplane and wing it back to America and the soft city life that awaited her there.

It had been all for the best, ten years before, when Jacy had returned his ring and gone home to the States, even though the pain had fractured something inside him. It was her coming back that was bad luck, that was a fact, and if he was smart, he'd stay the hell away from her.

His own place came into view, a large block homestead with a wraparound veranda and shutters on all the windows, and the familiar sight quieted his spirit a little and gave him comfort. Beyond were the various sheds and the farmyards, the paddocks, the horses he bred and trained to work on stations all over Australia.

He parked the truck in back and grinned to see his son, nine-year-old Chris, leading his piebald pony out of the main shed. The boy looked just like his mother, with his glossy chestnut hair and round hazel eyes, but Ian loved him with all of his heart.

"Did you see Jake?" Chris asked, swinging deftly up into the saddle. He'd been riding since before he could walk; Ian had made certain of that.

Ian nodded and reached out to stroke the horse's muscled neck with one hand. "Jake's on the mend, all right, though he looks a bit puny. Don't go far, now—Mrs. Wigget'll have dinner ready soon, and you've got your lessons to do."

Chris beamed. "I don't have any lessons," he said. "Mr. Ryerson's gone off on another of his walkabouts."

Ryerson was the teacher at Yolanda's one-room schoolhouse, and he was about as dependable as a street rat. He disappeared regularly, leaving his handful of students to fend for themselves, and yet the town had felt fortunate to have him. Not many teachers wanted to work in such an isolated place, and they'd taken special care to hire a man for the job. The idealistic young women who had preceded Ryerson had all either gotten themselves married to some bushman in the middle of the term and resigned or been overwhelmed by the isolation and the spareness of the accommodations and gone scurrying back home to Adelaide or Melbourne or Sydney, where life was tame and safe.

"At this rate," Ian told his son, "you'll end up too ignorant to look after yourself. I'll have to support you until you're a hundred and three."

Chris laughed, and the sound reminded Ian of the chimes that hung on the front veranda and sang softly whenever a breeze came up. God in heaven, he loved that boy, loved him so much that it scared him. "You won't have to support me," he assured his father, grinning. "I'm going to be your partner when I grow up. And when you're old I'll take care of you."

The words made Ian's throat tighten and his eyes sting. With the drought, and Merimbula trying to squeeze him out, and the economy the way it was, he sometimes wondered if he'd have a property to turn over to his son when the time came. His grandfather had settled this land, and Ian would have sworn there were grains of it in his blood. He didn't want to be the one who lost it.

"Thanks, mate," he teased. "It'll be nice to give all the work over to you one day and just sit there on the veranda and rock and watch the 'roos go hopping by."

He slapped Chris's blue-jeaned leg. "Go on, get out of here," he said. "But mind what I said, and have yourself washed up and at the table in half an hour."

Chris gave him a cocky salute, reined the game little pony away, and headed off toward his favorite haunt, an old mining camp a few kilometers from the house. He knew to stay away from the mine shaft itself, and Blue, Ian's best sheepdog, trotted along behind. The mutt was tame as a canary most of the time, but at the first sign that Chris was in danger he'd turn vicious.

Ian watched them go and then went into the house to change out of his good clothes.

His room was large, taking up almost a third of the homestead. The roof slanted over his bed, and there were shelves everywhere, stuffed with books. He'd read most of them more than once, being largely self-educated, and many were dog-eared and falling apart.

A few pictures hung on the wall, one of his mother as a young bride, and one of Chris, taken when a roving photographer had come through Yolanda the spring before.

Ian had always liked his room, especially when it rained. He'd never thought of moving into the master bedroom after his father died. Just then, though, as the light was beginning to change, it seemed a lonely place, too big and too plain and too empty.

He swore softly as he changed into battered jeans and a work shirt. He was getting sentimental, probably because he'd kissed Jacy in her father's kitchen and because he still ached, inside and out, with the wanting of her.

He was determined to think with his head this time, instead of his pecker, but he knew only too well what would happen to that noble resolution if he found himself kissing Jacy again, touching her breasts, pressing her close against him. . . .

Ian cursed once more and slammed the door of his room when he went out.

Jacy was like a person in a daze. She kept reliving Ian's kiss, the feel of his hands on her, the weight and heat of his body crushed against hers. While Jake took another of his naps she put away the groceries, tidied up the living room, and washed the cups and glasses the guests had used. She would think about dinner later.

Slipping out of the house, she headed for the place she'd longed for so many times back in the States, when she'd been troubled, confused, grief-stricken.

Jacy went to Corroboree Springs, the large, fresh pool that had given the property its name. Long ago, perhaps as far back as the Dream Time, the aborigines had used the site for ceremonial gatherings and celebrations. The name Corroboree had stuck.

Eucalyptus trees grew on three sides of the springs, sheltering the banks from the wind and, at that time of day at least, from the sun. The sheep had trampled the grass around the pool, but there was a high, flat rock at the water's edge, and Jacy sat upon it, stretching out her legs, closing her eyes, and tilting back her head.

The place was curative, it seemed to her. She had often gone there when visiting Jake as a young girl—to dream, to think, to read poetry and romance novels. After she'd found out about Ian and Elaine she'd come there to lay sprawled on the sun-warmed rock, to cry and wish she were dead.

She felt like crying now, as a matter of fact, and laughing at the same time. It was official, she decided. She was losing her mind.

When she returned to the house twilight had gathered and the night music was beginning. A lamp burned in the window—because electrical power was supplied by a generator, they were careful to conserve—as if Jake had feared she would lose her way.

She went inside and found him in the kitchen, making scrambled eggs and heating "bully beef," a canned meat concoction, for the meal he generally referred to as "tea." He actually smiled full out when she went in to set the table.

"A man who cooks," she said. "I could learn to like this."

"You didn't think I was going to let you do all the work, did you?" he teased, and Jacy was moved because he sounded more like the Jake she'd always known and loved.

"I was beginning to wonder," she retorted with a grin.

He laughed, the sound more precious than stardust to Jacy, and gestured with the spatula in his hand. "Sit down, sheila, and mind your manners." Jake went back to his stirring, leaning on the cane at the same time, and when he looked at Jacy again his expression had turned serious.

"Tell me about your mother," he said. "Is she well?"

Whenever Jacy returned to Corroboree Springs Jake invariably presented that same question. It was as awkward for him to ask, she knew, as it was for her to answer.

"She's well," Jacy said, seated obediently at the table, tracing a flower pattern on the worn-out oilcloth cover with the tip of one finger. "Busy with her clubs and classes and charity projects."

"That doctor bloke she married—he treats her the way he should?"

Jacy nodded. Although she knew Jake and Regina's decision to divorce had been a mutual one, she had guessed that their relationship was passionate while it lasted. "Michael is very kind," she said. But he isn't my father. He isn't you, Jake Tiernan, and I could never love him as much, or in the same way.

Jake brought the eggs and bully beef to the table in their enamel pans and sank gratefully into his chair. He looked strained and pale; the visit from his friends and the effort of cooking the meal had drained him, but Jacy would not have deprived him of either experience.

"What about that young man—Paul?" he asked out of the blue. "The one who died a few years ago. Did you love him?"

Jacy's fork hung suspended in midair. She had stopped making references to Paul in her letters to Jake long ago, because even writing about him had been too painful. "I loved him," she confirmed hoarsely. "But not in the way you're thinking. We were friends, that's all. Mates."

"Sometimes that's a lot," Jake answered, searching her face with his pale blue eyes. How she missed the sparkle and mischief that used to dance in those eyes. "You look all right on the outside, sheila," he went on gently, "but inside you're all bruised and broken. Do you think I don't see that? Or is it that I'm too fragile, in your opinion, to listen to your troubles?" He paused. "I'm still your old dad, Jacy-girl, and I love you."

Jacy set down her fork and swallowed the sob that had risen to her throat. "There's so much—"

"What?" Jake urged. "I know all about the trouble with Ian, of course, though from the way the pair of you were trying to swallow each other this afternoon, I daresay there's still hope in that direction. But there's more, isn't there? More even than your friend dying the way he did."

Jacy looked away, then made herself meet her father's eyes. "I've failed at so many things," she confessed. "I've never seen anything through to the finish—I always run away when it gets too hard. I don't want to be that kind of person, but I am."

"People change," Jake commented between bites of scrambled egg. "And you're young. If you don't like the way you are, then work on yourself."

"It isn't quite that simple," Jacy protested.

"Isn't it?" Jake countered. He took a drink from his coffee mug, then went on. "They'll be wanting a teacher in Yolanda now that the last one's gone wandering. Maybe you could help them out."

Jacy was instantly intrigued; she'd loved teaching once. After a moment, though, she shook her head. "You need looking after. That's why I'm here, after all."

Jake pretended to glower at her, and his accent thickened. "Who says I want you under me feet all the time? A man needs a moment to himself now and then, you know."

Jacy smiled. "You're not fooling me, old man. All men like to be waited on, hand and foot, whether they're sick or well, and you're no exception. You're trying to be noble and save me from myself." Her smile faded. "And how I wish you could."

They finished their meal in companionable silence, and then Jacy washed the dishes while her dad listened to the news on the portable radio. When he'd found out what was going on in the world he turned it off and raised himself from his chair with a difficulty that made Jacy ache. This was a man who had climbed into the tops of trees to save kittens, who had won prizes for shearing the most sheep in a day and broken wild horses to ride.

He cleared his throat. "You ought to be more patient with Ian, you know," he said. "He isn't a bad sort, and he was young when that other went on."

Jacy didn't answer because she couldn't say what she knew her dad wanted to hear.

Jake lingered a few moments, then said good night and shuffled off to get ready for bed.

Jacy was exhausted—she hadn't slept well since before she'd left New York. The endless flight certainly hadn't been restful, and after she'd reached Adelaide and the hospital she hadn't wanted to leave Jake's side. She'd gone to her hotel only to shower and change clothes, and most nights she'd slept in a chair in her father's room, fearing he would slip away, as Paul had.

For all of that, as Jacy went into her room, undressed, and stretched out on her bed with a book, she dreaded turning out the light and closing her eyes. When she did she would remember Ian's kiss and relive it, and all the painful desires, all the things that could never be, would rise up around her like ghosts.

3

THE YOLANDA SCHOOL COMMITTEE CONVENED IN THE
Dog and Goose Pub the following afternoon, with Ian Yarbro presiding.

He sat at a scarred wooden table with his hands folded,
regarding his three fellow committee members solemnly.
He had showered for the occasion, and put on a white
shirt, and his hair was still wet.

"We've got to do something about replacing Ryerson,"
Ian announced. "He's gone off chasing moonbeams again
and left the nippers all on their own."

Bram McCulley, who owned the pub as well as the grocery shop, settled back in his chair with a great sigh. He
wore a torn T-shirt, jeans so old they were practically color-
less, and biker's boots. On his right biceps a tattoo of a
well-endowed mermaid waved an Australian flag. For all of
that, Bram was a devoted father to his only child, a daughter named Jasmine.

"At this rate," he said, "our little ones is bound to come
out just a shade smarter than those sheep Ian here is always
chasing from one paddock to another."

Wilson Tate, who worked on Merimbula Station looking after their prize horses and cattle, had three little boys enrolled in the school at Yolanda. Relations between him and Ian were on the bristly side, given Ian's antipathy toward Tate's employers.

A thin man with spare features and plain clothes, Tate wet his whistle with a big draught from his beer mug, wiped his mouth with one arm, and frowned. "We must have used up every teacher who was willin' to come out this far by now. I'm thinking of sending my own boys into Melbourne to live with my sister and go to school there."

The pit of Ian's stomach clenched painfully at the thought of packing Chris off to the city. Even though the boy had never truly known his mother—Elaine had long since gone off in search of other worlds to conquer, and her father no longer managed Merimbula—the lad had a deep fear of abandonment. More nights than he could count, Chris had come hurtling out of the darkness to land in the middle of Ian's bed, frantic because he'd dreamed yet again that he'd been left on his own.

"My son stays with me," Ian said. "Even if I have to teach him his lessons myself."

"Do you have time for that?" Bram asked reasonably. "Seems to me that you've got your hands full between the woollies and your horses."

"Chris is more important," Ian replied, but even as he said the words he wondered how he could support his son and tutor him at the same time. Times were hard, and it took all Ian's strength and determination just to get by. His days were often fourteen to eighteen hours long as it was.

"Jake's been braggin' on his daughter's teaching certificate for years. We could try to hire her, couldn't we?" Wilson Tate suggested, avoiding Ian's gaze. "She's plannin' to stay about and look after her old dad. Maybe she'd like a job to break the monotony."

Ian stiffened. God knew he was as desperate to solve Yolanda's education problem as anyone in the whole countryside, but as far as he was concerned, Jacy Tiernan was not the solution. She'd just abandon the post as soon as she got weary of life in the bush, and then the children would be without a teacher again, and the committee would be simmering in the same old kettle of stew. Besides that, Jacy was hotheaded, and she had a lot of radical Yankee ideas into the bargain. In no time she'd have the women of Yolanda standing up for their rights and all like that, and every sort of grief would come of it.

"She's a bad choice," he told his companions.

Bram folded his burly, tattooed arms and smiled. "Is she, now? You didn't think so once upon a time, or so it seems to me."

Ian was in no mood for a ribbing. "Let's tend to business, shall we? I don't have all day to sit around flapping my jaws with you lot."

"What have you got against the Tiernan woman?" Wilson pressed. "Oh, I know all about that other, but it's been a long while, hasn't it?" He allowed himself a scant grin. "Imagine the sheila's gotten over you by this time, for all your charms."

Ian set his jaw for a moment in an effort to put a clamp on his rising temper. "I'll not tell you again," he warned at length. "Whatever might have happened between Jacy and me all those years ago is none of your concern. Now could we get back to the problem at hand?"

Bram shrugged one beefy shoulder. "There isn't much choice as far as I can see. We can send the nippers away to school or teach them ourselves—and we all know that might be worse than givin' the poor little blighters no education at all—or we can ask Jacy Tiernan for a bit of help."

Both Bram and Wilson watched with ill-concealed amusement as Ian's color rose.

"What'll it be, mate?" Wilson asked.

Ian swore.

Bram grinned. "You should be the one to ask her, don't

you think? You bein' the head of the committee and all like that.''

Ian knew there was no choice—maybe he hadn't had one in the first place. He'd just been forestalling the inevitable, arguing against hiring Jacy. Sure as February would follow January, though, there was trouble ahead.

"She's no great admirer of mine," he said, after a long breath. "Better to send one of you."

Bram smiled all the harder, and Wilson had the balls to laugh out loud. "Not likely, mate," Bram said.

Wilson stood, slapping Ian on the shoulder as he did so. "Give it some hard thought. You'll remember how you got her to say yes."

Ian closed his fists momentarily. Bad as things were between him and Jacy, he wouldn't stand for any insinuations about her character. Yes, she'd given herself to him all those years ago, willingly and often, but he'd done some fancy persuading in the first place. And they'd cared for each other in a way that still made Ian ache when he thought about it.

"Not another word," he counseled, rising from his chair. "I'll talk to Jacy about taking over the school." His gaze lingered a moment on Bram's face, then swung to Wilson's, silently conveying the message that his next words would be as earnest as any he'd ever spoken. "Remember, when this grand folly blows up in your faces and you wish you'd never laid eyes on the Tiernan woman, that I warned you off."

Bram just shrugged and ambled off to polish the bar while Wilson headed for the door. He touched the brim of his stockman's hat in a gesture of farewell, chuckled at Ian's dilemma, and left.

"Give Jake me best," Bram called as Ian slammed his own hat back onto his head and strode in the direction Tate had gone. "Tell him there's a mug of grog here with his name on it."

Ian didn't trust himself to answer.

* * *

Jacy was just climbing out of the springs, naked as the moment she'd drawn her first breath, when she heard dogs barking and the unmistakable bleating of sheep. Frantically she grabbed up the towel she'd brought from the house, along with her cotton sundress, and dodged into the bushes. When she came out, damp-skinned and irritated by the interruption, she encountered Ian again, mounted on that half-wild horse he seemed to value so highly.

He tugged at his hat, his eyes invisible under the brim, swung down from the saddle, and left the stallion to drink while he approached the high, grassy ground where she stood. The sheep closed in around the water, giving the brumby a wide berth.

Even though Jacy could not see Ian's eyes she felt his gaze touch her lips and then her breasts, which were straining against the thin fabric of the old dress. He might as well have touched her intimately; her skin felt hot all over, and her face throbbed with defiant chagrin.

For those reasons she wasn't exactly diplomatic. "What do you want?" she blurted.

Ian's grin flashed white in his tanned face, and for a moment Jacy felt as though someone had wrenched the hillside from beneath her bare feet. She curled her toes under in an effort to hold on.

"Water," he answered, in his own good time.

Jacy sighed and struggled for some kind of equanimity. She'd made a fool out of herself over this man once, but she wasn't going to make the same mistake again. If it was the last thing she ever did, she'd get her animal instincts under control and stop reacting so violently whenever she encountered him.

She pushed her wet hair back from her face with a hand that trembled only a little, took a deep breath, and let it out again. "Jake's up at the house, if you're looking for him," she managed to say. "I suppose he could do with a visit."

Ian tugged at the brim of his stockman's hat, a gesture

of nervousness Jacy remembered from the old days, and cleared his throat. "I've had a word with Jake," he said gruffly. "It's you I've come to see."

Jacy's heart took a sudden pitching lurch at his words, and she despised herself for still caring so much after all this time. After the way Ian had let her down.

Because she couldn't speak she simply looked at him questioningly and waited.

He swept off his hat and then put it on again in almost the same motion. "It isn't easy to ask you for a favor, Jacy," he said. "Not with all that went before."

"I don't imagine so," Jacy replied, none too generously.

Ian murmured an impolite word, then came to stand very close—painfully, deliciously close—and look straight into her eyes. "You never gave me a chance to explain," he said.

Jacy was stunned. What was this, she wondered—a crack in the fierce, immovable Yarbro pride? Inconceivable. She struggled to speak in a cool, collected manner. "Explain what?" she inquired.

A muscle pulsed in his jawline. "Damn it, Jacy, don't make this any harder than it has to be. Chris is my son— I've never denied that—but he was conceived before you and I started spending time together. Elaine and I had already parted ways."

Time supposedly heals all wounds, and yet the pain of Elaine's spiteful revelation that night in front of the picture theater in Yolanda was still brutally fresh. Tears sprang to Jacy's eyes—tears she hated and would have done anything to hide.

She tried to turn away, in fact, but Ian grasped her shoulders and made her look at him.

"I never told you one thing that wasn't true, Jacy Tiernan," he said hoarsely. "Not once."

Jacy bit her lower lip and struggled desperately for control. Logically, at least, she'd worked it all out during the years apart. She just hadn't been able to convince her broken and fearful heart that her conclusions were true.

"I know," she said.

Ian was plainly startled. "What?"

"I know you and Elaine had already broken up before you and I—before we were together the first time."

A series of unreadable emotions moved in the depths of Ian's changeable eyes, and his fingers tightened on Jacy's shoulders, almost bruising her. *"You knew?* And you still left, still put me through all the tortures of hell?"

"I didn't leave because of what you had done with Elaine, Ian. It was your cussed pride that drove me away—you claim now that you wanted a chance to explain, but back then you weren't ready to admit to any mistake. If you'd loved me the way you said you did, you would have *talked to me,* Ian. Maybe you would even have come after me, tried to stop me from leaving. . . ."

Fury brewed in his eyes like some inner storm and was promptly replaced by contempt. He practically threw her away from him, so quickly did he withdraw his hands. "Sweet God in heaven," he hissed. "You wanted me to run after you and beg, is that it? Do you have any idea what I went through after you left me standing there in your back garden with my hat in my hands and my guts lying on the ground? Did you even give a damn?"

Jacy felt an urge to touch his face, but some other part of her mind counseled restraint. "Yes, Ian," she said with gentle regret. "I did give a damn. But I was young, like you, and so caught up in my own pain that I couldn't begin to think about anything you might have been feeling."

Ian averted his gaze for a few moments, and Jacy wondered what was going on in his mind. When he looked at her again she was chilled by the coldness she saw in his face. "Let me tell you about what I was feeling, Jacy," he said in low, raw tones. "There were times when I truly thought I'd perish of it, I hurt so much. It was as if you'd *died,* for God's sake—I couldn't eat, I couldn't sleep, I couldn't think. Sometimes I rode out into the bush, far enough so no one would hear me, and I yelled until I had no voice left.''

Jacy raised the fingertips of both hands to her temples and closed her eyes. ''I suffered, too, Ian. I suffered, too.'' She sighed and lifted her gaze to his face, mourning all that might have been. ''You didn't come here to talk about the past, did you?''

He shoved one hand through his hair, fingers splayed. ''No,'' he admitted, and the word was rough as gravel. ''No, damn it, I didn't. It's about the school in Yolanda— we can't seem to keep a teacher—and Bram and Wilson thought you might do.''

Jacy couldn't help the grin that formed on her lips, even though her vital organs still felt as though they'd done a turn or two in a cement mixer. ''How kind of Bram and Wilson to think I could possibly be adequate. Tell me, Mr. Yarbro—what was your opinion?''

His jawline tightened, and his wonderful eyes flashed with the innate stubbornness that sustains a bushman in a harsh environment. ''I argued against it,'' he said plainly. ''You'll just go dashing off when the mood strikes you, and besides that, you're bound to give the nippers ideas. Especially the girls.''

Jacy was both furious and amused. Here was another reason—perhaps the *real* reason, she mused—why she and Ian could never have made a good life together. She was independent, and although he could charm the starch out of a woman's knees if he put his mind to it, Ian was basically a chauvinist. He truly believed that females were fragile creatures who needed someone of the opposite sex to sort out their problems and fight off their dragons.

''You don't have very much confidence in me, do you?'' she asked.

He put his hands on his hips. ''Why should I?'' he countered. ''You're like your mother—at the first sign of trouble you head for the hills. You've done it before, and you'll do it again.''

Ian's words struck their mark; Jacy had run away too many times, from too many things. More things than he would ever know about, in fact. She put out her chin. "That sounds like a challenge to me. And kindly leave my mother out of this.''

He narrowed his eyes and slammed his hat back on. "Do you want the job or not? The wages are next to nothing, the hours are long, and you'll have to travel over one of the worst roads in Australia to get there.''

Jacy smiled, even though she wanted just as much to weep. "Yes, I want the job. To spite you, if for no other reason.''

"That sounds like your kind of logic,'' Ian snapped. Then he turned and strode off toward his horse, which had raised its magnificent head from the springs by then and was looking on with what might have been alarm. "Have yourself at the school by eight-thirty tomorrow morning,'' Ian barked as he swung up into the saddle. "And one more thing: This isn't the United States. Don't go starting any revolutions.''

With that he turned and rode away. The two dogs who had accompanied the mob, lying in the shade on either side of the springs until then, immediately went into action, dashing about and barking. Soon the sheep were moving back in the direction from which they'd come, complaining all the way.

Jacy sank to the grass, drew up her knees, and pressed her forehead against them.

"What was that all about?''

Kindly though it was, Jake's voice startled her.

She lifted her head and tried to manage a smile. Jake looked shaky; even such a short walk was a monumental task for him, she knew, and he must have been very concerned to make the effort.

Jacy patted the ground beside her, and Jake sat down

with a grateful sigh. "It seems they need a teacher in Yolanda. Ian came to tell me that while the town wants me for the job, he most certainly doesn't."

Jake chuckled and shook his head. "He's a good lad, Ian is, but sometimes he's about as obliging as a mule up to its knees in molasses. Are you going to accept the town's offer?"

She looked at her father closely. "That depends on you, Dad. You're my first priority."

"It's enough having you in the house again, darlin'," Jake replied, his eyes glistening with pride and love and perhaps a few tears in the bargain. "I don't need you there twenty-four hours a day, fussing and cooking and fluffing up me pillows. You take that job, if that's what you want to do. You can use the truck to go back and forth."

Jacy felt a surge of delight—and trepidation. Teaching, after all, was one of the things she'd run away from; she'd left the last school without even giving notice, after Paul's death. Perhaps it was time to prove to herself that she could be responsible, that she could stick with a task or a commitment until it had been fulfilled.

"I'm scared," she said.

Jake put an arm around her shoulders and gave her a brief, fatherly hug. "Why, sheila? I don't reckon Yolanda kids are any meaner than the ones in America."

She thought she saw the old mischief flicker far back in Jake's eyes, though she couldn't be sure. "You know, Dad—we talked about it last night at dinner. When things go wrong, well, I tend to bail out. Maybe I'm an incurable coward."

"Not a chance," Jake said. "You're as tough as Ian. You just haven't had to prove it yet."

Jacy laid her head against the outside of her dad's shoulder and sighed. "Nobody's as tough as Ian," she argued ruefully. "Or as bullheaded, or opinionated, or—"

Jake chuckled again. "I see you're still wild about him," he said.

Much as she wanted to, Jacy couldn't deny her father's remark. She offered a silent prayer, though, that the tempestuous passion she felt for Ian Yarbro was anything, *anything* but love.

Ian sweated under the hot sun, and under his annoyance with himself, as he dug post holes for a new line of fence. It was brutally hard work, for the ground was dry and hard as stone, and it made the muscles in his arms and torso throb with a sensation that was a close cousin to pain. Worse, it provided no distraction from his thoughts.

Why, he asked himself yet again, had he said all those things to Jacy? Why had he told her about the times he'd gone off by himself and bellowed at the sky until his throat was raw? Christ, he'd gone to Corroboree Springs to water the sheep and to offer Jacy a job, and he'd ended up spilling his insides at her feet like one of those fools in the silly radio plays Mrs. Wigget liked to listen to while she was doing her housework.

He jammed the post-hole digger against the relentless ground, and the shock reverberated through his arms to throb in his shoulders. He cursed and flung the tool down to go back to his truck for the water bag.

He was drinking deeply of the lukewarm contents when he spotted the big Land Rover jolting over the rugged terrain toward him. The rig belonged at Merimbula, and the feelings that arose in Ian in response to that discovery were not those of a friendly neighbor.

The rover came to a dusty halt a few yards away, and Andrew Carruthers got out and started in his direction. Carruthers was a Yank, and a particularly irritating one at that. He was about Ian's age, a graduate of some fancy college, and dressed in khakis and a pith helmet, like a Pom on safari.

Ian didn't offer his hand, as he would have to Wilson Tate or Jake Tiernan or any of the others. He just leaned on his post-hole digger, drenched in sweat from the top of his head to the soles of his feet, and waited.

"Hard work," Carruthers commented charitably, his gaze skimming the line of holes Ian had already dug.

Ian held his tongue and shrugged. Words, like water, were precious to a bushman—not to be spent just for the sake of making a noise.

Carruthers sighed. "All right, then, Yarbro—have it your way. We'll skip the polite remarks, and I'll come straight to the point. Why do you refuse to sell your land when you know we're going to squeeze you out eventually?" The American pushed out a loud breath in exasperation. "The price we're offering is more than fair. You could take the money and start over somewhere else."

"There's nowhere else I want to be," Ian said, and he went back to his digging.

Carruthers moved alongside him. "What about your son?" he pressed. "Think of the boy's future."

Ian slammed the tool into the ground and left it there, like a knife swaying in a wound. "My son will work this land like his father and his grandfather and his great-grandfather."

The other man retreated a step, ready to dash back to the safety of the expensive vehicle provided by his employers. "Maybe," he agreed belatedly, and with a degree of diplomacy. "But what if the drought goes on for another year or two? What if you lose even one more watering hole? What will you have to give the boy then?"

Ian considered stuffing Carruthers's head into the Land Rover's exhaust pipe, then decided the pleasure wouldn't equal the effort. "Get out of here," he growled.

Carruthers reached the vehicle and wrenched open the door on the driver's side. "You're using the water at Corroboree Springs now," he persisted. "But Merimbula is about to make an offer on that property as well as yours. Tiernan's tired and sick. He's been talking about going to Queensland and lying on the beach for years." The little worm slammed and locked the door, opening the window a crack and talking through the opening. "Old Jake's been willing to share his water, but Merimbula won't be so generous."

Ian stood close by the Land Rover, glaring at Carruthers through the glass. "I've told you once to get off my property," he said evenly. "I won't say it a second time."

Muttering, Carruthers started the rover's engine, jammed it into gear, and drove off, a plume of red dust swirling behind him.

Ian turned away, putting all his frustration and fury into his work. Carruthers was right, though Ian wouldn't have said so to save his own hide. If Jake sold his property, with its spring of fresh water, Ian wouldn't be able to stand against Merimbula for long.

He leaned on the digger's handle and lowered his head to his forearm, imagining what it would be like to leave his land forever, to take Chris away from everything he knew and begin again in some city, or as a hand on another man's station.

He couldn't let it happen.

That night after supper Jacy went out to sit in the swing on the front veranda, where she'd dreamed so many dreams as a girl. Jake joined her presently, his walking stick making the familiar clumping sound as he moved.

"You'll be off to Yolanda in the morning," he said, lowering himself into a wooden chair that sat at a right angle to the swing.

"Yes," Jacy replied, sighing the word. "Is there still a telephone in the Dog and Goose? I'll need to let Mother know I'm all right."

"We've kept up with the times better than that," he said lightly. " Mamie Dinter's got a facsimile machine over at the post office, and there's a public telephone in the Yolanda Café, too. The restaurant's got a new owner—Nancy somebody. She's a lively thing, about your age. You'll like her.''

They just sat for a while after that, in what Jacy thought was a companionable silence. Then Jake spoke, and it was evident that he'd been working up his courage all the while.

"There are things I need to say to you, Jacy. In case—in case I don't make it through.''

She stiffened and started to protest that he'd surely recover, that he was getting stronger every day, but he stopped her by holding up one hand.

"I don't know what your mother's told you about our splitting up, but I want to tell you my side of things. I was a good husband to Regina, so far as it went, and God knows I loved her. But I was hard and stubborn like Ian—the bush makes a man like that, if it doesn't kill him first. I forgot, if I ever knew it before then, that a woman needs tender attentions once in a while. Especially one that's been gently raised, the way she was.''

Jacy felt her throat tighten. What was it about this day that made everyone want to bring up the past? "You did the best you could," she said. "Even Mom says that. And I think she has a few regrets of her own.''

There was a sad smile in Jake's voice, if not on his lips. "She might have kept you away from me after the divorce—it would have been easy, with her living so far off in the States and everything—but she let you come to visit. That was something in her favor.''

Jacy didn't speak again. She'd fought her mother tooth and nail before every trip Down Under, but Jake didn't need to know that. Let him have his illusions about the woman he'd loved in his youth.

He went on, staring straight out at the dark sky, with its silver scattering of stars, keeping his eyes away from Jacy, though he did reach over and clasp her hand in his own callused one.

"My mother and father settled and held this land in spite

48

of bushfires and droughts and depressions," he said. "I don't want to give it up."

Jacy waited, full of pain. She probably wouldn't stay in Australia for the rest of her life, but it wounded her to imagine Corroboree Springs not being home anymore. It was the center of her existence, really, the place she thought about when she was far away. She'd wandered over every inch and acre in her mind when everything went wrong, and she had taken comfort from the knowledge that she could always go back.

Always. Now there was a concept; she might as well go looking for Camelot, or Brigadoon.

"I don't see you running a property," Jake continued, "though plenty of women have done just that—including your own grandmother, until I got to an age where I could be of use." He paused, probably remembering his strong, brave mother. "Fact is, I don't like the thought of selling to strangers, and it isn't as if I needed the money, either. I've got all I need put by." Another pause followed; then, at last, Jake met his daughter's gaze and saw the tears glistening in her eyes. "Ian Yarbro's been a mate to me— closest thing I've got to a son—and he needs the water on this land to survive. I'm thinking, Jacy-me-girl, of signing Corroboree Springs over to him."

4

FOR A MOMENT IT WAS AS IF THE WHOLE WORLD HAD SUD-
denly frozen solid; Jacy just sat there listening to her own
heartbeat thump in her ears. Jake wanted to turn Corroboree Springs over to Ian—forever?

"No," she whispered after a very long time. "No."

Jake squeezed her hand once more. "Listen, love," he
said gently. "I know you and Ian have had your differences, but he's a fine man. He'll make this property productive again—"

Jacy felt a dizzying variety of emotions. She was jealous
of Jake's obviously high regard for Ian. She was angry, and
she was sad, too. Sad because a daughter wasn't enough
for Jake; somewhere deep inside he wanted a son. And
despite the old and wicked attraction she and Ian felt for
each other, Yarbro was not her friend. Once Corroboree
Springs was legally his, he might even forbid her to set foot
on the property ever again.

She turned to face her father squarely in the dim light
that spilled from the living room window. "Don't do this,

Dad," she pleaded quietly. "Please—don't let Corroboree Springs pass out of the family."

Jake rubbed his chin thoughtfully, gazing out toward the springs and the stream they fed, a stream that flowed straight on to Merimbula, the neighboring station. "I can't manage the place any longer," he said.

Jacy was on the edge of the porch swing. "That doesn't mean you have to sign it away," she argued desperately. "You could hire a caretaker."

"What would be the point of that, Jacy-girl?" Jake countered in a quiet voice. "I'd only be putting off the inevitable." He patted her knee indulgently, as if she were a fretful child. "There now, you'll learn to accept it. Life's always changing, after all."

Jacy surprised even herself with her reaction. She bolted to her feet. "I'll never accept it," she cried. "Maybe I'm not the son you really wanted, but I'm not an idiot, either. I can learn to manage the property if you give me half a chance! And if you turn Corroboree Springs over to *that man,* Jake Tiernan, I'll never forgive you!"

Jake raised himself shakily from his chair, his face grim and pale, and Jacy regretted her outburst even before he spoke.

"I wouldn't have traded you for a hundred boys," he said. "There's never been a moment of your life that I haven't been grateful to be your father. But for all your good intentions, you haven't the experience to run a place like this. It wouldn't be a lark, something you could put aside when you hit a hard patch."

There are times when the truth hurts, Jacy thought, stricken, and this is one of those times. Jake didn't want to entrust her with Corroboree Springs because he was afraid she'd give up at the first sign of trouble, and there was nothing she could say in her defense.

Tears stung her eyes, and she would have turned away from her father to hide them, but he laid a hand on her shoulder. "You'd better get some rest, love. You have a big day ahead of you."

Jacy nodded, because she couldn't speak, and watched numbly as Jake made his laborious way into the house.

She slept fitfully that night and rose early the next morning. Her eyes were still puffy from crying, and her nose was distinctly red even after several splashes of cold water. Great, she reflected as she went into the kitchen to start breakfast. In an hour she'd be facing her class in Yolanda. What a terrific first impression she'd make!

Jake was already seated at the table when she arrived, sipping his morning tea, a half-written letter spread out before him. The look he gave Jacy was both tender and cautious.

"You're a sight this morning," he said.

Jacy chuckled at his frankness in spite of her bruised feelings and irritable mood. "Thanks, Dad. I needed a little confidence-builder, and you came through."

He smiled. "There's another solution to your dilemma, you know," he said. "You could marry Ian. Corroboree Creek would be yours then, but you'd have a husband to help you."

Jacy had been pouring coffee for herself, and she nearly dropped both the cup and the percolator. "How can you suggest a thing like that?" she demanded, setting everything aside in her consternation. "Good God, Dad, I know Australia is behind the times when it comes to women's rights, but a marriage of convenience? That's straight out of the Middle Ages!"

Jake was clearly undaunted, and he looked more like his old self than ever. "I've worked it all through," he said, as if she hadn't spoken. "You're a Tiernan, and by rights the land should belong to you. On the other hand, Ian needs the springs more than ever, with his own watering holes drying up right and left. So I've decided to sign the property itself over to you, and the springs to Ian. The whole thing would be easier for the both of you, of course, if you were married."

Jacy gaped at him, appalled, even though the idea of being Ian Yarbro's wife was not without its attractions. The right to share his bed, for example . . .

She shook off the thought with a toss of her head, though the accompanying sensations lingered, and drew a deep breath. "All right, Dad, let's assume, for just a moment, that I'd be willing to go along with this scheme of yours. What makes you think Ian would? He dislikes me intensely, in case you've forgotten."

"No," Jake answered. "Ian's afraid of you, that's the truth of it."

A headache took shape at the back of Jacy's head and slithered down into her nape and then the muscles of her shoulders and upper back. "Ian isn't afraid of anything," she argued. "And you still haven't answered my question. Why should he agree?"

The old mischievous grin rested on Jake's mouth. "He needs the water," he said blithely.

Jacy sagged into her chair. "But you said last night that you were willing to sign Corroboree Springs over to Ian lock, stock, and barrel."

Jake shrugged bitterly, then patted the top of her head. "I've changed me mind," he said. "You get the land, he gets the water. The two of you will have to work out the rest between yourselves, I guess."

A glance at the noisy plastic clock above the stove told Jacy that she didn't have time for further arguments. It was the equivalent of ten miles to Yolanda, and she wanted at least a few minutes to acclimate herself before the school day began.

She grabbed an apple from the fruit bowl on the counter and a carton of yogurt from the refrigerator and started toward the front door. "We'll talk about this later," she called to her dad.

"Nothing to talk about," Jake responded cheerfully.

"The land is mine, Jacy-girl, and I'll do with it as I see fit."

Jacy made an exasperated sound and hurried out to the truck.

The drive to Yolanda was dusty and rough, but Jacy enjoyed it all the same. At one point a mob of kangaroos crossed in front of her, and she was struck by the realization that she loved this unique and primitive land with her whole heart. Perhaps she *could* make a life here, living at Corroboree Springs, and teaching in Yolanda. . . .

Ian came to mind as she pulled to a stop in front of Yolanda's one-room schoolhouse, a squat and ugly building made of concrete blocks, and she forcibly put him out.

She had work to do.

The inside of the school was just as dismal as the outside, with its out-of-date world map, its old-fashioned inkwell desks and obsolete reference books, and yet Jacy felt real excitement and anticipation as she looked around. She could make a difference in the lives of these children, and she meant to do just that.

She dusted off the teacher's desk and was thumbing through one of the textbooks she'd found behind it when the first student arrived.

She recognized Chris Yarbro instantly, even though he didn't resemble his father physically. His hair was light in color, his eyes a changeable shade of hazel, and he had one of those choirboy faces that would almost certainly bring on a fistfight or two before he was grown. Small for his age, and slight, Chris hesitated in the doorway.

In those brief moments Jacy wondered what she'd expected to feel when she saw Ian and Elaine's son for the first time. The reality was that she liked the boy right off and wanted to be his friend.

"Won't you come in?" she asked. "My name is Miss Tiernan."

Chris waited a moment longer, then stepped over the

threshold. Only then did Jacy realize that Ian was behind him.

"He knows who you are," Ian said, leaving the boy and approaching Jacy's desk. His face was set and hard, and he loomed over her. "I told him."

"How kind of you," Jacy said when she found her voice. She supposed it was too much to hope that Ian hadn't noticed how taken aback she'd been.

Ian braced his hands against the edge of the old desk—Jacy saw that they were scarred with both old wounds and new—and leaned toward her, his voice low and ominous.

"Mind you teach this lad the things you're supposed to, and nothing else," he warned.

Jacy swallowed a rush of fury. "Such as?" she asked, with a lightness she most certainly did not feel.

A muscle leapt in Ian's jaw, and his indigo eyes flashed with some deeply cherished conviction. "Don't be putting any radical American ideas in his head. I won't have him turned 'sensitive.' "

"In other words," Jacy began, speaking moderately, in a voice barely above a whisper, "you want your son to be raised as a thoughtless, unfeeling barbarian?" She leaned to one side to look around Ian and smiled reassuringly at the boy, who was pretending disinterest in the scene at the front of the schoolroom. "Too late, Ian. I think the damage has already been done—Chris looks like a gentle, intelligent boy to me. Where do you suppose you went wrong?"

Again that muscle in Ian's cheek clenched, and one of his hands knotted momentarily into a fist. "Just remember," he said, after an internal struggle that was a delight to watch. "Chris is not a Yank. He's an Aussie."

With that Ian turned and, with a brisk wave to the boy, walked out.

Jacy watched him go, feeling both irritation and triumph, but then the sounds of other children's voices gathered into a sort of happy crescendo outside, and she set her mind on her work. Chris had taken a seat at the back of the room, and now others rambled in to take their places—three small boys, each a head taller than the last; a shy girl of about twelve with a ragged stuffed giraffe in her hand; another, more outgoing one, well-dressed and obviously secure in herself. By the time Jacy rang the old-fashioned bell there were nine children seated in the antique desks.

There should have been at least twenty, by Jacy's calculations, and she was troubled. Plainly, quite a few parents in and around Yolanda had chosen to keep their children at home.

For the moment, however, there was nothing to do but concentrate on the tasks at hand. Jacy introduced herself and said she'd come to Australia to stay with her father for a while. She'd spent most of her life in the United States, she told them, but the land Down Under was her home, too; she had roots there, and her grandparents had settled at Corroboree Springs.

When Jacy had finished speaking she asked the children to come up to the front—one at a time, of course—say their names, and tell a little about themselves.

Not surprisingly, the confident little girl went first. She had dark pigtails, lovely brown-gold eyes, and freckles, and she announced that her name was Jasmine McCulley. She wanted to live in Sydney when she grew up and have her own dress shop.

After Jasmine sat down there were no more volunteers, so Jacy scanned the room and let her gaze come to rest on the eldest of the three brothers. Like his siblings, he had slicked-back hair and wore a clean shirt and new jeans.

"Would you like to come forward, please?" Jacy said to him.

He remained in his desk chair. "Everybody knows my name," he grumbled.

"I don't," Jacy pointed out.

At last the boy got up and swaggered forward to stand with his back to Jacy's desk. "I'm Linus Tate," he said with elaborate reluctance, "and those are my brothers, Lionel and Liander. We live at Merimbula—my dad's foreman there."

Having spoken his piece, Linus returned to his seat.

As a matter of principle, Jacy made Lionel and Liander come to the front separately and speak for themselves. Then she turned to Chris Yarbro.

He slid down in his seat and averted his eyes.

Later, Jacy thought, and she invited the girl with the toy giraffe to come and stand beside her.

Painfully thin, her dress long overdue for the ragbag, the adolescent trundled forward with all the enthusiasm of a French aristocrat approaching the guillotine.

"Baby!" Linus—or one of his matching brothers—called out. "Got to have her dolly."

Jacy swept all three of the Tate boys up in a quelling glance, perfected in Connecticut with help from Paul, and laid one hand gently on her student's thin shoulder.

The child looked up at her once, in plain misery, then bravely faced her classmates and said, "My name is Gladys Shifflet. I like to read books about castles and princesses." She turned her gaze to Jacy again, silently pleading, and Jacy nodded permission for Gladys to go back to her desk.

Chris was the last to speak, and in his own way he looked as uncomfortable as Gladys. "Christopher Yarbro," he said, without preamble. "I like to ride my horse, and someday my dad and I'll be partners."

"You mean someday you'll work on Merimbula, if they'll take you on," said Linus Tate in a sly voice. "They're bound to force you out, those Yanks that own the big station."

Chris, so shy before, so unlike his bold father, suddenly exuded Ian's fierce determination. He bolted toward Linus, and Jacy hurried down the aisle to keep the two boys apart.

"That will be enough, Linus," she said calmly. "And you, Christopher, will please keep your temper."

The rest of the morning was fairly quiet; Jacy had each child read aloud and tested their knowledge of math. While they were outside for noon recess she sat at her desk, working out lesson plans suited to each child's needs. At the same time she nibbled her runny, lukewarm yogurt and munched on the apple she'd brought from home.

When the shadow fell across her desk she raised her eyes and smiled, expecting to see one of her students. Instead she found herself looking into the narrow, avid face of Redley Shifflet, the one man she'd ever known her affable father to actively dislike.

Redley was older and thinner, his clothes were shabbier, and he was probably meaner, too. Jacy remembered him well from her visits in the old days. Now he leaned against the edge of her desk, rife with the smells of motor oil, sweat, and cheap liquor.

"May I help you?" she asked politely. After all, Redley was the father of one of her students, and she would afford him the appropriate courtesies.

Redley smiled, showing an assortment of brown, crooked teeth. "You're Jake Tiernan's girl," he said.

She was getting tired of being known only as her father's daughter, but she didn't care enough about Shifflet's opinion to say anything about it. "Yes," she replied. "And you're Gladys's father."

The cheerful and patently offensive smile faded to a look of resolve. He nodded. "I've come to fetch the girl. Her mother's out workin', and Gladys is needed at home."

Jacy had known that teaching in this backward place would be a challenge, of course, but she hadn't expected to run into a snag quite so soon. "Class will be dismissed at three o'clock," she said in pleasant yet firm tones. "Perhaps you could pick Gladys up then."

Redley leaned closer, and the smells intensified, taking on new and disturbing nuances. "Maybe you didn't understand me," he said. "Gladys is needed at home."

She was about to protest when it occurred to her that if she made this cretin angry, he might take out his frustrations on Gladys. "Very well," she said stiffly. "I hope

58

you'll keep in mind, Mr. Shifflet, that your daughter needs an education. In order to get one, she will have to attend school regularly."

"Gladys doesn't need to know much," Redley said, pushing away from the desk, a spark of triumph gleaming in his feral eyes. "She'll just marry a farmer and start turning out nippers anyhow."

For Gladys's sake, Jacy held her temper. Don't start any revolutions, Ian had said. As far as she was concerned, it was time to begin gathering recruits and planning battle strategies. "The world is changing," she pointed out moderately.

Redley didn't reply, and in the end there was nothing Jacy could do to prevent him from taking Gladys out of school. She watched from the doorway, a chill settling into her soul, as the visitor summoned his daughter. Gladys tossed one baleful glance in Jacy's direction and then followed him to his truck, which sat chortling and smoking at the schoolhouse gate.

Jacy felt more than frustration, more than fury. She felt ill, though this was a malady of the spirit, not the body.

She was relieved when three o'clock came around, though her students had had a busy and productive afternoon. The incident with Redley had shaken her, and she had self-doubts aplenty. Maybe she shouldn't have tackled this job after all, she thought.

Jacy caught herself. One thing was certain; she wouldn't be able to back out without proving that Ian had been right in not wanting to hire her, and she wasn't going to let that happen.

Although his classmates had dashed out into the afternoon sunshine the moment Jacy dismissed them, Chris lingered, working industriously at his desk.

Jacy approached cautiously, not wanting to startle him. "I could give you a lift home if you need one," she offered. "It wouldn't be out of my way."

Chris raised his eyes from the picture he'd been drawing—it showed a man and a boy and a kangaroo—and the expression Jacy saw in them was a wary one. "My dad will come and get me," he said. "I usually ride old Meathead, but he threw a shoe."

Before Jacy could respond she heard a car door slam out by the road and braced herself.

Ian was back. Why did that come as such a surprise to her?

She could actually feel his approach, as though he were a missile homing in on her, set to explode on impact. Her skin grew damp everywhere and tingled, and her heart tripped into a faster beat. Although it hadn't entered her mind during their earlier encounter, her dad's insane plan to divide his property between her and Ian came back to Jacy suddenly.

On the heels of that thought, with no warning at all, came the disturbing image of herself as Ian's wife, lying beneath him in a tangle of sheets. . . .

Her face was hot when he filled the open doorway, framed by the glaring sunlight, his stockman's hat in one hand.

Jacy wanted to look away, but she found herself staring at Ian all the same, noticing the V of sweat that soaked the front of his light-colored work shirt, noticing his battered jeans and scuffed boots.

He acknowledged Chris with a quick, flashing grin and, stepping out of the doorway, cocked a thumb toward the front gate. "Wait in the truck," he told the boy. "We'll get some ice cream before we start for home."

Chris hurtled toward the door, dashed back to snatch up the drawing he'd left on his desk, and went outside.

The moment they were alone Ian's face changed. Gone was the grin, the wonderful light in his eyes, the easy warmth of his manner. His features seemed to harden as he regarded Jacy, and she felt a poignant grief, mourning the time when he'd looked at her with love.

"Well?" he demanded bluntly. "How was it?"

She swallowed, wanting to cry but quickly quelling the urge. "The lessons went fine," she replied in a tone as clipped and cool as Ian's had been. She squared her shoulders. "There's one problem, though—Redley Shifflet."

Ian straightened, listening with solemn interest, idly turning his disreputable hat in one hand. His eyes narrowed. "What about him?"

Jacy sighed. "His attitude toward education, especially where females are concerned, isn't exactly modern, even by *your* standards. He took Gladys out of school early today—said she was 'needed at home.' Lots of other kids didn't show up at all." She'd been turning an old chipped globe with her fingertips as she talked and was startled when Ian's callused hand covered hers, stopping the motion.

It was innocent, ordinary sort of contact, and yet another wave of heat rose up out of some secret place inside Jacy and swamped her with sensation. She swayed slightly and pulled her hand away.

"I warned you that the people 'round Yolanda weren't the forward-thinking types you're used to," Ian said, his voice quiet and oddly hoarse.

"It's more than that," Jacy argued, impatient again, and glad of it. She took refuge in that emotion, because the one that had just passed—a passionate longing to be taken into this man's arms and never released—was unacceptable. She met his eyes and, for a dizzying moment, thought she'd drown in them. "There's something terribly wrong in that family."

Ian sighed ruefully. "Yes, there is—it's Redley. He's a son of a bitch; there's no question of that. But out here we don't meddle in one another's business."

Jacy remembered the pleading expression in Gladys's eyes, and the hopelessness, and felt a surge of anger. "Not even when a child's safety might be at stake?"

His dark brows drew together for a moment. "You don't know that."

She threw up her hands in a burst of frustration. "Oh, for God's sake, Ian, think! Everybody knows Redley beats Darlis up on a regular basis. Is it so hard to believe that he might be abusing his daughter as well?"

Jacy watched as Ian's expression closed against her like some huge, intangible door, and she longed to pound on his chest with her fists and shout at him until he listened. Until he let her in.

"That's a serious accusation, sheila," he said. "Mind you have some proof before you bring it up again."

With that Ian turned and strode out, leaving Jacy to stare after him in mute fury.

She took her sweet time closing up the schoolhouse for the day.

She wanted to telephone her mother before she drove back to Corroboree Springs—New York was fifteen hours ahead, which meant it was about seven in the morning on the eastern coast of the United States. She might have chosen to use the telephone in the Yolanda Café, but she was sure Ian and Chris were there, enjoying the promised ice cream, and she'd be damned if she'd let Ian think she'd come trailing after him.

Jacy parked her dad's truck in front of the Dog and Goose, the only pub in Yolanda and probably the seediest one in all South Australia. It was an unwritten rule, if she remembered correctly, that no "sheilas" were allowed in the place, on the theory that a man needs a place to hide out in once in a while.

Climbing the rickety steps and heading toward the doors with their rusted hinges, Jacy wondered where women were supposed to hide out when they needed a little time to themselves.

She paused, for she wasn't nearly as brave as she usually pretended she was, and took a deep, resolute breath. The Dog and Goose was a public building, she reminded herself. She had a moral right to go inside, if not a civil one.

The interior was cool and gloomy, lit only by a few dim

bulbs and the glow of a vintage jukebox. An American country/western tune was playing, and three or four tough-looking types, probably farmhands, were gathered around the pool table.

At Jacy's entrance Bram McCulley, the burly proprietor, stopped polishing the bar in midwipe, and the pool players turned as one to stare.

Bram cleared his throat, plainly prepared to be tolerant of "Jake's girl," but firm as well. "We don't serve ladies," he said.

Jacy only wanted to use the telephone—the idea of actually ordering a drink had never entered her mind—but Bram's words struck her like a slap. She'd never experienced direct prejudice before, however polite, and she found it hard to take. In fact, it brought up a lot of old emotions tied to the injustices her best friend Paul had suffered after he was diagnosed.

She stood there in the middle of that tacky pub with her chin sticking out and her heart pounding. She hadn't understood before how demeaning it was to be denied access to a place because of who she was, and she was both angry and scared.

"I want to use the telephone," she said after a difficult silence, during which Bram looked at her pityingly, as if being a woman, and an American one in the bargain, was some sort of affliction.

Bram wouldn't hurt her physically, she knew—he was her father's friend and a good-natured person in the first place—but she still felt as though she'd been knocked down and stepped on.

"There's one over at the café," one of the pool players put in.

Jacy didn't know any of the other men, and the way they were looking at her only increased her nervousness.

"I'm going to use this one," she managed to say. Then, somehow, she broke the inertia that had kept her paralyzed and, rummaging in her purse for her calling card, she started toward the old pay telephone on the wall. The silence behind her had weight and substance like a living thing.

As she lifted the telephone's plain black receiver and asked for an international operator Jacy thought she heard the door open and close again, but she didn't turn to look. Her momentum even now, when she had the receiver in her hand, was fragile; she couldn't afford a distraction.

The call went through quickly, an unexpected blessing that made Jacy sag against the pub wall, with its carved initials and assorted graffiti, and breathe a silent prayer of gratitude.

Her voice must have trembled when she answered her mother's cheerful hello, because Regina Walsh responded with an alarmed, "Are you all right?"

The disapproval behind her seemed to pulse in the room like a giant heartbeat. Jacy made herself smile. "Terrific," she said in a somewhat brittle tone.

"Is your father feeling better?"

"Yes and no," Jacy said, and after that her words tumbled out, one falling over the other in her anxiety to complete the call and leave. "I'll explain in a letter. I mainly wanted to tell you that I plan to stay a while—I have a teaching job, and I'm not ready to leave Dad just yet. Listen, Mom, I really am in a rush, but I promise to write before the end of the week. Say hello to Michael. Goodbye, I love you."

She heard her mother say, "Jacy!" just before she hung up.

When Jacy turned at last, feeling a lot like a known witch facing a tribunal of Puritans, she got another shock. Ian was standing just behind her, his hands on his hips, his hat pulled low over his eyes, and he was glowering.

"What do you do," he muttered, taking her arm in a none-too-gracious grasp and marching her toward the door, "sit down every night before you go to bed and make a list of ways you can piss people off?"

Out of the corner of her eye Jacy saw the pool players, who were looking at her the way a starving dingo might look at road kill. Glumly they went back to their game.

"Sorry, mate," Ian called back with cheerful chagrin, probably addressing Bram. "It won't happen again." With that he propelled Jacy out onto the street.

Jacy was angry, but she was also glad to be outside in the sunshine. The relief made her high, and annoyance renewed her bravado. She wrenched her arm free of Ian's grip and glared up at him. "Don't you *ever* apologize for my actions, Ian Yarbro!" she hissed. "Furthermore, if you manhandle me like that a second time, I'll devote the rest of my life to making you regret it!"

"That pub has been standing right there for fifty years," Ian retorted, gesturing wildly with one muscular arm, "and in all that time not one sheila has ever set foot inside! Damn it, woman, that was a *tradition!*"

Jacy surged up onto the balls of her feet so that she was nose to nose with Ian. She was vaguely aware that the two of them were making a public spectacle, standing outside the Dog and Goose and yelling at each other, but at the moment she didn't give a damn.

"Do you want me to tell you what you can do with your dumb-ass tradition?" she yelled.

Ian whipped off his hat, slapped it against his thigh, and then put it on again with what looked like enough force to rip the top of his head off. He drew in a breath to shout some retort, then stopped himself. "Go home," he said, his voice dangerously calm. "If you don't, I swear by all the angels in heaven and all the devils in hell that I'll take you over my knee right here and now!"

Jacy narrowed her eyes and drew her lips into a tight, stubborn line, but she knew when she was pushing her luck. She gave Ian the most impudent and disdainful once-over she could manage, then stormed down the street to the truck.

As she sped toward Corroboree Springs, her face dusty and streaked with angry tears, she wondered why she still wanted Ian so much, why she cared what he thought of her, when there wasn't a hope in Hades that the two of them could ever get along for more than five minutes running.

5

WHEN JACY ARRIVED AT CORROBOREE SPRINGS SHE found Jake all decked out in khaki slacks and a spiffy striped sport shirt. He took one look at her splotchy face and sized up the whole situation in a single word.

"Ian."

Jacy went to the sink and splashed her face with tepid water before speaking. When she'd done that she was a little more composed, and the fury that had made her tremble before had subsided to a quivering sensation in the pit of her stomach. "I don't want to talk about that arrogant, opinionated, chauvinistic jerk!"

Jake allowed himself a fraction of a smile. "Seems to me you just did," he replied. He gestured toward the kitchen table. "Sit down, love."

Jacy wrenched back a chair and collapsed, watching as her dad took two bottles of beer from the fridge and set one down before her. "Where are you going all dressed up?"

His answer startled her. "I've got business in Adelaide,"

he said. "Legal stuff. Collie's taking me there in his airplane."

"You're in no shape to go flying off—"

Jake interrupted the flow of her protest by raising one hand, palm toward her. "Enough. I'm still in charge of me own life, Jacy-girl, and you'll not be telling me what to do."

Jacy took a big, desperate gulp of her own icy-cold brew. It wasn't so, she thought irritably, what people said about drowning their worries in alcohol. Hers were all afloat. "Dad—"

Again Jake broke in before she could finish. "I'm off to the big smoke, and that's that, so accept it. When I get home we'll have a long talk, you and I and Ian, and then I believe I'll take myself off to Cairns or someplace like that." A dreamy expression entered his eyes. "I don't imagine I'll ever get weary of looking at the sea."

Jacy felt a sudden wild sadness; she wanted to cling to Jake, to somehow make him stay at Corroboree Springs and be the father she'd always known, but of course she wasn't about to do that. Any sort of pleading would only make the inevitable parting harder for them both, and besides, she could always visit him in the tropics. They'd look at the sea together.

"How on earth did you manage to get in touch with Collie?" she asked, taking refuge in the practical.

"He came by to see if I was wanting anything," Jake said with a grin. "He's a good mate, is old Collie. He'll be flying me up north when the time comes."

There was something of the permanent in the way Jake was talking, and Jacy found that difficult to handle. She didn't do well with separations—after saying good-bye to Ian when she was eighteen she'd turned into a world-class wallflower and spent the next five or six years actively grieving. Following Paul's death, the ultimate farewell, she'd lost all confidence in her ability to see even the sim-

plest thing through to its finish. Now she would not even
have Jake to lean on.

He reached across the table and touched her hand. "No
worries, love," he said. "You'll be just fine, and so will
I."

Jacy nodded, left her beer unfinished, and went off to
shower and change clothes. When she returned to the
kitchen Collie was there, seated at the table, hoisting a
brew with Jake.

Collie was half crazy even without beer. The idea of the
two of them flying off into the blue made Jacy's stomach
muscles clench, but by then she'd accepted the fact that it
would be futile to protest.

She made a light dinner for Jake and Collie, though she
couldn't choke down a bite herself, and managed to smile
when she said good-bye to her dad. Jacy watched them get
into a truck Collie had borrowed in town and drive off.

Though it was nearly seven, the sun was still shining
brightly. Jacy left the supper dishes and went out to the
stable, remembering when it had been populated with half
a dozen horses. Now the place looked as though it would
tumble down at any moment. The air smelled of mice, stale
hay, and dust.

Jacy thought of her grandmother, Matty Tiernan, and
even though she'd never met her, she was sure the woman
wouldn't have approved of the state the property had fallen
into.

The decision to order timber, hire workmen, and have
the stables renovated was made in an instant, and Jacy's
spirits rose a little at the prospect of taking direct action.
If the land was to be hers, then she would make the most
of it. There would be horses in the stalls and paddocks
again, and perhaps she would even put some of the for-
saken acres into wheat. Even with the drought crops were
being raised all over South Australia.

Jacy lingered in the barn, although she had things to do
in the house, making plans and taking mental measure-

ments. The ladder to the loft looked steady, and she started up it, recalling that some of her grandmother's things had been stored up there.

It was only when she reached the top that the memory came out of left field and nearly crushed her with its bittersweet force.

She and Ian had lain together in the then-sweet straw, exchanging dreams and secrets, one rainy summer afternoon when Jake was off tending his stock. Ian had kissed her, innocently at first, but then they'd both been caught up in youthful passion, and they had made love. Even though that had been Jacy's first time, she'd known incredible pleasure, because Ian had been so patient and so gentle.

Jacy clung to the ladder, enduring the memory, and when the worst had passed she finished the climb. In a corner of the loft she noticed a trunk draped in cobwebs, an old dressmaking form, and something that might have been a bedrail or a quilting frame.

The contents of the trunk, mostly dresses and various linens, had long since dissolved into rags, aided by time and mice. To Jacy's disappointment, there were no old photographs, letters, or diaries.

It would have been a comfort to know some of Matty's thoughts and hopes and dreams, she thought, eyeing the quilting frame. Jake's mother had probably used that very one while stitching the lovely, faded coverlet Jacy cherished—the one she'd had to wash twice because of the dust Ian's sheep had raised.

Feeling a little less lonely, perhaps because of the tenuous link she'd forged with Matty, Jacy climbed carefully down the ladder again. She went back to the house, did the dishes, and wiped the table and counter. Since she was feeling so efficient, she decided she would sketch out a teaching plan for the next day before tumbling into bed with a book. She found a pen and tablet in a drawer and made herself a cup of tea. When she was settled and ready to write she lifted the cover of the notebook and found the pages of an unfinished letter inside.

Even though she had no intention of reading anything so private, she recognized her father's handwriting, and in the split second before she closed the notebook again a few random lines and phrases made the leap from the paper to her mind. "We should be together . . . a day never goes by that I don't think of you . . . home to Queensland soon . . ."

Home to Queensland? Jacy thought. Since when was Queensland home?

She felt exaltation, though, along with a daughter's jealousy, as she put the pad back where she'd found it. Jake was waxing poetic; there was a woman waiting for him in Queensland. Why hadn't he mentioned her? When Jacy had fallen in love with Ian so long before she'd talked and thought of nothing and no one else.

But then, she thought with some embarrassment, she'd been a naïve girl at the time. Jake was a man, and a sophisticated one, despite his lifetime of relative isolation.

The story had been read, the brief and earnest little-boy prayers offered, and Chris was obviously having a hard time keeping his eyes open.

"She's pretty," he announced out of nowhere just as Ian was about to switch off the light and leave the room.

Ian felt a rushing sensation, then a powerful lurch, both of which were involuntary, and was annoyed with himself. "Who?" he asked, even though he already knew. Oh, God help him, he definitely knew.

"Miss Tiernan, my teacher." Worry flickered in Chris's eyes. "You don't like her, do you? You weren't very polite to her when you took me to school. Then you went over to the Dog and Goose and brought her outside and shouted at her."

Ian winced. Guilty, he thought.

He'd seen Jacy enter the pub through the window of the Yolanda Café while he and Chris had been having their ice cream and, knowing there would be trouble, had gone after her. His intentions had been good, even noble, he thought irritably, but despite that the whole situation had blown up in his face.

"I wouldn't exactly say I don't like Ja—Miss Tiernan. It's just that she and I don't agree about some things."

Chris frowned, clearly puzzled. "When I got in a row with Linus Tate that time you said people don't have to fight every time they have a difference of opinion."

A mental gavel came down in Ian's mind, and its echo reverberated through his conscience. "I did say that, mate," he confessed. "And I meant it. Maybe I'll tell Miss Tiernan I'm sorry." Like hell I'm sorry, he thought grimly. If he'd been the sort of man who believed in laying his hands on a woman in anger, he'd have cheerfully paddled her even then.

Still, raising nippers was tricky business. Just talking a good line wasn't enough; a bloke had to set a proper example and do the right thing whenever and wherever he could.

Chris gave him a bright, sleepy smile. "I'll bet you'd even like her if you tried," he said. "She's nice."

Ian made no comment, because if he'd tried to agree that Jacy was nice he'd choke on the words. In his opinion she was a saucy little troublemaker with a true gift for making enemies. So he simply leaned forward, kissed his son on the forehead, and turned off the light.

When he paused in the doorway to look back he saw that Chris was already asleep. A fierce love for the boy welled up in Ian in those moments, and he made a silent vow that he would save the land and pass it on to the lad no matter what he had to do to make it happen.

At the end of the long hallway in his vast kitchen Ian lit a kerosene lamp and set it on the trestle table, then went outside to shut down the generator. Petrol, like everything else, was expensive.

He paused after completing the task to look up at the star-scattered sky. The spectacle never ceased to amaze him; he was part of the land as surely as the scrubby gum trees were, with their roots reaching deep into the hard earth.

Back inside the house Ian settled down at the table and went over his books. He'd gotten a decent price for the wool, and he had a respectable sum put by for Chris's education. Still, the line between prosperity and total ruin was alarmingly thin. He wouldn't be able to hold out for more than a year if Merimbula got hold of Corroboree Springs and fenced off the water.

After an hour Ian closed the books. The lamp was flickering, low on kerosene, but still he lingered, the fingers of his right hand threaded through his hair. He'd tried to keep Jacy out of his mind, but she'd been there all along, troubling him, enticing him, forcing him to remember better times.

It was an irony; things that had been almost unbearably delicious when they happened were torturous in retrospect. Despite consistent efforts to forget he could recall only too well what it was like to feel Jacy's soft body beneath his own, trusting and supple. The memory of her stroking fingers lingered on the skin of his back; he heard her muffled cries of pleasure as clearly as if she'd just uttered them, saw her eyes, glazed with ecstasy, in his mind. She'd made him feel like a king every time he touched her. . . .

Ian knotted his hand into a fist and slammed it down onto the table. When would the remembering and the hurting stop? How much was enough?

He sighed, standing and reaching for the lamp. Maybe the only solution, he thought as he made his way along the hallway to his empty bed, was to make love to Jacy again. Perhaps then he could get her out of his system.

He smiled humorlessly as he entered his room and closed the door behind him. As if Jacy would agree to a seduction. "The woman hates your guts, mate," he reminded himself aloud as he stripped to the skin. "And you'll do well to remember that."

73

Ian was exhausted, having put in well over a day's worth of work, so he blew out the lamp, tossed back the covers, and collapsed onto the sheets facedown.

With a muttered curse he finally gave up and flung himself onto his back. Might as well have tried to sleep straddling a fallen tree, he thought just before weariness rose mercifully to enfold his mind.

The next day Ian brought Chris to school again, and Jacy wondered unncharitably if he meant to make a habit of that. She hoped not; the effect he had on her heart was practically aerobic, and it always took at least an hour to get over any encounter with him.

She gave Ian a level look when he entered the schoolhouse and approached her desk, his hat in his hands. She wasn't going to let him forget for a moment that he'd been an ass the day before, inside the Dog and Goose and out.

Chris took his seat and opened his reader, but his ears were practically stretching, he was listening so intently.

Ian, meanwhile, looked both chagrined and furious, and Jacy couldn't help a slight, wicked smile at his discomfort. It didn't take a nuclear physicist to figure out that Chris had witnessed and probably overheard their shouting match the day before—the confrontation would have been almost impossible to miss. Now Ian was no doubt trying to make up for the unfortunate example he'd set.

For all of it, the expression in his eyes told her plainly that he wasn't the least bit sorry even before he spoke. The apology he was about to offer was a complete sham.

"I shouldn't have raised my voice to you yesterday, Miss Tiernan," he said. "It wasn't polite, and I apologize."

Jacy smiled sweetly and relished a brief, vivid fantasy in which she had a barbed-wire fence put up between Ian's property line and the springs. For Chris's sake, and to nettle the impossible man looming in front of her desk, she said magnanimously, "You are forgiven, Mr. Yarbro."

His jawline tightened, and blue-gold fireworks sparked in

his eyes. He put on his hat with a controlled motion of his arm, turned, and walked out.

Jacy wondered how he would react when Jake told him how he meant to divide Corroboree Springs between them. Ian's water problems would be solved, for all intents and purposes, but he was insufferably proud, and he'd surely hate the idea of having to work out a partnership with her.

Soon Jacy was too busy to think about Ian or Jake's plan for the family property. She had projects planned for the whole day, which was a Friday, and while the children worked she made lists of things they needed—accurate maps and textbooks, art materials, novels and nonfiction books for a small library, perhaps even some playground equipment. As it was they had only a swing made from an old tire and suspended from a rusty metal pole.

It might have been a nearly perfect day, in fact, except that Gladys Shifflet didn't come to school.

At three o'clock the children left. There had been a few new students, and Jacy had hopes that more would enroll. Even so, she would have to start making home visits soon, asking people directly to make sure their kids came to class.

To Jacy's mingled relief and disappointment, Alice Wigget came to collect Chris, not Ian.

Jacy closed up the schoolhouse and walked over to the grocery store, hoping she wouldn't encounter Bran McCulley, who owned the shop along with the infamous Dog and Goose. As it happened, there was at least one shopper in each of the narrow aisles. Some were strangers; some were people Jacy remembered from old times.

She took a basket and, keeping an eye out for Darlis, selected a package of hamburger, the makings of a salad, and some diet cola. Only when she went up to the counter to pay did Darlis finally come out of hiding, and even then the other woman kept her gaze carefully averted.

"We missed Gladys at school today," Jacy said as pleasantly as possible.

A slender young woman with short brown hair was standing beside Jacy, watching her with large eyes. Her mouth looked ready to smile.

"Redley said Gladys had to stay home," Darlis replied in response to Jacy's remark. She ignored the brown-haired woman. "He doesn't want our girl getting any fancy ideas." There were small yellowish-blue bruises under her jawline, as if she'd been throttled.

Jacy knew a stone wall when she collided with one, but she couldn't give up because that would mean abandoning Gladys, even betraying her. "Your daughter is an intelligent child," she said quietly. "She'll have a good life if you'll only stand by her."

For just a moment Darlis raised her eyes, and Jacy saw in them a plea and the same heartrending misery she'd glimpsed in Gladys's little face.

Depressed, Jacy picked up her small bag of groceries and started for the door, but the woman who had been standing beside her was in the way.

She smiled and put out her hand. "Nancy McPatrick," she said. "I own the Yolanda Café."

Jacy's flagging spirits rose a little; she needed a friend her own age, a woman she could confide in, and Nancy looked like a good candidate. "Jacy Tiernan," she said, shaking Nancy's hand.

Nancy beamed. "I know," she replied. "I wanted to meet you before, but after yesterday—well, I just had to get a close look at the woman who crashed the Dog and Goose."

Jacy flushed at the memory, feeling both renewed conviction and embarrassment. No doubt Nancy, and probably the whole of Yolanda as well, had witnessed the spectacle she and Ian had made of themselves, standing on the sidewalk and yelling. "I'm no crusader," she said. "I wanted to prove a point, it's true, but I have to admit that I was partly motivated by plain, ordinary stubbornness." Why couldn't she have confessed as much to Ian, for the sake of the peace, she wondered, fairly certain at the same time that she would have died before giving an inch of ground.

She and Nancy left the store together.

"It's the end result that matters," Nancy said, "in this instance at least. Maybe Bram and the rest of that lot will get the idea that times are changing."

Jacy put her bag on the floor of the truck. "I'm not sure things will ever change that much, out here at least," she mused.

"Come in and chat awhile, won't you?" Nancy pleaded good-naturedly, gesturing toward the Yolanda Café, which was a metal quonset hut covered in tar paper. In that part of the country the termite problem was so bad that virtually nothing was ever built of wood. "I do get lonesome."

Since she was fairly certain Ian wouldn't be inside treating his son to ice cream, Jacy followed her new friend into the small restaurant. The Formica tables and vinyl chairs from ten years ago were still there, along with the same signs and forlorn vending machines. Only the management had changed, it seemed.

Jacy took a seat at the counter—the slow-moving fan overhead produced a welcome breeze—and glanced over the menu. She asked for a chocolate sundae, and Nancy talked while she filled the order.

"How's that dad of yours, then? I've always liked him, though for some reason he's never been able to remember my last name."

Jacy smiled. Jake hadn't been gone long, and already she missed him as sorely as if he'd left the planet in a rocket ship. Nancy somebody, he'd said, speaking of the new owner of the Yolanda Café. You'll like her.

"He's off to Adelaide with Collie Kilbride," she answered.

"Now there's a pair for you," Nancy observed, setting the sundae in front of Jacy. She remained behind the counter, elbow propped on the edge, chin resting on one palm. "It was glorious watching you hold your own with

Ian Yarbro yesterday. Not just anybody can do that, now, can they, and it was about time somebody stood up to him."

"Don't you like Ian?" Jacy asked, not sure what she wanted the answer to be.

Another dazzling smile. "Oh, he's a good bloke, Ian is. It's just that he's stubborn as a blind ox sometimes, and for some reason he thinks he ought to have his way about everything. He and Bram McCulley and Wilson Tate practically run the town."

Jacy had no doubt that that was true, and a soft sadness stole over her. She'd known another Ian once, one who'd spoken gently, and valued her ideas about things, and touched her with fingertips that left fire in their wake.

Dear God, how she missed him.

"Here now, cheer up," Nancy commanded. "You look as if the sun's just blinked out and there's no hope of it ever lighting up again."

Jacy's smile was real, if a bit tentative. "Sorry. I didn't mean to be glum." Again she wondered why it would be impossible to say something similar to Ian: "Sorry. I know you were trying to protect me, in your own misguided and officious way, when you hauled me bodily out of the Dog and Goose. . . ."

"So then sometimes the telly works, and sometimes it doesn't," Nancy finished. Obviously she'd taken the conversation onward while Jacy was framing an apology she would never offer. "Anyway, you're welcome to come by of a night and look at it with me, if you'd like."

Jacy pushed the remains of her sundae away and smiled. She wasn't a great TV enthusiast. Jake didn't own a set, since the house at Corroboree Springs was powered by a generator and electricity was used sparingly, and so far Jacy hadn't missed watching. Still, she wanted Nancy for a friend, and an invitation was an invitation. In Yolanda social events were thin on the ground.

"Say the word," she replied. "I'll bring the pizza." She

paused and frowned. She hadn't really looked at Yolanda, and suddenly she was curious. "What about the picture theater? Is it still open?"

Nancy shook her head and sighed wistfully. "No, it's been closed up since I came here. There was some talk of starting a theater group and putting on plays, but nothing ever came of it." She laughed. "Can you imagine any of these louts dressing up in tights and tunics and learning Shakespeare?"

The thought was too ridiculous. Or was it?

Ian in tights.

The temperature, already scorching, seemed to rise a few degrees. Jacy reached out and reclaimed her chocolate sundae.

Jacy kept herself busy all weekend. She washed clothes on Saturday, and when she found a current mail order catalog among the mysteries and cowboy novels on Jake's bookshelf she spent several happy hours planning a general facelift for the house.

On Sunday she put on a dress and drove into Yolanda to attend church. Since Paul's death she'd been on awkward terms with God, but she was willing to make a move in His direction. Although she saw Chris at services with Alice Wigget, a thin, sun-baked woman who shared a trailer on Ian's property—or a caravan, as the Aussies said—with half a dozen cats, there was no sign of Ian.

Not surprising, Jacy thought with a righteous sniff.

On Monday Gladys Shifflet came to school, though she didn't meet Jacy's eyes once during the whole day. Liander Tate wet his pants and had to be consoled, and Chris smiled a couple of times, though very shyly. Attendance in general was disappointingly sparse.

In the evening Jacy bought a frozen pizza at the grocery shop and went to Nancy's flat, which was behind the café. There they watched a rerun of an American TV movie, the screen so fuzzy at times that the characters looked like ghosts. Yolanda was a long way from any of the television transmitters, after all, and reception was a catch-as-catch-can kind of proposition.

Still, Jacy had a wonderful time, and she was in a fairly cheerful mood as she drove home late that night. When she arrived at Corroboree Springs lamps were burning in the kitchen, and Ian's truck was parked in the backyard.

Jake was home, and he'd evidently lost no time summoning Ian to tell him about his scheme to split the property. He'd probably sent Collie over to issue the invitation.

Jacy gave a ragged sigh, snatched her purse off the passenger seat of the jeep, and slammed the door when she got out. She was glad her dad was back, but she didn't want to see Ian. She hadn't had a chance to prepare herself.

When she stepped into the kitchen she heard Jake's voice from the living room, and then Ian's. She tossed her purse onto her bed, splashed her face with cool water, combed her hair, and then went out to join them.

Jake's eyes lit up with some secret merriment at the sight of her—what was he up to now?—but Ian looked as though he might still carry out his threat to turn her over his knee. To his credit, though, he grumbled and rose briefly from his chair.

Jacy responded with a cool nod and crossed the room to stand beside Jake. "Hiya, handsome," she said, bending to kiss his cheek. "I missed you."

Jake looked pleased, and his color was unusually high, it seemed to Jacy. Maybe he'd had a few too many drinks with Collie, or spent a lot of time outdoors while he was away. "Sit down, Jacy-me-girl," he said. "I was just about to tell Ian me grand plan."

Just don't mention the marriage of convenience, Jacy begged silently, giving her dad a pained smile and sinking into a chair. If you do that, I'll fall over in a quivering heap of humiliation. "Right," she said aloud.

She felt Ian's gaze touch her, warming her skin and mak-

80

ing her ache deep inside, in private places. She didn't dare look at him and, mercifully, he didn't speak.

Not then, at least.

Producing legal papers to back up his offer, Jake announced that he'd already signed his land over to Jacy and the springs themselves over to Ian.

Ian's surprise was palpable. He caught Jacy's eye for a moment, though she'd tried to evade him, and she saw a question forming in his face. He didn't ask it aloud, however. "You can't mean it," he told Jake. "This is your property—the land needs you to look after it."

Jacy didn't miss the way Ian spoke of the farm, as if the dirt itself were hallowed, a living thing with wishes and wants. She bit her lower lip and stayed quiet.

Jake shook his head. "No, Ian. I'm tired, and this is the only way I can lay down me burden without regret. There are other things I want to do."

Jacy thought, a little uncharitably perhaps, of the mystery woman waiting in Queensland.

Ian was still flustered, although on some level he had to be feeling relief, even jubilation. Jake had said Ian needed water for his sheep, that he would lose his property without it, and now he had water aplenty. It seemed to Jacy that he should have been satisfied.

"But I'm not—"

"My son," Jake finished for him. The gentle affection he bore his friend was visible in his face, and the sight of it brought tears to Jacy's eyes. "No, you're not. But you've been as fine a mate as a man could ever hope to have, and I know I can trust you to look after things around here."

Jacy winced. Oh, no, she thought wildly. Oh, Dad, please don't say it. . . .

"Of course, if I had me dearest wish, you'd marry me daughter," she heard Jake say in his affably blunt way. She gave an audible groan, unable to look at Ian, and the silence that followed was an immense and resounding one.

At long last Ian spoke.

"When hell freezes over," he said adamantly.

81

6

WHEN HELL FREEZES OVER.

Jacy was stung, and color surged into her face in a fiery rush. She responded quickly.

"As if I'd ever agree to marry the likes of you in the first place, Yarbro!"

Ian leaned forward in his chair. "As if I'd ever ask!"

"Stop it, both of you!" Jake broke in. "You sound like a pair of children." He sighed and looked at them both in exasperation. "Is it so hard to imagine a wedding? There was a time when you loved each other."

Jacy bit her lower lip and sank back in her chair, dangerously close to tears, and Ian gave an irritable sigh.

"That time is gone, Jake," he said after a short silence. He glanced at Jacy, dismissed her, and looked Jake straight in the eye. "Do I have to marry your daughter to get the springs?"

Jake studied his friend despairingly for a few seconds and, after that, Jacy. Then he replied hoarsely, "No. No, the water's yours, Ian, no matter what."

Jacy wanted to tell Ian that he'd have to get across her land first, not to mention her dead body, but she dismissed the idea as spiteful and infantile. In the end, she knew, she would go back to the United States, leaving Ian in control of the whole property.

The idea galled her.

Ian regarded Jake in solemn amazement. "I can't believe you'd do this. You could get a good price for this land from Merimbula."

"They're bastards at Merimbula," Jake said. Although he was trying to be a good sport, Jacy could see that her dad was disappointed in the evening's outcome. He had obviously expected Ian and Jacy to put their deep and long-standing differences aside and agree to a marriage based on water rights, fence lines, and easements.

Men!

Ian, damn his arrogant hide, looked relieved that Jake agreed with his assessment of the management of the area's largest station. He apparently felt no chagrin for his earlier rudeness. He extended his hand to Jake and rose from his chair at the same time.

"Thank you," Ian told his friend. "I don't know what else to say."

Jake's smile was a bit weak; he was plainly tired. "How about good night?" he suggested. "I'm tuckered."

Ian hesitated a moment, still clasping Jake's hand, then turned to retrieve his ever-present stockman's hat from the table beside his chair. In the middle of the motion, and probably quite by accident, he met Jacy's gaze, and the stark hostility in his eyes was wounding to see.

"Show Ian out, will you, darlin'?" Jake said, already making his way toward his room. "I'm off to me bed."

Jacy led Ian through the house to the back door out of spite, because she knew he'd rather she let him leave on his own.

At the bottom of the porch steps he turned to look back

at her, the brim of his hat and the shadows of the night hiding his expression. Jacy figured that was just as well.

Both of them stood there for a long moment, neither speaking. Jacy felt a deep sorrow; she'd known Ian disliked her, but until that moment in the living room when their eyes had met she hadn't begun to guess how much.

Finally Jacy broke the silence, never consciously planning the words she said. "Don't worry, Ian—I won't make things difficult for you. You'll have access to the springs—your springs—anytime you want it."

His voice was taut, as ruthlessly unyielding as the land that stretched out around them in every direction. "Good." With that, he got back into his rig and drove off.

Jacy sat down on the steps, drew up her knees, and laid her forehead against them. She didn't want to marry Ian Yarbro, she insisted to herself, not for a minute. But if that was the truth, why had his brusque rejection left her feeling as though she'd been torn apart by a pack of wild dogs?

As soon as Ian was out of sight of the house at Corroboree Springs, and out of earshot, he stopped the truck with a lurch, got out, and threw his hat down on the ground. He should have been celebrating, because Jake Tiernan had just saved his ass by giving him the springs, but instead he was furious with himself, with his old friend, and with the world in general.

He wanted Jacy with every muscle and fiber, and the idea of making her his wife, with all the sweet, fiery privileges that implied, made his blood sizzle. In his determination to resist those dangerous desires he'd treated Jacy as if he hated her.

And that, whether he would admit it to another living soul or not, was a long way from the truth.

With a curse Ian bent, snatched his hat up, and flung it into the rig. He'd be damned to hell, stripped naked, and dunked in sheep dip before he'd go back and apologize—

the last time he'd told that woman he was sorry she'd repaid him for the courtesy by taunting him.

Ian got behind the wheel again and sped toward home. It was getting on into the evening, and he still had plenty of work to do in the stables.

While he was feeding and watering the horses, though, he got to thinking about the seemingly inexhaustible supply of water at Corroboree Springs, and gradually his mood changed. He was whistling when he went into the house to wash and take his dried-up supper out of the warming oven.

Alice had stayed with Chris, and seeing that Ian was home, she prepared to get into her old car and leave to go back to her caravan.

"Time and past that you got yourself home, Ian Yarbro," she fussed. She'd been to America once, and there she'd gotten her right forearm tattooed with a cowboy on a bucking bronco. Ian was full of questions about that tattoo, but he didn't have the nerve to ask them.

"The boy's long since bathed and gone to bed," Alice said when Ian didn't speak.

He averted his gaze from the cowboy and the bronco and crossed the room. After taking up a pot holder he reached into the oven for his plate and peered cautiously under the foil that covered it. "Don't nag, Alice," he replied good-naturedly, heading for the table. "That's a privilege reserved for wives, and thank God I don't have one of those." Yet. The word floated unexpectedly to the surface of his mind, and he promptly pushed it back down.

"What are you so cheerful about, anyhow?" Alice demanded. It was clear that she wasn't going anywhere until she had the whole story. "I could hear you whistling before you were halfway up the back walk."

Ian was ravenous; he took a drumstick from his plate and eyed it with anticipation. "Jake Tiernan gave me the rights to the springs on his property tonight," he said, watching his housekeeper's reaction as he bit into the piece of chicken.

"He did what?" Her words were more an expression of disbelief than a question. "Go on with you! Jake loves that land. His own mother and father settled it. Why, he's been through fires and floods—"

Ian swallowed and wiped his mouth with the paper napkin Alice had left at his place at the table. He frowned, grasping for the first time the extent of the sacrifice Jake was making, walking away from his family homestead like that. "He's tired, he says."

Alice made a huffing sound, but her eyes were sad. "Sounds to me like Jake's made up his mind to go ahead and die," she said. Then she grabbed her handbag and a crumpled package of unfiltered cigarettes and left.

Ian's appetite went with her. He had a nagging suspicion that Alice was right—Jake was through trying.

He carried his plate to the trash bin, scraped what remained of his dinner into it, and went into the seldom-used front room. There he sat down in his mother's old rocking chair without bothering to light a lamp against the thick darkness, and he thought.

Jake had wanted Ian to marry Jacy and look after her because he knew he wouldn't be around much longer.

Ian rubbed his temples with a thumb and forefinger. Hell and damnation. Jake Tiernan had given him the precious supply of water that would make the difference between survival and failure, and he'd been counting on Ian to take care of his daughter in return. Not only had Ian let him down, he'd been flippant about it.

He sighed raggedly there in the darkness and wondered what in hell he was supposed to do next. Even if he did ask Jacy to marry him, as Jake wanted, she'd only laugh in his face.

"Dad?"

The sound of Chris's voice startled Ian. He stopped rocking and turned toward the doorway, where his son's small frame made a dark shape in the shadows. "Hello, lad."

Chris stayed where he was. "I heard Alice say Jake was

going to die," he said shakily. "We're mates, Jake and me. He showed me how to throw a boomerang."

Ian crossed the room, put an arm around the lad's shoulders, and guided him in the direction of the main hallway. It was time they both put the troubles and worries of the day aside and got some sleep.

"We're all worried about Jake," Ian admitted, wanting to be as honest with Chris as he could without laying a heavy burden on him. "He's been sick, after all, and he's tuckered out most of the time. Still, there's no way any of us can guess what's going to happen, and Mrs. Wigget was only speculating."

The room was drenched in moonlight, and when Chris was settled in bed again Ian could plainly see the fear in the little boy's face. "You won't die, will you, Dad?"

Ian drew a deep breath and let it out as a heavy sigh. "Sure I will, lad—you know that. We all have to go when our turn comes."

Chris's eyes looked huge, and Ian ached for him. "What if you die before you get old—like tomorrow or next month? What will happen to me then?"

It was a hard question to field, since all Ian and Chris really had was each other. Elaine hadn't wanted the boy; in fact, she'd have had him aborted if Ian hadn't begged her, practically on his knees, to see the pregnancy through to the end and let him raise the child. Chris didn't know his mother's parents, the Bennetts, and Ian couldn't guess where they'd gone after Mr. Bennett had resigned his post as manager of Merimbula. Perhaps they had even returned to the States. For all he knew, they would be no more interested in their grandchild than their daughter had been.

But Chris was watching his face, and Ian had to make a stab at answering. "Mrs. Wigget would look after you," he said. "And don't lie here worrying about it, do you hear me? I'm not planning to turn up my toes in the immediate future." To lighten the moment he tickled Chris, but instead of laughing as he usually did, the poor little nipper

87

hurled his arms around Ian's neck and clung with all his might.

Only when Ian stretched out beside Chris in the small bed, still fully clothed right down to his boots, did the lad relax and finally go to sleep.

Ian lay there thinking for a long time, watching the moon make shadows on the ceiling. He had promised Chris he wouldn't die, though of course he had no real control over that.

What *would* happen to the boy if he, Ian, died before his time? Mrs. Wigget wasn't the sort to raise another child; she meant to retire one of these days anyway. She'd been saving her money for years, planning to go traveling as soon as the last of her cats died of old age.

No, Chris would probably be put into a foster home or an orphanage, even though he had an inheritance, until he was eighteen.

Jacy came unbidden to Ian's mind. She might have despised him, but she was gentle and affectionate with her students; Ian had seen that even during his brief visits to the schoolhouse. If he did marry her—and he had by no means decided to humiliate himself by proposing—she would be a fair mother to Chris.

Ian left his son's room as quietly as he could, and proceeded to his own. There he stripped and lay down on his bed, his hands clasped together behind his head. He could hear the wind coming up now, whispering around the sides of the house and beneath the eaves.

There was yet another reason, if he were to be completely honest with himself, why he would consider biting the proverbial bullet and asking Jacy to marry him. He wanted her in his bed.

"You're out of your mind, Ian Yarbro," he told himself aloud. "Jacy Tiernan wouldn't have you if a band of angels argued in your favor."

The wind rose, the whisper replaced by a low whistle. Normally he would have gotten up, dressed, and gone outside to see if the weather was turning, but that night he just lay there, lonesome as hell and more confused than ever before.

The sound of the wind kept rising in pitch throughout the night, and by morning it was a dry, screeching storm, blotting out the sky, flinging coarse dust at the walls and windows. Jacy got up at dawn and found dirt sifting in under the kitchen door, reaching further and further across the floor.

Dust storms were one of the things she *didn't* love about Australia. They usually lasted only a few hours, but they had been known to go on for days on end. People had been driven insane by the incessant shrieking, the gloom, the confinement.

Jake came in as she was turning up the flame beneath the teakettle, and he had a reassuring, if weary, smile on his face. Dear God in heaven, Jacy wondered, how could he have aged so much in only ten years? And how could she have stayed away all that time, thinking only of herself?

"Don't be scared, Jacy-me-girl," her father said, touching her shoulder briefly as he passed her on his way to the kitchen window. "It's a natural thing, a storm like this— just the land resituating itself."

Jacy consciously released the tension in her neck and shoulders. The truth was, there was more than the storm bothering her; she had hardly slept the night before for remembering how quickly Ian had rejected the idea of marrying her, remembering the cold distaste she'd seen in his eyes. She didn't want him—by all that was holy, *she didn't*—but it hurt to know he didn't want her either.

She got out eggs and milk and started an omelet to share with Jake. "It'll seem strange not going to school," she said. She was skirting the subject of Ian, even though she wanted to talk about him, wanted to rail at her dad for putting her in such an embarrassing position.

"The nippers always welcome a holiday from their lessons," Jake observed, still standing at the window, looking out. He'd filled his mug from the kettle, and now he was taking slow, leisurely sips of tea. When he spoke again it was almost as if he were just musing aloud, not talking to Jacy at all. "If I still had me strength, I'd go out and see how Ian's farin' with those sheep of his. He'll lose a few, no doubt."

Jacy closed her eyes for a moment, not out of concern for Ian's sheep, but because it hurt even hearing his name. She wondered what she had to do to get over this stupid obsession with a man who had taught her the finer points of heartache.

"Surely even he won't go out in this," she commented. The howling of the wind was growing more unnerving with each passing moment.

"He'll be out, all right, and so will the men who work for him," Jake responded with quiet certainty. "Ian Yarbro looks after what's his."

Jacy cut the omelet down the middle with the side of the spatula, then slid the parts onto two plates. "Yes," she murmured irritably. "He's a paragon, all right. An inspiration to us all."

Jake turned at that and stumped over to the table. There was a kindly, sorrowful light in his eyes as he sat down across from Jacy. "I don't believe for a moment that you truly hate Ian," he said, "but for some reason you want the rest of us—especially him—to think you do."

A fine layer of dust covered their food, and since they both knew there was no escaping it, they ate anyway.

Jacy took her time answering. "It would be pretty stupid to let myself care about him again, wouldn't it?" she reasoned, watching the dirt swirl dark beyond the window. "It's plain to see how he feels about me."

"Is it?" Jake inquired gently, leaning forward in his chair. "He was all but destroyed after you left him, Jacy-girl. Maybe he doesn't want to risk going through that again."

90

She shifted her gaze to the food on her plate, unable to meet her father's eyes. There was an unwritten code in the Australian bush, she knew; the land was cruel, the weather unpredictable and often violent, and the worst thing you could do to another person, mate or lover, was abandon him.

"I didn't leave without good reason," she said, but her words sounded lame even to her. "Ian had fathered a baby with another woman—"

"A woman he'd stopped seeing. Doesn't it make a difference to you, knowing Ian would take in a little bit of a baby, and him barely nineteen when the nipper was born, to raise all alone? That should tell you that he doesn't take his responsibilities lightly, and that's a rare quality these days."

Ian was a good father to Chris; that much Jacy had already determined by watching the man and boy interact. It was clear that Ian loved his son, and, unlike a lot of men, he wasn't afraid to show his affection.

Jacy bent her head and sighed, pressing her fingertips to her temples. "Okay, Dad—you win. It's true that I never got over Ian, never had a real relationship with a man after we broke up. I'm one of the walking wounded. I'm terrified of opening myself up to him—you heard the things he said last night—because if he knocks me down again, I'm not sure I'll be able to get back up." Her vision was blurred by tears when she met Jake's gaze at last. "And you know what? This is the pitiful part—if he'd agreed to marry me, even as a business proposition, I might have said yes."

"And gone right on pretending you didn't care for him?" Jake marveled quietly.

She plunged her fork into her gritty omelet again, determined to finish even though she'd temporarily lost her appetite. At Corroboree Springs just coping took energy, and she had to sustain herself.

"Yes," she admitted.

"For how long?"

"Until I knew he loved me back," Jacy retorted stubbornly. "And that might be forever."

Jake let out his breath. "That it might," he agreed with a certain sad resignation. He gave up on his breakfast and carried his plate to the sink, then wandered into the front room without another word. He wasn't ignoring Jacy; he was distracted, as if her presence had slipped his mind.

When Jacy joined him, making a pretense of reading, he was sitting at the desk, turning the dial on the radio. Now, on top of the screaming barrage of wind buffeting the walls and rattling the windows, Jacy's ears were assaulted by intermittent static.

She tried to concentrate on her book, having settled into her grandmother's rocking chair with her legs curled beneath her, but between the radio and the storm itself she finally gave up. She was pacing when a blast of wind *whooshed* down the chimney and sent ashes billowing out of the fireplace.

Conversation was useless, for as the day progressed, so did the storm. It was as if the wind were determined to sweep all traces of humankind from the surface of the earth.

Ian wore a kerchief over his nose and mouth, but the grit got through anyway, and soon his lungs and nasal passages burned with the stuff. The assault on his eyes was relentless, and he had to battle his horse—he'd trained the animal personally to work under almost any circumstances—to keep it from bolting.

He didn't blame the beast for wanting shelter; just then Ian would have given almost anything to be out of the grating wind. All the same, he kept going, and so did the sheepdogs, because the flocks were out in the open.

Sheep weren't God's most brilliant creatures, and as likely as not they would panic and scatter in terror. He could trust his men, Killgoran and Bates, to look after the mobs they normally tended, but the ones in the paddock closest to the house were Ian's personal responsibility.

He found them huddled into a mass, heads toward the center, bleating and struggling to climb over one another.

There was a fairly deep gully a short distance away where the woollies could take refuge until the bad weather let up a little, but getting them there would be the trick. They were half frenzied in their fear.

The dogs—by some magic Ian had divined but never come to understand, though he had seen the phenomenon time and time again—went into immediate action, flanking the sheep and attempting to muster them in the right direction. Ian swung off his horse, which immediately fled into the spinning gloom, and waded into the center of the sheep, shouting until his throat was raw, trying to push the writhing, leaping bodies toward safety.

Between the dogs and his own blind but earnest efforts they finally got the animals moving. When the majority were in the gully, still carrying on as if they were being skinned alive, Ian went back to look for stragglers.

It was impossible to see, and by that time he couldn't hear the dogs, Blue and Mustard, though he knew he could trust them to patrol the edges of the mob.

Ian had been raised in the bush, and this wasn't the first dust storm he'd been through by any means, but for a moment, standing there in the raging void, he was afraid. He'd lost his bearings and the house might have been in any direction. The vague bleating of ewes, a sound he felt rather than heard, drew him deeper and deeper into the encompassing darkness.

He found a sheep caught in some brush and freed it by rote. The frightened animal squirmed and tried to run away, and Ian held it against his chest, arms wrapped around its middle, and buried his face in its side.

The wind, sharp with dirt, pelted him from every quarter. It dug through the fabric of his shirt, abraded the back of his neck, got under his hat to grind against his scalp. After a while Ian struggled to his feet and started moving again, carrying the small ewe in his arms, listening for the dogs or the rest of the mob. He heard nothing but the bawling of the animal he carried and the unearthly screech of the wind.

Keep walking, he told himself. He didn't like to think that he might be stumbling deeper into the bush, where a man could die of thirst or exposure without going to any real trouble at all. There were brown snakes and wild boars to contend with, too, but Ian preferred to believe they had gone to ground, like the other wild creatures, to escape the slicing ferocity of the wind.

The storm kept rising in intensity, and finally the roar of it drowned out even the bleating of the sheep in Ian's arms. Breathing grew more and more difficult until he felt as though he were choking.

He thought frantically of Chris and the conversation they'd had only the night before, when he'd rashly promised not to die. What a hell of an irony it would be if fate made a liar of him so soon.

Ian was tired. His knees gave out; he got back up again, still carrying the ewe. When something struck him hard in the back of the head he went down a second time. The sheep scrambled free and ran off in a panic, and Ian stayed where he was, half conscious and breathing dirt.

He awakened sometime later to the feeling of a long tongue lashing the back of his neck. The wind had stopped, darkness had fallen, and he was half buried.

Grinning, delighted to be alive even though his head felt like it was about to cave in on itself, Ian rolled over onto his back and saw one blue eye and one green one staring back at him. Blue. His best dog.

With a hoarse laugh Ian yanked the kerchief from his face and sat up to ruffle the fur on top of the mutt's head.

"Came out looking for me, did you?" he said. "Thanks, mate. I owe you for that one." Ian got to his feet, staggered, and righted himself. It was night, but a big, hazy moon spilled light over the landscape, and the familiar pattern of stars told him the way home.

As it was, he was closer to Jake Tiernan's place than his own, and he was still a little dazed and unsteady from the blow to the back of his head. Even though he knew it meant encountering Jacy—the last person on earth he wanted to deal with just then—he realized he had no choice but to stop there. He wouldn't be able to make it to his own house on foot.

The lights of Jake's house lifted his heart; the older man had been a good friend to Ian, especially after his father died. He could be counted upon to welcome a mate, no matter how late the hour.

He crossed the yard, stopping once and grasping the pole at one end of the clothesline until the ground stopped spinning and he could focus on his destination. Had he not been on the verge of collapsing again, Ian would have laughed at the expression on Jacy's face when she answered his knock. He must have looked like a red ghost, covered from head to foot with dust.

He lurched forward, and she caught him—she was strong for a sheila—and her voice seemed to echo through a tube when she turned her head to call out to her dad.

Ian dropped into a chair at the table, and Jacy immediately began poking and prodding at the sore spot on the back of his head.

"What happened?" she demanded, and it sounded as though she were in another room instead of just behind him.

He flinched and then cursed as she pulled the hair of his head aside to examine his injury. "I was hit by a train," he replied with all the mockery he could manage, and then Jake was in the room, too, frowning, banging pots about, filling one from the teakettle.

Jacy got even for his sarcasm by going after the gash with hot water and a cloth. "Time out," she said in that same peculiar, distorted voice. "We'll exchange barbs later. Right now, Ian, you're hurt, and you need looking after.''

A strange, embarrassing kind of tenderness swept over Ian; he couldn't remember the last time a woman had taken care of him. "Something hit me—a shingle or something caught up in the wind," he said with a hoarseness he attributed to all the dust he'd swallowed in the last few hours. He sat up a little straighter in the chair. "I'm all right. It's Chris I care about—Alice is there with him, but he'll be that worried that I didn't come home." Again Ian thought of the conversation he had had with his son about death. He started to rise, set on going to the boy right then, but Jacy put her hands on his shoulders and pushed him back down.

Jake, in the meantime, had come round to have a look at the wound. "This wants stitches," he said. "Two, maybe three."

He went off to fetch the appropriate instruments of torture.

Jacy sat down in a chair next to Ian's and put her hands on either side of his dirt-caked face. He had no doubt that even his eyebrows and his lashes were thick with the stuff, and he found himself wishing that he looked his best.

"Relax," she told him with a smile resting on her lips and, at the same time, dancing in her eyes. Ian felt a painful tightening sensation deep in his gut. "I'll drive over and let Chris know you're all right."

Ian nodded, wanting to hold Jacy close, to seek sweet sanction in her embrace. Maybe the injury was worse than he'd guessed, because he was suddenly swamped with tender sentiments. He'd have gone ahead and kissed her, in fact, if Jake hadn't come in with a needle and thread and a bottle of rum and announced that he was ready to start sewing.

7

As Jacy drove toward Ian's house she marveled to herself at the chilling beauty of the land. It seemed surreal, in the sweep of her headlights and the glow of the moon, like the landscape of some strange, distant planet. Dust lay in drifts, not only on the ground but on the posts of the rail fence edging Jake's empty paddock. In places the stuff rose in shifting mounds on the road itself, and she had to downshift and accelerate to get through it.

The Yarbro property was fairly close by, and Jacy reached it within ten minutes. Lantern lights glowed inside the large house—no doubt the storm had clogged up the generator, as it had done at Corroboree Springs—and the back door flew open the moment Jacy stepped out of the truck.

Chris stood on the porch, and his expression was one of frank disappointment.

Jacy laid her hands on the boy's small, thin shoulders. "Your dad's okay, Chris—he's at Corroboree Springs right now, with Jake."

Alice Wigget filled the doorway behind him, and Jacy

saw tears of relief in the older woman's eyes. Though she looked tough enough to wrestle a wild boar and win, Alice was a kindly sort—Jacy had figured that out long ago.

"Nothing would keep that hardheaded fool from going out into the storm—"

Chris's eyes were solemn as he looked up at Jacy. "Why did Dad stay with Jake? Why didn't you bring him with you?"

Jacy gave the boy a quick hug and ushered him into the spacious kitchen. The familiarity of the place gave her a pang, for she'd eaten many meals in that room, at that very table, with Ian and his father, Mike.

She sat down beside Chris on the bench and shook her head when Mrs. Wigget silently offered tea.

"Ian had a small accident," Jacy said carefully. "Something struck him in the back of the head during the storm, and he was knocked out, as well as cut." Seeing the rising alarm in Chris's face, she hastened to go on. "Your dad will be all right, I promise. He just needs a little looking after, that's all. I'll bring him home in the morning."

Chris looked only slightly mollified. "I could go back to Corroboree Springs with you and spend the night. Just in case Dad needs me for something."

Jacy's heart twisted, but the memory of Jake getting ready to stitch up Ian's gash stopped her from agreeing to the plan. There would be considerable pain involved, and the whole process was bound to be upsetting to a child.

"Just this once," she said gently, slipping one arm around Chris, "will you trust me to look after him?" She crossed her heart with her free hand and held it up in an oath. "I swear I'll protect Ian for you."

At last, and warily, Chris smiled. "All right," he agreed. "But don't forget to bring him home first thing."

Jacy planted a light kiss on his forehead. "Word of honor," she said. "And now I'd better be getting back. Sleep tight, Chris—there'll be school tomorrow if the roads are passable, and you'll need your rest."

Chris looked up at Jacy with his beautiful hazel eyes, and in that very moment he took permanent possession of her heart. "Tell my dad I'm glad he didn't die," he said.

Jacy's throat tightened, and she and Alice exchanged looks. The fact was, Ian could easily have been killed; many experienced bushmen before him had perished in such storms. "I'm glad, too," she answered gently.

On the way over Jacy had been able to distract herself from thoughts of Ian by concentrating on the aftermath of the tempest, but on the trip back it was a different story. What if Ian *had* died, with all the bad feeling between them? If that had happened, she'd have been left with remorse to deal with, as well as grief.

She shifted the truck into a lower gear, since the dust was still deep on the road, and sighed. Suppose she did try to make peace with Ian? He might very well laugh in her face.

Just the prospect made her narrow her eyes and set her jaw. It would be just like that mule-headed son of a dingo to scorn her. . . .

The pain was worse than anything Ian had suffered up to that point, and even the half bottle of rum he'd consumed didn't help. The cleaning of the wound had been bad enough, but when Jake shoved the needle through his flesh for the first time he nearly bolted out of his chair.

"Here now, sit still," Jake scolded. "Swear if you want to, but no more of that bouncing about."

Ian swore roundly, but he sat still and endured his mate's ministrations until the thread was tied off.

"We'll have to keep an eye on that," Jake said, frowning. "An infection might take hold."

Ian took another long draught of rum. Liquor, like strong emotion, caused his speech to thicken into the broguelike meter typical of bushmen. "If you're through torturin' me, Jake Tiernan, I'll be on me way."

"You're goin' nowhere," Jake answered, surveying Ian's

dirt-covered frame. "Probably should have hosed you down before we did any sewin'. I'd offer you the use of the shower, but you're wearin' half the outback, and you'd no doubt clog up the drain. Go down and dip yourself in the springs, if you've got the strength to take yourself that far, and I'll see about makin' up a bed for you."

Ian rose, pushing his chair back, glared at Jake for a moment, and then wove his way through the house to the front door. If he had the strength to take himself that far indeed, he thought as he crossed the seemingly interminable distance to the springs.

There, as everywhere, the dust coated the grass and even the leaves in the trees, but the force of the water had already carried away any grit that might have settled on the surface.

Slowly, painfully, Ian took off his clothes and walked into the pool just to one side of the springs. It was like a cool caress, and for a few moments he forgot everything but the pure sensual pleasure of the water against his wind-scoured flesh.

Washing the dirt from his hair proved a painful process, however, and he was cursing when he felt a sudden stillness inside. Usually the sensation was a warning of danger, but when Ian turned his head he saw Jacy standing on the bank.

"Brought you some of Jake's clothes and a towel," she said, holding up a bundle. Her words had been offered cautiously, as though she'd expected to be rebuffed, and a swift, piercing sensation of regret struck Ian at his center.

Ian's response came out sounding as rough as the dirt that had ground itself into his skin. "Thanks," he said. "Chris is all right, then?"

Jacy nodded, just standing there bathed in moonlight, holding the clothes against her chest. Ian wished she'd go away and, conversely, that she would strip off her jeans and blouse and wade in to join him.

For a time they just stared at each other, and the silence seemed as vast as the "wide brown country" itself.

Jacy finally broke it, setting the bundle carefully on the grass. "Good night," she said, too brightly, as though there had never been fire between them, as though they hadn't loved and hated each other, as though they hadn't created whole new universes when they made love.

She turned, and Ian, his body stone weary, his head throbbing with pain, his gut writhing in protest against the rum he'd consumed, found that he couldn't bear to see her walk away.

"Jacy," he said, and she stopped without turning to face him. Even in the moonlight he saw her shoulders tense beneath the thin fabric of her blouse. "Don't go—please."

She hesitated; for a few treacherous moments he thought she would ignore him, or spin about, blue eyes flashing, and tell him to go straight to hell.

"You said it earlier," Ian went on, quietly desperate. " 'Time out.' Just for tonight let's agree to a truce."

At last she rounded to look him in the face, and the depth of Ian's gratitude was ridiculous. Her manner was wary, but the suppressed anger that usually crackled in every muscle was gone. "Is this a joke?"

Ian looked away a moment, stricken to know that she suspected a verbal ambush. At the same time he had to admit she had every reason to expect just that. "I thought we could talk, that's all. We're going to be business partners after this, you know. We ought to learn to exchange a civil word, don't you think?"

Jacy took a step forward, but she was still cautious, braced to do battle or to flee. She squinted, and the beginnings of a smile touched her mouth. Her soft, luscious, inviting mouth . . .

"Is that Ian Yarbro talking?" she teased.

He laughed for an answer and splashed a little water her way with one hand, and for a few golden seconds it seemed they were eighteen again, safe in their sweet, youthful love.

He yearned to capture the magic, but he knew it was a fleeting thing, and all the more precious for the fact.

Jacy bent and sent a responding spray flying over him like liquid crystal. Then she crouched beside the pool and looked at him with sad curiosity. She wanted an explanation for the change in his attitude toward her, and it was only fair to give her one.

"I've been thinking over what Jake said—about our getting married, I mean."

She went absolutely still, like a wild thing sensing peril.

Ian let out a ragged sigh. Obviously, the burden was on him. "Maybe it's not such a bad idea."

Jacy put her hand over her heart and spread her fingers. Her mouth opened once, then closed again. Finally she spoke. *"Not such a bad idea?* Ian, you said not twenty-four hours ago that hell would freeze over first. Frankly, I have to wonder just how bad that head wound of yours really is."

He felt the magic toppling, ready to fall and splinter at their feet, and he grasped it with all his strength of spirit. "I was wrong," he said.

Jacy stared at him in bewilderment for a long time, plainly wondering what he was up to. "We're not in love with each other," she pointed out. "That would be a problem."

Ian shrugged and held out one arm, and Jacy tossed the towel to him. "Why? It wouldn't be the first time a couple married for practical reasons, especially out here."

"What's in this for you?" she asked suspiciously, watching as he came toward the bank. He took his time wrapping the towel around his middle.

"There's the land, for one thing. Our two properties joined together would be on a par with Merimbula." He sat down on the grass beside her, moving slowly partly because he was lightheaded from the day's ordeal and partly because he didn't want to scare her away. Finally, wearing nothing but the towel, he found the courage to look her directly in the face. "I won't deny that I want you, Jacy Tiernan. I kept waiting for it to stop—the wanting, I mean—but it never did."

Jacy was quiet. He saw her throat move as she swallowed, and he wanted to kiss her there, at the pulse point. Among other places.

"Do I have to do all the talking, Tiernan?" he finally demanded with a half grin. "Or are you going to help me out a little here?"

She wet her lips, and Ian felt another grinding clench far down inside him. "It's just that you caught me off guard, that's all. I don't really know what to say."

Ian couldn't resist any longer. He bent his head and brushed her mouth lightly with his, then paused, a breath away, giving her time to draw back if she wanted.

Jubilation coursed through him when she slipped her arms around his neck instead and pulled him toward her.

The kiss was deep and wet and completely mutual, and the old desire flared within Ian, then blazed across his soul like a bushfire devouring dry grass. He knew he couldn't take her—not there, with Jake so close by—but at the same time he wondered if he'd be able to stop, because she was offering herself.

With a groan Ian pressed her back onto the ground, kissing her throat, and her hands moved on his bare shoulder blades, his spine, the small of his back. He raised his head with a gasp. "Oh, God, Jacy—we've got to stop this now—"

She was opening the buttons of her blouse, spreading the fabric apart. Only sheer silk and lace hid her breasts from him, and he saw her nipples plainly, tightening for him. Asking.

He groaned again, rasped a second plea. "Jacy—"

She undid the front catch of her bra, and then she was bared to him, and Ian was lost. He fell to her with a low cry, greedy for her, and she arched slightly to accommodate him. With one hand she stroked his hair, careful to avoid the wound, and that was as electrifying anything she could have done.

Her breaths were quick and shallow, and Ian opened the front of her jeans with one hand while he enjoyed her breasts, each in turn. He slid his fingers between her skin and her clothes, and when he found the soft, hidden nubbin of her femininity, she cried out softly and raised herself to him.

As badly as Ian wanted this woman, writhing warm and willing beneath him, he knew he couldn't take her—not then, not there, just a stone's throw from her father's door. But he could please her, and make her yearn for his bed, and he set his mind to those things.

He knew how to touch her, and where—it all came back.

"Ian," she whispered, pleading.

"Shhh," he said gently, wanting to soothe her even as he inflamed her. "There now, it's all right, love—I'll see to your pleasure, I promise—"

Jacy made a soft, strangled sound, one of desperation and surrender.

It was music to Ian's soul. He slipped downward and kissed her soft, trembling belly even as he smoothed her jeans over her hips and thighs. She whimpered when he teased her, stroking the silken tangle lightly with his fingers, and she gave herself up completely when he took her with his mouth.

Jacy writhed in the dusty grass, her breasts bared to the night sky, her jeans and underpants gone and forgotten. All she knew in those wild, fevered moments was Ian—Ian's hands, Ian's mouth, Ian's tongue.

He satisfied her in stages, just as he had always done, bringing her to a shattering climax only to carry her higher after that, to another plain of pleasure. And while he consumed her he raised his hands to her breasts, fondling them, alternately stroking and lightly pinching the nipples.

She came with a long, low cry, rising high, and before

she touched the ground she was climbing again, toward another pinnacle.

Ian might have kept her going from one response to the next throughout the night if she hadn't finally broken down and begged him to let her rest.

She expected him to mount her, wanted him to do that, but instead he withdrew, avoiding her gaze, and started wrenching on his clothes.

Jacy stared at him in disbelief; it was plain enough that he wanted her, and just as plain that he meant to turn away.

"Ian?" She found her jeans, put them on, and started to button her blouse. "What is it?"

He glanced toward the house. "Jake is the best friend I've ever had," he said, fastening his pants with some difficulty. "I don't know what I was thinking, making love to the man's daughter in his front yard."

Jacy was frustrated, but she was relieved, too. She'd feared on some level that Ian was rejecting her, and that would have been unbearable just then. "You've changed," she teased. "It never bothered you to make love to me in the loft of Jake's hay shed, if I remember correctly."

"I was a kid then," Ian said, irritable. He came over, extended his hand, and pulled Jacy to her feet. She tumbled, by accident or design, against his chest, and his grin flashed white in the darkness. "I'd ask if I pleased you," he said, "but the way you carried on answered all my questions."

Jacy was amazed to realize that she could have melted into him, could have and surely *would* have responded yet again if he'd laid her down on the ground and entered her. It was disturbing to think that a man had that much power over her, especially one who didn't love her.

She looked up into his eyes, hoping the night would camouflage the hot blush that had surged into her face. "You're no gentleman, Ian Yarbro."

He curved one hand around her breast and bent to kiss her lightly on the mouth. However fleeting, it was a prophecy of other seductions, of long, delicious hours of total surrender. "You wouldn't want a gentleman in your bed, at least not all the time," he answered at long last as her nipple pressed eagerly against his palm, "any more than I'd want a lady."

It was only too true. She liked the commanding way Ian made love to her, and when she was intimate with him, she was anything but a lady.

She touched the front of his pants, where his rod still pressed against the rough cloth, powerful and hard. "You owe me," she warned in a sultry voice, "and I'm going to make sure you pay up."

Ian groaned and let his head fall back, surrendering to her stroking fingers. "Oh, I'll pay, all right," he breathed as he clasped her wrist and pulled her hand away. "Believe me."

When they entered the house there was a single lamp burning, and the couch was made up with blankets and a pillow. Jake had obviously gone to bed.

Leaving Ian to go and lie down in her own bed was one of the hardest things Jacy had ever done. Her body still pulsed and throbbed in places, alive with the aftershocks of the merciless pleasure Ian had shown her. She felt hypersensitive, as though even the merest touch would be too much, and when she had taken off her clothes she lay down naked on the bed and closed her eyes.

An instant later she was asleep.

It was hard facing him the next morning at breakfast. Jake had gone down to the springs, Ian told Jacy, to meditate. They both knew the truth—Jake wanted them to be alone together.

Jacy went to the percolator, her color high as she recalled the events of the night before, and poured coffee with a shaky hand.

She drew in her breath when she felt Ian behind her. He

laid his hands on her hips possessively and kissed the side of her neck.

"We're not going to pretend last night didn't happen, love," he warned gently. "It was magic, and I've never wanted a woman the way I wanted you."

Jacy turned and looked up into his eyes, searching desperately for a lie, for any indication that he was about to hurt her again. Her blush heightened, but she blurted out her question all the same. "So when are we going to do something about that, Mr. Yarbro?"

He grinned, amused by her embarrassment, and though the light in his eyes was kindly, she saw an elemental passion blazing behind that. "As soon as possible," he said. "I'll get in touch with Collie and have him fly in a magistrate. As soon as you're my wife we'll have Alice take Chris home for the night, and you and I will complete our transaction." He touched the tip of her nose with his index finger. "We'll need the house to ourselves that first time, because you're going to make a whole lot of noise."

Jacy smiled, leaning closer. "You might have to holler a couple of times yourself," she predicted. She tilted her head back then, and Ian kissed her, and neither of them heard Jake come into the house.

He was in the kitchen with them before they noticed him, and that was only because he cleared his throat loudly.

Ian looked at his friend and frowned, and when Jacy turned to face her father she felt a flash of sudden, piercing fear. It was almost a premonition, and she pushed it away immediately.

Jake grinned; the ghost of the old mischief appeared briefly in his eyes. "Well? Is there something either of you would like to tell me?"

Jacy lowered her eyes, afraid even after all Ian's reassurances to say the words aloud. It might jinx things, or maybe she would find herself back in bed, alone, waking up from a dream.

"I asked Jacy to marry me last night," Ian said. He

smiled down into her eyes, his hands resting on either side of her waist. "If she says no, I won't be responsible for the consequences."

"I won't say no," she said.

And so it was settled.

Jacy drove Ian home in the truck, and Chris came hurtling out the back door the moment she'd brought the vehicle to a stop. Before opening the door to greet his son Ian reached over and passed his fingers ever so lightly across the top of Jacy's thigh.

A hot shiver went through her, and despite her effort to hide it, Ian was completely aware of her response. In fact, it was almost as though he were inside her skin with her, sharing her breath and her heartbeat and every sensation that played in her nerve endings.

"Don't worry, sheila," he teased as Chris drew nearer. "I'll take proper care of you, and soon."

Jacy was trembling, glad she didn't have to get out of the truck because she wasn't sure her knees would hold her. She smiled as Chris flung himself into Ian's arms.

"Remember," she called to Chris in what she prayed was an ordinary voice, "school today."

Chris made a face, and Ian ruffled the boy's hair with a tenderness that touched a soft place in Jacy's heart. Ian's gaze, when he raised it to her face, was a man's gaze, full of scandalous promises.

"I'll bring him into town myself," he told her. "I've some business with Collie, and with any luck he'll be found in the Dog and Goose."

She swallowed once and then nodded stupidly, not knowing what to say. Everything had happened so fast, and she couldn't help fearing that Ian would suddenly change his mind and treat her with cold disdain again.

It would be too terrible, too humiliating to lose Ian again now, after the way she'd responded to him the night before. He'd heated her blood, and the underlying need of him was a warm, persistent ache, a desire only he could satisfy.

Jacy taught school that day, and the next, and the one after that. Every moment of that time Ian was in her mind, taking her over, preparing her for his conquering.

It was the following Saturday when Collie flew in with a magistrate in tow. The wedding itself was quiet, held in the living room of Ian's homestead, with only Jake and Collie and Alice and Chris present, but it was understood that there would have to be a party soon. The community would expect to share in the celebration at some point, and disappointing so many old and loyal friends was unthinkable.

As it was, it seemed to Jacy that the festivities stretched interminably. In truth, the words were said, and they all had some of the cake Alice Wigget had made for the occasion, along with punch and a round or two of cold beer, and then Collie and the magistrate were ready to go.

"I'll catch a lift with you, if you don't mind," Jake said to his old friend, the crazy bush pilot. "Just give me a moment to kiss the bride and shake the groom's hand."

His blue eyes shone as Jake looked deep in Jacy's soul and smiled at whatever he saw there. "Behave yourself," he said. He didn't need to say he loved her; the emotion was almost palpable between them. He kissed her forehead and turned to shake Ian's hand. "Be good to her, or so help me, I'll set the devil himself on your trail and pay him overtime for his trouble."

A light rain had started up, tapping gently at the windows and the porch roof. Maybe it was a trick of the light, but Jacy thought she saw a deep sorrow in her new husband's eyes as he said good-bye to Jake.

Mrs. Wigget and Chris were the next to leave. Chris was one big smile, and he'd already asked Jacy if he could call her Mum—except at school, of course. She'd hugged him close and kissed him soundly on top of the head and told him she'd always wanted somebody just about his size to call her Mum. Wasn't it convenient that he'd offered?

"Come along now, Chris," Alice nagged in her blustery but benign way. "We've got to stay ahead of this rain, and my cats will be expecting us back." With that, they were gone, and the house was empty except for the bride and groom.

For one paralyzing moment Jacy wondered what she'd gotten herself into. She didn't love this man, however much he stirred her senses, and yet she'd married him. And she was committed to Chris now, too; a little boy was counting on her to be there for him.

Ian came to stand facing her, in the shadowy living room draped with sagging crepe paper streamers, and curved a finger under her chin. "No doubts, my love," he ordered gruffly. "This is a night for believing in miracles."

He touched his lips to hers then, not with passion but with a devastating tenderness, and Jacy believed, because that kiss was a miracle in and of itself.

"And now," he said, when at last he drew back, "you have a promise or two to keep." He lifted her easily into his arms and started toward the stairs, and Jacy thought the anticipation alone would be the end of her. "Or do you plan to go back on your word?"

Jacy gave her groom a saucy smile. "Let's just say it's a good thing we're alone, Mr. Yarbro, because in about five minutes I'll be the one doing the loving, and you'll be the one making all the noise."

He grinned wickedly. "We'll see," he said.

Ian carried her the length of the hallway and into his room, where the rain played lively, welcome music on the roof, and Jacy was determined to make good on her promise.

8

ONCE THE DOOR OF IAN'S ROOM—NOW *THEIR* ROOM—
closed behind them, Jacy's misgivings and insecurities vanished as if by bush magic, and she slid both arms around her husband's neck as he set her on her feet. All the doubts would return in their own good time, she knew, but that night, that enchanted, rainy night, belonged only to her and to Ian, and she meant to make use of it.

She leaned against him, reveling in the hard strength of his body and at the same time well aware that she was arousing him with the softness of her own.

A sound escaped Ian, part chuckle and part groan. "Stop that wriggling, sheila," he said, "or I swear I'll take you right here, in the middle of the floor."

She laughed at him, because hers was the power. For once.

Without speaking she slid his suit coat off his shoulders and tossed it away. His tie followed soon after, and then she began opening the buttons of his shirt, smoothing the fabric aside. His flesh was warm beneath her palms, rough

111

with a matting of dark hair, and as ungiving as the land itself.

I love you, Jacy thought. She stopped herself from saying the words, but just barely.

Slowly, ever so slowly, she stripped away Ian's shirt and dispensed with it. Even then, in the midst of a frantic wanting, she marveled at his strength, his confidence in his own masculinity. It wasn't every man who could allow a woman to take the lead in lovemaking and relish the experience instead of being threatened.

Ian closed his eyes and tilted his head back slightly as Jacy made small, feather-light circles around his hardened nipples with the tips of her fingers.

"God in heaven," he breathed.

Jacy leaned forward and kissed the places she'd been touching only a moment before, and Ian drew in a sharp breath. In the next instant he closed his work-roughened hands over her ears, his thumbs stroking the delicate skin at her temples, and raised her head to look deep into her eyes.

His expression was solemn, almost reverent, but there was bewilderment in the way Ian regarded Jacy, too. It was as if he couldn't quite believe he was holding her, that they were married and about to make love for the first time as man and wife—indeed, that she was there with him at all.

When he started to speak she touched her fingers to his lips and shook her head. The magic was fragile; even a word could splinter it.

She stood on tiptoe to touch her mouth to his, and he kissed her then, gently at first, questioningly, and then with a hunger that sent a warm ache streaking through her system. As easily as that, Jacy was lost.

It was as though every stitch in the seams of her dress had suddenly dissolved, so easily did the garment fall away into the void all around and beneath them. Her slip, bra, panties, and pantyhose vanished in much the same way.

Jacy had no memory of undressing Ian, but he stood naked and magnificent before her nonetheless, and she could not keep herself from touching him.

He endured her caresses, sometimes flinching as if her hands had turned to fire, her fingers to flames, for a long interval. Then, with a primitive, barely audible cry, he lifted her into his arms and carried her to the bed.

Jacy wanted her husband, was desperate for him, and she arched under the slow strokes of his hand that followed, making a soft, whimpering sound in the depths of her throat.

"Not yet," Ian said gruffly, bending to capture her nipple with his mouth.

Jacy plunged her fingers into his hair and cried out, "Oh, God, Ian, *please* . . ."

He made no move to increase his pace but instead made a bridge of her breastbone, kissing his way across to the other nipple, which awaited him eagerly. He teased the morsel mercilessly with the tip of his tongue before settling down to suckle.

Jacy writhed on the bed like some wild creature driven to the edge of reason. "Ian," she pleaded over and over again, unable to form any word besides his name.

Finally, when she thought she'd die if he did not appease her, he poised himself over her, his fingers interlocked with hers, pressing the backs of her hands into the mattress. His gaze reached beyond all the barriers she'd erected, into the shadowy corners of her very soul.

"Do you want me?" he asked in a rough whisper.

She nodded, her eyes brimming with joyous tears.

"Say it," Ian insisted, not unkindly. Jacy understood that he was asking permission to enter her body.

"I . . . I want you," she said.

Ian settled between her legs then, and heat rolled over her, permeating every cell, when she felt the size and power of him throbbing against the flesh of her inner thigh.

She gasped with pleasure and raised her hips when he

found her and pushed a little way inside. Her whole being, physical and spiritual, seemed to pulse with the need to be one with him.

"Please," she said again.

He plunged deep, in one hard, sure stroke, his gaze locked with hers, and Jacy went wild beneath him. It was as though she had been shut outside herself all these years apart from him. Now that they were together again she was able to come home to her body, home to her mind and heart and soul.

She sobbed, flailing, hurling herself frantically against Ian, and he understood. Slipping his hands beneath her buttocks, he lifted her to himself and had her well, holding nothing back.

It was benignly violent, that first joining; their bodies slammed together again and again, harder and harder, until in one final, furious flexing they both shouted with the sweet agony of their satisfaction.

They slept when it was over, intertwined, consumed by the fire they themselves had stirred to life.

Later they awakened and made love again, artfully this time, and with excruciating leisure. Other sessions followed, some inventive, some graceful, as if their two spirits waltzed together.

It was a long night.

Jacy awakened in stages the following morning, stretching luxuriously, her whole body pulsing with the lingering glory of Ian's attentions, and finally opening her eyes.

The loud pounding started suddenly—or had it been going on for a while? Jacy didn't know. Beside her Ian cursed and rolled out of bed to pull on a pair of jeans and tug a T-shirt over his head.

There was a frightening urgency in the noise, and Jacy got up, too, taking shorts and a summer top from the suitcase she'd brought from Corroboree Springs. She paused only briefly in front of the bureau mirror, fluffed her tousled hair with her fingers, and dashed along the hallway toward the kitchen.

The knocking ceased, and an ominous silence took its place. Jacy froze in the kitchen doorway, seeing Ian and Collie standing across the room, and her stomach muscles clenched in violent resistance to the inevitable.

Ian leaned against the counter, his head down, while Collie fidgeted just inside the door, his eyes red-rimmed and too bright. The two men became aware of Jacy's presence in the same instant, and Collie gulped, evidently too overcome to speak. Ian came toward her, his expression solemn.

Jacy knew what had to have happened—Jake was gone— but nothing could have prepared her for the devastating shock she felt.

"No," she whispered. She made it to the end of the bench at the trestle table and, closing her eyes, sat. She shook her head, because it wasn't fair, because it couldn't be true. "No."

She wouldn't let Ian tell her, she decided frantically. If he didn't say the words aloud, maybe Jake would still be alive.

Ian came to stand beside her; she felt the warmth and solidity of his body as he rested both his hands on her shoulders.

"No," Jacy said again in a soft, wild, pleading voice, turning to stare up into her husband's grim face.

Ian hesitated, as if gathering his own internal forces, and then said hoarsely, "Collie found him down by the springs a little while ago."

Smothering pain welled up in Jacy. It was real now; her father was dead. She sobbed and leaned forward, touching her forehead to the tabletop and clutching her middle. Ian lifted her into his arms and held her against him; she gripped the fabric of his T-shirt in her fists and clung to him.

"I'm sorry, sheila," he murmured, his voice gruff with controlled emotion. "I'm so sorry."

Ian held Jacy for a long time, until the first furor of her grief had passed. After a while she sniffled, dashed at her tears with the back of one hand, and pulled away from Ian to cross the room and stand facing Collie.

"Did you leave him there—by the springs, I mean?" she asked.

Collie shook his head. "No, lass," he ground out. "Jake was me mate—I carried him into the house and covered him with a blanket." He turned his gaze to Ian, imploring. "What do I do now?"

Ian stood behind Jacy, looped his arms loosely around her waist. She leaned back, depending on his steadiness and strength, allowing him to support her. "We'll have to get a doctor out here to issue a death certificate," he said with quiet resolve. "After that the parson will want to say a few words, of course."

Jacy knew all those things were necessary, but she felt her knees weaken because this was *her father* they were talking about, not some acquaintance or shirttail relative. Instantly Ian's hold tightened; he would not let her fall.

She shuddered to think of what it would be to face such shattering news without him.

"I have to go to Jake," she said. "Right now."

Collie's dismay was evident. "Now, miss . . ."

Ian turned her gently to face him. "Maybe that's not such a good idea, love," he said. His eyes were filled with suffering and earnestness. "Collie will fetch a doctor. Let me see to Jake—please?"

She rested her forehead against his shoulder. "He knew," she choked out. "The way Dad said good-bye after the wedding—he knew." She raised her head to look into Ian's eyes again. There was no accusation in her voice. "And you knew, too. I saw it in your face when you watched him walk away."

Ian sighed, raising one hand to caress her face, his thumb

116

tenderly tracing the outline of her jaw. "I didn't know," he rasped. "Not really. But I felt something, I admit that."

Fresh tears welled in Jacy's eyes, and she managed a slight nod. She was agreeing to Ian's request that she let him go to Corroboree Springs alone. "I'll wait here," she said.

He kissed her on the forehead. "I won't be long, I promise."

Collie lingered, searching awkwardly within himself for the right words. Finally he put out his hand to Jacy and blurted, "Jake was a good sort. He'll be missed."

Jacy squeezed his fingers and dropped her hand back to her side. "Thanks."

Ian returned to the bedroom to put on socks and boots, and Collie hurried out to his borrowed car. Jacy went back to the trestle table and sank onto the bench, dazed. Pictures of Jake in all the phases of their lives together rushed through her mind, vivid, searing in their simple beauty.

Ian came into the kitchen again and took his stockman's hat from the peg next to the door. He hesitated there, looking back at Jacy over one broad shoulder.

"You'll be all right while I'm gone, then?"

She nodded, though she wasn't at all sure she was telling the truth. In some ways Jacy felt as if she were about to explode in all directions; she was wildly restless and, at the same time, locked into the strange inertia of shock.

When the door closed behind Ian a primitive cry of protest surged into her throat, but she swallowed it and sat rigid on the bench, hands folded in her lap. It was harder to be alone than she'd expected.

After a few moments Jacy began to cry again, hugging herself and rocking slightly as she wept. The loud tick of the old mantel clock above the kitchen fireplace was a metronome marking off the notes and pauses and crescendos of her grief.

Jacy was still sitting in that same place when Ian returned perhaps an hour later, afraid to move outside the small space she occupied. It was an unpredictable world, it seemed to her, a deadly place where anguish could strike without warning.

Ian sat down beside her on the bench without a word and lifted her onto his lap. She buried her face against his chest, trembling, fresh out of tears and feeling more pain than she knew what to do with.

Alice arrived with Chris to find them like that, Jacy clinging to Ian, too broken to speak. The stricken look on the older woman's face made it plain that the news had already reached her in that quick, uncanny way of the bush.

Chris approached Jacy with the innocent directness so typical of children and shyly touched her arm. "I liked Jake," he said in tribute. "We were mates. He was going to send me a postal card from Queensland. One with a shark on it."

Jacy smiled, sniffled once, and reached out to ruffle Chris's silky blond hair. He might have been her own child, she thought, as the bond between them tightened with another bittersweet tug.

Alice approached in her abrupt, forceful way, carrying a medicine bottle and a spoon. "You'll want some of this, Mrs. Yarbro," she announced, filling the spoon and holding it out. "It'll make you sleep, and that's what you need just now."

Jacy couldn't have argued, for sleep or against, but she accepted the bitter stuff. The phrase "Mrs. Yarbro" was a comfort to her; she spread it over her spirit like a child's favorite blanket.

Ian carried her back to their bed and tucked her in, then drew up a chair and sat. He didn't speak, and neither did Jacy, but they had no need for words. They were both missing Jake, both struggling to accept the fact that he was gone forever.

Jacy reached out just as she was dropping off to sleep and felt Ian's callused hand close around hers. She dreamed she was a child again, running to Jake, being lifted high in his strong arms.

Ian didn't leave Jacy's side until Alice came to the door to say that Collie was back. He'd found a doctor over in Willoughby, the next town, and brought him to view the body and sign the necessary paper. The two of them were on their way to Corroboree Springs.

Ian smoothed the blankets over Jacy and bent to kiss her soft, pale forehead. He met Chris in the hallway; the boy was just coming out of his room. In his small hands he held the toy boat Jake had given him for Christmas the year before.

"Is Jake in heaven?" Chris asked, his eyes huge as he looked up at his father.

Ian touched the child's face. He'd been busy helping Jacy through the first shock of her father's death and working out minor details, and he hadn't had a chance to talk things over with Chris. In fact, he was holding his own grief at bay, to be dealt with later. In the meantime he'd keep his feelings locked up inside him, in that place where he stored things that hurt.

"Yeah," he said, his voice rough. "Jake's in heaven."

Chris nodded, apparently satisfied for the moment, and went back into his room, still carrying the boat.

Alice was in the kitchen, mercilessly rolling out dough for her legendary meat pies, and she looked at Ian with dry, swollen eyes. "It's not right," she mourned. "Jake Tiernan was still a young man, and a good one."

Ian sighed. "When you work out where we can go to complain," he said, taking up his hat again, "let me know."

Alice frowned, plainly disapproving. But then, she'd never been shy about expressing her opinions, whether they were favorable or not. "You're off again, are you? Well, I don't mind saying that Collie and the doctor can take Jake's remains to town without any help from you."

Ian quelled his housekeeper's rising rebellion with a stern look. He'd be damned if he'd stop to explain wanting to be close to Jake when he traveled the road from Corroboree Springs to Yolanda one last time. It was the least he could do.

"I'll be back in time for tea if I can manage it," he said. And then he went out.

Jake was buried the next day, at the edge of the churchyard in Yolanda, in a spot next to the fence. Just beyond, the bush stretched away toward the horizon, wild and raw and starkly beautiful.

Ian had selected the site, Jacy knew, because he thought Jake would want to be within sight of the land. He'd never cared much for towns, even little ones like Yolanda.

The entire population turned out for the service, and although Jake hadn't been a member of the congregation, being, as he'd have put it, "no kind of joiner," the place was filled. Even the Shifflets were there, seated in the pew closest to the open door. Bram McCulley stood in front, by the casket, and spoke up for Jake, and so did Collie and several other men.

Jacy sat through the ceremony with dry eyes and a straight back until Ian left her side to offer a brief eulogy of his own. The words he said were simple ones, not particularly poetic, but Jacy listened with tears running down her face because during those moments she glimpsed the inner reaches of her husband's heart.

When it was over Jake's coffin was carried outside by Collie and Ian and Bram and three other men and lowered carefully into the grave on ropes. In New York or Sydney things would have been done differently, with more decorum, but that was the bush. People there lived close to the land, elbow to elbow with reality, and they gave up their dead personally, instead of leaving the task to strangers. Moreover, they followed the funeral with a wake, a way of thumbing their noses at the specter of death, of celebrating the life that had just ended.

Ian, Jacy, and Chris hadn't been back home for fifteen minutes before the townspeople and farmers began arriving with casseroles and pies and all sorts of other dishes.

Jake's friends filled the house, the veranda, and much of the yard. They ate and played a coin-tossing game called two-up and told each other stories about their mate, Jake Tiernan. Jacy was numb, but she held up through the day, and she circulated, greeting the guests. That, after all, was what Jake would have wanted. He'd have been gratified, too, to know that such a huge crowd had turned out to bid him farewell.

Still, it was a relief when the day finally ended. The visitors offered solemn consolations, took their empty pie plates and baking dishes, and left.

"Shouldn't you lie down or something?" Ian asked when he and Jacy were alone in the big bedroom. He was changing into his work clothes, since the chores needed doing no matter what else might be going on at the same time. Jacy, standing at the window, looking out at the land, glanced back at him over her shoulder.

"I'm not so fragile as you seem to think," she said with a soft smile. "I'll miss Jake every day of my life, and right now I'd give almost anything to see him again, but I'll make it through this."

He crossed the room to stand behind her, his arms resting lightly around her waist. "Just remember that you don't have to work it through alone." With that he bent to kiss the side of her neck, then turned and went out, closing the door softly behind him.

Jacy lingered at the window for a few moments, her eyes closed, thinking of Jake. He'd gotten what he wanted in the end, her father had, because he'd seen his daughter marry the man he would have chosen for her. Too, they'd had some time together, she and Jake, before the end came.

Maybe, just maybe, Jake Tiernan had been happy when he died.

She unfastened the big fabric-covered buttons of her navy blue linen dress, the only suitable garment she'd brought from the States, slipped out of it, and hung it carefully in the huge antique wardrobe that held Ian's clothes and some of her own.

After putting on her favorite, most comfortable pair of jeans, an open-necked cotton blouse, and sneakers, she returned to the main part of the house. Alice was clearing away the litter left behind by Jake's mourners, and Jacy helped, though her gaze kept straying to the nearest window, seeing the light fade by degrees.

"You don't have to do this, Mrs. Yarbro," Alice scolded. She put her hand on Jacy's forearm and gave her a gentle, sympathetic squeeze. A sorrowful sort of mischief flickered in the older woman's eyes. 'If you insist on doing all the work around here, then I'll soon be out of a job, now, won't I?"

Jacy covered Alice's hand with her own. "Nonsense. If Ian won't pay your salary, I will." The words reminded her that there were things she had to do if she was going to stay in Australia permanently. She needed to transfer her trust fund from New York, for one, and have her clothes, books, and personal belongings shipped. There was the house in Connecticut, still needing to be closed and sold. . . .

It was all too much. For now, all Jacy could really manage was putting one foot in front of the other, following each breath and each heartbeat with another.

They were in the vast living room, and Mrs. Wigget tugged Jacy over to a large leather chair that faced the fireplace. "Here, now, sit yourself down. You look pale as milk, and you'll not move a muscle again until you've swallowed some good, strong tea."

It was nice to be fussed over, so Jacy didn't resist. "Only if you'll join me," she said.

Alice smiled and nodded. Minutes later she returned with a tray. The porcelain cups and teapot she'd arranged upon it were fragile and translucent, an uncommon luxury in the Australian bush. The housekeeper set the tea things on a sturdy table and dragged another chair over to face Jacy's.

"It's what they've needed, a woman 'round this place," Alice whispered confidentially, her breath smelling of tobacco smoke and perhaps a nip or two of gin, as she poured steaming tea into the delicate cups. "Ian and Chris, I mean. Oh, it's clean, I see to that, and they have good food and clothes to wear"—her gaze strayed to the piano standing silent at the other end of the long room—"Ian's a good man, and he loves that little boy to distraction. But there's been no music. No flowers or soft things. It's been a purely masculine household all this time, and I don't mind admitting that it's worried me some. A child needs a female influence when it's coming up as much as a male one."

"I agree," Jacy said, settling back in her chair and regarding the loyal housekeeper thoughtfully. "But I think you've done a very good job looking after Chris. Ian's a fine father to him, but he's been away from the house a lot, I should think, with his sheep and those wild horses he loves so much."

Tears welled in Alice's eyes, and she straightened her back in a bid for dignity. "I'm sorry," she said. "I'm not fit for anything today. It wasn't right, Jake's leaving us so soon."

Jacy glanced at the window again and saw that darkness had fallen. An overwhelming sense of grief bore down on her, rather like the homesickness she'd felt as a child that one summer when Michael and her mother had made her go to camp instead of sending her to Australia for the customary visit with Jake.

"No," she whispered. "It wasn't right." She would have to write her mother soon and tell her about her marriage to Ian, as well as informing her of Jake's death.

Regina would hide whatever grief she might feel for the

husband of her youth, thinking it inappropriate, but her reaction to news of the wedding was likely to be volatile. Regina might even fly down to try and persuade Jacy that it was a mistake.

She closed her eyes against the thought, imagining the arguments Regina would use. Her own history of marrying an Australian—probably in a fit of passion—and then finding life in the bush too difficult would be the first. Then there was Jacy's undeniable history of running away from things.

Alice must have been alarmed by something she saw in Jacy's face or manner, because she reached out and rescued the cup and saucer from her hands. "You're tuckered out, poor thing," she scolded gently. "Take yourself off, have a nice, warm bath, and get into bed. I'll bring you tea when you're settled."

It sounded like a good plan.

In the stables Ian moved from one stall to the next, feeding each of the horses in its turn, filling each water trough by hand, taking his time. He had performed the simple tasks so many times that he did them automatically now, and his mind wandered free.

He grieved for Jake in those private minutes, his face wet with tears he didn't bother to wipe away. Memories trailed through his mind, one after another. . . .

After Jacy had gone back to America in a fury ten years before and left Ian behind with a broken heart, Jake had played endless games of cards and cribbage with him and told him things would get better. Jake had been there for Ian when his father had died suddenly, leaving him with enormous responsibilities and a pile of debts. Jake had stood by him when he'd become a father at nineteen, taking his side against the gossips, and he'd been at the house waiting to admire the new infant when Ian first brought Chris home from Adelaide.

Ian had to smile, remembering that day. Neither he nor

Jake had known the first thing about babies, but Alice Wigget had been there, too, God be thanked, to show him how to change nappies and mix formula. He'd taken a lot of guff from the stockmen and the blokes at the Dog and Goose for doing women's work, but Jake stepped in again. He'd said it didn't take a man to make a baby—any lad who'd reached puberty could do that—but it sure as hell took a man to raise one.

Finished with the horses, Ian climbed into the loft to pitch down enough hay for the next day, breaking open bales and then wielding the fork with a steady, practiced rhythm. He recalled more recent events as he worked—like going over to Corroboree Springs the day before and finding Jake laid out on the living room couch, where Collie had left him, covered by a blanket.

He'd looked downright tranquil, Jake had, when Ian pulled back the blanket's edge for a look at his face. Ian had brought a chair in from the kitchen and sat beside his old friend for the better part of an hour, holding Jake's lifeless hand between his own.

Ian hadn't wept then; he'd been numb. Later he'd held himself together because Jacy needed him.

"Dad?"

Chris. Ian took a deep breath and dragged his right forearm across his face.

"Up here," he said, and his voice came out gruff. "Just stay where you are and I'll be right down."

Leaning the pitchfork against the wall of the loft, Ian descended the long ladder to find his son waiting at the bottom. Chris was wearing his favorite pajamas, ones printed with tiny images of Yosemite Sam, along with sneakers and the sweater Alice had probably insisted on.

He frowned, looking up at Ian. "You've been crying," he said. It was a phenomenon Chris had never seen and perhaps never even imagined.

Well, Ian concluded, it was time the boy knew that sometimes a man needed to let out his emotions. He ruffled the lad's hair and smiled sadly. "Yes. I'll miss Jake a lot."

The two of them sat down side by side on a wooden trunk filled with old bridle fittings, nails and horseshoes, and other miscellaneous items.

Although the grief showed plainly, there was a new light in Chris's eyes, some secret hope Ian had never glimpsed before. It buoyed Ian's heart and, at the same time, made him afraid for his son.

"I'm glad Miss Tiernan lives with us now," the boy said. He lowered his voice to a whisper, as if to impart a bit of solemn news. "She said I could call her Mum." He paused, evidently considering the ramifications of that. "Do you think she'll be sad for a long time?"

Ian smiled and laid a hand on Chris's small shoulder. "She'll be sad for a while—we all will." For a moment it was as if Jake was standing somewhere nearby, silently encouraging him, just like always. "Once some time has passed we'll be able to think about Jake without hurting."

Chris considered again. "If Miss—Mum is your wife now, does that mean you'll have babies together?"

The idea warmed Ian inside. You were so right, Jake, he thought. Life does go on. "I hope so."

The boy slid closer to Ian on the tool chest. "But you'll still like me."

With one arm Ian pressed Chris against his side for a moment. "You'll always be my mate," he said. "In fact, I'll be counting on you to look after the little nippers, and teach them how to throw a boomerang and where to find colored rocks and fossils and all that sort of thing."

He felt Chris relax against him and closed his eyes for a moment, savoring the sense of deep, poignant love that washed over him.

"You can depend on me, Dad," Chris said stalwartly.

Ian thought for a moment, that he would weep again. This time, though, it would have been joy that moved him so deeply instead of sorrow. What a marvel life was, full of complexities and complications.

"That's good," he said when he could trust himself to speak.

The work was done, but they sat there for a time anyway, in companionable silence. After a while Alice came outside and called to them, and they walked back to the house together, through the cool night air. Just before they stepped inside Ian looked up at the sky glittering with stars.

He felt his roots move still deeper into the earth and offered a silent prayer of thanks for all that he had. For all his troubles, Ian reflected, he was a rich man.

Alice had set out a light meal for him—Chris had already eaten—and there was no sign of Jacy. He went to tuck the boy in, then moved on to the room he and his wife shared.

Jacy was sitting up in bed, awash in moonlight, her fair hair still moist from her bath. Ian felt his heart constrict as he looked at her, and he knew he would gladly have borne the pain of her grief, as well as his own, if that had been possible.

"Hi," she said.

He saw her soft smile and, despite all that he would have spared her, thanked God that he didn't love this woman. That foolishness lay behind him, in his youth; never again would he let himself be vulnerable to the kind of anguish she had brought to him. Never.

He didn't approach the bed. Jacy was fragile now, and he didn't know whether to touch her or stand back. He would wait and let the decision be hers.

"You're all right, then?" he asked.

"I'll live," she answered. The night before she'd pressed herself against Ian as if trying to lose herself in him, and their lovemaking had had a ferocious tenderness about it.

Ian swallowed, feeling like a schoolboy calling on his first great love. "Alice made tea," he said. "It'll be getting cold about now."

Jacy bit her lower lip, and he wished he could see the

expression in her eyes, but the glow of the moon masked it. "Ian," she began, her voice light and yet fragile, too, "are you trying to ask me whether or not I want you to sleep in our bed tonight?"

He *had* been wondering that, without consciously realizing it. Feeling his neck grow warm, Ian was glad of the relative darkness. "Yes." To his further embarrassment, the word came out sounding rough and rusted.

Jacy rose to her knees, stepped off the bed, and approached him. She laid her hands on his chest, and he felt the warmth of her palms and fingers through his shirt.

"I want you with me," she said.

It was a simple conversation between a man and his wife. Ian wondered why he felt as though he'd been strapped to the cowcatcher on the steam engine of a speeding train. He couldn't speak, so he bent his head and kissed her lightly on the mouth in parting.

When he came back from dinner, having stopped along the way for a quick shower, Jacy was waiting for him. She watched as he took off his terry cloth robe and tossed it over the back of a chair, pulled back the covers as he approached the bed.

"You've been uncommonly good to me, Ian Yarbro," she said. "And I'm grateful."

Ian wasn't sure it was gratitude he wanted, exactly, but he didn't stop to work through the question. He needed Jacy as he never had, needed to take refuge in her arms and in the warm, tight depths of her femininity.

He slid into bed beside his wife and drew her to him, kissing her gently at first, and then with growing hunger. "Just how grateful are you?" he asked, breathless, when they finally broke apart.

"Pay attention, Mr. Yarbro," Jacy replied. "I'm about to show you."

9

BAD THINGS COME IN THREES.

Ian couldn't help think of the old superstition as he drove a mob of sheep across the Tiernan paddock to Corroboree Springs the morning after Jake's funeral. First there had been the storm, which had cost him several ewes and lambs. He still hadn't found the horse he'd been riding that day, and he'd very nearly lost his life. Right after that his best friend had sat himself down under a gum tree and given up the ghost.

Ian pushed his hat off and scratched the back of his neck in the same motion, with the same hand, being careful to avoid the place Jake had stitched. He shifted uncomfortably in the saddle, afraid to think what the third disaster might be.

Maybe, Ian reflected as the woollies closed in on the springs, it was marrying Jacy.

The new horse, skittish and green, danced nervously as the sheep surged around its legs. Ian and the dogs relaxed; the creatures had caught the scent of water, and their own thirst would drive them the rest of the way.

Ian looked back over his shoulder toward the house. He knew Jacy was there, sorting through her father's things, deciding which were to be kept and which were to be given away. It was lonely and painful work by its very nature, but she had refused his offer to help.

He understood that, too. The ritual belonged to Jacy, to hold close or to share, whichever she chose. Still, Ian had an ache rooted either in his gut or his heart—he couldn't tell which—because she wouldn't let him inside the circle of her grief.

He swung down from the saddle and left the horse's reins dangling. At first Jacy had allowed him to comfort her— she'd leaned on him, clung to him, wept in his arms. They'd both taken refuge in the one thing in their relationship that could be counted upon to work—their explosive love-making.

That morning, however, when Jacy had announced her intention to start emptying the house at Corroboree, there had been a certain coolness in her manner, and she'd avoided Ian's eyes. Clearing out Jake's things was her job, she'd said, and when he had gone so far as to suggest that she might need some help she'd cut him off with a look.

He stood on the grass now, hat in hand, gazing up at the house where he had played so many games of cards, losing most of the time. The place had been his second home, Jake his second father. He had gone there to share triumphs and, once or twice, to weep. He could deal with all of that; it was knowing Jacy didn't want him around that hurt.

Jacy started sorting things in the kitchen, since she wasn't quite ready to face going through Jake's books, papers, and other personal belongings. The letter she'd come across earlier, the one directed to some woman in Queensland, found its way into her hands immediately.

She sank into a chair at the table, staring at the words— so many words—moving neatly across the paper. She had to find out who this woman was and let her know about

130

Jake's death, but for all of that she still felt as if she were intruding. Letters were so private, especially love letters.

Drawing a deep breath, Jacy flipped back the pages of the tablet until she came to the opening: "Dear Margaret . . ."

A flood of unfounded resentment swamped Jacy's heart. Dear Margaret, indeed. In between her visits to Australia her father had never written a line—he hadn't even sent birthday or Christmas cards. And yet he'd penned pages to this woman.

"Get a grip, Jacy," she said aloud. Whatever his failings, Jake had been a good father when she was with him, if a poor correspondent when they were apart, and he'd certainly had a right to a private life.

She folded the rest of the letter without reading it, having already absorbed the central message of the thing. Jake had been in love with Margaret, whoever she was. He'd planned to join her in Queensland. What else was there to know?

Resigned, Jacy left the kitchen and went into the living room. Jake's desk was there against one wall, covered with clutter, although the rest of the house was characteristically neat. The first thing she had to do, if she was to have any peace, was to find Margaret's address and write her.

While searching Jake's desk for an address book or even an envelope with the label still on it, she came across a stack of letters tied with plain string. A curious sense of alarm and happiness surged through her when she realized that the envelopes were all addressed to her. Each one had a stamp neatly affixed and never canceled. Jake *had* written to her, then—but why hadn't he posted the letters?

She held the thick packet against her heart for a moment, then tucked it carefully into her handbag. She would read Jake's letters later, in a private place, when she'd had time to prepare herself for the emotional jolt.

She'd heard Ian's sheep passing the house, of course, and as she went by the window to return to her dad's desk and the task of tracking down the mysterious Margaret, she caught a glimpse of her husband.

Ian was standing near the springs in almost the very spot where he had, for all intents and purposes, made love to her. He held the trademark hat in one hand and gazed toward the house with an expression Jacy couldn't read.

She didn't know whether or not he could see her, and in the final analysis it didn't matter. She wanted Ian to help her with Jake's things; she could even admit, at least to herself, that she *needed* him. Still, for some unfathomable reason, she couldn't let him inside the smothering wall of grief and regret that surrounded her.

Jacy bit her lower lip, fighting the urge to go out onto the veranda and call out to Ian, and finally found the strength to turn away. She could grant Ian admission to her body, even welcome him eagerly, but her spirit, the most vital and private part of her, was closed to him. And to everyone else.

She came across papers, receipts for paid bills, newspaper clippings, and, finally, an empty envelope with an address in the upper left-hand corner. The woman's name was Margaret Wynne, and she lived in a small town on the northern coast of Queensland.

Jacy smoothed the old envelope out on the desktop, running her hand over the thin paper as if she could divine something by touching it, like a psychic. What, she wondered, knowing it was foolish even as she entertained the question, had Margaret Wynne offered Jake that her mother, Regina, had not?

Unfair question, she said to herself. Jacy didn't know much about her parents' parting all those years ago, but she was clear on one thing: The divorce had mostly been Regina's idea. She'd left Jake in a fury, taking their small daughter with her, but Jacy had never been able to get either her mother or her father to tell her why it had happened.

Like most everyone else, Jacy had speculated that it was

because Regina's wealthy widowed mother had raised her to be a pampered princess. The only time Regina had ever rebelled, to Jacy's knowledge, was when she married "that Australian man," as her grandmother had ever after referred to Jake. Regina had just completed college and had come to Australia on a world tour. She'd made the trip to Yolanda because her former roommate, an exchange student, lived there. During the visit Regina had met Jake Tiernan and fallen head over heels in love with him.

"What happened?" Jacy wondered aloud. She couldn't help thinking of her own unconventional courtship and marriage. God knew what she felt for Ian was powerful, whether it could be classified as true love or not. And she wanted it to work—oh, dear heaven, she prayed, let it work.

She squeezed her eyes shut. When Paul was sick she'd prayed frantically, and God hadn't listened. If He wouldn't save a good person's life in answer to a prayer, why would He care about the outcome of one relationship?

Jacy had lost more than a friend when Paul died. She'd lost her faith.

Shaking off a lot of troublesome thoughts, Jacy went back to work. She heard the sheep pass the house again, bleating and baaing, heard the dogs barking, but she didn't go back to the window. Seeing Ian just then would weaken her, and she couldn't allow that to happen.

By one o'clock that afternoon Jacy had packed Jake's clothes into boxes Alice had save up, stripped his bed and folded the blankets and sheets, cleaned out his bureau drawers and the medicine cabinet. She had no memory of crying, but her eyes felt sore and swollen, and the skin on her face was chapped.

She put the boxes in a neat stack and went out to get into Jake's truck. She'd appropriated that, along with some books, a couple of photo albums, and the packet of letters in her purse.

Jacy felt hollowed out inside as she drove toward Ian's

133

house—she still couldn't think of it as her home, but maybe that would come in time. On Monday morning, she resolved school would start again. She would visit her students' families personally, in fact, to let them know. The Shifflets were at the top of her list.

Thinking about her job gave her a way to escape missing Jake for a little while, to dodge all her doubts and regrets.

She had not expected to encounter Ian before dinner time, but when she arrived at the homestead the area in back was choked with ewes and their woolly little lambs, and Ian was leading his horse into the barn. The dogs, ever faithful, sat panting at their separate posts like furry sentinels awaiting their orders.

Jacy hesitated, torn between the desire to avoid Ian and the need to be close to him. Finally she took a deep breath, let it out, and started wading through the sheep.

Ian was just inside the hay shed door, muttering to the fitful horse while he unbuckled the cinch to remove the saddle.

"Is that one of your wild ones?" Jacy asked, because that seemed safe.

He looked at her, though the brim of his hat hid his expression. "Yes," he said. "Some of the lads catch them out in the bush. I buy and train them to work sheep and cattle."

Jacy bit her lip, at a loss. She wanted to be close to Ian, but she was afraid, so afraid. No one else on the face of the earth had the power to hurt her that he did, and making herself vulnerable to him felt like baring her bosom to the sword.

Ian pulled the saddle off the horse's back and set it on the rail of a stall gate, along with the blanket beneath. He was removing the bridle, the hat still cloaking his emotions, when he spoke again. "Did you make any progress over at Jake's place?"

Jacy came a little closer, though not much, and perched on the edge of a bale of hay. Strange, she reflected, how she could respond to Ian in bed and be so wary of him in the daylight. But then exposing the body was quite a different matter from exposing the soul.

"He didn't have a whole lot," she said, knotting her fingers together. "It's kind of sad the way the space we occupy fills in so soon after we're gone."

Ian kept his distance, perhaps sensing the odd fragility she felt. Pushing back his hat, leaning against a support beam, he folded his muscular arms across his chest. He regarded her solemnly for a long moment, and when he spoke his voice was hoarse. "Jake was a good man. He left a lot behind to remember him by."

Jacy felt her throat constrict, felt tears sting her already ravaged eyes. "Like what? A few acres of land, some letters and papers . . ."

Ian crossed the space between them and crouched in front of Jacy, catching hold of her chin and forcing her to look at him. "Like you," he said. He gestured in the general direction of the homestead. "Like a little boy who'll always remember the man who taught him to catch frogs and then set them free. Like a lot of people who are proud to say they were his mates. That's what Jake left behind."

Jacy slumped forward, her forehead resting on Ian's strong shoulder, and started to sob. "I thought I was past this!" she babbled between pitiful, snuffly wails.

Ian rubbed her back with both hands, cautiously at first, and then with something almost like relief. "It'll be a while, sheila, before the storm blows over. All we can do is ride it out."

She raised her head after a few minutes of pure, unadulterated grief and studied his face with burning, heavy-lidded eyes. "Why did you marry me, Ian? Was it to make sure I wouldn't put up a fence so you couldn't drive your sheep to the springs?"

He stiffened for just a fraction of a moment, but it was long enough for Jacy to know that she'd touched on the truth. He drew back, his hands strong on her shoulders, and searched her face with those marvelous, heart-stopping blue eyes of his.

"I wanted you," he said in the blunt, plain way so typical of him. "It drove me crazy thinking of you, wanting you, remembering how it was when things were good between us. . . ."

Wanting me, thinking of me, Jacy thought. What about loving me, Ian Yarbro? Did that ever enter your mind?

In that instant she realized that she did indeed love Ian with all her heart and soul. She'd never stopped caring for him, not for a single breath or heartbeat, though she'd managed to delude herself for a long time.

Instead of comforting Jacy, the knowledge terrified her. She was vulnerable, her soul as naked as a snail caught outside its shell. It made her all the more determined to protect herself.

She would have gotten up off that bale of hay and run away, but Ian held her in place.

"Why did you marry me?" Ian countered. It was a fair question, a reasonable question, and the very last one Jacy wanted to answer just then.

Because I love you, you idiot, she thought in fury and pain. What she actually said was very different. "Same thing," she relied flippantly. "I wanted to go to bed with you. One thing about you, Ian—you're a hell of a lover."

He narrowed his eyes for a moment, obviously confused, and the realization did Jacy's bruised heart good. For thousands of years, she thought, men had been evaluating women on that basis; let them see how they liked it!

"Who were you comparing me with?" he asked, catching her off guard all over again. "Paul?"

A flush climbed Jacy's neck and throbbed in her face. "Since I've never slept with anyone but you, I can't make a comparison. For all I know, you're on the low end of the scale."

He considered that, and if Jacy hadn't been so torn up about other things she might have laughed at his confounded expression. "What about Paul?" he persisted after a moment.

Jacy sighed. "I wondered if you knew about him," she said. "I guess Dad must have told you, huh?"

Ian looked honestly worried, and that raised Jacy's spirits a bit. Maybe he cared just a little under all that pride and uncompromising masculinity. "He didn't say much. That wasn't Jake's way."

Jacy slid her teeth over her lower lip before answering. "No, it wasn't. And he didn't know the whole truth anyway."

Ian tensed; she felt it through his hands, saw it in the set of his jaw and the tightening of his shoulder muscles. "I don't suppose you'd care to share that—the whole truth, I mean."

She smiled. Ah, power. It was so fleeting, but so intoxicating while it lasted. "Paul was the very best friend I've ever had," she said when she couldn't sustain the silence any longer. "He was also gay."

Ian arched one dark eyebrow; for a moment Jacy thought he was going to ask what Paul's being happy had to do with anything, but then he let out his breath in a rush. His grin was blinding, and more than a little cocky. "So you didn't sleep with him?"

She was exasperated. "Don't be a peacock, Yarbro," she said. "I might have slept with Paul if he hadn't been dating a bellman at the Waldorf-Astoria."

Ian's grin faded. "He died . . ."

"Of AIDS," Jacy said with soft ferocity, preparing herself for battle. The macho types like Ian were sometimes very quick to condemn or to minimize, and she wasn't going to stand for it for a moment. Paul had been her friend—he'd been a victim, not a criminal—and she wouldn't let anyone tarnish his memory or make light of the pain and indignity he'd suffered.

Ian paled. "Dear God," he said, and then he pulled Jacy

close and held her very tightly. "Oh, God, sheila, I'm so sorry."

Jacy closed her eyes. Thank you, she thought, and one bruise, tucked away in a shadowy region of her heart, began to heal. She pushed away from Ian in the next instant, though, afraid to hide out in his embrace for too long.

"Aren't you scared that I might be contaminated or something?"

He frowned. "Are you trying to goad me into a fight?" he countered.

She looked away, unable to deny the charge.

Ian cupped her face in his hands and gazed deep into her eyes. His own were dancing with mischief and a cautious tenderness. "No fights, sheila. I could win easily, you know, and I don't like taking advantage of weaker minds. No sport in it."

Jacy laughed, placed both palms on Ian's chest, and pushed him backward. " 'Weaker minds,' is it?" she demanded as Ian scrambled to catch his balance and landed on his backside in the straw just the same. "You've met your match this time, Ian Yarbro—I can be every bit as cussed as you."

He got to his feet, and so did Jacy. She wriggled her fingers in farewell and turned to go, but Ian caught her by the waistband of her jeans and whirled her around so that she collided with him. Hard.

Bold as only he could be, Ian cupped her backside in his hands and thrust her against him. Her nipples went hard when her breasts were pressed to his chest, and heat curled up through her like smoke. She hated his power over her, and feared it, but she couldn't have broken free of his embrace to save civilization itself.

He kissed her, thoroughly and hard, until she sagged against him, helpless with her need. When he led her into a shadowy corner of an empty stall where the straw smelled fresh and sweet, she made no attempt to resist him. In fact, the idea didn't even cross her mind; if she was worried about anything, it was being caught.

"Remember, sheila?" Ian whispered, opening the buttons of her blouse with damnable grace. "Remember all the places we hid away and made love until nothing else mattered? Well, that's what's going to happen now. For a little while you and I are both going to forget all our troubles."

She moaned as he pushed away her blouse and brought down her bra so that her breasts bounced free, their tips already puckered and hot. "Oh, God, Ian," she gasped.

"Remember," he repeated, opening her jeans, reaching inside to caress her most intimate place, to stroke the small nubbin of flesh, with its cluster of nerves, until it throbbed and seemed to strain toward him the way her nipples did. His own breath came shallow and quick as he bent to nibble hungrily at the side of her neck, the underside of her jaw, the rounded tops of both her breasts. "Oh, God, Jacy, say you haven't forgotten how it was."

She was trembling. "I couldn't have," she admitted breathlessly, tilting her head back, stiffening as he took a nipple into his mouth and sucked greedily. His hand stroked and teased her all the while; she was wet, her insides already expanding to receive him, but it would be a long time before he appeased her. "Oh, God—*oh, God*—I remember."

When he knelt before her and pulled her jeans and panties the rest of the way down, Jacy was completely lost. She leaned back against the wall of the barn, her eyes closed, waiting, offering herself, and yet a little afraid because every time Ian made love to her he carried her to new heights and made her give more and more of herself.

He pulled off her shoes, her socks, and then the jeans and panties were gone, too. Her only clothing was a blouse, hanging wide open, and a bra that hung loose from her shoulders.

"Remember this, sheila?" he asked, parting her with his

fingers. She felt his breath on that most tender and intimate part of her, that part that had hardened with yearning.

She gasped and threaded her fingers through his hair, being careful of the half-healed wound at the back of his head, tensing because she did remember. God help her, for ten years she'd relived other encounters with Ian and awakened in a torment of aching heat. It had only receded, that heat; it had never been assuaged.

He nibbled at her, and she gave a low, helpless moan. "Shall I stop?" he teased after sending silver flames shooting through Jacy like fireworks.

She tightened her fingers in his hair. "No," she whimpered, as she always had, long ago, when Ian had loved her this way. "No, please—"

His tongue flicked over her, and she swallowed a long animal cry, tossing her head back and forth, feeling perspiration on her skin. Ian put one of her legs over his shoulder, and then the other, her bare back pressed against the wall. He was going to have her, in the same methodical, torturously beautiful way he always did, and the prospect was an exquisite conquering in its own right.

"Hold on, sheila," Ian said, his voice muffled by her own moist, aching flesh. "You're in for the ride of your life."

Jacy bucked against his mouth—there was no escaping Ian's quick tongue, his lips, the heat of his breath. He gave her no quarter but pursued her relentlessly and drove her into an explosive climax. Her cries were primitive, like those of a she-wolf with her mate, and she could no more hold them back than she could stop the sweet, violent convulsions of her response.

When at last she was finished and sagged back against the wall, her skin slick with perspiration, her breath coming in ragged gasps, he started in on her again.

"No, Ian," she pleaded, tossing her head. "No, really—" But even as she said the words she was burrowing her fingers into his thick hair again and drawing him closer.

He brought her to three different releases, each one more piercingly pleasurable than the last, before laying her down in the straw. Jacy was exhausted, and yet, as she watched Ian shed his clothes, there was a quickening deep inside her, a brazen readiness that baffled her. When he stretched out over her, naked and magnificent, she welcomed him, her hands moving soothingly up and down his back.

Ian's kisses were feverish and quick; Jacy's pleasure had aroused him far more than anything she could have done. Speaking gently, tenderly, as though consoling him, she guided Ian to the center of her womanhood, put her hands on his buttocks, and ushered him slowly, slowly inside her.

He held himself high, push-up style, his head back like a stallion's, his teeth bared as he struggled with forces even he could not control. She saw the muscles in his neck and throat form quivering cords as she stroked his buttocks lightly, urging him.

For a while, Ian remained deep inside Jacy, but then he withdrew and came into her again, and withdrew. She had thought, up until then, that she'd given him everything, but the friction ignited her most primitive instincts all over again. Soon she was pitching beneath Ian, flinging herself at him, trying to make him move faster.

His control was consummate. He kept his strokes long, slow, and even, until Jacy came apart beneath him, thrusting herself upward, abandoning the many and complex defenses that stood between them at all other times. When she'd settled down and stopped crying out, Ian sought his own satisfaction, driving deep inside her again and again, his gaze locked with hers. Finally, with a low cry, he stiffened upon her, and she felt his warmth spilling into her and arched her back to receive him.

When Ian's magnificent body had stopped its wondrous, spasmodic flexing he collapsed beside her in the fragrant straw, burying his face in her neck.

She wished he would say he loved her—it would have been the perfect time—but he didn't, and Jacy couldn't take the chance of being first to say the words. They were too powerful, too full of dark magic.

So she just lay there waiting, holding her husband close, her whole body reverberating with the shattering effects of his lovemaking, her breathing and heartbeat in overdrive. Probably fifteen minutes had passed before Ian raised himself onto an elbow, eyed her breasts with a distinct twinkle in his eyes, and ran his tongue across his upper lip.

Jacy hiked up her bra and pulled her blouse closed. "Oh, no you don't," she said. "I'll have a heart attack if we do that again."

Ian didn't speak. He simply took her by the waist and lifted her so that she sat astraddle of him. She felt his impressive manhood under her, already rising to the occasion.

"Ian, I mean it," she whimpered. But an ache was starting way up inside her, where only Ian could reach.

He said nothing but simply parted her blouse again, pushed it down over her shoulders, tossed it aside. Her bra followed, while she just stared into his hypnotic gaze with wide, worried eyes.

"I'm *serious,*" she whimpered.

Ian pulled her head down for his kiss. "So am I," he replied when he'd given her a small preview of what would happen next.

"You're going to kill me."

Grasping her hips, he slid her forward, and she had to plant her hands in the straw to keep from landing on her head. Her breasts dangled helplessly over his face. "But as they say," he teased, "what a way to go." He caught a nipple lightly between his teeth then, following up with a few quick passes of his tongue.

"Oh, God," Jacy moaned, tilting her head back.

"I wouldn't look for any help from that quarter," Ian responded, breathing the words rather than speaking them, grasping her buttocks in his hands and arranging her just the way he wanted her.

"Ian," she whined, "I *mean* it—if you make me do all that again—"

He took a good long time suckling one of her breasts before answering. "I am going to make you do all that again, sheila—and then some." He slid her forward and kissed her belly, teasing her mercilessly with his fingers. When she was panting, half out of her mind with renewed desire, he lowered her onto the tip of his manhood and looked up into her eyes. "Still, I'm a gentleman," he said with a sultry, mocking grin. "If you say no, I'll honor your wishes."

"Damn you," Jacy moaned. She couldn't have said no if her life depended upon it, and Ian knew that full well. Still, he waited, and he made her ask for him. "I want you!" she finally cried in a fury, and he gave her what she'd requested.

10

JACY TOOK CARE NOT TO LOOK AT IAN WHILE SHE WAS PUT-
ting her clothes back on. Her face felt hot, her body so
weak that she wondered if she could walk the distance
between the hay shed and the house. It mortified her to
think of the way she lost herself when they were intimate;
she became another person entirely during those long, fiery
minutes—a woman she didn't begin to know or understand.

Mercifully, Ian didn't try to engage her in conversation;
he simply got dressed and waited patiently for Jacy to finish. Just when she thought there was a hope of not having
to look into his eyes, however, he reached out to pluck
bits of straw from her hair.

She grew even more embarrassed, thinking that Alice
Wigget or, God forbid, Chris might have guessed what she
and Ian had been doing in the stables.

Ian put his hand under her chin and lifted. "As they say
in the States, sheila, lighten up. We're married, and there
is no shame in what just happened between us."

Jacy shoved her fingers through her undoubtedly tousled

hair. She wasn't ashamed of their lovemaking, never that; it was her own wanton, mindless responses that worried her. It was the fact that Ian could cause her to put aside all her doubts, however reasonable, just by touching her in ways he knew would arouse her.

She looked into his intensely blue eyes, wet her lips nervously with the tip of her tongue, and said, "I become someone else when you and I make love. Someone I don't recognize."

Ian smiled softly and kissed the crown of her head. "No, sheila," he replied in a gentle, amused voice. "You become the woman you really are—a little warrior, made of fire and fury."

Jacy absorbed his words, though she tried not to reveal the way they'd affected her. "You're quite a poet, Ian Yarbro," she said, ducking around him and heading for the stall door. "And you know how to use a line."

He chuckled. "Among other things," he said.

Jacy's blush deepened, and she walked out of the barn and back to the house at a fast clip.

Alice was in the spacious kitchen, making the initial preparations for dinner, and Chris sat at the long trestle table, absorbed in a picture he was drawing.

Jacy didn't want to face either one of them just then and tried to cross the kitchen to the hall without attracting attention.

Of course, the attempt failed.

"Will there be school on Monday?" her stepson inquired in his lilting Aussie accent.

Jacy stopped, her hand on the door frame, and assembled her features into a smile before she turned to face him. At least she could be grateful that Alice and Chris had been in the house and thus would not have heard her carrying on while Ian loved her on a bed of straw.

"Sure will," she replied, feeling a sweet tug in a corner of her heart as she looked at the little boy. She loved Chris more every day and wondered how she would manage to avoid showing favoritism at school. "We'll go over your spelling after we eat, if you like."

Chris's face brightened. It came home to Jacy with a wallop that the child had high hopes for their relationship, that he'd dreamed of having a mother. If she let him down, he would be devastated. "Thanks," he chirped. "Would you like to see my picture?"

Jacy and Mrs. Wigget exchanged a look over his head.

"Sure," Jacy answered, hardly missing a beat. She went to stand beside Chris and felt her breath catch when she saw that he'd drawn another family portrait—a father, a child, and a mother with wild yellow-crayon curls. For a moment she was too moved to comment. Then she got out, "Wow, Chris. That's a really terrific drawing."

At almost that same moment the back door opened and Ian came in, casting one glance of mocking appreciation in his wife's direction before hanging that blasted hat of his on its peg. For a moment it was as though the whole universe had lurched to a stop, and the air seemed to undulate with invisible fire.

Jacy caught herself staring and lowered her eyes, just in time for Chris to point to an open spot on his drawing and say, "I could put the baby right here. When we get a baby, I mean."

Jacy tried her best not to fall into the trap of Ian's gaze a second time, but she couldn't help herself. The reaction was automatic.

He smiled as if to say that if there wasn't a child growing under Jacy's heart, it hadn't been for lack of effort on his part. Her cheeks were hot again.

"Right," she said to Chris in a distracted tone when she realized she'd left his remark hanging. She had been planning to hide out in the master bedroom for a while and perhaps read the packet of letters she'd found in Jake's desk, but she wasn't about to take the chance that Ian might follow her.

She'd had all the pleasure she could handle—for the time

being, at least—and she knew only too well how persuasive her husband could be.

Yanking her gaze from Ian's, she walked across the kitchen, perhaps too purposefully, and took a colander full of potatoes off the counter. She carried it to the sink and began peeling with a vengeance.

Ian, with typical audacity, came to stand behind her. Apparently heedless of the housekeeper's presence, not to mention Chris's, he lifted her hair and lightly kissed the back of her neck. Then, still without saying a word, he let her curls fall, swatted her lightly on the bottom, and walked away whistling.

Jacy accidentally caught Alice's eye and saw an approving twinkle there. For Jacy's part, she wanted to go after Ian, fling herself onto his back, and start pulling his hair out with both hands. *Damn* him for his cheerful arrogance!

Chris was bent over his drawing again, busily adding a picture of a baby to the family portrait.

Jacy peeled potatoes for all she was worth until finally Alice reached out and stopped her.

"At this rate," the older woman teased gently, "we'll have nothing but peelings, and no potatoes to speak of. Why don't you go and sit on the veranda for a while, Mrs. Yarbro, and read a book or something?"

Mixed in with Jacy's chagrin—it seemed to her that a grown woman should be able to peel potatoes without instruction—was a sense of relief. She nodded, took Jake's letters from her purse, and walked through the living room and out onto the long porch at the front of the house.

There was an old-fashioned swing there, like the one at Corroboree Springs, and Jacy sat down with relief. After watching the spectacular changes in the late afternoon sky for a time she opened her purse and brought out the letters her dad had written to her but, for some reason, never mailed.

The first was dated almost twenty-three years before, when Jacy had been a little girl of five. She expected to feel renewed grief as she read the words Jake had written, but instead his letters were comforting. He'd loved her all along, that was plain, but there was no self-pity or resentment in the things he'd put to paper. Instead Jake had given detailed accounts of the changing Australian sky, the glorious subtleties of the light, the passing of the seasons.

For Jacy, reading those letters was like having Jake sitting right beside her in the porch swing, pouring out his heart to her. She sat with the last one pressed to her heart, the one written after she and Ian had broken up and she'd fled back to the States. It had begun then, Jacy knew, her tendency to skip out when things got too difficult.

She didn't look up when the screen door squeaked open, though she was well aware of Ian's presence. He'd showered, and she caught the unique scent of his skin, the soap Alice had used to wash his clothes, and the separate perfume of the shampoo he'd used. Jacy wondered with quiet amusement when she'd gotten to be such an expert on detecting and defining fragrances.

He sat on the porch rail a few feet away, guessing, perhaps, that Jacy's senses were already on overload from the session in the barn, that she needed a little time to let her nerve endings stop crackling.

"It might have happened, you know." Ian spoke quietly, and Jacy saw out of the corner of her eye that he was gazing out over the land he battled every day of his life, the land he loved and hated, cursed and worshipped.

Jacy set the last letter with the others, in a little stack beside her on the swing seat, sighed, and pushed her hair back from her face. She didn't need to ask Ian what he was talking about; she knew.

"Yes," she said, after a long, easy silence. "There could be a baby."

Ian's gaze shifted to her face at last; she felt it and responded, having no choice in the matter. "You aren't taking the pill or anything like that?"

Jacy laughed softly. "Now's a fine time to ask, Yarbro,"

she said. His answering grin warmed her heart. She drew one knee up and wrapped both arms around her leg, tilting her head to the side. "No," she said, squinting a little in the late-afternoon sun. "I'm not taking anything. I had no reason to, since I wasn't sleeping with anybody, and—let's face it—you and I didn't exactly enjoy a long courtship. I didn't have time to plan."

Ian's smile told her how he felt about the possibility, and Jacy suddenly felt shy, like a virgin bride. It pleased her inordinately to know that Ian liked the idea of their having a child together, but underneath that was a quiet, insistent fear. If she ever wanted to leave him, and Australia, Ian wouldn't let her take their son or daughter without a hell of a fight; he'd proven that at nineteen, when he'd claimed Chris at the hospital in Adelaide and brought him home to raise alone.

She felt compelled to steer the conversation onto another subject. "Does the school committee have any funds stashed away?" she asked, delighted to note that, for once, she'd been the one to catch Ian off guard, instead of the other way around. "We could use new desks and playground equipment at the schoolhouse, and we're downright desperate for current textbooks, maps, reference material, and study guides."

Ian's eyes narrowed slowly, then widened again with the same lack of haste before he answered. "There might be a few dollars," he admitted. A frown made two tiny lines between his eyebrows. "What do you care, anyway?"

Jacy tensed, then bristled. They hadn't discussed the fact that she planned to continue working; it had never occurred to her that Ian would object. But it should have, she thought with rising ire as she looked into his face. Dear Lord, it should have. The man was anything but a progressive thinker, at least when it came to women and their careers.

She kept her temper, kept herself from panicking. "You mean besides in my capacity as a stepparent to one of the students?'' Jacy asked evenly. Let him say it, if he had the nerve. Let Ian come right out and hit her with the old no-wife-of-mine routine.

"I mean as a teacher,'' he said. "We've got books aplenty right here at the house, and you know I'll buy whatever Chris needs for his studies.''

Jacy just watched him, waiting.

Ian scowled, fidgeted a little, then left the rail to pace the length of the veranda, his boot heels marking the meter of his mounting frustration. On the return round he stopped square in front of Jacy and glared down at her.

"Damn it, you're going to make a crusade out of this, aren't you?'' he spat. "You're going to insist on working, as if I can't support me own wife.''

Jacy regarded him steadily. She was intimidated, but she wasn't about to show it. "I never needed either the job or you to support me, Ian,'' she said evenly. "I have a trust fund the size of Tasmania, in case you've forgotten.''

Ian clamped his jaw down tight, then made a visible effort to get hold of himself. "And in case *you've* forgotten, sheila, you were hired on a temporary basis.''

She sat up a little straighter, knowing that if she gave too much ground now she would be in real danger of turning into a meek and obedient mouse. "Ian Yarbro, if you're threatening to use your place on the school committee to get me fired, you'd just better back off and think about it first. If you do that to me, I swear by all that's holy I'll never forgive you!''

He subsided, though Jacy could see it was only a temporary retreat. Ian wasn't getting ready to wave a white flag; he was merely regrouping. His blue eyes snapped with quiet fury, and his jawline was edged in crimson.

Jacy refused to look away, and she knew her own gaze was probably full of fire.

"You were only hired to fill in until we could find someone else,'' Ian insisted, breaking the silence after a long staring match.

She rose, her backbone stiff, her chin sticking out. "Well, you can stop looking. That someone else is me!"

They were standing close together, almost nose to nose, but this time the energy ricocheting back and forth between them was anger, not desire.

"We'll talk about this another time," Ian growled. "When you've had a chance to come to your senses."

"I never left my senses," Jacy retorted. Then she flung her hands out in a burst of frustration and slapped them against her sides. "Can't you pick something else to be bullheaded about?" she demanded. She turned the fingers of her hand inward and tapped herself hard on the chest. "I'm the best thing that ever happened to those kids, and I'll be damned if I'll stay home and pick ticks off sheep just because of your overblown masculine ego!"

A look of sorrowful rage moved in Ian's eyes. "How does this happen?" he rasped. He gestured in the general direction of the outbuildings. "Not an hour ago, Jacy, we were one person. We traded souls, at least for a little while. And now we're ready to tear into each other like a couple of dingoes fighting over the same piece of meat!"

She sagged back onto the bench and gathered up her precious letters. "Why are you surprised, Ian?" she asked, keeping her eyes down because seeing his pain and anger would only compound her own. "When it comes to sex, we've always been good together. It's when we try to relate in any other way that we get into trouble."

Ian was silent for a long moment, and Jacy still didn't look at him, but she could feel his heat and substance. It seemed to her that they were joined by some invisible cord, sharing the same heartbeat, the same breath.

When he spoke at last, in a low rumble of a voice, his words struck Jacy like a lash. "I want more than that," he said. "Good sex isn't enough."

Jacy nodded, full of despair. "You're right," she replied. "It isn't." What had she expected, she asked herself miserably. She'd come into this marriage knowing Ian didn't love

151

her, and yet love was the vital element, the missing link, their only hope of making the union work. "I'm not going to make all the concessions, Ian," she said softly to his back as he started down the steps to walk away from her. "You'll have to give a little ground, too."

Ian didn't turn around, didn't look back. Instead he settled that infernal hat on his head, stared off toward the horizon for what seemed like an eternity, and finally asked, "Are you planning to leave already?"

The resignation she heard in his voice made Jacy want to cry, but she couldn't. She'd exhausted her supply of tears; perhaps she would never weep again. "No, Ian. I'm not planning to leave. Not unless you drive me away."

He rounded slowly and looked at her, but Jacy couldn't make out his expression because of the shadow covering his face. Damn that hat, she thought. First chance she got, she was going to flush it.

"And all I have to do to keep from 'driving you away' is agree with everything you say, right?"

Jacy went over to stand directly in front of her husband, pushing the hat back from his face. She saw angry mockery in his eyes, but there was a certain fragility, too, and a stubborn stoicism that twisted her heart.

"You should be so lucky, Yarbro. I'm going to stay right here and fight it out with you, toe to toe."

A muscle pulsed in his jaw, but Ian's expression softened ever so slightly. "You don't think you'll win, do you?"

Jacy grinned and folded her arms. "Maybe not every time," she admitted. "But I'll have my share of victories— you can count on it."

He almost smiled. He could control his mouth, Jacy thought with satisfaction, but not the look in his eyes. "I'm still against your teaching school," he said. "There's bound to be trouble from that quarter."

She touched the cleft in his chin with the tip of one index finger. "Maybe a good dose of trouble is just what the Yolanda school system needs. In case you and Bram and whoever else is on that committee haven't noticed, we're fast approaching the twenty-first century. You people have completely missed the twentieth." Jacy shook the same finger she'd stroked Ian's chin with in front of his nose. "And by the way, how come there aren't any women in that elite little group of decision makers?"

Despite an obvious effort to resist, Ian raised one corner of his mouth in the briefest sketch of a grin. "The women don't have time for such things. They've got bread to bake and clothes to wash, and, of course, their men need looking after."

Jacy narrowed her eyes, folded her arms across her chest, and drummed her fingers on her elbows. "Their men need horsewhipping," she countered, grateful that the storm between them had blown over—and well aware that the respite was only temporary.

Ian's lips twitched again, but then he bent toward Jacy until they were nose to nose and warned, "Take my advice, sheila, and don't stir the wasps' nest. You're bound to get stung."

Jacy didn't back off. In fact, she was mentally pushing up her sleeves. "Tomorrow I'm going to call on all the parents and let them know that school will start again on Monday. Exactly where do the Shifflets live?"

All semblance of amusement faded from Ian's features. "That family's got trouble enough without you sticking your nose in," he observed grimly. "Besides, you might as well prod a wild boar with a pointed stick as pester Redley Shifflet—he's just about that friendly."

Jacy felt a cold trembling in the pit of her stomach—she *was* a little afraid of Gladys's father—but she was determined to learn to stick with things to the finish, and this was as good a place to start as any. "I was thinking you might go with me," she ventured, sounding more timid than she would have liked.

Ian swept off his hat and put it on again, a familiar gesture of exasperation. "I have a property to run, you know.

And since you own every inch of land between my paddock fence and Corroboree Springs, so do you. You might give a thought to putting the place to some use!"

She hadn't thought about her inheritance at all, in fact, and the mention of it brought a frown to her face. "You're right," she muttered. "I'd better work that out." She turned, biting her lower lip, and gathered up Jake's letters. When she looked back Ian was gone.

He didn't come to tea.

Jacy made herself eat, washed the dishes afterward so Mrs. Wigget could go home to her cats, then sat down at the trestle table to help Chris with his spelling. Occasionally she cast a nervous glance toward the door, dreading Ian's return and, at one and the same time, wondering what the devil was keeping him.

When the lesson was done Chris went to his room to put on his pajamas and brush his teeth. He came back afterward to bid Jacy good night.

She hugged him. "Does your dad always stay out this late?" she asked, trying to sound casual.

Chris nodded. "It takes a lot of work running a property like ours," he said knowingly. "In the first part of summer, when we shear the sheep, Dad practically never sleeps."

"Great," she said.

Jacy stayed up for a while after Chris went off to bed, writing letters. She addressed the first to her mother and stepfather, telling them about not only Jake's death, but also her marriage to Ian. *That* was bound to start a riot. The second letter—the one to Margaret Wynne, her father's friend in Queensland—was harder to compose. The message would be necessarily brief, since the woman was a stranger, but Jacy didn't want to be too abrupt, either. The news was bound to come as a terrible shock.

It was nearly midnight when Jacy finished the task, and still there was no sign of Ian. She looked out the window over the sink and saw that there were lights burning in the stables, but she didn't go out to see what was keeping her husband. In the first place, she didn't want to be the kind of wife who's always scanning the horizon for some sign of her man, and in the second, she wasn't up to another session of lovemaking like the last one.

In the end Jacy took a long bath, read for a while by the light of a kerosene lamp, and finally dropped off. Ian joined her somewhere toward morning, though she was too deeply mired in sleep to look at the clock or say anything. All she remembered when she awakened was that he'd fitted her into his arms, her back to his chest, rested his chin on the top of her head, and fallen into an exhausted slumber of his own.

She sat up in bed, amazed. Ian was already gone.

After sitting there for a moment, trying to decide how she felt about that, Jacy realized that there was more noise than usual. She went to the window and saw two strangers herding half a dozen wild horses into the yard by the stables. Ian was approaching one of the terrified animals with a bridle of some sort, and Chris was perched on the rail fence, watching.

Jacy scrambled into her clothes, brushed her hair and teeth, and splashed her face with water. A strange excitement filled her, an emotion composed of both wonder and fear. She dashed down the hallway and across the kitchen, calling a greeting to Mrs. Wigget as she passed, and barreled outside.

Soon she was next to Chris, her feet on the bottom rail of the fence, gripping the top one with both hands. Her mouth dropped open when Ian slipped the bridle over the head of the horse he'd selected and, in almost the same motion, swung up onto its back.

The dun-colored beast planted its forelegs in the dirt, quivering, and then, like a package tied too tightly with string, it came undone, spinning and bucking and pitching with all the force it possessed.

A cry of terror escaped Jacy, but Ian was laughing—*laughing* as he rode that wild horse—and Chris and the two strangers were shouting encouragement. Finally the animal went one way and Ian the other. He soared through the air, landed hard, and rolled to his feet with a grace that could only have come of long practice.

The horse stood in the middle of the yard trembling, its hide glistening with sweat, its eyes rolled back so far that only the whites showed. Jacy felt its fear and its fury, and she couldn't believe it when she saw Ian moving close again, murmuring something to the beast, catching up the loose reins, getting a grip on the animal's mane to swing right back up onto its back.

She started to climb the fence, to yell in protest, but Chris stopped her by laying a hand on her shoulder.

"You might get trampled if you go in there," the child said in a reasonable tone.

Jacy swallowed hard and then froze, her eyes widening with horror as she watched the horse trying with all its considerable might to hurl Ian off its back. The remaining five animals, also wild, were panicky, nickering and crowding one another at the other end of the corral. Jacy had a graphic vision of Ian being flung into their midst and stomped to a bloody mash, and for a few moments she thought she was going to disgrace herself by throwing up right there in front of everybody.

Ian was busy being a macho bronco buster and didn't notice that his wife was clinging to the fence, weak with terror. The horse bucked and whirled until it was exhausted, then it simply stood still in the middle of the corral, its flanks and withers quivering, its hide slick and wet.

The two men, still mounted on their own horses, whistled and shouted their approbation as Ian swung his right leg over the animal's neck and slid gracefully to the ground. There was a cocky grin on his sun-browned face, and when he saw Jacy he tugged once at the brim of his hat, then strode toward her and Chris.

Chris was delighted by his father's performance, but he was a child and didn't know any better. Jacy was a grown

woman, and she could imagine a crushed shoulder or collapsed rib cage all too vividly.

Ian pushed his hat to the back of his head and grinned.
"Thought you were going to sleep the day away, sheila."

Jacy held her tongue. She wanted to tell Ian he was a
fool for risking his life like that, and tell him she would,
but not in front of Chris.

Ian adjusted his leather gloves—they were as worn as
that infernal hat of his—a shadow of the grin lingering on
his mouth. As if on cue, Chris got down from the fence
and hurried into the shed, probably meaning to saddle his
own horse.

Jacy gestured wildly toward the wild animals huddled at
the far end of the corral, with their ears back and their
eyes rolling. She did manage to keep her voice down to a
hiss. "I suppose you think you're some big deal of a cowboy or something!"

Ian just laughed. He plainly enjoyed her anger, and that
made her even madder.

"I'm not even going to *try* to talk sense into your head,
Ian Yarbro, because it would be a waste of my valuable
time! But I will say this: You are an idiot!"

He arched one dark eyebrow, gloved hands on his hips.
He was filthy and sweaty from the top of his head to the
soles of his scuffed boots, and Jacy thought he'd never
looked more damnably attractive. "You don't like my
breaking the brumbies to ride, love?" he asked innocently.

Jacy climbed over the fence and walked over to face him.
"For the record, no, Ian, I don't like it. I'd feel roughly
the same way about watching you jump out of Collie's
plane without a parachute. But I'll be *damned* if I'm going
to let you suck me into another argument. If you want to
kill yourself, go ahead!" With that she turned to storm
away, but Ian caught her by the arm and pulled her back.

To her surprise, there was no anger in his eyes or the
set of his face. "This is what I do, Jacy," he said, with
eminent reason. "I run this property. I muster sheep. I

shear them and dip them so the blowflies won't eat them alive. And I break brumbies to sell to stationers all over South Australia.''

Jacy wasn't appeased, but she knew there would be no changing this man, and in fact, she wasn't at all sure she wanted him to change. Ian thrived on hard work, and the more dangerous it was, the more he liked it; but just as he'd said, that was who he was.

She gave a great sigh. "All right, Ian. I can accept that this is what you do." She put her hands on her hips and tilted her head to one side. "The question is, can you do the same for me? Because teaching is what *I* do."

11

THE MIDDLE OF THE FARMYARD IS HARDLY THE PLACE TO talk about our personal problems," Ian pointed out.

Jacy let out a long sigh. He was right, damn him. "Fine. We can argue later. Right now I have things to do." With that she turned and walked away, going through the gate this time instead of over the fence rail, and marched into the house.

She took a quick shower, then put on pantyhose, makeup, a light blue linen dress, and sandals. She was fluffing out her hair when Ian came into the bedroom looking as though he'd been dragged through the barnyard muck.

"You look nice," he said in a grudging tone. Gazing into the bureau mirror, Jacy could see that his eyes were narrow, and his jawline looked a little tight, too.

Jacy felt a rush of private pleasure; Ian was jealous. She wanted to celebrate, to throw a party, to send up flares. It was a passing fancy, quickly gone. "Thanks." She let her eyes move over his image in the glass, a tube of lip gloss in one hand. "You'll understand if I don't return the compliment, I hope."

Ian took a step toward her, then stopped, his frown deepening. "Where are you going dressed up like that?"

At last she turned. "Ian," she began patiently, "I've already told you. I'm calling on as many of my students' families as I can to let them know school will begin again on Monday morning."

His throat worked visibly, and even though his voice was quiet there were sparks in his eyes. "Starting with the Shifflets, I suppose?"

"Yes," she replied. "I thought I'd take the most difficult case first—just as you probably chose the wildest and meanest of those brumbies out there to break before all the others."

Again Ian swallowed. "That's different."

Jacy turned her back on him, gave herself a final inspection in the mirror—she looked every inch the modern educator—and then reached for her purse. "It isn't," she said. She stood facing her husband; everything hinged on whether he barred her way or stepped aside.

He swore. "Just let me wash up, and I'll go with you."

Jacy shook her head, though a sense of loving triumph swept through her. There was hope for the both of them, she thought. "No. I've been thinking about that, and I decided it wasn't a good idea. After all, you didn't ask me to help you break those wild horses of yours to ride."

He opened his mouth and would have said it again—"that's different"—but Jacy stopped him by laying a finger to his lips.

"It's the same," she insisted softly. "Now tell me. Where do the Shifflets live?"

Ian was stubbornly silent.

"All right," Jacy said finally. She walked past her husband and stood at the door, one hand on the knob. "Fine. I'll just ask Mrs. Wigget, or Nancy. Or Bram McCulley."

"They're camped out in that old homestead just south

160

of Yolanda. We stopped there for a picnic once, you and I. . . ."

Jacy closed her eyes, remembering. She and Ian had pretended the ancient, crumbling house was their own to fix up and live in, but they'd never gotten around to eating lunch. They'd been too busy making love in the shade of several gnarled old mulga trees.

"I know the place you mean," she said without looking back at Ian. Just as she turned the knob Ian's hand closed over hers, callused and strong.

"Just be careful," he told her hoarsely.

She looked up at him. He wasn't going to try to stop her, and for him that was an enormous concession. The love Jacy felt for Ian just then was piercing and sweet. "I will," she said, almost whispering.

Ian frowned. "I want your promise on something, Sheila. If Redley's been in his cups, you'll get into Jake's truck and come straight back here."

Jacy nodded. It was little enough to ask in return for the ground he'd given. Besides, Redley Shifflet was frightening enough when he was sober; drunk, he'd be a horror. "I promise," she said, and standing on her tiptoes, careful not to brush against his dirty clothes, she kissed him lightly on the mouth.

A half hour later Jacy arrived at the Shifflet place. Another, more industrious man might have fixed up the house and grounds a little, but Redley was obviously no ball of fire. The roof tilted precariously—it was a miracle the dust storm hadn't torn it off like a loose toupee—and bits of cardboard had been taped over the broken panes in the windows. There were chickens on the porch and, Jacy feared, inside the house as well, since the rickety door was hanging wide open.

She smoothed her good linen dress and worked up a smile before leaving the truck. Darlis came out, shooing clucking hens out of her way and wiping her hands on an apron as dirty as Ian's horse-breaking clothes. There was a tentative smile on her face, and Jacy's heart twisted as she read the other woman's emotions—Darlis was pleased to have company, but she was scared, too. Her hand trembled as she raised it to shade her eyes from the wicked sun.

"Jacy," she said, with some surprise.

Jacy smiled and approached, holding out one hand, hoping to reassure Darlis a little. No doubt the few visitors who came to that house were bill collectors, tax people, and Redley's riffraff friends. "Hello, Darlis," she said. "I just came to tell you that there will be classes on Monday. I hope Gladys can be there."

Darlis must have been pretty as a young girl, but time and hardship had made her gaunt. She looked far older than her real age, which was probably about thirty-five. She nodded hard, pathetically eager to appease and nervous as a spider. "Gladys is under the weather just now," she said quickly. "Lying down, she is. I'd ask you in, but I don't like to disturb her."

Jacy felt a chill despite the brutal heat. She glanced toward the house, silently debating with herself. She wanted a firsthand look at her student, and yet she knew the rules were strict in the bush. If she pushed too hard, she might never have another chance to win Darlis's confidence.

"If I could just say hello—"

Darlis's face actually contorted. She reached out and clasped Jacy's upper arms hard. "Please," she begged with plain desperation. "Just leave us be. I'll get Gladdy to school if that's what you want, but—"

Jacy's uneasiness congealed into cold alarm, but before she could think of anything to say, Gladys appeared in the open doorway of the house. Even from that distance Jacy could see that one of the girl's eyes was blackened, and there were bruises on her arms and legs.

"My God," Jacy whispered, forgetting Darlis, forgetting

all the social rules of the outback, and moving toward the child. "Gladys, sweetheart, what happened?"

Gladys stood still, her lower lip trembling. It was clear that she wanted to run to Jacy, seeking safety, but there was a too-wise expression in her eyes as well. The child knew she couldn't be rescued like the beautiful princesses in the books she loved to read. In Gladys's world the dragons always won.

Jacy took another step toward her, but then the sound of a truck's horn shattered the undulating silence, and dread wrapped itself around Jacy's heart like a vine. Gladys slammed the door, and Darlis looked absolutely panic-stricken.

"It's Redley," she said quickly, unnecessarily. "He's been doggin' with his mates, and they always drink when they go after dingoes. Spend the bounty money the government offers before they see it. *Please,* Jacy—he won't do nothin' to you because he's too scared of Ian, but he'll hurt Gladys and me."

Jacy's eyes burned with tears of frustration, fury, and, most of all, pity. Redley and his buddies were bearing down fast, their old truck throwing up a spiral of red dust, their drunken songs audible even over the grinding roar of the worn-out engine.

"You can't let him do this, Darlis!" Jacy whispered desperately. "Let me help Gladys, I beg of you!"

"How?" All the heartache and hopelessness of Darlis's life echoed in that single word.

Jacy glanced nervously toward the new arrivals. Redley was pulling in behind the truck now, as if to block her way out. "Write a note releasing Gladys to my custody for a few weeks, and then just bring her to school on Monday. I'll take it from there."

Darlis bit her lower lip, half wild with fear, barely able to hold herself still. "What will you do?"

Jacy squeezed the other woman's hands. "I'll get her out of this place—send her somewhere where Redley can't hurt

163

her anymore. But I need your help—and your permission—to do it.''

An unconscious whimpering sound came from Darlis's throat as Redley brought the old truck to a clattering, smoky stop. Her eyes were on her husband, frantic and fearful, and Jacy shuddered inwardly to think what it must be like being trapped in such a place at the mercy of such a man.

"I'll try," Darlis whispered.

Jacy had to settle for that, at least for the time being. She squared her shoulders, locked all the fear and revulsion she felt deep inside her, and faced Redley.

He carried a rifle in one hand and a bottle in the other. His two friends, whom Jacy recognized from her visit to the woman-free Dog and Goose, got out of the truck and came to stand beside their mate, leering at her.

Jacy reminded herself of what Darlis had just said: Redley wouldn't hurt Jacy because he was too afraid of what Ian would do to him in retaliation. Her terror was under control, to a degree at least, but her stomach was churning so badly that she thought she might vomit. Nothing in her life had ever galled her as much as the knowledge that Darlis and Gladys were doomed to suffer every indignity, every deprivation Redley might decide to dish out simply because they were female.

Mockingly, almost losing his balance in the process, Redley swept off his hat—it was in even worse shape than Ian's—with the hand that held the bottle and clutched them both to his scrawny chest in a parody of good manners. "Get a look at this, mates," he called to his friends, slurring the words. "It's the lovely Mrs. Yarbro come to visit." His eyes roved over her with insulting slowness. When he spoke again he was addressing Jacy. "Ain't you just as pretty and cool as a bowl of ice cream on a hot day."

Jacy was heartened to see one of the goons behind Redley stop leering and turn pale under the filth that covered his skin.

"Wait a minute," he interrupted, gripping Redley's gun arm. "Did you say Mrs. Yarbro? This lady is married to *Ian Yarbro?*"

"Holy shit," breathed the other one, backing away and tugging at his hat at the same time. "No offense meant, ma'am."

The other fellow wrenched at Redley's arm again, whispering loudly. "Leave the bird alone, Redley—you know what a temper Ian's got. You mess with her, and he'll cut your balls off!"

Redley jerked free of his mate's grasp and held the rifle out in front of him, running a grubby finger along the length of the barrel. "I ain't afraid of Yarbro," he said, watching the slow progress of his finger. "He might get me once, but it won't happen twice."

Jacy went cold at the implication, but she would have died before letting Redley know how afraid she was. Terrible images filled her mind—Ian lying on the ground somewhere, bleeding to death from a gunshot wound, ambushed by Redley Shifflet. The smile she managed, in spite of that vision, was a grand-scale accomplishment.

"I'll be sure and give your regards to Ian," she said, casually opening the door of her truck. "He wanted to come along today, you know, but he was busy with those brumbies of his. By now he's probably got all six of them not only broken to ride, but eating out of his hand." The implication was clear, even to a dunce like Redley. Ian was a man in every sense of the word, more than capable of defending himself against three drunken doggers. She got into the vehicle, cast one meaningful look in Darlis's direction, and left, making a horseshoe turn in the Shifflets' front yard because Redley's truck was still in the way.

In the rearview mirror, even through the inevitable tailspin of dust, Jacy saw Redley standing in the middle of the road watching her go, the rifle in both hands. His hatred was so real, so virulent, that she could feel it following her, clutching at her.

She was terrified, for she knew now that Redley was not just bad, not just lazy and mean; he was evil. And maybe, just maybe, he was smart enough to know that hurting Ian was the best way in the world to get back at the schoolmistress for meddling in his personal business.

On the other hand, remembering Gladys's black eye and bruised body, Jacy knew she had no choice but to interfere. She couldn't turn her back on the child and pretend she didn't know what was happening to her. No, this time a fairy godmother was going to step in and work her shaky magic.

As soon as Jacy was out of sight of the Shifflet place she pulled the truck over to the side of the dirt track, got out, and was violently ill. Her stomach was still contracting painfully when she pulled into Yolanda and stopped at Nancy's café.

Her friend came out of the restaurant, beaming, to greet her, but Nancy was perceptive, and her wide Aussie smile instantly faded.

"Look at you!" she crowed in that lovely, musical accent. "Good heavens, Jacy, you're white as July in the Blue Mountains—what's happened?"

Jacy was seated at one of the café tables and had swallowed half a glass of water before she answered. "It's Redley Shifflet," she croaked, shaking. "I've made myself an enemy, Nancy. And I'm so afraid he's going to hurt Ian."

"Here, now," Nancy scoffed. "If any bloke about can look after himself, it's Ian Yarbro!" She sat down across from Jacy, frowning. "Tell us what's happened, then."

Jacy told, starting with Darlis's nervousness, then going on to Gladys's appearance in the doorway, all battered and beaten, and finishing with Redley's implied threat.

Nancy put one hand over her mouth. "Good Lord, Jacy, you've made a day's work of it, haven't you? And what do you plan to do about that poor little girl?"

Jacy bit her lower lip. She wasn't shaking quite so badly now, and it was easier to talk. "I was thinking I'd take her

back to our house after school. You haven't seen Collie
lately, have you? We could get him to take Gladys out of
here in his airplane—''

Nancy's face brightened. "She could stay with my Aunt
Molly up in Darwin! She's always taking chicks under her
wing, is Aunt Molly—how do you think I grew up to be so
fine a lady?'' She struck a comically elegant pose.

Jacy gave a strangled laugh of mingled relief and joy.
"Oh, Nancy—that would be wonderful. Will you tell Collie
I want to see him if he happens to come in for a landing
in the next few days?'' Some of her good cheer waned.
Sometimes Collie didn't land at Yolanda for a month at a
stretch; she wouldn't be able to hide Gladys at the property
forever, even if Ian backed her up. And she wasn't at all
sure he would.

Nancy reached across to pat Jacy's hand. "There now,
love—you're doing the right thing. We women have got to
look out for each other in this hard world.'' She paused,
and her expressive brown eyes widened. "Did you know
that in India young women are burned alive by their own
fathers just because there's no money for a dowry?''

Jacy felt sick all over again. "You're right, Nancy,'' she
said grimly. "We women have got to stick together. Get in
touch with your aunt if you can, and keep an eye out for
Collie. I'll be at school bright and early Monday morning.''
She started to rise, faltered, and fell back into her chair.

"You need to sit awhile!'' Nancy cried. "I won't let you
leave looking so white.''

Jacy took a few deep breaths, then stood up again. "I'm
okay,'' she insisted. "I'm going to stop by the churchyard
and say hello to Jake, then I guess I'll go home. I've got
tomorrow to see all the other parents—most of them will
be at services in the morning.''

It was clear that Nancy was still worried. "Maybe you
should just spend the night here in town,'' she said. "I
could get word to Ian somehow.''

Jacy saw the image of Ian again, shot by Redley, left to

die in the lonely expanse of the bush, and made up her mind. "No," she said. "I want to go home. To my family."

Despite her eagerness to get back to the property, to see for herself that Ian and Chris were both safe and well, Jacy stuck by her original plan and stopped by Jake's grave. The fancy stone she'd ordered through Bram McCulley's store hadn't arrived yet; there was only a wooden cross made by one of Jake's mates, and of course the ground covering the grave itself was still raw. There had been no time for a carpet of sweet green grass to grow.

Jacy knelt, paying no mind to her linen dress and panty-hose, and touched the cross. "Hey, Dad," she said, trying to smile, "I got your letters." She still didn't understand why he hadn't mailed them and accepted that she might never know.

A blessedly cool breeze flowed through the small church-yard. It was like the caress of a guardian angel, and it soothed Jacy's frayed nerves a little.

"I love you, Dad," she said. "I wish I'd told you that more often." She went on talking softly, stumbling over her words now and then, until she'd told Jake all about her discovery that she still loved Ian—indeed, that she'd never stopped. She told him her hopes—for a lifetime of happi-ness and a houseful of children—her problems and her fears. Then, feeling better, she got into the truck and set out for home.

She was composed when she arrived to find her husband and stepson in the kitchen, calmly eating lunch. Still, there was no hiding her pallor or her crumpled, dirt-stained dress, and she probably had a sour smell about her, too, from being sick by the roadside.

Ian was seated at the head of the table instead of on one of the benches beside it, and he immediately slid back his chair, rose, and came toward her.

"What the hell—"

Jacy offered a crooked, fleeting smile. "I look that bad, huh?" she joked, but her voice trembled.

Ian gripped her shoulders gently, supporting her. There was no hint of humor in his eyes, and his mouth looked as if it had never shaped itself into a cocky grin. "What happened?" he demanded in a hoarse whisper.

"It's all *right,* Ian," Jacy said tightly, trying to remind him of Chris's presence with a motion of her eyes.

Mercifully, he subsided. "Well, go on and clean yourself up," he ordered.

She gave him a grateful look, mouthed the words *I'll explain later,* and hurried down the hall. She returned after half an hour or so, clean and cool in a light cotton jumpsuit. She'd brushed her teeth, washed her face, and reapplied her makeup, but on the inside she still felt like a condemned building. One blast and she'd fold in on herself with a magnificent crash and lots of flying debris.

Ian was there waiting in the kitchen, though there was no sign of Chris or Mrs. Wigget. He'd cleaned up, too, and he was leaning against the counter, a glass of cold lemonade in one hand, watching her. "Shall I go off straightaway and beat Redley into a powder, or shall I let him live?"

Jacy didn't want to talk about Redley, didn't want to think about him, though she knew she didn't have much choice. She went over to Ian and put her arms around him. "Let him live," she answered, trying to smile.

Ian's expression was still grim, but he relented a little by setting aside the glass and embracing Jacy lightly, his hands clasped at the small of her back. "What happened over there?"

She sighed. "Nothing, really. I just got a clear view of what a son of a bitch Redley Shifflet truly is. He's been beating that child, Ian."

A muscle bunched in Ian's cheek. "You're sure?"

She nodded. Relief washed through her like a flash flood, and she realized that on some level she'd feared that Ian would think beating his child was Redley's province, if not his right. "I know you asked me not to make trouble, but I have to do something."

169

He touched her mouth with his index finger. "Yes, I suppose you do. What are you planning?"

She told him the scheme she and Nancy had come up with—Jacy would bring Gladys home with her after school on Monday and keep the child until Collie could fly down to Adelaide. From there Gladys would catch a connecting flight to Darwin, where Nancy's aunt would take her in until some permanent arrangement could be made. Hopefully, Darlis would join her daughter, and they could start their lives over in safety.

"Are you aware that that's kidnapping?" Ian demanded when she was finished.

Jacy was scared. "Darlis is going to cooperate."

"And once Redley gets to her, he'll make her swear you're lying, that any paper she signed, she signed under duress."

"Are you backing out on me, Ian Yarbro? That child is being *beaten,* and maybe worse, and I don't care if they throw me in prison for a hundred years. I won't just stand by and pretend it isn't happening!"

He grinned and bent his head to place a brief, light kiss on her mouth. "God help me," he said. "I guess this is what I get for taking up with a Yankee."

She looked deeply into his eyes, unsmiling and worried. "You'll help me?"

"I'll help you," he confirmed.

Jacy threw her arms around his neck. She almost blurted out that she loved him, in fact, but then she remembered that he didn't feel the same way about her and stopped herself just in time. "Thanks," she said instead, a little breathless from the close contact with him, knowing that what she felt for this man was shining brightly in her eyes, wondering if he saw it and recognized it for what it was.

To keep from making a complete fool of herself, she babbled on. "Don't tell me you've broken all those horses to ride already."

Jacy went red the instant the words were out of her

mouth, and all hope that Ian had missed the connection was lost when she saw the laughter in his eyes.

"Aye, love," he teased, holding her still closer. "I'm the master of all I survey. And I'm good at taming wild creatures of all sorts."

Jacy gave a low, involuntary moan. "Oh, no!"

Ian kissed her thoroughly, and the laughter lingered in his eyes when he lifted his head to look at her. " 'Oh, no' what?" he rumbled.

"You're going to make love to me again, aren't you?"

He fitted her against him with damnably skillful hands. "Do you hate it so much—my lovemaking, I mean?"

She was trembling; if Ian hadn't been holding her up, she probably would have slid to the floor like a noodle. "It's—well, it's the middle of the day—and you know how I get—"

Ian threw back his head and laughed out loud.

Somewhere inside herself Jacy found the will to double up her fists and pound at his chest.

Once.

Weakly.

He looked down at her, his eyes still twinkling, his broad shoulders trembling with the effort to control his amusement. "You can make all the noise you want, sheila," he told her. "Alice took Chris to town to have ice cream and pick up the mail. They won't be back for a while."

Jacy sagged against him. "I'm lost," she said.

Ian swept her easily up into his arms and started toward the stairs. "Completely," he agreed. "Just don't scare the sheep."

Jacy laughed and pretended to strike him again. Ian was so utterly impossible, and she was grateful that he was who he was, for all his faults and foibles, and she loved him so very much.

Alice Wigget smiled to herself as she peeled carrots for tea that night. Ian had been going about the place whistling, and Mrs. Yarbro had a glow about her, she did. One that promised there'd soon be a babe or two underfoot, and it was about time.

Alice began to think, with longing, of Arizona and cowboys and other pleasures. She was ready to move on, and lonely way out there in the bush. Ian was all grown up, of course, and Chris didn't need her any longer either, now that he had a mum to look after him proper-like.

Remembering that little problem ten years ago, with Mrs. Yarbro—she'd been just plain Jacy Tiernan back then, of course—Alice frowned to herself. Suppose the girl up and flew off again. Why, Ian would never trust another woman as long as he lived, and as for the lad—well, it didn't bear thinking about, what her leaving would do to little Chris!

She cast a worried look in Mrs. Yarbro's direction and saw that the younger woman was gazing back at her with a curious expression in her eyes. It was almost as if Jake's girl knew what she, Alice, was thinking.

Ian's wife ruffled Chris's pale hair—he was sitting at the table, making another of his drawings—and came over to stand beside Alice. Ian remained at the table, reading the week's accumulation of mail.

Mrs. Yarbro took a stack of plates down from the cupboard. Alice liked her for that; she didn't expect to be waited on hand and foot, as some new brides would have done.

"You love those two very much, don't you, Alice?" she asked in a voice too soft to carry as far as the table.

"With all my heart," Alice said stalwartly. And it was true, too, even if she did yearn to go to Arizona and take up with a cowboy.

Jacy ran her fingertip around the golden edge of the first Mrs. Yarbro's wedding china. "Here's a little secret for you," she said in that same low tone. "So do I. You needn't worry, because I'm going to look after them. You have my solemn promise."

Alice felt unaccustomed tears burn in her eyes. She

hadn't wept often, though her life had been a hard one in many ways, and she'd been on her own for most of it.

"They think they're so strong," Alice confided in a snuffly whisper. "But they need you, Mrs. Yarbro. Both of them."

Ian's wife laid her hand gently on Alice's forearm. "Please, Alice—we're friends, I hope. Won't you call me Jacy?" She glanced toward Ian and the boy, Jacy Yarbro did, and there was a warm shimmer in her blue eyes. Behind that Alice saw the fiercely protective love of a young tigress. It was still there, in fact, when Jacy looked at Alice again. "Don't worry," she said. "Nothing and no one could make me leave them."

Alice yearned to believe the girl, but she was still fearful. She hadn't forgotten, and never would, heaven help her, what losing Jacy had done to Ian the first time around. Why, if it hadn't been for Jake pulling and pushing and sometimes dragging him back from the edge, the lad would have been ruined for certain.

Again Jacy read her thoughts, and she touched Alice's arm reassuringly. "I don't blame you for not trusting me," she said. "There have been a lot of times when I haven't trusted myself. But I'm going to make a life right here, no matter how much yelling and crying and loving it takes."

Alice couldn't help smiling, for she'd certainly heard the yelling, and some of the loving besides, bless their hearts. Maybe it was wishful thinking on her part, but Alice wanted to believe there would be a whole family living under that roof at long last, so she did.

12

Ian accompanied Jacy, Alice, and Chris to church services the next morning. Jacy knew his motivation wasn't purely spiritual; he wanted to be nearby if there was trouble, and even though his mood was downright irascible, she was touched. Obviously he was determined to look out for her.

Except for the Shifflets and Bram McCulley, all the students' families were present. Redley was probably chasing dingoes across the bush for the bounty, and Bram was guarding the sacred threshold of the Dog and Goose, no doubt, in case another misguided female should attempt to step over it.

Jacy sighed and settled back in the pew. It wasn't the parson's week to be in Yolanda, so one of the congregation members was conducting the services. As a result the sermon was exquisitely dull, and Jacy's mind wandered.

She thought about Jake, wondered if there truly was a heaven and if her dad had gone there. When her stepson stirred restlessly beside her she thought about his birth

174

mother. Did Elaine Bennett ever wonder about the child she'd given up? Or the man who'd fathered that child?

Jacy frowned and glanced at Ian out of the corner of her eye. His temple was throbbing slightly; he'd rather have been at home, she knew, taming those brumbies of his, or mustering sheep. Anything except sitting in a crowded building, wearing a suit that probably only came out of the closet for weddings and funerals.

My knight in wool and starched cotton, Jacy thought with tender amusement. She let her head rest against his shoulder for a moment.

Even sermons eventually come to an end, and finally that one did. The congregation sang the closing hymn, put their meager contributions into the basket, and adjourned to the shade of the gum and pepper trees out in the yard.

Ian got into a conversation about the last plague of locusts, and Jacy slipped away to approach her students' parents one by one. All of them promised to have their children at school in the morning, though they seemed to regard the teacher with a certain wary curiosity.

She was still an outsider after all, Jacy reminded herself, suddenly feeling sad. Even though she was the daughter of a native son, she'd lived elsewhere for much of her life, and that made her suspect. For all the hardships of scratching out an existence in the bush, few of the locals would have dreamed of leaving, and they didn't identify with people who did.

Jacy felt drawn to Jake's grave, and she was standing there looking out over the stark landscape when a man she didn't recognize walked toward her across the grass. He was probably in his mid-forties, attractive in an Ivy League sort of way, and very well-dressed.

"Andrew Carruthers," he said in an American accent, extending a hand to her. "I'm the current manager of Merimbula."

"Jacy Tier—Yarbro," Jacy replied, feeling tense. Jake

had never trusted the people at Merimbula, and Ian bristled at any mention of the massive station or its management.

Carruthers smiled and glanced back over one shoulder, scanning the milling congregation. A game of two-up had been started, and women were spreading blankets on the ground and opening picnic baskets.

After a moment his icy blue eyes shifted back to her face. "Yes," he said, as if no time had elapsed since the beginning of the conversation, "I know. You're Jake Tiernan's daughter, aren't you? As well as Ian Yarbro's wife."

Jacy smiled coolly. "All that and more. I have qualities all my own, Mr. Carruthers—ones that have nothing whatsoever to do with my husband or my late father."

Carruthers sighed, glanced back toward the crowd again. Jacy wondered if he was keeping an eye out for Ian, who might not be particularly glad to see him.

"Right," he agreed. "I won't waste any more of your time, Mrs. Yarbro. Merimbula—the corporation, I mean—is willing to offer you a sizable amount of money for the land Mr. Tiernan left you." Before Jacy could offer a response he named a figure that took her breath away.

Over Mr. Carruthers's right shoulder she saw Ian approaching, and he didn't look any too happy. Although she'd appreciated his protective mood earlier, she felt a little defensive now.

"I don't plan to sell my land," she said just as Carruthers turned again and spotted Ian. He stiffened, and for a few moments Jacy thought he was going to bolt and run.

The manager of Merimbula collected himself just as Ian reached Jacy's side, but he couldn't hide the glimmer of perspiration on his upper lip. He cleared his throat and, to his credit, managed to look Ian straight in the eye.

"Your wife was just turning down our offer to buy her land," he said.

Ian was ominously still, like the ground just before an earthquake or the sky prior to a thunderstorm. "Her property wouldn't do you any good even if she did sell," he said after a moment's silence. "It's the spring you really want, and that's mine."

Carruthers closed his eyes and squeezed the bridge of his nose between his thumb and forefinger just briefly, then stared piercingly at Jacy. "Is that true, Mrs. Yarbro?"

Jacy flushed. Carruthers was her countryman, and she wanted to like him. There was something in his nature or his attitude, however, that made it difficult. "Of course it's true," she snapped. "Why would Ian say it if it wasn't?"

In answer to that, Carruthers simply raised his eyebrows and assumed a wry expression.

Ian stepped between Jacy and Carruthers, his broad shoulders blocking out her view of the exchange that followed. She finally bent around Ian's arm to see him jabbing a forefinger into Mr. Carruthers's neatly pressed shirtfront. "Don't be hounding my wife about Corroboree Springs," he warned in a furious undertone. "She's not going to sell, now or ever!"

It was true that Jacy didn't plan to sell, but she felt a niggling resentment as she listened to Ian. The property, if not the spring itself, was still her own, to do with as she chose, with or without her husband's approval.

Or was it? Jacy didn't really know much about Australian law; perhaps just by marrying Ian she'd made the land half his. That would have been the case in the United States.

She closed her eyes as a new and painful suspicion touched the edge of her heart. Ian had the spring he'd needed to survive, but he might well have wanted Jake's land, too. There was a lot of it, room for wheat and twice the number of sheep he ran on his own place.

And the best way to get his hands on all those fallow acres was to marry his neighbor's daughter.

She swayed slightly and blinked. No, protested some deep part of her that wanted, needed to believe in Ian. Please don't let it be that.

Jacy drew a deep breath and gave herself an inward shake. What else could it be? Ian had never pretended that he loved her. In fact, they'd practically been at war until that night beside the springs, after the dust storm, when he'd charmed her into a truce. . . .

"Jacy?"

She felt Ian's hands on her arms, looked up into his worried face. At the edge of her vision she saw Andrew Carruthers making a beeline for his fancy Land Rover, which was parked on the far side of the churchyard, well away from the other vehicles.

For an instant Jacy felt sorry for the manager of Merimbula. Even though the people of Yolanda had been friendly to her, for the most part, she understood what it was not to belong.

"Are you all right?" Ian asked, loosening his tie with one finger. "For a moment there I thought you were going to keel over or something."

Jacy swallowed hard and summoned up a smile, though she felt a fissure streak across her heart, breaking open all the mended places. "I'm fine," she lied. She glanced toward the departing Carruthers. "Why do you hate that poor guy so much?" she asked, in an effort to shift Ian's attention away from her. "It isn't a sin to try to buy property, you know. He's just doing his job."

Ian's face tightened, and he watched as his adversary disappeared in a billow of red dust. "It's more than that," he said quietly. "Merimbula would suck up the whole area if they could. They've driven more than one grazier out of business in the last few years."

They were moving back toward the church. Alice had laid out a picnic, and Chris was watching Jacy and Ian's approach with a wary sort of interest, as if he sensed the tension between them and feared it.

Jacy wanted to know more about Merimbula. "That's pretty ominous, Ian. What do you mean, they've driven people out of business? How?"

He flung another grim look in Carruthers's direction. "It was nothing we could prove," he admitted. "There were a few suspicious fires, and some loans were called in at inconvenient times. Then there were the poisoned water holes."

Jacy's curiosity turned to alarm. "And you think Carruthers is behind all that?"

Ian stopped, gave a heavy sigh. "He's just a go-between for the big Yankee corporation that owns Merimbula. It's never been any great secret that they wanted to take over all the land around here and put it into wheat. Even Yolanda would be plowed under if they had their way."

"But why?"

"Money," Ian answered, tugging at his tie again. "And they've already got enough of that to put the pinch on all of us, believe me."

Jacy caught hold of Ian's arm, stopping him just out of earshot of the Sunday picnickers. "Even you, Ian? Have you got a mortgage they could call?"

He shook his head. "No," he said hoarsely. "But if they got hold of your land, they could cut me off from the springs easily enough, couldn't they? If that happens, I'll be finished in a matter of months."

Ian's words reconfirmed Jacy's earlier suspicions. He loved his land; it was in his blood. And it was plain enough that he would have done almost anything to save it.

Her face must have fallen, because Ian cupped his hand over her chin and demanded, "What is it, sheila?" When she hesitated, unable to voice her very private heartache, he leapt to a logical conclusion. "Are you missing Jake?"

"Yes," she said, although it was only part of the truth. She couldn't ask Ian if he'd married her just to get control of the land between his property line and the springs; it would be too devastating if he answered in the affirmative. "Yes, I miss him very much."

The gentleness of Ian's reply twisted her heart. "So do I, sheila," he said. Then he took her hand and led her to the family picnic that awaited them.

Ian took off his suit coat with great relief, then tossed

his tie aside, too, and undid the top three buttons of his snowy white shirt. Then he sat cross-legged at one end of the blanket, grinning, and Jacy wondered, just looking at him, how she'd ever managed to stay away for ten whole years.

After they had eaten Alice's delicious fried chicken, potato salad, and pie, Ian and Chris joined in the two-up tournament as a team. Alice remained seated primly on the blanket, along with Jacy.

"You do love him, then," the housekeeper said with quiet satisfaction.

Jacy flung a startled look at the other woman, who smiled and added, "Your heart's right there in your eyes for anybody to see. Anybody but Ian Yarbro, that is."

Jacy frowned. "What do you mean, anybody but Ian?"

Alice busied herself gathering up the debris of the picnic. "It'll take him a little time to believe you truly care for him, I think," she said. "He's built a wall up around his feelings over the years." The older woman paused, staring thoughtfully at Ian as he threw the two coins into the air, laughing at something one of the other men had said. "I guess what I'm saying is, give him a while to learn to trust again."

Jacy ached inside. "And I'm the reason he's afraid, right?"

Alice surprised her. "No," she said. "Ian needs to learn to trust his own feelings again. It's himself he's fighting, Jacy, not you. If you'll remember that and be patient, he'll come round in time."

Tears stung Jacy's eyes. "I hope you're right."

"But you don't think I am?" Alice prompted gently.

Jacy picked up a cloth napkin and dried her tears before they could spoil her makeup. "Ian married me for entirely practical reasons. He was really quite straightforward about the whole thing. He wanted a woman to share his bed, and a mother for Chris. Most of all, I think he wanted the land between his place and the springs."

Alice smiled to herself as she resumed the process of clearing away the mess. "Ian may *think* that's what he wants—the land, I mean. Give him a chance, dearie. He'll work through to the truth of it all."

Jacy watched him ruffle Chris's hair and bend to lend the boy advice on tossing the coins. "I guess I deserve this," she said in a thick whisper. "I love him so much that sometimes I think I can't bear it. When he felt that same way about me ten years ago, I abandoned him."

"You were young," Alice reminded her brusquely. "Besides, it would have come as a shock to anyone, learning about the baby that way. That Elaine was a piece of work, she was. Loved stirring up trouble, the little minx. Imagine giving up your own child that way, just walking away and not asking after him even once!"

Jacy longed to change the past, to somehow wave a magic wand and make Chris her own natural son. If only she'd stayed and worked things out with Ian in the first place; there would probably be several children by now, and she and Ian might have built a relationship they could both trust.

"Ian must have worried," she finally said. "That Elaine would come back and want to take Chris away, I mean."

Mrs. Wigget made a soft, contemptuous sound. "Not a bit of it. Ian would die before he'd give that child up, and she was smart enough to know that much, at least. Besides, Miss Bennett wanted a whole different sort of life, I think, one full of parties and men and loud music. No room in her schedule for a nipper."

Jacy laid a hand to her own abdomen and wondered, not for the first time, if there was a baby growing inside her even then. She set her jaw. She wasn't Elaine, and if she was ever lucky enough to have a child, she would raise it herself. With or without Ian Yarbro.

"You don't look as though you feel very well," Mrs. Wigget remarked with a hint of speculation in her manner and tone. "Maybe it's time we got you home, where you could get out of the heat and put your feet up."

It sounded marvelous, but Jacy shook her head. Normally her husband worked like a maniac, and it was good to see him laughing with his friends and his son. She would wait until Ian and Chris were ready to leave.

Soon Ian began casting looks in Jacy's direction. She couldn't help being pleased, even reassured, but she would have given anything to know what was actually going on in his mind.

Finally, he came over to Jacy with Chris in tow and held out one hand to help her to her feet. "I guess we'd better start for home," he said.

The words sounded like music to Jacy. She was well aware that Ian could be stubborn and hardheaded, that he was a raving chauvinist, and yet she adored him. She would have stood beside him through anything, if only there was hope that he would one day trust her again and—please God—allow himself to love her.

At home Jacy took Alice's advice and went off to lie down in the shadowy coolness of the bedroom. Ian was there for a little while, though only to exchange his suit for worn blue jeans and a chambray shirt. He sat on the edge of the bed to pull on his work boots.

"Would you do it, Jacy?" he asked. His expression was somber and a bit wary.

"Do what?" she countered, teasing. She was sleepy and comfortable, though her heart still felt bruised.

Ian frowned, brushed a lock of hair back from her forehead in a distracted way, as if he weren't quite conscious of the action. "Would you sell your land?"

Jacy felt a stab of fear and hoped to God it didn't show in her face, because Ian was looking at her intently now. He probably wouldn't miss much, so she had to be careful what she revealed. "No," she answered. There was a sob trembling behind the word, but she swallowed that and even managed a shaky smile. "I think we should put our two properties together, as you suggested once, and make the most of it.''

What an actress you are, Tiernan, she thought to herself. And what a fool.

She'd expected Ian's frown to smooth out, but it remained, creasing his tanned forehead. ''Really?''

She sat up, exasperated and ridiculously close to tears. Maybe she *was* pregnant; she was certainly feeling overemotional. ''What did you think I was going to do, Ian?'' she snapped. ''Build a stone wall between you and your precious goddamned water?''

''I wouldn't have been a bit surprised,'' he said frankly. But Ian's hand was gentle as it curved around her face. ''Relax, sheila,'' he went on. ''I'm on your side, remember?''

Jacy looked away. She wished she could believe him, but the truth was that, with Jake gone, she felt alone and more than a little out of place. After a few moments she was able to look at him again, and she thought of Redley Shifflet running his fingertip along the length of his gun barrel and claiming he wasn't afraid of Ian.

''You're going out?'' she asked, alarmed.

Ian pressed her back onto the pillows tenderly, as if she were a distraught child and not the woman he'd made love to so often and so well. ''I've things to do, sheila,'' he said reasonably, ''even if it is Sunday.''

She clutched at his shirt with one hand, thinking of Redley and his rifle again, feeling terrified. ''You'll be careful?''

He frowned. ''I'm always careful,'' he said. He bent and kissed her on the forehead. ''Rest now, love. I'll see you at teatime.''

Jacy closed her eyes, but only because she was too weary to keep them open any longer. Within moments she tumbled into a fitful sleep and dreamed that Ian had been shot dead and laid to rest in a grave beside Jake's.

She awakened sobbing, to find shadows taking over the room one by one. She felt a small hand touch her arm and focused on Chris, standing beside the bed, searching her face with troubled eyes.

"It's all right, Mum," he said cautiously. "I get bad dreams sometimes, too. Everybody does."

Jacy sniffled, a little embarrassed. She was supposed to be the adult there, the strong one. Instead she was falling apart, and a schoolboy was trying to comfort her. She nodded and sat up, smoothing her hair.

Chris went out, returning a few moments later with a glass of water. Jacy took it gratefully, murmuring her thanks, and after a few sips she felt calmer.

"You're quite the gentleman, Chris Yarbro," she told the child with an unsteady smile. "Thank you for trying to make me feel better."

He risked a slight smile, then looked solemn again. "Are you going to stay here with us?"

The question left Jacy as breathless as if the bed had suddenly been yanked from beneath her, and maybe the floor, too. "Why wouldn't I stay, Chris?"

The boy chewed on his lower lip for a few seconds, then answered in a rush of words. "Linus Tate said you and my dad almost got married once before, a long time ago. Then you got mad at him because I was going to be born, and you went home to America."

Jacy closed her eyes just briefly, in an effort to recover. She made a mental note to strangle Linus first thing in the morning, then scooted over and patted the mattress. "Sit down," she said.

He obeyed, watching her earnestly. Waiting.

She took one of his hands. "Your dad and I did know each other when we were younger, and we were in love. There was a problem, and I ran away, and I will always be sorry that I did that, because it was a mistake. But—and it's very important that you listen to this and believe it, Chris—none of it was your fault."

His eyes were huge. "But you did run away."

Jacy nodded. "That was pretty stupid, wasn't it?" She

frowned pensively. "Did you ever do something foolish, Chris, and then wish with all your heart that you hadn't?"

He shifted uncomfortably. "Yeah," he confessed.

"But you wouldn't do that same thing over again, would you? Because you know now that it was a blunder?"

Understanding shone in his eyes, and he smiled tentatively. "Then you won't leave us?"

Jacy drew the child into her arms, as she had often longed to do, and held him close for a few moments. "Not if it's my choice," she replied after some careful thought. "But life can be pretty unpredictable, Chris. You've probably discovered that for yourself."

He pulled away far enough to look into her face. "Do you love us, my dad and me?"

She felt her throat constrict. "Oh, yes. Very, very much."

"But sometimes you and Dad yell at each other. I've heard you."

"People can be in love and still disagree, Chris." She closed her eyes for a moment, wishing that love went two ways, knowing that it had died long ago, at least on Ian's side. And she had no one to blame but herself. "A little yelling can be healthy sometimes."

Chris began to feel uncomfortable then, apparently, because he withdrew from Jacy's arms and stood. "Okay," he said. All his trust and faith were there in that one word, and Jacy vowed, to herself and to heaven, that she wouldn't betray him.

When he was gone Jacy got up, went into the bathroom, and splashed cold water on her face. She looked pale, and her eyes were puffy and red. Resigned, she combed her hair, exchanged the dress she'd fallen asleep in for jeans and a T-shirt, and went into the kitchen.

Mrs. Wigget had left a stew bubbling on the stove, but the house was quiet and filled with evening shadows. Chris had apparently gone outside.

Jacy lit a few lamps and was standing in the living room,

185

her hands on her hips, when Ian came in through the kitchen.

"What we need," she announced, "is a television set."

Ian was leaning against the door frame, grinning wearily. It was plain that while she'd been sleeping, and having nightmares, he'd put in a day's work. "Right," he said. "Never mind that you couldn't pick up anything way out here, other than static."

"We could get a satellite dish," Jacy reflected.

"They're expensive."

"I have money."

Ian sighed. "I can see I'm going to lose this argument," he admitted good-naturedly. "Do what you want, sheila."

Chris, who had obviously been eavesdropping from the kitchen, started jumping around and emitting shrieks of joy.

"You've won him over, I'd say," Ian said wryly.

How about you, Ian? Jacy wanted to ask. Have I won you over? But she couldn't take the risk, not yet.

They had stew for tea, and while Jacy and Chris washed the dishes, Ian took a bath. Jacy tried not to think too much about that.

When they went to bed that night Ian seemed to understand that she needed to be held. He tucked her against him, kissed the back of her head, and promptly dropped off to sleep.

Jacy wondered what it was like to rest so deeply, and so peacefully. Her own slumber was shallow and troubled, and she awakened the next morning feeling as if she hadn't slept at all.

Ian was already gone, as usual. Jacy dressed for school, put on light makeup, and went into the kitchen to find Mrs. Wigget making tea and Chris seated at the table eating oatmeal.

"I told Mrs. Wigget we're getting a telly," he said excitedly. "Just like they've got over at Merimbula."

Jacy was tense, her mind on the day ahead. She wondered if Darlis would follow through with her plan or lose

186

her courage. And what if Gladys didn't want to leave her family? Many abused children lied for their parents, after all, and were willing to suffer most anything just to stay.

"How would you know what they've got at Merimbula?" Alice asked Chris, though she was looking at Jacy while she spoke.

"Linus told me," Chris answered without missing a beat. "There's a swimming pool there, too. And a place to play golf."

Jacy met Alice's gaze and raised her eyebrows. "Pretty fancy," she said, helping herself to a cup of coffee and mussing Chris's hair when she returned to the table.

"Linus doesn't get to swim or play golf, though," Chris was quick to explain. "That's just for Mr. Carruthers and his wife and their two daughters."

Jacy stopped, intrigued. "Mr. Carruthers has children? And they live on Merimbula?"

Chris nodded, pleased to be the bearer of news. "They're Yanks," he said, as if that were the key to myriad mysteries.

"Why don't they come to school?"

Chris hesitated and had the grace to blush a little. "I guess it's not good enough for them," he answered uncomfortably. "They've got a governess from England."

Jacy looked to Alice for confirmation, and the housekeeper nodded.

"Snobs they are, those people at Merimbula," Alice said. "Don't give them another thought."

That was asking too much. The Carruthers children were probably getting a fine education from their English governess, but what about their social needs? It was Jacy's experience that kids needed other kids to interact with. "I think I'll pay the Carutherses a visit one of these days," she reflected. "Maybe their daughters could come to the schoolhouse to play with the other children, if nothing else."

"You'd go there?" Alice asked, appalled. "To Merimbula?"

Jacy was surprised. "Why not?" she countered with a puzzled smile. "Is there a drawbridge? A moat, perhaps, with alligators?"

Chris laughed, but Alice was plainly flustered. "First she goes to the Shifflets'," she muttered to herself, turning away to rattle dishes and silverware in the sink. "Then to Merimbula, of all places! Where will it end?"

Where indeed, Jacy wondered, winking at Chris.

He grinned and winked back.

13

GLADYS SHIFFLET DID NOT COME TO SCHOOL THAT MORN-
ing, and neither did many of the children whose parents
had promised better attendance when Jacy had spoken to
them after church. Her frustration was only heightened by
the note she found on her desk.

"Not today," Darlis had written, in a painfully childish
scrawl. "Redley's mean. Wait till he goes hunting 'roos.''
With it, though, was another message, carefully written on
cheap paper, giving Darlis's permission to take Gladys to
another part of the country.

Jacy bit her lower lip and fought back tears of pure irritation and fear. Darlis wanted to wait until her no-gooder of
a husband had gone off with his drunken friends, clipping
kangaroos for the bounty the government was offering. But
what horrors would Gladys be forced to endure in the meantime? The possibilities made Jacy frantic.

She resigned herself to paying another visit to the Shifflets that very day, directly after school. Maybe a miracle
would happen and she would find a way to reason with

Redley; the only thing she knew for certain was that she had to try.

Jacy set the other children to working on their school-work that morning, then went out to stand on the porch. The breeze she'd hoped for didn't materialize; the air was as hot and humid as the steam from a boiling teakettle. While she was standing there, though, fanning herself with an outdated lesson planning book, an old rattletrap of a truck pulled up at the gate, and out spilled an eager little boy about Chris's age. He hit the ground running, as Jake would have said.

The lad was followed by his parents, a young couple in shabby clothes. They seemed outrageously happy, given the surely difficult circumstances of their lives, and approached Jacy with almost as much enthusiasm as their son did. She felt a touch of envy, as well as an instant liking.

"I'm Tom McAllister," the man announced. "This is my wife, Ellie, and here's our boy." He paused to gesture toward the child with his old felt hat as though Jacy might somehow have missed him. "Thomas Jr.'s his name."

Jacy smiled. "Hello, Thomas. Would you like to come in and join our classes?"

Thomas Jr. wrinkled his freckled nose, but it was clear that he could barely contain himself. He wanted to go barreling past Jacy and plunge into whatever experiences might await him. "Yes, mum," he said.

Jacy gestured toward the open doorway, where all of her other students had crowded in to peer at the newcomer. "There are several empty desks. Choose the one you like best."

The kids moved aside, still reserving judgment, from their expressions, and Thomas Jr. walked between them with all the confidence of Moses passing through the parted waters of the Red Sea.

Mr. and Mrs. McAllister remained outside the gate. Their belongings, including a mattress that had seen better days, filled the back of the rusted-out, sputtering old truck. For an awful moment Jacy wondered if they meant to abandon Thomas Jr., but she put the idea aside quickly.

The McAllisters fairly glowed with love, for each other and for their son.

"Do you know where a man could get work, mum?" Tom Sr. asked.

A brilliant idea dawned on Jacy. Ian would have said she was being rash, and he'd have been right, but there were times when a person had to take a calculated risk. "Yes," she said, stepping down from the rickety porch to go and stand facing the McAllisters over the equally rickety fence. "I've recently gotten married, and my husband's property adjoins the one I inherited from my father. He'll need more help now that there's twice the land to deal with. There's a perfectly good homestead at Corroboree Springs, and you could live there. If you want to take the job, I mean."

Mrs. McAllister's face, already beaming, had brightened visibly at the mention of a house, and Tom Sr. looked painfully hopeful. "Wouldn't he want to meet us first?" he asked. "Your husband, I mean?"

Jacy smiled, imagining the way Ian would react to having a family of strangers installed on their property without so much as a nod from him. "I can't think why he should," she lied pleasantly. "The land is mine, and so is the house."

Tom Sr. regarded her in wonder for a few moments, then cleared his throat. "If you'll excuse us, Mrs.—?"

"Yarbro," Jacy answered. "Jacy Tiernan Yarbro."

Tom Sr. nodded. "Mrs. Yarbro," he repeated dutifully. "We'll just talk this over a bit, my wife and me."

With that the McAllisters went around to the other side of the truck to confer. Jacy waited patiently until they returned, both their smiles on high beam.

"We'll take the job, Mrs. Yarbro," Tom Sr. announced.

"With pleasure," Ellie added.

Jacy offered her hand over the fence, and they shook on it, she and Tom Sr. and then she and Ellie. She told Ellie there were still a few canned goods on the shelves at Corroboree Springs, gave them detailed directions to the place, and promised to bring Thomas Jr. home when school was over for the day.

Returning to the schoolhouse, Jacy found that the new boy had chosen a seat next to Chris's. Another good omen, she thought. Chris needed a special friend, and Thomas Jr. was an excellent candidate.

Jacy spent the rest of the morning analyzing what Thomas Jr. had already learned. He'd studied by school-of-the-air, like many children in the Australian outback, living on a big station up in Queensland until just a month before. Tom Sr. had been a roustabout, and he'd lost his job when the owner sold the place.

At noon recess Chris shared his lunch with Tom Jr., and the other children accepted the boy readily into their schoolyard games. Jacy sat on the step, watching them while she ate her chicken noodle soup from a thermos lid. Until then she'd been too busy to think about Gladys Shifflet's predicament, but now the little girl's plight filled her thoughts.

As much as she would have liked to avoid the confrontation, Jacy knew she had no choice but to approach Redley herself. After school she would leave Chris and Thomas Jr. in town with Nancy and drive out to the Shifflet place again.

As it happened, that wasn't necessary. Pulling up in front of the Yolanda Café, Jacy saw Redley's truck parked in front of the Dog and Goose. She shepherded the boys into Nancy's place of business and up to the counter and ordered chocolate milkshakes for them both.

"You have a look about you," Nancy fussed, watching Jacy over one shoulder while she mixed up ice cream, milk, and syrup in the American fashion. "Don't you dare step outside that door without telling me what you mean to do."

Jacy sighed and pushed her hair back with one hand. She wished there was some way to avoid the task ahead of her, but couldn't think what it would be. Someone had to take

Gladys's part—the child's fate and perhaps even her life depended upon it—and apparently Jacy was that someone.

While the boys were talking and enjoying their milk-shakes Nancy took Jacy's arm and hustled her into the corner next to the jukebox.

"You're white as flour," Nancy accused in a whisper. "What's going on?"

"Gladys didn't come to school today," Jacy answered in a soft, despairing voice. "I just saw Redley's truck outside the Dog and Goose, so I'm on my way over there to talk to him."

Nancy's face reddened, then paled in the space of a moment. She started to speak, swallowed hard, and tried again. "I don't suppose there's any way to talk you out of this."

Jacy shook her head. God, how she wished Ian were around. Even though he'd probably be annoyed at her for breaching hallowed ground again by venturing inside Bram McCulley's pub, he would have kept her safe.

"I'll go with you, then," Nancy sputtered, pacing back and forth in front of the jukebox.

"No," Jacy said quickly, shaking her head again.

Nancy stopped, hands on her hips, eyes narrowed, cheeks flushed with conviction and anger. "And why not?"

"Because someone needs to stay here and look after the boys," Jacy answered, keeping her voice soft. "I'm dealing with Redley Shifflet, remember? Anything could happen."

Nancy's eyes were the size of the pancakes she served for breakfast. "Then go and find Ian first—have him go with you to talk with Redley—"

"No time," Jacy interrupted. "Ian could be anywhere on the property—it might take hours to find him. No, Gladys is trapped in hell, and every passing second counts."

With that, Jacy squared her shoulders and headed resolutely for the door. Hey, Jake, she said silently, if you happen to be hanging around, I could use a hand with this.

Jacy felt like Gary Cooper in *High Noon* as she crossed

the dusty street toward the Dog and Goose. The trouble was, she wasn't wearing six-guns, and Redley wasn't going to meet her out in the open. She had to seek out a man who hated her, in a place she was forbidden to go.

Outside the door of the pub Jacy paused, took a deep breath, and glanced back over one shoulder. She could see Nancy's face, a white circle at the window of the Yolanda Café.

Letting out her breath, Jacy pushed open the door and stepped inside the Dog and Goose.

She was aware of the cool, shadowy atmosphere first, then the abrupt cessation of sound. The pool balls stopped clicking together, and the flow of laughter and talk might have been sliced off with a sharp knife.

Bram McCulley was behind the bar, and he rolled his eyes as if to say, "Not again."

Jacy acknowledged him with a crisp nod and turned to search the darkness for Redley.

He was at the pool table, leaning on his cue stick and watching her with a strange mingling of hatred and mirth. His thin face was dirty, roughened by a new beard, and his dark eyes gleamed with meanness.

Jacy took another deep breath and started toward him. "I'd like to talk to you, Mr. Shifflet." She almost choked on the polite salutation, but under the circumstances, a few such concessions were definitely in order. Redley's buddies, other doggers and kangaroo hunters like him, were staring at her in angry bafflement. "In private."

Redley's grin was obscene. "In private?" He gave the words a suggestive spin.

Jacy was trembling inside, but she made a point of standing tall and pretending she wasn't scared. "It's about Gladys," she said.

Instantly the grin faded. "My girl? What about her?"

Now, Jacy thought wildly, would be a good time for Ian to walk in. Of course, he didn't; he was probably riding a fence line or working with one of those damned horses of his. "I want to see Gladys. I want to talk to her. Alone."

Redley looked coldly furious now; Jacy figured even the obnoxious grin would have been better. "Maybe in the States men let their women run all over, poking their noses in other people's business, but here we make them mind their manners."

Dear God, Jacy prayed, help me keep my temper. "I won't be going home and minding my manners, Redley," she said quietly, evenly. "Not while I know a child is being abused. If you refuse to let me see her, I'll bring the authorities in. You can bet your rum money on it."

A murmur rose among Redley's friends, and Jacy felt someone standing behind her. She knew it wasn't Ian this time and didn't dare dwell on the other possibilities.

The cords in Redley's skinny, unwashed neck flexed dangerously, and his right temple seemed about to leap right out of his greasy hair. "I guess you don't understand the rules here," he drawled, his eyes glittering with barely controlled malice. "Your man had better explain them to you—usin' the back of his hand, to start with."

Jacy lost it. She put her hands on her hips and leaned in toward Redley, despite the smell of his flesh and the rot in his soul. "Listen to me, you Neanderthal," she breathed. "Ian Yarbro is ten times the man you are, and he doesn't need to hit women and children to prove he's strong."

In a lightning-quick motion Redley buried a grubby hand in Jacy's hair and yanked. The pain made her gasp and brought stinging tears to her eyes. "No, *you listen to me, you Yankee bitch!* Maybe you've got a ring in Yarbro's nose, but I ain't him. *I* take care of my women, and with no interference from the likes of you!"

Jacy had caught her inner balance and dealt with the pain, but before she could speak she heard the sharp click of a rifle being cocked behind her. For a heart-stopping moment she thought someone was actually going to shoot her.

Instead, Bram spoke in his deep, laconic voice. "Let the sheila go, Redley," he said. "If you don't, I swear by the queen's best nightie, I'll shoot your balls off right here."

Redley tightened his grasp for an instant, purposely intensifying the pain, and then flung Jacy away from him with such force that she collided with Bram. The tavern keeper steadied her by taking a none-too-gentle hold on her upper arm.

She was half sick with relief and, conversely, with the terrible knowledge that she'd accomplished nothing by this visit except to make matters infinitely worse. It didn't take a genius to figure out that Redley would go straight home from the Dog and Goose and take his fury out on his wife and daughter.

Bram marched her to the exit and "helped" her outside with a subtle thrust. "Tell Ian I'll be wanting a word with him," he said grimly. And then he slammed the door in her face.

Nancy was waiting on the sidewalk in front of the café, and Jacy saw with a sinking heart that Chris and Thomas Jr. had taken her place at the window.

"Well?" Nancy demanded.

"I've made everything worse!" Jacy half sobbed the words. "Why did I think that monster would listen to reason? Why?"

Nancy put a firm arm around her friend. "There, now, your heart was in the right place, and I don't know what else you could have done."

Jacy knew what else she could have done, with the cruel clarity of hindsight, and so did Nancy, who had suggested the other option. She should have waited, found Ian, asked for his help, maybe even let him talk to Redley on his own.

As it was, Ian was going to hear the story from Bram, and he would be furious. She could imagine the lecture to come only too well, and she certainly wasn't looking forward to it, but she'd survive that. No, the worst thing was knowing that Gladys, innocent Gladys, was probably going to pay dearly for her teacher's bumbling attempts to help her.

"Come inside," Nancy pleaded. "I'll get you something cool to drink, and you'll feel better."

"I've got to go out there—to the Shifflet place, I mean—and get Gladys. Right now!"

"No," Nancy said quickly. "Are you daft? Redley would know where you were headed. He'd follow you out there and kill you as *well* as poor little Gladys!"

Jacy knew her friend was right. She wanted to crumple to that dusty cement sidewalk and wail in despair, but she held herself upright by sheer force of will. She had to think, to do things in order. First she needed to get Chris and Thomas Jr. home. Then she would find Ian and beg him to help Gladys.

If he refused—well, that just didn't bear thinking about. Ian wouldn't, *couldn't,* turn his back on that child.

Running on hysterical energy and not much else, Jacy gathered up the boys, got into the truck, and headed for Corroboree Springs. The McAllisters had unloaded their belongings, and Tom Sr. was understandably eager to discuss his new duties, but Jacy couldn't take the time to talk business just then. She promised to get in touch soon.

Chris gave her yet another sidelong look as they sped toward home. "You went inside the Dog and Goose again," he said. There was no disapproval in his tone, only amazement. "Dad's going to yell."

Jacy sighed. She knew she looked a sight by then—her hair was mussed, her face was puffy and probably covered with road dust in the bargain. "You're right," she said. "Your dad is definitely going to yell." And after that—please God—he'll help me save Gladys, she thought.

Jacy's feelings were mixed when they pulled to a stop behind the house just as Ian was coming out of the stables.

" 'Bye," Chris said quickly, ready to bolt and make a dash for shelter.

"Coward," Jacy teased with forlorn humor.

Ian was grinning when he came to the door of the truck and stood looking in at his wife. "Are you going to sit there all day, woman?"

The moment Jacy's eyes connected with his, however, Ian's smile evaporated. A glower began to take shape in his face, like summer storm clouds on the horizon.

"What have you done?" he demanded when she couldn't bring herself to speak.

"My sins are many," Jacy said. The joke died without a whimper.

Ian opened the truck door and pulled her out. His grasp wasn't rough, but it wasn't gentle, either. "Let's hear your confession, then," he answered without a trace of humor.

Jacy straightened. "Bram wants to see you," she began with weary resignation. "He's going to tell you how I came into the Dog and Goose this afternoon. He had to save me from Redley Shifflet—threatened to shoot his balls off, in fact—but I've got no illusions about our friendly local pub owner. He'd have killed me himself if he hadn't felt some kind of loyalty to you."

Ian looked pained. He shuffled Jacy around to the front of the house and sat her down in the grassy place shaded by a clump of tall eucalyptus trees. "What did Shifflet do to you?" he growled.

"That isn't important, Ian," she answered sorrowfully. "Not right now, at least. He's going to hurt Gladys if we— if you don't do something. Fast."

Ian swore furiously. "What happened?"

She told him the whole story, how she'd gone into the pub again because she hoped she could reason with Redley, how Redley had grabbed her by the hair, how Bram had interceded with his rifle.

Ian, who had been crouching beside her, shot to his feet. "I'll kill that son of a bitch," he rasped, his eyes shooting blue fire. He glared down at Jacy, shaking one finger. "And when I'm through with him, sheila, I'm going to start in on you!"

He wasn't threatening her physically, Jacy knew, but she'd heard Ian tell off station hands and shearers before. His lectures were loud, and they were blistering, and the prospect made her want to hide somewhere until his legendary temper had cooled down.

For all of that, Jacy couldn't afford to think of herself then. She grabbed Ian's hand with both of her own, on her knees in the fragrant grass, and held on. "Ian, please—I'll plead if that's what you want—I'll grovel, even—but first do something to help Gladys. Please!"

Ian was frighteningly still for a long time. His hand felt stiff and unyielding between Jacy's fingers. Finally he asked, in a hoarse and raspy voice, "Like what?"

Jacy began to cry. "I don't know," she wailed in soft desperation. "Oh, God, Ian, I don't know! All I can be sure of is that if that little girl gets hurt, it's going to be my fault, and I can't live with that!"

After a few moments of stiff resistance Ian crouched again and put his hands on both sides of Jacy's face. With a simultaneous motion of his thumbs he wiped the tears from her cheeks. "You look a mess," he said in all seriousness. "Go inside and wash and calm yourself a bit. I'll go over to Redley's place and see what I can do about clearing this up."

Jacy gave a strangled cry of joy. "I want to go with you."

Ian allowed himself the merest shadow of a smile. "Not a chance, sheila. You'll stay right here and behave yourself."

She remembered Redley's rifle. He was probably a good shot, since he made his living, if you could call it that, shooting dingoes and kangaroos for the bounty. "No," she whispered, clutching at Ian's sleeve. What if Gladys wasn't the only one to suffer for her rash actions? What if Ian *died* because of the things she'd said and done?

"Ian, you don't understand—he's crazy—"

Gently, Ian removed her fingers from his arm. "I'll handle this," he said. "Do you have some kind of paper from Darlis?"

When she nodded he rose, turned, and walked away.

Jacy sat there in shock for a few minutes while a series of truly horrible pictures played like movies in her mind. When she heard Ian drive away she was seized by sudden, violent nausea. How could things have gone so horribly wrong when her intentions had been so honorable?

Redley had left the Dog and Goose by the time Ian arrived. He brushed off Bram's attempts to tell him that he needed to take his wife in hand—he knew that well enough, God help him—and set out for the Shifflet place.

Redley's truck was gone, the front door was closed, and there was no sign of Darlis. No doubt she was still in town, working at the grocery. A flutter at one of the patched windows made Ian get out of his truck and approach the house.

He knocked, scanning the horizon for Shifflet's truck. Ian was bitterly disappointed by the other man's absence; he wanted to get his hands on the bastard. Nobody, but nobody, was going to treat Jacy the way Redley had without a good many scars to show for it.

There was a shuffling sound within—the child, no doubt—and Ian rapped at the door again, this time with less force. He wanted to reassure the little girl somehow, let her know he didn't mean to hurt her, but he hadn't the first idea what to say.

"Go 'way!" Gladys finally called out, her voice high-pitched and tremulous.

Ian rested his forehead against the weathered door frame and drew a deep breath. He might have been able to get through to a lad, but what was there to say to a girl? Especially one who had every reason to be terrified of men.

"I'm your teacher's husband." It was all that came to him, and he hoped none of his mates ever got wind of it, his defining himself that way. If they did, he'd never hear the finish.

The door creaked open ever so slowly, and a tiny freckled face peered around the edge. Ian's heart twisted at the fear etched in those small features, the knowledge.

He lowered himself to one knee to look up at Gladys in an effort to show that he meant her no harm.

"Did Mrs. Yarbro send you here?" she asked.

Ian nodded. Mrs. Yarbro was going to get a talking-to she'd never forget once he'd dealt with the situation at hand. In fact, if he'd been a man to strike a woman, which he wasn't, he would have relished turning Jacy over his knee and blistering her backside.

As it was, he had to be content with the fantasy.

"It's all up to you, Gladys," he said gently, aching inside at the sight of the fading bruise around her eye. "You don't have to stay here if you don't want to. I'll take you to Mrs. Yarbro right now."

Gladys's lower lip trembled, but other than that she held herself as stiffly as a soldier on the parade grounds. And that wounded Ian more than sobs would have done. "He'll just come and get me."

Ian shook his head and swallowed once before he answered. He felt like he was choking. "Not this time," he said quietly. "We'll get you away to a safe place. If you want to go."

"I'd miss my mama."

Ian looked away, watched a lizard skitter through the dirt, then made himself meet the child's gaze again. "I know," he said gravely. "You might not see her for a while. But when she can, I'm sure she'll come for you."

"He'll hurt her."

Ian didn't avert his eyes, though he wanted to, because the little girl's suffering was so hard to face and acknowledge. "You can't take care of your mama, love," he said after long moments of despairing silence. "Not even if you stay here. You know that, don't you?"

At last she began to cry, this little one who had so much right to weep, so much reason. Had she been any other child, Ian would have taken her into his arms, but his deepest instincts warned him against touching her. If he did, he might lose her fragile trust.

"I'll get my giraffe," she said.

Ian waited while Gladys Shifflet collected the one possession that mattered to her, an old, ragged toy. She didn't have a single extra dress, or a hair ribbon, or any of the things he imagined a little girl would own. It seared his heart.

By the time Gladys was settled in the passenger seat of Ian's truck, clutching the pathetic stuffed animal to her thin little chest, Ian had decided that maybe he'd let Jacy off the hook just this once.

Redley Shifflet, now—there was another matter altogether.

Passing through town, Ian kept an eye out for Redley's truck. There was no trace of it, but he supposed that was for the best, given the fact that Gladys was with him. Even if he did spot Shifflet, Ian thought grimly, he couldn't very well brake to a screeching halt, jump out, and beat the shit out of the child's father right in front of her.

Darlis was working in the grocery, as usual; Ian caught a glimpse of her through the glass at the front of the shop, and even from a distance her misery was plain to see. He'd known Darlis as long as he'd known anybody in or around Yolanda, and Redley, too, for that matter, but he'd never given any real thought to the tragedy of their lives. He'd been too busy working out his own problems, he supposed, and while he knew there was nothing wrong in that, he still felt a little remiss for not noticing.

He smiled slightly. He had Jacy to thank, as well as to blame, for the constant uproar. Everywhere she went, it seemed, she started a fire of some kind. And he guessed it was his job to put them out.

Nancy ran out of the Yolanda Café as he passed and

stopped him by climbing right up onto the running board
of his truck and sticking her head through the window. Ian
liked Nancy, had even paired up with her at the odd shear-
er's dance a time or two, but there had never been any
excitement in their relationship. They'd made a tacit
agreement to be good friends and stopped trying to strike
up a romance long before Jacy's return.

"Hello, love," Nancy said to Gladys, smiling and wag-
gling her fingers in a wave.

Gladys only nodded and gripped her giraffe a little
tighter.

Nancy turned her attention on Ian. "Two things, my
friend," she said, in her bright, lilting voice. "First, I've
gotten in touch with my aunt by telephone, and she'll be
happy to take Gladys for a foster child. We're to send her
straight to Darwin. Second"—she paused and crinkled up
her nose—"well, just don't be too hard on that wife of
yours, all right? She's a lovely thing, Jacy is, with a fine
heart—far better than you deserve, Ian Yarbro."

He frowned. "That she is—a lovely thing with a fine
heart, I mean. She's also a meddling little hellcat in dire
need of an attitude adjustment. Furthermore, Nancy-me-
girl, I'm out-and-out insulted that you think I'd hurt her."

Nancy beamed. "Knew you'd never strike her, didn't
I?" she chimed. She mocked Ian's frown by mimicking it.
"But you can be stern when you're not thinking, and like
the rest of the men around here, you're still living in the
nineteenth century." She shoved a bit of folded paper
through the window while Ian was still reeling from her
whirlwind assessment of his personal nature. "Here's the
aunt's name, address, and telephone number up in Darwin.
Oh—and I did manage to track down Collie as well. He'll
be here tomorrow night, 'round teatime."

"You've been busy," Ian said with a smile.

"You'll be nice to Jacy? I have your promise, don't I?"

Ian shifted into first gear to let Nancy know he was ready
to move on. "I'll make you two promises—one, I won't

lay a hand on her, and two, I'll give her a talking-to she'll never forget. G'day, Nance. And thanks.''

She stepped down off the running board, but a glance at the rearview mirror showed her standing in the middle of the street, watching them go, an expression of consternation on her face.

14

JACY WATCHED FROM HER POST AT ONE OF THE KITCHEN
windows as Ian drove in, bringing Gladys with him. Seeing
her husband whole and unscathed, she swayed slightly and
let out her breath in a rush. She'd been terrified every
moment of his absence, tortured by images of him lying in
the Shifflets' front yard, bleeding from a variety of gunshot
wounds.

She rushed to the door, flung it open, and hurtled into Ian's
embrace, her arms tight around his neck. He grinned down
at her in that familiar, cocky way of his that mocked her for
worrying—didn't she realize that he could handle anything?

"You're impossible," she said, but there was little conviction in the words.

At last Jacy turned her gaze on Gladys, who stood a
few feet behind Ian, clutching the ever-present giraffe and
watching the scene with a guarded expression in her eyes.
Jacy's heart clenched; for Gladys, life had been dangerous
and unpredictable, and the little girl had plainly decided
that no place was really safe.

Maybe, in some ways, she was right.

Jacy held out her hand to the child.

Gladys stood still for a long moment, fighting some inner battle, and then stepped closer and clasped Jacy's fingers with her own. It was a small and fragile victory, but it was sweet.

"Let's go around to the front veranda and talk, just you and I," Jacy said gently. "Mrs. Wigget has some sugar biscuits and cold lemonade for us." The thought crossed her mind, as she led Gladys through the side yard, that the child might be hungry and need something more nutritious. "Would you like a sandwich, sweetheart, or some soup?"

Gladys shook her head, and tension was visible in her thin shoulders as she trudged along beside Jacy. Her eyes kept darting this way and that—she probably expected Redley to spring out at her from some unlikely hiding place—and she held on to her giraffe for dear life.

Jacy blinked back tears of pure fury, considering what Redley had probably put this child through. No doubt the abuse hadn't truly begun with him, however—he'd almost surely been badly mistreated in his own childhood. Darlis had been trained to be a victim and conditioned to believe there was no way out. Probably, on some level, she thought she deserved to suffer.

Since it was relatively late in the day, the veranda was comfortably shady. Jacy gestured for Gladys to sit down in the porch swing, then leaned back against the rail, arms folded, facing the child.

"I guess you're pretty scared," she said quietly. Gladys was like a deer; any sudden noise or motion might frighten her into emotional retreat.

Gladys fidgeted, pressing the giraffe hard against her chest. She swallowed once and nodded.

Jacy crouched, slowly, and looked up into Gladys's fitful eyes. "You're safe here, sweetheart. Nobody is going to hurt you."

Gladys looked skeptical, her glance flitting over Jacy's

slender frame. "He's strong." For the first time it struck Jacy that Gladys always referred to Redley with the masculine pronoun, never as Daddy or Dad.

With a half smile, Jacy replied, "And I'm not?"

"You don't have muscles," Gladys pointed out. "And you aren't mean."

Ever so carefully, Jacy reached out to touch the child's hair. "You don't have to be mean to be strong, love. Cruelty weakens a person in the long run. But you're right about the muscles—we'll have to depend on Mr. Yarbro for those."

For a moment Gladys actually looked hopeful. "Mr. Yarbro won't let him hurt me?"

It was a promise Jacy felt safe in making; there was nothing impulsive about her reply. "Not in a million years, darling." After that she moved to sit beside the girl and held her close, though not too tightly. "Now let's talk about the adventure you're about to have. First you'll get to fly in an airplane . . ."

Gladys's eyes widened as she listened, and although Jacy couldn't be sure, she seemed to loosen her hold on the giraffe just slightly.

Jacy told her about the lending libraries in Darwin, where there were undoubtedly lots of books about princesses and castles, about the new clothes and toys Gladys would have, and the school where she would make lots of friends. Jacy meant to pay for the clothing and playthings herself, and when the time came she'd see that Darlis had a plane ticket to join her.

At tea Chris drew Gladys into conversation, and afterward they played Chinese checkers at the trestle table. Jacy was touched and a little amused to notice that Gladys kept casting surreptitious glances at Ian—checking out his muscles, no doubt.

Alice Wigget stayed until after the children were in bed, which meant she had something on her mind. In fact, she'd been building up to an announcement all evening.

"We can't just send that child soaring off into the blue with the likes of Collie Kilbride," she blurted out, her gaze moving earnestly from Ian to Jacy and then back again.

Ian's mouth quirked slightly at one corner, but he kept his expression solemn. "Collie's a good sort," he said. "Any child would be safe with him."

"It isn't that," Alice countered with a wave of one hand. At the same time she pulled off her apron. "Of course he's harmless. But he hasn't the sense to pour tea down a rabbit hole. Why, he might put that poor little thing on a flight to Tahiti or Africa, just because he wasn't paying attention!"

Jacy bit her lower lip, uneasy. "She has a point, Ian."

Ian offered no comment. He simply gazed at Alice, waiting for her to go on.

She did. "What I'm proposing is that—well, I'd like to go along. See her safe to Darwin and get a good look at this aunt of Nancy's. I'm sure she's a brick, but we'd all feel better for knowing, now, wouldn't we?"

"You're right," Jacy said. "Yes. You'll go along, and of course I'll pay your expenses."

Ian turned to his wife, still suppressing a smile, and arched one eyebrow. "And who'll do the cooking and cleaning while Mrs. Wigget's away?"

Jacy flushed; she knew exactly what he was thinking. "I have a job," she pointed out, bristling.

"And I'm a gentleman farmer?"

Alice waved both hands in a burst of frustration. "Let the place fall down around your ears until I get back—I don't care! Whatever happens, we can't let that little girl travel all that way alone."

"We'll make do," Jacy said a bit stiffly. Her tone was directed entirely at Ian, not at the gruff but undeniably bighearted Mrs. Wigget. "Right now Gladys is our most important consideration."

"Very well, then," Alice said after expelling a long breath. "I'll be on my way home. If Collie turns up sooner than expected, one of you can come for me."

Jacy nodded, and Ian walked the housekeeper out to her car. It was an unusual courtesy on his part, and Jacy felt even more uneasy. If Ian was being extra cautious, it meant he expected trouble.

As it happened, several hours passed before the trouble came. Jacy was sound asleep—she and Ian had made slow, quiet love earlier—and the room was in complete darkness.

Maybe it was the contrast that awakened her—the sweep of headlights across the dark ceiling. The blasting horn came afterward.

"Here he is," Ian said with a resigned sigh, sliding out of bed and starting to pull his clothes on. Jacy marveled at his calm; she knew their visitor was Redley, and that he was probably crazy drunk and bursting with his version of righteous indignation. "Go and sit with the little girl," he added from the doorway. "My guess is he'll be in a rage."

Jacy swung out of bed and grabbed for her robe. She was trembling violently as she pulled it on. "Ian—what if Redley has a gun?"

He shrugged. "Then he has one. Just do as I tell you—for once. Look after the kids."

Jacy nodded, but she stood in the hallway watching as Ian disappeared. For a few moments she just leaned against the wall, too terrified to move; indeed, she might have stayed there for the duration, paralyzed, if it hadn't been for the children. Chris and Gladys needed her; she had to be strong.

Redley was already pounding on the back door and bellowing incoherent oaths when Jacy reached Gladys's room, which was just beyond Chris's. The child was huddled in a corner, shaking visibly and making an animallike whimpering sound low in her throat.

Jacy overcame her own fears in that moment and rushed across the floor to gather Gladys in her arms. Chris stood in the doorway, tousle-haired, clad in his Batman pajamas.

"No worries," he said to the other child. "My dad won't let anybody hurt us." His confidence was utter, absolute, and so very innocent. Jacy prayed Chris wasn't going to lose his father to a gunshot or knife wound in the next few minutes.

Gladys gave a wailing cry and tried to burrow into Jacy, half wild with terror.

"Shhh," Jacy whispered, holding her tightly and stroking her hair. "Shhh, baby, you'll be all right—I promise."

There was more yelling, some of it Ian's, and Jacy steeled herself to keep her promise or die in the attempt. Her eyes scanned the spare room for anything that could serve as a weapon; if Redley got past Ian, she would have to protect the children.

When the sounds of a brawl came rolling through the house Chris bolted into the hallway, evidently planning to go to his dad's aid.

Jacy spoke sternly to him for the first time ever. "Christopher Yarbro, you get back here right now!"

He hesitated, then returned, obviously torn.

Jacy made an attempt to salve his masculine pride. "We need you here with us," she said, looking at him over Gladys's head.

"I just want to know what's happening out there," Chris whispered, pale now. Evidently he'd already worked out some of the possibilities for himself.

"So do I," Jacy answered as Gladys settled into soft, plaintive sobs against her chest. "Believe me, so do I. But your dad said we were to stay here no matter what, and I think this would be a really bad time to cross him."

Chris considered that, then gave a reluctant nod. Things were quieter in the house; there was no shouting now, and no sounds of things crashing to the floor or the ground, but they could still hear the asthmatic chortle of the motor in Redley's truck. It was idling.

Jacy swallowed once and tried to sound calm. "Is there a gun handy, Chris?"

Chris ran his tongue over his lips once, still looking as though he wanted to bolt out of the door and down the hall to his father's side. "There's a hunting rifle in Dad's room. But he told me he'd tan my hide if I ever touched it."

Jacy listened to the relative silence. She was drenched with sweat, and she couldn't tell where Gladys's trembling stopped and her own began. She'd never, at any time in her life, been more frightened.

God in heaven, what was happening out there?

"Is it loaded?" she asked after rocking Gladys in thoughtful silence for a little while.

Chris shook his head. "No. But there's a box of shells next to it."

Jacy took a deep breath, closed her eyes for a moment, then exhaled softly. "Get the rifle and the bullets and bring them to me. Quickly."

"But Dad said—"

"I'll take the responsibility for this, Chris. Just do as I say. Please."

He studied her face for a moment, looked at Gladys, who huddled, terrified, in Jacy's embrace, and then ran off. Jacy heard his bare feet pounding against the bare floor of the hall.

Before Chris returned, Ian appeared in the doorway. He was sweating and covered with dirt. His lip was bleeding, and one of his eyes was starting to swell shut, but he grinned as he leaned against the jamb.

"You should see the other guy," he said.

Jacy's relief was like a storm inside her. She wanted to shout with it, to run to Ian and take him into her arms and never let him go, but she had Gladys to think about.

"Is he gone?" she asked her husband.

Just then Chris returned, carrying the rifle. He stopped and looked up at his dad with an expression of defiant guilt on his face, and Jacy thought the boy had never resembled his father so much.

They heard the truck roar away into the night as Ian gently took the gun and the box of bullets from his son's hands.

"He's gone," Ian confirmed for them all.

Only then did Gladys lift her head from Jacy's bosom. She turned her gaze on Ian, and Jacy felt her stiffen.

"He hurt you?"

Ian smiled at the girl. "No, love. He just dented me a bit." With that he turned and left the room.

Chris hurried after him, his voice trailing back to Jacy's ears, which were still pounding with the force of her heartbeat.

"It wasn't my idea to fetch the rifle. Mum said to do it."

Jacy smiled to herself. Ian was alive.

It took thirty minutes and a cup of warm milk to bring Gladys around, and Jacy lay with her on the spare room bed for more than two hours before the child finally went to sleep. Even then the little girl was fitful, tossing and turning, murmuring and crying out.

Jacy left her only temporarily, making sure the light was on and the door was open. Chris was in his own room, slumbering soundly in the firm belief that his dad could and would protect him from anything. Ian was in their bed, propped up against the pillows, his right eye disappearing into a fold of blue-green flesh.

Jacy practically fell on him. "What happened?" she demanded.

"Thought you'd never ask," he teased.

"Ian!"

He shrugged. "Redley and I got into it. The fight started in the kitchen doorway and progressed to the backyard and the vegetable patch. And I think it's safe to say that I won."

Jacy felt a niggling twist of alarm, along with a sort of hysterical gratitude that the fates had spared the man she loved. "For tonight," she said. "I don't trust Redley."

Ian touched her nose and grinned a comical, twisted grin, made misshapen by the slant of his bruised eye. "Smart girl," he replied. He drew her close and kissed her, but it

212

was the end of the evening, not the beginning, and they were both aware of the fact.

"I've got to sleep with Gladys," Jacy said when she caught her breath. "She'll be terrified—"

He stopped the flow of words by touching her lips with his index finger. "It's all right, love—you needn't explain. I'll see you in the morning."

Jacy kissed him again, tenderly, grimaced at his sore eye, and left their bedroom.

When she awakened in the wee small hours she found Collie in the kitchen, along with Ian and Mrs. Wigget, consuming a man-sized breakfast. He looked up when Jacy entered the room and gave her a roguish wink.

"Mornin', Mrs. Yarbro," he said.

Jacy felt grumpy and tense. Life was never simple—at least not for her. As soon as Gladys and Mrs. Wigget were safely away there would be another tussle between her and Ian. Despite the danger from Redley, there would be school that day, and Ian was certain to go through the roof when he found out.

Presently the children came out of their rooms. Gladys was quietly petrified, and Chris was bursting with confidence. When he saw his father's shiner, however, he stopped short and whistled in admiration.

Ian smiled and ruffled his hair. "It looks worse than it is, mate," he said gently.

Chris seemed reassured, though Jacy hadn't forgotten how upset he'd been after the dust storm, when he'd feared something had happened to his dad. She made a point of squeezing the boy's small shoulder once after he'd taken his place at the table next to Collie.

Soon it was time to say good-bye to Gladys and, at least temporarily, to Alice Wigget. Jacy gave Alice her credit card, along with the personal identification number that would give her access to various cash machines, plus several endorsed traveler's checks—the last of the money she'd brought to Australia. There were tears in Jacy's eyes when she embraced Gladys in farewell, and she stood on the veranda watching as they all got into Collie's borrowed car and drove away.

Chris went out to the stables to feed his horse, and as quickly as that, Jacy was alone with Ian.

He looked at her neat cotton dress and light makeup with grave comprehension. "You actually think you're going to town today and teach?"

Jacy nodded.

"Well, you're wrong," Ian countered. He came and stood close, glaring down at her.

"Ian—"

"No," he said, coldly, laying his hands on both sides of her face and gazing straight into her eyes, straight into her soul. "Listen to me. As soon as Redley sobers up he'll go directly to the schoolhouse, looking for you. And he'll be out for blood."

Jacy took a deep breath and then released it slowly. "It's an impossible situation," she admitted. Then she raised her eyes to his imploringly. "Don't you see, Ian? I can't hide out from Redley Shifflet for the rest of my life, any more than you can."

He dropped his hands to his sides, but she could see that he had made up his mind. There would be no moving him— not this time. "I've given a lot of ground where you're concerned," he said in a low yet thunderous voice. "But today I forbid you to leave my sight. Do you understand that?"

Jacy's face felt hot. Even if she'd wanted to comply with his wishes—and a part of her did, because just then it would have been so much easier to give in—she couldn't afford the luxury. "Fine," she hissed. "We'll both hide in the house like a pair of scared rabbits!"

He swore in a swift, furious rush of words, then took control of his temper with a visible effort.

"I have a property to run," he reminded her at last. "You can sit in the truck while I work—"

"The hell I will, Ian Yarbro—I have classes to teach!"

"Damn it all to hell, I'll tie you to the steering wheel if I have to!"

"You wouldn't dare!"

Just then there was a soft, tentative rap at the glass in the kitchen door. Jacy shifted her gaze, saw Tom McAllister standing there, and wondered if there was some kind of cosmic plot against her. In all the excitement she hadn't had a chance to mention hiring the McAllisters and installing them in the house at Corroboree Springs.

Ian was going to be outraged that she hadn't consulted him.

He gave her a scorching, suspicious look and went to the door, wrenching it open and barking, "Yes?"

McAllister smiled in that winning way of his, but Ian's back was to Jacy, and she couldn't tell if Tom Sr.'s charm was working or not. "You must be Mr. Yarbro," he said, jutting out a hand. "I'm Tom McAllister, and I'm pleased to be working for you."

Ian turned just far enough to look at Jacy over one shoulder, and his expression was downright acidic. Just you wait, his look said plainly, but when he spoke to Tom his tone was polite, even friendly.

"Call me Ian," he said, shaking Tom's hand.

"I thought I'd start by fixing up the hay shed over at the other place, if that's all right with you. I could drive to Willoughby in my truck and pick up the supplies that's wanted."

"Good idea," Ian replied, sending another sour glare back over his shoulder. "Come inside, and I'll make out a check."

McAllister stepped over the threshold, but just barely. He looked eager to make good, and Jacy's heart went out to him. Times were hard in Australia; fine men and women were finding themselves out of work.

"How is Ellie getting along?" Jacy asked, but her voice and her smile were both a little thin. She'd had a hell of a night, after all, and now she and Ian had locked horns again. Which meant it might be a hell of a *day* in the bargain.

Tom Sr. beamed. "She's that pleased," he said. "And Thomas Jr.'s outside talking to your boy."

No doubt Thomas Jr. was all spruced up for school, too. He was terminally happy, like his parents, and Jacy adored him. She didn't say anything, because Ian returned from the living room just then with a check in his hand.

Tom Sr. thanked Ian and left.

Jacy squeezed her eyes shut and braced herself, but Chris and Thomas Sr. saved her from the blowup by bursting into the house. Chris was in the middle of a dramatic account of the exciting events of the night before.

Ian looked fit to be tied.

Jacy smiled broadly, then stood on tiptoe to kiss him lightly on the mouth. "Have a wonderful day," she said cheerfully, then turned to walk away.

Ian grabbed her by the elbow and subtly wrenched her back to his side. His gaze was on Chris. "Go outside like a good lad and make sure I closed the yard gate last night," he said.

Chris knew he was being gotten rid of, and he didn't quibble. He just fled the scene, with Thomas Jr. right behind him.

"Who the hell are those people?" he rasped.

Jacy sighed. She'd hired Tom McAllister because Ian needed the help now that there was twice as much land as before, and she was getting tired of being grilled. "Their name is McAllister," she said. "They brought Thomas Jr. to school yesterday, and Tom Sr. asked if I knew where he could find work. I figured you could use his help."

Ian was ominously still; he looked as though he might be silently counting to ten. "And who's going to pay his wages?" he asked after a long time. He knew the answer, of course, even before she responded.

"I am. Corroboree Springs is mine, and I don't intend

216

to let my property go to waste. If you're not going to use it, then I will."

Ian turned away rather abruptly and poured himself a cup of coffee Jacy knew he didn't want. "McAllister seems like a good man," he allowed, though only at length, and in a grudging tone.

"I liked him immediately," Jacy said. She was glad Ian wasn't looking at her just then, because she couldn't seem to help grinning.

He set his coffee down on the counter rather forcefully, and some of it slopped over, but he kept his back to her. It was plain that Ian was struggling with emotions of his own, though she doubted that amusement was among them.

"I suppose the minute I turn my back you're going to head straight for the schoolhouse, even if you have to hitchhike?"

"That's right," Jacy agreed moderately. She'd won another round, but there was no sense in pushing her luck. "I'm not staying here unless you do, too."

Ian rubbed the back of his neck with one hand, and even through the fabric of his shirt she could see that his shoulder muscles were tense—those delightful muscles that she and Gladys had put such confidence in. "Hell," he breathed. Then he slowly turned to face Jacy, and she saw a mixture of fury and admiration in his poor bruised face.

She tilted her head to one side and didn't even try to resist the smile tugging at the corners of her mouth. "Are you sure you won the fight, Ian?"

He made a growling sound, but in the next moment he was grinning. He crossed the room, gripped Jacy by the waist, lifted her onto her toes, and kissed her soundly. So soundly that she thought her bones would dissolve.

When that was done, and she was dazed and wondering if she had the strength to defy him by leaving the homestead after all, he held her away from him and warned hoarsely, "Don't be thinking I'm through with you, sheila. I'm not."

217

Jacy figured her eyes were glazed and her smile was probably a bit lopsided, if not downright daffy. "Right," she answered cheerfully. "I'm in big trouble."

"The biggest," Ian replied readily, and he didn't look or sound like he was kidding.

Jacy felt a tremor of nervousness, a sort of dizzy anticipation, like the sensation that always preceded their lovemaking.

Kinky, she thought with a sort of drunken amusement.

Ian's frown deepened. He really *was* serious. "Don't forget where you are, love," he warned. "This is Australia, and I am still the head of this family. I've let you get by with a lot because of Jake passing on and like that, but I won't take much more."

"What's that supposed to mean?" Jacy hissed, instantly sober. She heard Chris and Thomas Jr. on the veranda, knew they would enter at any second, thus terminating the conversation.

Ian's voice was at once evenly modulated and ominous. "You're a smart lady," he said, strolling across the room and taking his hat from the peg. "Work it out for yourself." With that, he left the house. Jacy watched him through the window above the sink, and he didn't look back once.

She got her purse and her lesson planning book, ushered Chris and Thomas Jr. into the truck, and headed for Yolanda, her emotions in an uproar. On the one hand, she loved Ian desperately, and she was so thankful that he was safe that she wanted to do everything he asked her to do. On the other, she thought he was the most arrogant man she'd ever encountered, and she longed to push him to the very brink, just for the sake of pushing.

When they arrived in Yolanda the schoolhouse was empty. Redley didn't show up that day, but neither did any of Jacy's students, besides Chris and Thomas Jr., of course. She was determined to keep things as normal as possible and didn't dismiss her two students until three o'clock on the dot.

After that, Jacy sent the boys to the post office to check for mail and walked over to the grocery shop, hoping to see Darlis and tell her that Gladys was safe with Collie and Mrs. Wigget.

Darlis wasn't around, as it happened, but Bram was. He frowned when Jacy walked in.

"Why didn't Jasmine come to school today?" she demanded, on the old theory that the best defense was a good offense.

"She don't need any of your wild Yankee ideas," Bram answered bluntly. "And you can tell Ian he can't put me off forever. We're going to have that talk."

Jacy was stung, and she raised her chin a notch. "Watch out, Bram. Ian just might tell you to stick your advice where the sun doesn't shine."

Bram made a disgusted gruntlike sound and resumed his sweeping. "Never thought I'd see the day," he muttered.

It was better, Jacy decided, not to pursue the subject. "Where's Darlis?" she asked.

"Back room," Bram replied at his leisure, giving Jacy a sidelong look. She felt a sick chill, a premonition. "My wife's looking after her." He paused, going for effect. "Redley took off most of her hide last night."

219

15

REDLEY HAD BEATEN DARLIS THE NIGHT BEFORE.

Jacy wasn't surprised, really, but she was horrified, and the reality was devastating. "I want to see her," she said, and without waiting for permission from Bram she headed for the back of the shop. Beyond a doorway covered by a green plastic curtain was a living room with a linoleum floor and fifties-style furniture.

Darlis lay on the overstuffed sofa, covered with a ratty crocheted afghan. Her face was so bruised and swollen that it took all Jacy's willpower not to avert her eyes.

She did raise one hand to her mouth, and for a moment she thought she would faint.

"Tell me about Gladys," Darlis said, and there was both desolation and pride in her manner. "Did she get away safe?"

Jacy's eyes filled with tears, she was so stricken by the enormity of Darlis's predicament, and she nodded her head once. "Gladys is perfectly all right," she managed to say. "You can join her as soon as you're ready."

The ghost of a smile touched Darlis's battered mouth and then disappeared as quickly as it had appeared. "That's fine, then," she said, plucking once at her cotton skirt.

Jacy took a hesitant step toward the other woman. Bram's wife, Sara, whom Jacy had met at church and at Jake's funeral, stood near Darlis like a reluctant sentinel. Sara was obviously a good-natured person, and it was plain that she disliked confrontations. It was just as clear that she was fiercely protective of Darlis.

Jacy rubbed her cheek with the back of one hand. "I'm so sorry you were hurt, Darlis. I would have given anything to prevent that."

Darlis looked away toward the filmy curtains at the window above the old-fashioned cabinet radio, and Jacy couldn't guess what she was thinking. Even when she spoke again the defeated woman did not meet Jacy's gaze.

"Redley's gone off doggin' with his mates," she said in a strange, detached voice. "Sometimes it's weeks before he comes home. But you mind your back all the same, Mrs. Yarbro, and you tell Ian to look out for himself, too. My Redley carries a grudge longer than most, and he'll want his revenge on the two of you if it takes the rest of his life."

The cool, quiet words sent a chill tripping down Jacy's spine. This was the bush, a place apart, with laws and customs all its own. There was no one to turn to for protection, for the nearest police were fifty kilometers away, in Willoughby.

"We'll be careful," Jacy said awkwardly. "What about you, Darlis? Are you going to stay here and wait for him to come back?"

At last Darlis looked her way again, and the hopelessness and despair Jacy saw in the other woman's eyes nearly brought her to her knees. "Where would I go?"

For one frenzied moment Jacy wanted to shake Darlis in frustration. "You can go to Gladys. Make a new start, just the two of you."

221

Darlis made a contemptuous sound, meant to pass as a laugh, though there was no trace of mirth in it. "It ain't easy for women such as me," she said. "I'm not smart like you are, or beautiful, or rich."

Jacy opened her mouth to protest, then closed it again without making a sound. Anything she knew to say would have sounded glib just then.

"You helped my girl," Darlis sighed. "I'm thankful to you for it. Beyond that, I don't know what there is to say."

Jacy ached. She'd always be something of an outsider, she knew, because she hadn't lived all her life in or near Yolanda, like the others. Still, she *had* hoped to be accepted, if not actually welcomed.

She nodded and turned to leave the room.

Sara McCulley caught up to her in the store proper. Bram was gone, and there were no customers.

"Don't take this too hard now," the stocky, florid woman whispered, taking Jacy's hand and patting it. "You're a brave woman, walking straight into the Dog and Goose—merciful heaven, I've never been in there myself, and my own husband owns the place—and standing up to the men of this town, too—*especially* that no-gooder Redley Shifflet. Don't think the rest of us haven't noticed."

Jacy searched Sara's plain, friendly face. "None of the children came to school today besides Chris and the McAllister boy, Thomas Jr. I assumed—"

"That the people of the town were taking a stand against you?" Sara finished for her. "Well, the men might be thinking some such thing. They've been the ones to balk all along, in case you hadn't guessed it. But we women have a different view—we want our little ones to get an education for themselves and have good lives. Most of us are on your side."

Hope touched Jacy's heart like a soft, fickle breeze, lingering a moment and then passing. She shoved a hand through her hair, which was already messy from a hundred preceding gestures just like that one. Then she sighed. "It may be a hopeless battle, Sara," she said. "The men can make things pretty hard for us. Look at poor Darlis in there—she should be in a hospital. I'm not sure I can live with any more of that."

Sara misunderstood. "Why, miss, Ian Yarbro would never lay a hand on you—he doesn't even spank the boy, as far as I know."

Jacy knew Sara was right; whatever form Ian's anger took—and he was angry—there would be no violence. "I'm not afraid of my husband," she said wearily. "It's the others—"

Sara shook her head. "They're stern, our men, and they like getting their own way, to be sure. They'd make all the rules if we let them, but most of them wouldn't strike a woman or a child."

Jacy nodded distractedly. She hoped the female population of Yolanda wasn't expecting her to lead a rebellion, because she wasn't up to it. Not just then, anyway. "I'm glad you're looking after Darlis," she said, and then she left.

By time she'd given Nancy a full report, collected Chris and Thomas Jr., and driven the dry and dusty distance between town and the property, she had a pounding headache and a sick stomach. Chris stayed at Corroboree Creek to play with his new friend, and the house was blessedly quiet when Jacy reached it.

She took two aspirin, retreated to the master bedroom, kicked off her shoes, and collapsed onto the mattress with a groan. The room was hot, so after a while Jacy got up and pulled off all her clothes except for her bra and panties.

She lay there and suffered for a few minutes, then dropped into a restless, slightly fevered sleep, and her dreams were a jumble of disjointed horrors. The one she remembered clearly on awakening was the worst—in that subconscious tableau, Ian was making sweet love to her, and they were reveling in each other. At the last moment

Ian turned into Shifflet, and their beautiful communion turned to something ugly and cruel.

The experience seemed frightfully real, and Jacy was ill and shaken as she got up from the bed and put on shorts and a top. The sense of terrified disgust was still with her while she splashed her face with cold water in the bathroom, and it pursued her when she went into the kitchen to start tea.

When Ian arrived Chris was with him, and the boy was chattering at top speed about all the plans he and Thomas Jr. had for the next school holiday. Ian, covered in dirt as usual, his blue cambric work shirt sweat-stained and grubby, listened with half an ear. His gaze followed Jacy as she moved between the gas-powered refrigerator, the stove, and the table.

Jacy's heart twisted, for Ian's blackened eye looked worse rather than better. After he'd washed and eaten she meant to examine his injury more closely. He probably needed to see a doctor, but she knew without asking that he would scoff at the idea. That roused her irritation.

She set a big bowl of mashed potatoes down on the table with a *thunk*, shoved a hand through her hair, which needed cutting, and shifted her gaze to Chris. It was something of a struggle, but she managed a smile.

"Go and get cleaned up, honey," she told the boy. "Dinner is ready."

Chris beamed, happy beneath his layer of dirt, and bounded down the hall to obey. Ian lingered, as Jacy had expected.

"You look like hell," he said in his forthright way.

"Thanks," she replied. "You've seen better days yourself." Within the moment she was busy again, taking the meat loaf from the oven, pouring the green beans she'd heated into a serving dish, tracking down the silverware.

Ian hesitated briefly, as if he wanted to say something, then followed Chris out of the room. By the time he came back some fifteen minutes later, taking his accustomed place at the table, the mashed potatoes were cold and the meat loaf was starting to congeal.

Jacy had waited for Ian, but Chris was nearly finished with his dinner. It was a good thing he lingered, rattling on about the plans he and Thomas Jr. had made to mine for opals and get rich. If he hadn't been there chattering away, the silence would have been deadly.

Chris finished describing the grand scheme, took a breath and a second piece of the shop-bought cake Jacy had found in the fridge, and shifted conversational gears.

"Nobody came to school today except for me and Thomas Jr.," he said. "Everybody else was scared Mr. Shifflet would be there."

Jacy's gaze collided with Ian's at the mention of Redley; her expression was defensive, and his plainly said I-told-you-so. He glowered at her for a few seconds, and she could not look away until, by some conscious decision, he released her.

She dumped her half-eaten dinner into the slop bucket, her appetite completely gone, and was standing at the sink rinsing her plate when she heard Ian tell Chris to leave the room for a little while.

Jacy kept her back to Ian, and he didn't make a sound as he crossed the floor, but still she felt him there when he finally stood behind her. She had absorbed some essence of Ian into every cell of her body, and now, by a magic as old as the aborigines' Dream Time, it often seemed that they were one person.

"Turn about and look at me, love," he said. It was a gentle command, but a command all the same.

Jacy turned and immediately winced. Ian's eye was badly swollen, bruised to glorious shades of purple and green, and perhaps because of the link between them she felt his pain.

"Oh, Ian," she whispered, gently touching his face. "I'm sorry I involved you—I'm so sorry."

He caught her wrist in his hand and held it, but his grasp

was gentle. With his thumb he caressed the heel of her palm. "Don't be regretting that," he said. "I'm your husband, sheila. Your troubles are mine as well, remember."

She nodded, but she was frazzled and very near tears, and when Ian pressed his hand against his hard chest she felt his heart beating strong and sure beneath. Her voice sounded choked and hoarse when she spoke.

"Ian, Redley beat Darlis. He practically killed her."

Ian said nothing and offered no judgment. He simply waited for Jacy to go on.

"I was so scared all day—I jumped at every sound, I was so sure Redley was going to show up at the school. At the same time I was certain he would go after you with that damn rifle of his."

Ian nodded, lifted her hand to his mouth, and lightly kissed her palm. The gesture was comforting rather than sensual. "I didn't have the easiest day myself," he confessed. "I wanted to let the property go hang and stand guard over you the whole time." He paused and sighed heavily. "I hate having you at that school, out in the open the way it is, but I've come to see that you wouldn't be any safer here, really."

Jacy waited. She knew what was coming and was ready to fight; for all her fear and trepidation, she had a new sense of her own strength and competence. She was facing what might be a life-and-death problem, and for the first time in her adult life, she wasn't running for cover.

Ian went on reluctantly. "I think you should go away for a while, Jacy. Back to the States, or at least to Sydney or Adelaide."

Jacy closed her eyes for a moment. Somehow, her anticipating his words hadn't taken the sting out of them. Whatever the reason, the fact was that he wanted her to leave, and that hurt. For all their philosophical differences, Jacy hated the thought of being apart from Ian.

"My mother and stepfather can arrange to have my house in Connecticut closed up and sold," she said softly at long last. There might have been a note of pleading in her voice, but she couldn't help that. "I would like to go to Adelaide at some point—to have my trust fund transferred, buy that satellite dish I promised Chris, get some things we need at the schoolhouse—but I was hoping we could make the trip together. During school holidays, maybe."

Ian's emotions, often so plainly visible in his handsome face, were unreadable now. "Jacy—"

She laid her hands on his shoulders. "It's useless to argue, Ian. I'm staying." She smiled tentatively, trying to lighten the mood a little. "Unless of course you throw me out bodily. In that case I'll just room with Nancy."

His grin appeared then, bright as the morning sun, and a little more crooked than usual because of the swelling. "You know, if I don't figure out how to handle you, and fast, I won't be able to show my face at the Dog and Goose."

Jacy stood on tiptoe and kissed him lightly on the mouth. "When it comes to handling, Ian Yarbro, you've got a way about you," she teased in a low voice. "As for your reputation at that hellhole of a bar, well, as they say in America, tough shit."

He laughed, hooked his index fingers in the belt loops on her shorts, and pulled her onto the balls of her feet and flush against his torso. He was kissing her in earnest when they heard Chris's bright voice.

"May I come back now?"

They broke apart, Jacy flushed and a little bedazzled, Ian amused and probably somewhat frustrated.

The next day, when Jacy went to the schoolhouse, bringing Chris and Thomas Jr. with her, all the lost students were waiting in the yard with their resolute mothers. The women's show of support lifted Jacy's spirits considerably, and as she was leaving Sara McCulley told her that there would be a meeting of the townswomen in the old institute—the Australian term for the movie house—the following night at seven-thirty.

Jacy nodded and lingered a moment at the gate while her students greeted each other with lilting chatter. "How is Darlis?"

Sara shook her head. "She insists on working—needs the money, you know. And she's gone back to that place of theirs, even though both Nancy and I offered to put her up for a while." She shuddered, and the expression on her ruddy, moon-shaped face betrayed her fears even before she went on. "Redley's off doggin', him and those other no-gooders he runs with, and there's no telling how long he'll be away. It scares me to death just thinking of what he might do to her when he gets back, though."

"Me, too," Jacy agreed sadly. "I wish we could have avoided this whole thing, but Gladys—"

"I know," Sara interrupted, patting Jacy's hand. "There was Gladys, living with that monster. It wasn't to be borne." She frowned, gazing thoughtfully off into the distance for a few moments. "Have a care, Mrs. Yarbro. Have a care."

The ominous warning notwithstanding, the rest of the day went well. There was no sign of Redley, and the children, once they'd settled in again, were attentive and even studious. After school Jacy picked up the mail and a few groceries and headed back to the property with Chris and Thomas Jr.

As it happened, Tom Sr. was there. He and Ian were on the roof of one of the sheds, evidently conferring about the state of the shingles. It was reassuring to know that Ian had accepted Tom Sr.'s presence at Corroboree Springs and was giving him work to do.

The boys ran into the house looking for milk and biscuits, and Jacy lingered in the dazzling late-day sunshine, shading her eyes with one hand and watching as the men descended the ladder and came toward her.

"How're things going over at the other place?" Jacy asked, meeting Tom Sr.'s smile with one of her own.

Tom Sr. beamed. "I've been hard at it all the day, mum," he told her. "Soon you'll be able to put up some horses over there if you want."

Jacy had ridden a lot when she was younger, during her visits to Jake, and she had been thinking about taking it up again. "Maybe I'll do that," she said, catching Ian's eye as he came to stand beside Tom Sr. "I could raise race-horses and give my husband a run for his money."

Ian's face was shadowed by the brim of his hat, and Jacy couldn't guess what he thought of the idea. It had appeared in her mind unexpectedly, and she wasn't entirely sure how she felt about it herself.

"When's tea?" he said.

Jacy loved the man to distraction, and she'd already committed herself to him heart and soul, but his question annoyed her. "Soon," she replied with acid sweetness. She couldn't resist adding, "I'll certainly be glad when Alice Wigget gets back."

"So will I," Ian retorted. He turned to Tom Sr., who had surely sensed the charge in the air but was doing his darnedest not to let on. "Stay for tucker, Tom?" Ian asked.

Tom Sr. shook his head. "Thanks, I'd like that, but Mrs. McAllister's been cooking up one of her special recipes today. She'll be a twin to herself if the boy and I aren't there to eat it."

Ian might have smiled—Jacy couldn't tell because of that infernal hat—but he did extend his hand to Tom Sr., and they shook. They were just two bewildered males, their manners seemed to say, doing their best to cope with the strange customs of womankind.

"G'day, then," Ian said.

Tom Sr. nodded, collected a biscuit-munching Thomas Jr. from the house, and set off for Corroboree Springs in his old truck.

Ian and Jacy lingered in the dooryard, that odd, intangible electricity arcing between them. They'd been in accord, since yesterday at least, and especially in bed, but now there was a certain well-mannered hostility in the air.

"So you've decided they'll do?" Jacy asked, to make conversation. "The McAllisters, I mean?"

Ian tugged at the brim of his hat, a sure sign that something was brewing behind that shadowed face. "They're good people," he allowed. "What's this about your raising horses?"

So that *was* it. Inwardly Jacy sagged with relief. "It was just a thought, Ian. I mean, if I've got a perfectly good stable over there—"

"If you want a horse, I'll give you one," he broke in. His tone was short, and from that point on, so was Jacy's patience.

"Oh, for God's sake, Ian," she whispered, starting toward the house, "will you stop acting like I was going to cut off your balls? I was just talking, that's all—I never intended to become your competition!"

He caught her arm and pulled her back, and silent thunder rolled through the hot stillness of the afternoon. Her nose was a quarter of an inch from his, and she could see his face plainly, despite the hat. His normal eye was shooting blue fire.

"I'm getting tired of hearing you talk like that," he informed her in an ominously quiet voice. "And you couldn't *hope* to compete with me when it comes to raising horses."

Jacy tried to pull free, but he held on. "Damn it, Ian, what is it with you?" she demanded in a soft hiss. Lately there had been entirely too much drama in the Yarbro home, and it wasn't good for Chris or any of the rest of them. "Are you stressed out by this Redley Shifflet thing, or are you actually chauvinistic enough to be threatened by any hint that I might presume to compete with you?"

"I wanted a wife when I married you," he argued back. "Not a station hand. Good God, if you get your way, I'll be the laughingstock of South Australia!"

Understanding dawned. Ian had been to the Dog and Goose for the momentous chat with Bram McCulley, and his male ego had been seriously bruised in the process.

Jacy softened her tone. "What did Bram say?" she asked.

Ian murmured a swear word, resettled his hat, and hustled her toward the shade trees in the front yard. "Let's get out of the sun, at least," he grumbled.

Jacy hid a smile. Poor Ian. His image as an incorrigible man of the outback had been tarnished. He would have to be handled very carefully.

When they reached the lawn Jacy sat down in the sweet grass, cross-legged, but Ian remained standing. He'd taken off his hat—that was something—but his manner was volatile, and some of Jacy's breezy confidence deserted her.

"What did McCulley say to you, Ian?" she persisted, even more gently than before.

He spat another barely audible curse, then met her eyes. "We've got our ways out here. A man looks after his own in the bush, and his woman doesn't go barging into pubs and stirring up trouble."

Jacy shrugged. "I admit to pub-barging, and you know I'm not going to apologize, so let's not waste time on it. And if by 'stirring up trouble' you mean my getting Gladys Shifflet out of that house, you're not being fair. You knew what I was planning. You even helped me."

At last Ian stopped his pacing and fretting and crouched in front of her. He tossed the hat aside into the grass without ever looking away from her face. "It's not that," he said with an obvious effort at diplomacy. "It's this meeting the women are planning."

Word gets around, Jacy thought. She sighed. "Sara McCulley told me about that," she said. "It wasn't my idea, Ian."

"Maybe not directly," Ian conceded furiously, "but if there's a rebellion afoot, you planted the seeds of it."

Jacy groaned and fell back against the trunk of the tree

behind her. "Or so the men of Yolanda have decided," she said.

"That's right," Ian replied. "And they're ready to strip my hide for letting you run wild the way you do. These are my mates, Jacy—people I've known all my life. It matters to me what they think."

She wanted to help him, she truly did, but she didn't know how. "What is it you want me to do?" she asked, laying her hands gently to either side of his face.

Enough of Ian's fury had faded for him to turn his head slightly and place a light kiss on her palm. Then he grinned, and half her heart melted then and there. "Nothing you'd be willing to go along with, sheila," he said, his good eye twinkling.

Jacy ached, despite the turnaround in Ian's mood, because she knew the issue was a serious one. He was an intelligent man, but his ideas were old-fashioned ones, and they were ingrained. He could not be expected to change in any fundamental way; the life he led called for strength and, yes, stubbornness. For her part, Jacy was just discovering her own power to make a difference, and there could be no going back.

What if we don't make it? she wondered to herself, and the question filled her with such despair that tears sprang to her eyes. "Do you ever wish I hadn't come here?" she asked aloud.

Ian allowed her to cry, and she loved him for that, among other things. "No, sheila," he replied without hesitation. "I wouldn't change that. I often wish you were different, though—more like Australian women in some ways."

His honesty left Jacy a little stricken, as usual.

"What ways, Ian?"

He sighed. "I'd like to be the head of my family again," he said.

"Fair enough. You're the head of the family." She took his hand. "Ian, I'm not trying to take over your position or make you subservient to me in any way. I simply want to be your partner. I want to share your problems and responsibilities as well as your authority. Is that really so difficult to understand?''

"No," Ian answered readily. And somewhat sadly. "It sounds grand in theory, sheila. But it's damnably hard to bring off in the real world."

She nodded. It might, in fact, be impossible. In those moments Jacy understood as never before the problems her mother and father had experienced in trying to blend two cultures and two very different mind-sets.

I'll die if I lose Ian, Jacy thought despairingly. But she knew the same fate awaited her if she lost herself.

Once again Ian and Jacy had reached an impasse, or so it seemed.

They went inside. Ian took a shower and put on clean clothes, and Jacy made tea. During the meal they talked around their differences, and when it was time for bed they both pretended their other problems didn't exist. The bedroom was enchanted, the one place where their relationship was perfect.

Ian was already up and gone when Jacy awakened the next morning. She'd slept well, perhaps because Ian had loved her so thoroughly during the night, and she felt rested and strong. Even optimistic.

After breakfast Jacy and Chris picked up Thomas Jr. at Corroboree Springs and headed for town.

Redley Shifflet stayed away that day, too, and Jacy began to think she'd been paranoid to fear him in the first place. He was obviously a coward, and it followed, after the beating he'd taken from Ian, that Shifflet would be afraid to make any more trouble.

She breathed easier after coming to that conclusion, taught the day's classes—the schoolroom was crowded with kids—and went home at the regular time. Ian wasn't around, but that didn't worry her. Their combined properties were far-ranging, and he could be anywhere.

Jacy made sandwiches for dinner, since it was so hot,

and she and Chris ate on the front veranda. She put Ian's food on a plate in the refrigerator, wrote a note explaining that she'd gone to Sara's meeting, then set out for Yolanda again, bringing the boy along. Undoubtedly, she wouldn't be the only one who'd brought a child; the kids could play outside while their mothers talked.

Surprisingly, there was quite a crowd at the institute that night. Word of the meeting had spread by bush telegraph, apparently, because there were women from faraway farms and properties. They sat in their plain dresses, sun-weathered and hardworking women, their jaws set with determination.

There was definitely a rebellion in the making, and Jacy was both afraid and honored when she realized she'd been appointed to lead the revolt.

They weren't asking for a great deal, these sturdy, practical females. They didn't seek careers, or even money of their own, in most cases. They wanted educations for their children, girls as well as boys, and they were willing to fight for them.

Once again Jacy was torn between her love for Ian and her principles. She bit her lip and, hoping he would understand, took her place in history.

16

THE BUSH GRASS WAS SO DRY IT CRACKLED, AND THE AIR
felt hot, oppressive, weighted. One spark, one match tossed
carelessly to the ground, Ian thought uneasily, and the
whole landscape would go up in a roaring blaze.

He couldn't help drawing a parallel between the weather
and the situation with Jacy—one was as volatile as the
other.

Ian stood next to the fence, watching as the shiny van
from Merimbula backed up to the gate. Wilson Tate got
out to unload the butternut-colored mare Ian had bought
as a gift for his wife.

With a practiced eye, his hat shielding his face from the
harsh sun, Ian assessed the animal as it clattered down the
ramp. Jacy might have supreme confidence in her ability
to manage a horse, but in truth she was an inexperienced
rider. If the mare wasn't tame enough, he'd send it straight
back to the fancy stables on the other side of Corroboree
Springs.

Tate slipped the bridle off over the horse's head and

sauntered toward Ian, grinning. "Never thought I'd see the day when you'd have dealings with Merimbula for any reason," he said. "Bram's right. That little Yank's got the measure of you, she has."

"Shut up," Ian grumbled, looking past his mate, still engaged in a critical inspection of the mare. He had tack waiting on the fence and began saddling the animal, hoping Tate would leave him be.

He should have known better.

"It's no wonder the rebel colonies broke away from Mother England," Tate commented sagely, "if the whole country's made up of people like your wife."

Ian was tightening the cinch, and he gave it an extra jerk, making the poor mare whinny in surprise and toss her head. Chagrined, he patted the creature's sweaty neck, murmured a few conciliatory words, and loosened the strap. Finally he turned and faced his mate, tugging at his worn leather gloves as he spoke.

"If you've got something to say about Mrs. Yarbro," he said evenly, "I'll be warning you to choose your words with care."

Tate took a cigarette from the packet in his shirt pocket, stuck it in his mouth, and lit it with a throw-away lighter. Again Ian thought apprehensively of the incendiary state of the bush grass.

"Don't get your balls in a wringer, Ian," Tate said, grinning through the acrid smoke wreathing his head. "It happens that I admire a spirited woman. Trouble is, she's got my wife and just about every other female between here and Willoughby all set for a mutiny."

Ian rubbed the back of his neck with one hand. "And you're wondering what I mean to do about her?"

Tate drew on his cigarette and exhaled leisurely before answering. "No. I figure you don't know what to do about her any more than any of the rest of us would. I guess I'm just trying to express my sympathy."

Ian chuckled—Tate's grasp on the situation was an accurate one—but then he was serious again. Behind him the mare pranced and nickered, evidently impatient to prove herself. "Maybe Jacy's right about some of it," he said. "For instance, there's Redley. All these years he's been knocking Darlis into next week and doing God only knows what to the little one, and the whole time we just looked the other way, the lot of us."

"Time was, a man could manage his family the way he saw fit," Tate reflected. "My own dad, now there was a one. He put his share of bruises on my brothers and me, and his word was law around our house. My mother, God rest her, wouldn't have dared to cross him."

Ian turned, thinking of his father, a good and decent man, if not one to show a lad any affection. He pulled the bridle on over the mare's head and swung up into the saddle. The animal fretted, and he calmed her with ease. "It's a new world," he told his friend. He leaned forward, resting his arm on the worn pommel. "To tell you the truth, I've never understood how slapping a sheila about could make a man feel big. Seems like a coward's way to me."

Before Tate could respond both men were distracted from the conversation. A car was approaching, flinging up a trail of reddish-brown dust in its wake, and it wasn't one Ian recognized.

"Who would that be?" he muttered, though he knew in advance that Tate wouldn't have an answer for him.

"No one from Merimbula," Tate affirmed. "Don't recognize it."

Ian nodded toward the gate, which was partly blocked by the horse trailer and the ramp, and Tate opened it up wider so Ian could ride through. The feeling in the pit of his stomach was made of the same stuff as his earlier anxiety about the dryness of the land.

This wasn't Collie bringing Alice Wigget home from the trip up to Darwin, nor, as Tate had already said, was it Andrew Carruthers come from Merimbula to make another of his fruitless offers on the property. Ian knew for a certainty that this was trouble come a-calling.

He rode the skittish little mare into the dooryard and bent to pat her neck while waiting for the car to arrive. It was long and shiny, a fancy English model of some sort with a uniformed driver. The back windows were tinted, however, and he couldn't see who else was inside.

Not that he didn't have a theory or two. Suppose his visitor was Elaine Bennett, Chris's natural mother, come to try and take the boy from him? Or, as was more likely, her wealthy parents, with the same aim in mind.

Ian set his jaw and waited. The devil would pass out ice cream in hell before he would give up his son.

The car came to a whispering stop in back of the house, and the driver got out, touched the brim of his fancy hat to acknowledge Ian, and went round to open the back door.

A woman stepped from the back, slender and expensively dressed, right down to a pair of white gloves. She had the good sense to wear a wide-brimmed hat, thus keeping the merciless sun off her head, but otherwise her clothes were more suited to a cooler climate.

"Ian Yarbro?" she demanded, and her voice had that peculiarly American twang, flat and slightly nasal.

Jacy's mother. Of course.

Ian pushed his hat to the back of his head and sighed. He'd almost have preferred to deal with Elaine or her parents.

"Yes," he said, dismounting and leaving the mare standing with her reins dangling in the dirt.

The woman extended a gloved hand with well-concealed reluctance and announced, "I'm Mrs. Michael Walsh—Regina—if you haven't guessed. Is my daughter around?"

Ian felt defensive, but he wasn't about to show weakness. "No," he said politely. "I'm afraid she's still in town, at some sort of meeting." He gestured grandly toward the house. "Why don't you and your driver come inside, out of the heat, and I'll see if I can find you something cold to drink."

Mrs. Walsh looked him over and plainly found him wanting. "Jacy led me to believe you had household help," she said coolly.

Ian was damned if he was going to explain Alice's absence, or mention her at all, for that matter. This, after all, was a woman who had abandoned her husband and separated him from his child—virtually unpardonable sins in the bush. Or anywhere else.

"I think I can manage to open the fridge," he said with exaggerated politeness.

Regina's eyes were the same pale blue-green as her daughter's, and they flashed with irritation now, though only briefly. "I should hope so," she said with the same hostile cordiality Ian had shown her.

He led the way toward the house, gesturing to the driver to join them. Wilson Tate, who had tied the butternut mare to a hitching post in the corral during the exchange between Ian and his mother-in-law, followed nonchalantly. He was a great one for gossip, was Tate; worse than any sheila ever thought of being.

For the first time in his memory that spacious, familiar kitchen seemed crowded to Ian, and strange. He remembered his manners and drew back a chair for Regina, but she stiffened, looking from the chauffeur to Wilson Tate and then back to Ian again. Her message was as plain as if it had been written in fire: Surely you don't expect me, a lady, to sit with these . . . men.

Ian felt a flush of irritation rise in his neck. "Perhaps you'd be more comfortable out on the veranda," he said to her, nodding for Tate and the driver to take seats at the trestle table.

With a huffy flourish Jacy's mother raised her aristocratic little chin and swept grandly off through the living room toward the veranda beyond. At first Ian was surprised that she knew the way; then he realized that she must have been in the Yarbro house with Jake before the divorce.

The driver, an overweight man who was plainly suffering in his chauffeur's uniform, rolled his eyes expressively.

"Got a fly up her nose," Wilson Tate commented.

Ian refrained from comment, though he figured Regina Walsh had something up *something,* for sure and certain. He ferreted about in the fridge until he'd found two bottles of beer and one of Jacy's beloved diet colas.

He carried the beer to the table, where Tate and the driver eagerly accepted their refreshment, then set off determinedly for the veranda with the cola.

Regina was seated in the swing, fanning herself with her narrow purse. She'd removed her hat, and her fair hair was moist with perspiration. She accepted the cola with a brisk and somewhat grudging "Thank you."

Ian nodded in response, leaning against the veranda's railing, his arms folded. "Jacy will be surprised to see you," he said.

Regina gave him another of her rich-bitch looks, but he caught a glimpse of softness in her, too, and realized that she wasn't nearly so mean as she would have him believe. In fact, she was probably capable of great tenderness and even greater passion, like her daughter.

If Jake Tiernan had loved this woman once, and he had, there was good in her.

"I have no doubt that my arrival will come as a shock to my daughter," she said, her tone colder than the beer Tate and the chauffeur were drinking. "You and I agree on that much, at least."

Ian scratched the back of his head, felt the rough place where Jake had stitched him up like a sheep cut in the shearing process. "I guess she must have written you about Jake," he said carefully.

Sadness cast a shadow over those porcelain features; if it hadn't been for her tendency to be ill-natured, Regina would have been a lovely woman. "Yes, I know that he passed away. I was sorry to hear it, of course."

Ian only shrugged; he wasn't about to offer further comment on the subject of Jake. The topic was too sensitive.

He took off his hat, shoved his hand through his hair. He resented this woman heartily, but he knew now that it wasn't because of what she'd done to Jake. That was old news, and although Jake had suffered, he'd come through the experience well enough. No, what bothered Ian was the knowledge that Mrs. Walsh had come to Yolanda, and to his property in particular, to convince Jacy that she didn't belong in the Australian bush.

The worst part was knowing that Regina might well be right. Life was hard in the outback, without any of the luxuries Jacy had probably enjoyed in the States, and she would be the first to agree that when it came to women's rights Yolanda was a hundred years behind the times. On top of that was the threat Redley Shifflet represented.

Regina must have divined some of his thoughts, because she smiled indulgently and then said, "You must understand that my daughter has been through a great deal these past few years. Jacy's told you about her friend, Paul, I'm sure—she was devastated by his death." She paused and sighed delicately, her attention focused on the landscape. After a moment her gaze swung back to Ian's face. "Jacy is in no condition to make long-term commitments."

Ian felt some new emotion akin to terror, but quieter and more calm. He didn't allow so much as a flicker of it to show in his face. "That's for Jacy to decide, don't you think?"

"No," Regina responded tartly, "I don't think. She's given to impulsive actions, ones she generally regrets. The problem is that Jacy is likely to suffer in silence, the way she did when Paul was dying."

Ian turned away, gripping the railing, because he felt his control over his facial expression slipping. Fortunately, he could still trust his voice. "That must have been very painful for her."

"It was," Regina agreed, sighing the words. "She hasn't been the same since."

"Grief does that to a person," Ian said, speaking to the land. Like a much-loved woman, it was capable, that terrible, beautiful terrain, of conferring the deepest of sorrows. He both revered it and feared its power over him.

"I quite agree," Regina replied. "I'll speak frankly, Mr. Yarbro—Ian—Jacy simply isn't ready for marriage. Especially not to a man who lives in this godforsaken outpost of nowhere."

At that Ian turned. His jawline felt tight; he consciously relaxed the muscles there. "We're not talking about a little girl, Mrs. Walsh," he pointed out. "Jacy is a grown woman. I think she knows what she's ready for and what she isn't."

They were both startled by the sound of soft applause from behind the screen door. Ian's heart stumbled and then righted itself when he saw Jacy standing there clapping her hands, partly because he hadn't heard her drive in and partly because he always felt a certain lurching wonder when he looked at her.

"Thank you, Ian," she said, pushing open the door. "Could I get you to put that in writing?"

He grinned crookedly, but he felt a pang of sorrow because he knew better than anyone how easy it would be to lose Jacy. She was like some beautiful tropical bird; if he tried to tame her, she might take wing and disappear into the blue sky. "Quote me," he teased, in response to her question, "and I'll deny everything."

Jacy stepped out onto the veranda then, and Regina, obviously thrilled to see her daughter, rose to her feet and held out her arms. "Baby," she said.

Jacy moved into her mother's embrace. "Hello, Mom," she said with a certain affectionate resignation in her voice. "What took you so long?"

That seemed like a good time to leave the two women alone, so Ian went back into the house and got himself a beer. Wilson Tate gave him a sympathetic slap on the back and said he thought he'd be settling the mare he'd brought into a stall and then getting back to Merimbula. With that he was gone.

Ian sat down at the trestle table for a chat with the chauffeur, but his mind wasn't on it. He was thinking about the two women on the front veranda. They looked alike, except for the obvious age difference. Did they think alike, too?

Jacy had been expecting her mother, on some level, but she wasn't prepared for the reality. There was so much going on in her life already, what with the small-scale revolution and Redley Shifflet out there in the bush someplace, no doubt plotting his revenge against both her and Ian. Now she would have her well-meaning parent to deal with in the bargain.

"I've got a hotel room—to use the term loosely—in Willoughby," Regina announced as soon as they were alone and seated on the swing, hands clasped. "You can come back with me tonight—we'll catch our breaths and then fly home. Michael will take care of the divorce."

Jacy flinched at the word. "First of all, Mom," she said patiently, "I'm not planning to go anywhere. I love Ian, and I'm going to stay with him. And second, Michael isn't an attorney, he's a pediatrician."

Regina's still-lovely face was pinched with jet lag and disappointment. "Don't be stubborn, darling," she pleaded. "This isn't the life for you, and you know it."

"It wasn't the life for you, Mother," Jacy pointed out, less patiently than before. "But I'm half Australian, and I've got this place in my blood, just like Ian does."

Regina gave a theatrical sigh. "Come, now—do you think I don't understand what's happened here? I know because I did the very same thing—I mistook a youthful passion for

243

real love. And because of that mistake I broke a good man's heart.''

Jacy didn't remember Regina speaking so kindly of Jake before that. Usually she referred to her ex-husband in far less complimentary terms. "What happened between you and Dad?'' she asked, her fingers comfortably interlaced with her mother's.

A sad, sweet smile touched Regina's mouth, and her gaze was on the distant horizon. After a long time she answered her daughter's question in a soft and hesitant voice. "We were just too different. He loved this dry, dusty place, and after the novelty wore off I was wildly homesick for Manhattan. We began to argue, and then . . .'' Regina looked at Jacy again, her brow furrowed with reluctance.

"And then?'' Jacy prompted gently.

"Jake met another woman.'' Regina closed her eyes for a moment; plainly, the memory still caused her pain. Seeing the shock and corresponding hurt in Jacy's face, Regina went on quickly. "It wasn't all his fault, sweetheart. He was young and very virile, and I refused to share his bed for the last six months of our marriage.''

Jacy's eyes burned with tears; she ached for both her parents. Regina must have felt like an outsider in this strange and hostile place, and Jake had probably just been looking for the love he'd had and then lost.

"Didn't you miss him at all after you left?''

Regina's smile was heartbreaking to see. "Miss Jake? I cried for a year. Every time the doorbell rang I prayed it was him.'' She sniffled. "Jake would have liked the United States, damn his stubborn Aussie hide, but he refused even to visit. It was as though he blamed the country—or specifically my being an American—for everything bad that happened between us.''

Jacy thought uneasily of Ian's remarks about her Yankee ideas and bit her lip for a moment. What if Ian grew disenchanted with their marriage—given their many differences, it didn't seem all that unlikely a prospect—and turned to another woman the way Jake had?

She'd die if that happened, she reflected. But only after killing Ian.

Her grip on her mother's hand tightened until Regina frowned and withdrew.

"I suppose you inherited Corroboree Springs," the older woman said.

Jacy was grateful for the change of subject, though she knew the respite was only temporary. Regina hadn't traveled halfway around the world not to accomplish her objective. "Sort of," Jacy said with a nod. "Ian got the springs, the land is mine."

Regina looked startled. "Ian inherited? Why on earth would Jake split up the property that way?"

Jacy smiled, missing Jake acutely, even though she felt a little disillusioned by what she'd learned about him. "Dad believed Ian and I were made for each other," she recalled. "My guess would be that he thought binding us in a partnership of sorts might lead to other things."

"And he got his way, the old devil," Regina reflected, studying the landscape again.

The sun was beginning to set, and there were familiar sounds coming from inside the house—masculine laughter, Chris's incessant chatter, a staticky newscast out of the big, old-fashioned radio in the front room.

"Yes," Jacy agreed. "He got his way."

"You're really not coming home."

"This is home," Jacy answered. "Right here, where Ian is."

Regina's mouth tightened for a moment before she replied. "You'll regret your rash choices, Jacy, when the passion fades—and it will, no matter what you think now. Then you'll come to hate this inhospitable place."

Jacy sighed. "There's no point in our discussing the subject, Mom," she said gently. "I'm staying."

"Until there's a child?" Regina demanded in a whisper,

suddenly angry. "That way the baby will be hurt, too, as well as that little boy in there, and Ian. And worst of all, you!"

"Mom—"

Regina was crying. She pushed away from Jacy and rose from the swing to walk to the other end of the veranda. "Just leave me alone," she said between soft, strangled sobs. "You can't imagine what it does to me—*you can't imagine*—seeing history repeat itself this way!"

Jacy opened the screen door but lingered on the threshold. "I'll have the driver bring in your bags."

Regina did not turn around. "Don't bother. I left my things in Willoughby, at the hotel, and I'll be returning there as soon as I pull myself together."

There was no point in arguing, although it broke Jacy's heart that Regina meant to leave so quickly. They had always been good friends, the two of them, as well as mother and daughter. It would hurt to part without laughing together, having a few heart-to-heart talks, and gossiping about all the fascinating people in Regina and Michael's lofty social circles.

"Did you see the horse?" Chris cried, unable to contain his excitement, when Jacy wandered into the kitchen in a spell, washed her hands, and automatically started dinner. She didn't mind cooking—she even enjoyed it sometimes—but she was definitely looking forward to Alice's return. "Did you see the horse Dad bought for you?"

Jacy went still, holding a frying pan six inches above the burner, and sought Ian's face. Wilson Tate was gone, but of course the driver her mother had hired in Willoughby remained, as well as Chris and her husband.

"Horse?" she echoed stupidly.

Ian looked shyly pleased, like a little boy offering a paste-speckled valentine. "You said you wanted to ride," he replied.

She set the skillet down with an unintentional bang and headed straight for the back door, all her doubts and problems momentarily forgotten. She'd noticed the Merimbula truck and trailer outside when she'd returned from the meeting in town, but she'd been more interested in the limousine. "Where is this horse?" she cried, breathless. "Where?"

She heard Ian laugh, felt him behind her even before he fell into step with her.

"In the shed, sheila," he answered, beaming. "Where else?"

They went into the barn together, not by way of the farmyard but through a side doorway. Jacy spotted the mare immediately—she was munching hay in a corner stall—and she startled every animal in the place with a shriek of pure joy.

Then she turned and flung her arms around Ian's neck, kissing him soundly on the mouth before telling him, "She's beautiful! Oh, Ian, I love you!"

He looked surprised by this declaration, but he offered no direct comment. "You'll have to wait to ride her—I haven't had a chance to make sure she's all right, what with your mother showing up and everything."

"Nonsense," Jacy said, striding toward the stall. "I'm not a novice, Ian. I don't need you to test-drive my horse."

"Jacy—"

She had already opened the stall door by the time Ian reached it and was inside slipping a bridle over the mare's head. Although Jacy had taken formal lessons in the States as a young girl, Jake had taught her to ride bareback, thinking it was safer, and that was the style she still preferred.

"Jacy," Ian repeated, more sternly this time.

She led the mare out of the stall and mounted. She grinned down at Ian when he took hold of the bridle. "Don't spoil this for me," she said shakily. "Please."

Ian hesitated, then released his grasp on the bridle. "Go ahead, then," he growled. "But be careful."

Jacy nodded, and she fully meant to comply with Ian's wishes, too, but once she got outside, into the twilight, she had a sudden, crazy impulse to outrun all her doubts and fears, all her inadequacies and failures. She leaned low over the mare's neck and goaded her into a gallop and then a dead run.

She didn't look back but simply headed straight out into the bush, spurring the horse with the heels of her sneakers, making the animal run faster and faster. And the mare seemed to delight in the exercise.

They must have traveled about a mile—Jacy couldn't see the house or remember exactly where it lay—when the animal stumbled and Jacy went flying off over its head. She rolled, unhurt, over the hot, sandy dirt and got up laughing.

The mare bolted, spooked by a lizard or some other small, quick creature, and ran off.

Jacy wasn't afraid, because she knew Ian was right behind her. Sure enough, he rode out of the thickening shadows within a couple of minutes, mounted on one of his tamed brumbies, leading her lathered mare behind him.

"Are you all right?" he asked when he reached her, swinging down from the saddle to grasp her shoulders in his hands.

She started to laugh and to cry, both at once. It was all too much—the threat from Redley, the rebellion brewing among Yolanda's women—a revolution of which she was the unwilling leader—Jake's death, and her mother's arrival.

Ian pulled her close and held her, and she clung to him, knotting her fingers in the back of his shirt, loving the man-smell of him, the strength and the substance and the warmth. Oh, God, if only he loved her, she thought, the world would be a perfect place.

"It's all right, sheila," he said gruffly.

She wailed, then laughed hysterically, then settled into a series of deep hiccups. "You're—going—to hate—me," she managed.

Ian chuckled, one hand buried in her hair. "No, sheila. Never that."

"The women—the women of Yolanda are going to refuse to—to sleep with their husbands," Jacy blurted, still hiccuping. "Until they agree to send all the children to school every day."

That got his attention, as she had known it would. He held her away from him, searching her face. It was then that she noticed his injured eye was almost back to normal. "Was that your idea?" he demanded.

Jacy shook her head. She held her breath, cheeks puffed out, in an effort to stop the spasmodic hiccups.

"Are you planning to leave our bed?" This was serious business to Ian, as it would be to most men.

Jacy let her breath out in a rush and waited, somewhat dazed, to see if the old trick had worked.

It had.

"No," she said. "I was going to ask you to leave it."

Ian narrowed his eyes. "What?"

Jacy laid one hand to her chest, fingers splayed, and sniffled loudly. "I'd be a hypocrite if I didn't, now, wouldn't I?" she reasoned.

"God damn," Ian hissed. Then he released her, turned away, and flung his hat down. "God damn, God damn, God *damn!*"

Jacy smiled, enjoying this display of masculine maturity. Then, mischievously, she said, "I didn't say I expected you to agree, Ian. I just said I had to ask, that's all."

He whirled, his face crimson beneath his deep tan. "You mean—"

She moved close to him, gripped the collar of his work shirt, and looked up into his eyes. "I mean," she teased shamelessly, "that if you refuse—well, there just won't be much I can do about it."

Ian glared. Then he laughed.

Then he kissed her. Hard.

17

To IAN'S RELIEF, REGINA INSISTED ON RETURNING TO HER hotel in Willoughby immediately after tea, though she made it plain enough that she meant to stay on for a while. He knew, as he stood on the front veranda reflecting on the matter, that Regina hoped Jacy would decide to return to America with her.

His feelings about that were mixed.

Ian had come to realize that he loved his wife, though the thought of telling her what he felt still terrified him, and he had not forgotten the ordeal he'd gone through the last time she'd left him.

On the other hand, Ian was afraid for Jacy to stay. Redley Shifflet might have vanished, but he'd be back one day, and he was just bastard enough to take his vengeance through Jacy. She could be hurt, or even killed, and if anything happened to her, Ian would never forgive himself.

Gripping the veranda post and gazing up at the Southern Cross, he recalled how it had been for him before Jacy's return. Life had been hard, yes—running a property in the bush was inherently difficult—but there had been a certain even rhythm to his days.

Get out of bed. Work. Eat. Chat with Chris. Sleep.

He smiled to remember how simple it all was. He'd actually believed he was living; instead, he'd been sleepwalking. Waiting for the show to start, for his life to begin.

Then Jacy had come back, and matters had been in almost constant upheaval ever since.

He heard the screen door creak behind him, knew it was her by her scent and her soft tread across the floorboards of the porch.

"Wishing on a star?" Jacy asked, coming to stand beside him at the rail.

Ian turned his head to look down into her sweet, mischievous face. How he loved this woman, how he needed her, how he regretted ever opening himself up to such dangerous emotions all over again. He'd been so vigilant . . . when had it happened?

"What would I wish for?" he countered, his voice low and perhaps a little hoarse.

Jacy shrugged. "Safety?"

"No such thing," Ian replied. "Might as well ask for a blue unicorn or a flying pig."

She laughed softly. "Only you could manage to sound both pragmatic and fanciful in one and the same sentence." She rested her head against the upper part of his arm, and he felt a rush of tenderness so poignant that it closed up his throat and made his eyes sting. "You're right, though. None of us are ever really safe." She paused, then looked up at him again, and he was grateful that she had more to say because he couldn't have spoken to save his hide. "That's one of the many reasons I mean to stay right here, Ian. Because no matter where I might go, there will be something or someone there who could do me in. So if you're thinking I should go home with my mother to avoid a confrontation with Redley Shifflet, forget it."

He studied her upturned face for a long moment, then

swung his gaze back to the moving pattern of stars. "Don't underestimate Shifflet," he warned quietly. "He's a sneaking, mean-spirited son of a bitch, and he's been hunting dingoes and 'roos all his life. He knows the bush, and when he's been drinking he might do anything."

Jacy sighed. "I know. But I'm tired of running away."

Ian felt proud of her for that, but his fears for her were as great as ever. He offered a silent, fervent prayer that if Redley struck out at anyone, it would be him, Ian, and not Chris or this stubborn, unfathomable woman.

He smelled the acrid dryness in the night air, and his disquiet deepened. "Something's coming," he muttered, unaware until afterward that he'd spoken out loud.

Jacy put an arm around him. "Yes," she agreed, but she didn't sound scared, just resigned.

As it turned out, nothing significant happened that night, or the next, or the next. Mrs. Walsh came to call each evening in her fancy hired car, escorted by the same long-suffering driver, and Jacy taught school every weekday. Mrs. Wigget returned from Darwin on a swell of triumph and reported with pleasure that Gladys Shifflet was safe and reasonably happy with Nancy's aunt. There was no sign of Redley—in fact, there were those who believed him dead—and the women of Yolanda, with one ironic exception, flatly refused to sleep with their husbands until such time as Jacy Yarbro should be made the final authority on all school matters. The men grumbled at the cruelties and injustices of fate and womanhood, and Ian stayed away from the Dog and Goose, even though there were times when he sorely wanted a mug of cold beer, a game of pool, and some masculine companionship.

The weather grew hotter, the grass got drier, and the sense of impending disaster heightened until everybody in the surrounding countryside was snappish and tense.

At last it was time for school holidays. For three weeks there would be no classes.

Jacy immediately announced that she was going to Adelaide to shop for clothes and school supplies, attend to her financial affairs, eat in restaurants, and take in some movies and live theater. She wanted Chris to go along, and Ian, of course.

He refused straightaway the night she raised the idea—they were sitting across from each other at the trestle table. Alice had gone home, Chris was in bed, and Regina, who had unbent herself just far enough to spend the night, had retired to the spare room with an oil lamp and a book.

Jacy leaned forward, her forehead creased. "What do you mean, you won't go?" she demanded in a low voice. "And don't tell me you have a property to run, because you known damn well the McAllisters would look after the whole place while we were gone!"

Ian squirmed a little. She was right—Tom Sr. was one of the best workers he'd ever seen, and under normal circumstances the man could be trusted to handle almost any crisis. The problem was, these weren't normal circumstances.

"Jacy, the bush is dry as tinder—it could go up at any time. Besides that, there's Shifflet."

"If there's going to be a bushfire," Jacy pointed out irritably, "there will be—whether we're here or not. And if you stay home because of Redley, then you're letting him control your life."

Ian set his jaw and glowered, refusing to respond. Maybe because he didn't have any workable arguments handy, though he preferred to think he was just being consistent with his personal nature.

Jacy curved her right index finger and thumped the table with it several times in rapid succession. "Do you know what I think, Ian Yarbro?" she hissed, her beautiful eyes blazing in the soft light. "I think you're scared!"

He flushed with fury, and with the painful knowledge that she was at least partly right. Just the same, he played stupid. *"What?"*

She wouldn't let him off the hook. "You're not used to

cities—or fancy restaurants, or theaters. You're afraid you'll make a fool of yourself.''

''The hell,'' he muttered.

''Save it,'' Jacy responded smugly. ''You're not fooling anybody but yourself.''

For a few moments Ian was too angry—with her and with himself—to speak. Finally he shook his head. ''No. You can take the boy, but I won't be going along. I've got things to do here, and besides, you need this time to square things with your mother and make up your mind what you want to do.''

Jacy's eyes widened, and she looked away quickly, then met his gaze again. ''I don't need to make up my mind about anything,'' she said. ''I'm staying. What is it with you, anyway? Are you trying to get rid of me or something? Because if that's the case, I'll just get myself a place in Yolanda.''

Ian reached across the table and clasped her hand in one of his—it was a quick gesture, largely involuntary, and a few more moments passed before he could trust himself to speak.

Tell her you love her, ordered a rational voice in his brain.

''I don't want you to go'' was as close as he could come to saying what he felt. ''Not forever, I mean.''

Her eyes glistened. ''You're so damn stubborn,'' she scolded, but there was affection in the way she shaped the words, and maybe something more than that. ''Is there any chance I can get you to change your mind and come to Adelaide with us?''

''None,'' Ian said. He could stand a lot of things, but looking like a bumbling idiot in front of this woman wasn't one of them. He supposed he shouldn't feel that way, but there it was. His one comfort, and it was a paradoxical one, was that some primal instinct warned him not to leave, not to let down his guard.

*   *   *

254

They'd made love again in the dry heat of the night, and Jacy awakened the next morning with a delicious sense of well-being. Beneath that, though, was a certain uneasiness with a measure of disappointment stirred in. She would miss Ian wildly during the upcoming week in Adelaide, but maybe he was right in thinking they needed a little time apart.

Not that she was going to change her mind about her marriage and her life in the bush. For all the trials and perils of the place, Jacy could feel her emotional roots spreading, stretching ever deeper into the ancient soil.

She belonged here, with this man, and his son, and all the people of the community—even those who despised and distrusted her.

It was glorious knowing that.

Because Ian had left their bed at the first hint of daylight, as always, Jacy had the spacious room to herself. She went to the armoire, took out one of Ian's work shirts, and put it on over her otherwise naked body.

She loved the feel of the worn fabric against her skin, and the Ian-scent that clung to it even after washing and ironing. One by one, standing there in front of that old-fashioned oak wardrobe, she touched each of his shirts, the sleeves of his one suit jacket, the fleece-lined leather coat he would wear in the cold days of June, July, and August.

After that strange and gentle communion Jacy took herself into the bathroom for a quick shower. Then she put on a red and white polka dot sundress, very short and clingy, and makeup. When she got downstairs, carrying a small suitcase and her cosmetics case, Chris was already there waiting. He was beaming, his fair hair slicked back, his freckled face scrubbed, and he looked very handsome in his traveling clothes.

"He's a bit excited, our Chris," Mrs. Wigget confided, from her post at the stove, with an affectionate smile.

Jacy's heart swelled with love as she looked at the little boy. She wanted to be a mother to him, not only then, but through all the years ahead. She wanted to watch him grow into a strong and intelligent man like his father, to see him married one day, with children of his own.

She bent to whisper in his ear. "I love you, Christopher Yarbro."

His face was bright with joy and trust; he put his arms around Jacy's waist and hugged her. He didn't say the words, being a boy, but there was really no need of that, because she knew.

"Where's your father?" Jacy asked after a few moments, when she'd composed herself a little.

Chris shrugged. "In the shed, I suppose, with the horses." Some of the delight faded from his face. "I wish Dad would go with us."

Regina came down the stairs just then, looking like a model in a white Armani jacket and matching trousers. A lustrous pearl pendant suspended on a long golden chain glowed against the pale blue silk of her camisole. "And leave his precious property?" she put in. *"Perish* the thought. The sky might fall."

Jacy gave her mother a you-stay-out-of-this look and laid her hands on Chris's slender shoulders. "Tell you what," she said to the child. "We'll have so much fun while we're in Adelaide, you and me and"—she took particular delight in saying it—*"Grandma* here, and we'll bring him such lovely presents, that the very next time we go away on holiday your dad will be begging to go with us."

There was a certain skepticism in Alice's face, Jacy noted in a glance, and Regina was clearly still smarting from being called Grandma. Not that she hadn't exhibited a sort of cautious fondness for Chris, because she had.

"Do you think so?" Chris asked eagerly.

"Absolutely," Jacy said, and neither Alice nor Regina had the heart to contradict her.

Regina's driver, who had spent the night in the quarters where the transient shearing crews stayed in early summer, was outside polishing his long, shiny car. He touched his

256

hat and smiled slightly when Jacy passed him on her way to the stables.

She found Ian there in one of the stalls with a brumby mare, examining the hoof of its left hind leg. He didn't look up when she came to stand at the gate.

Jacy wasn't about to be ignored. She wanted him to think about her while she was away, and she'd chosen the slinky red sundress especially for the purpose.

"If you think I'm going to leave without a good-bye kiss, Ian Yarbro," she said in a teasing croon, "think again."

He glanced at her and did an immediate double-take. Then he gave a low, grudging whistle and let the mare's foot down. He tried to speak, but the effort was a colossal failure, and Jacy watched with satisfaction as her husband's Adam's apple rose like an elevator and dropped back to the base of his throat.

"Like it?"

Ian managed an endearingly lopsided grin. "Ummm— you could put it that way."

Jacy gave her hair a theatrical toss and proceeded to bat her eyelashes, her mouth curved all the while into a mischievous smile. "Maybe you'd better come along to Adelaide with us after all," she said. "Just to make sure I behave myself."

He laughed. "If I did, the last thing you'd do is behave yourself. Fact is, love, we'd never get out of the hotel if I had anything to say about it."

Ian came out of the stall to stand facing her, and she pretended his collar needed straightening. "Sounds like a honeymoon to me," she said in a deliberately throaty tone. "We never had one of those, did we, Mr. Yarbro?"

He bent his head, nibbled at her mouth, and, as easily as that, sent a series of electrical charges crackling through her veins. "No, love, we didn't. And we won't—not with Chris and your mother about, anyway." With brazen leisure he smoothed the strap of her dress off over her shoulder, then pushed down the lacy bra beneath.

Jacy drew in her breath and closed her eyes as he cupped her bare breast in his hand, stroking the nipple with the rough pad of his thumb. When he leaned down to taste her she gasped and cried out softly.

Ian withdrew, chuckling, and put her bra and dress back in place. "Think about that while you're away, sheila," he told her. "That and all the other things I'm going to do to you when you get back."

Jacy swayed slightly because her knees were unsteady, and she knew her face was flushed. "Damn you, Ian—I came out here to make sure *you* thought about *me* while I was gone!"

He smiled. "No worries there, love. I won't be able to get you out of my mind." He smoothed her hair with one hand. "Now take yourself off to the big smoke before I throw you down in the straw and have my way with you."

Jacy's blush deepened. Such a session was out of the question, of course, in broad daylight, with her mother and Chris and the chauffeur waiting to leave, but the idea had its appeal all the same.

"At least come and say good-bye to your son," she said, bristling a bit. She needed to distance herself a little or she wouldn't be able to bear leaving him, even for such a short time.

Ian grinned again, put his arms around her loosely, and cupped her backside in his hands. Then he hoisted her against him and kissed her with a thoroughness that left her feeling dizzy and disoriented.

In fact, Ian had swatted her lightly and left the stables to speak to Chris before she was able to move again.

Soon enough, though, she was in the blessedly cool and shadowy interior of the limo beside her elegant mother, with Chris sitting across from them, on her way to Adelaide by way of Willoughby. The muted strains of Mozart came from the speaker system, and there was a cellular telephone handy, as well as a well-stocked bar.

Jacy felt as though she'd been taken aboard an alien

spacecraft. No doubt the painful medical experiments would begin shortly.

"Champagne?" Regina asked in a chiming tone, holding up a small green bottle. Her expression was mischievous.

Jacy laughed. "For heaven's sake, Mother—it's ten-thirty in the morning."

Chris's eyes were huge. "May I have some?"

"Not on your life," Jacy answered. "Is there any juice in there, or diet cola?"

Chris made a face.

"Like it or lump it, fella," Jacy told him. She was happy at the prospect of a holiday, but she'd left her heart behind with Ian, and she felt incomplete, like an impostor, only posing as Jacy Tiernan Yarbro.

In Willoughby, a bustling town in its own right, Jacy and Chris went on a brief foray of exploration while Regina was checking out of her hotel room. There was a bookstore stocked with fairly current titles, and Jacy bought a stack of paperbacks, some for herself and some for Chris.

The three of them had lunch in the hotel restaurant and then set off in the limousine for Adelaide. The drive would take several hours.

Chris fell asleep in the middle of the afternoon, the adventure story he'd been reading slipping silently to the floor of the car, and Jacy picked it up, marked his place, and tucked the volume lovingly beneath his hand.

Regina spoke softly, not wanting to awaken the child. "I've been meaning to ask," she began sweetly. "Where *did* you get that dress? It looks like it came from one of those mail order places that sell edible underwear and flavored body lotions."

Caught off guard, Jacy gasped and then put one hand over her mouth to stifle an embarrassed giggle. "Mother! Maybe you shop for things like that, but I don't. I bought this outfit in Honolulu five years ago, if you must know, and I happen to like it."

"You wore it," Regina said, undaunted, "to torture that

poor husband of yours for refusing to come to Adelaide with you.''

Jacy blushed again and looked away, unable to deny the charge.

"What happened?" Regina pressed, leaning forward slightly, a hint of laughter in her voice. "Did the plan backfire?"

Jacy still didn't answer.

There was silence for a while, except for the Mozart and the almost indiscernible purr of the car's expensive engine. The tinted windows kept out the sun, and there was a panel separating them from the driver.

When Regina spoke again she sounded serious. And sad. "Ian won't change, you know," she told her daughter. "He's like Jake was. He'll never love any woman as much as he loves that land of his.''

"Maybe so," Jacy admitted with a sigh, "but love was never part of the bargain Ian and I made anyway.''

Regina frowned. "What?" she whispered.

Jacy shrugged. "I love Ian," she answered, somewhat sadly. "I guess I probably never really stopped caring for him, even while we were apart those ten years. And while I'd be thrilled if he loved me in return, I don't need that to be happy. And I don't have to compete with the property.''

"That's what you think," Regina said after a few moments of reflection, but she neither looked nor sounded so certain as before. "Ian Yarbro would die for that damned patch of red dirt," she went on presently. "And believe me, if it ever came to a choice, he'd take the land.''

"Why should he have to make a choice?" Jacy asked, settling back against the plush seat and closing her eyes. She was feeling tired all of a sudden, and maybe a little carsick.

"He won't have to," Regina persisted. "You will. This trip will remind you of everything you left behind, and then the novelty of living with Crocodile Dundee back there will wear off in short order.''

Jacy opened her eyes again. Without a word to her mother she leaned forward and tapped on the panel between the front and back seats. "Would you stop for a moment, please?"

The sleek vehicle came to a smooth halt at the side of the road. Jacy pushed open the door, leapt out, and ran around the back to throw up.

Regina was there for her, in the way only a mother could be, with a bottle of fancy water and a handkerchief.

"Good heavens," she said. "This is worse than I thought."

Jacy rinsed out her mouth, then moistened the handkerchief and laid it over the back of her neck. "What?" she asked impatiently.

"You're pregnant, you ninny," Regina said.

Jacy drew in her breath, and her eyes went wide as she did a mental count. She hadn't had a period since before she'd left the States. Why hadn't she noticed that?

"Oh, God," Jacy said, covering her mouth. She began to laugh, and yet tears stung her eyes. "Oh, God—you're right! Oh, Mother, this is wonderful—we have to go back and tell Ian right now!"

"Nonsense," Regina said, taking Jacy's arm and ushering her back to the car. "The news will keep until you get back from Adelaide. If I don't manage to talk you out of staying here first, that is."

Chris had awakened, as luck would have it, and he was sitting up and rubbing his eyes. "You're not going to stay with us?" he asked in a heartbreakingly small voice, staring at Jacy.

She moved to the other seat and gathered him close, since he was too big a boy to hold on her lap. "You bet I'm going to stay," she said, ruffling his hair and kissing his temple lightly. "Didn't I promise when you asked me about that before?"

He nodded, tilting his head back to search her face. "I guess you did." He looked at Regina, and his eyes narrowed. The two had been well on the way to friendship, but now Chris was clearly suspicious. "Why does *she* want you to leave us?"

"Oh, Lord," Regina murmured, sinking back in her seat and covering her eyes with one hand.

"That's a good question," Jacy said, holding him tighter for a moment.

Regina wailed comically. "The guilt!" she cried. "You're making me feel like some kind of homewrecker—both of you!"

Jacy raised her eyebrows and ruffled Chris's hair again, but she wasn't really thinking about her mother's well-intentioned meddling. The certainty that she was carrying a child, hers and Ian's, pounded inside her like an extra heartbeat.

Chris was cool toward Regina from then on, though unfailingly polite, and, to her credit, Jacy's mother didn't say another word about taking her daughter home to America.

They stopped for dinner in a small town some distance from Adelaide and arrived in that gracious city at around eight o'clock.

Regina had made reservations at a fine hotel, and Jacy had to admit the place was a treat after living in the bush. Chris walked through the lobby with his head tilted back and his mouth wide open.

He shared Jacy's room, and Regina had her own suite down the hall.

"I wish Dad could be here," Chris said, bouncing cautiously on the bed and watching intently for Jacy's reaction. When she didn't scold him he began to gain momentum.

"Me, too," she answered, opening her suitcase. She was exhausted and full of the sweet secret of her pregnancy, and more than anything she wanted to take a warm bath and fall into bed.

Chris, mercifully, was distracted from his mattress jumping when the television set caught his attention.

"Is this a telly? Are we getting one of these?"

Jacy smiled. "Yes and yes," she said, switching on the set, locating a colorful cartoon, and selecting low volume. "We'll get a lot of stations with the satellite dish, but the reception might not be this good."

Chris's face was a study in delight as he watched Fred Flintstone cavorting with Barney Rubble.

"Are you hungry?" Jacy asked.

He nodded without looking away from the screen, and Jacy went to the telephone and ordered room service. She had taken her bath and was watching television with Chris, comfortably wrapped in a terry cloth robe provided by the hotel, when the food arrived.

Chris gobbled up half a sandwich while watching a rerun of "I Love Lucy," and Jacy ate the other half.

After an hour she insisted that Chris take a bath of his own and, amid protest, and turned off the set. When he was settled in his own bed, next to hers, Jacy went to the window to gaze out at the spectacular city lights. She was wearing cotton pajamas.

She found herself wishing for a glimpse of the stars she'd looked at with Ian back home. If only he were there, so that she could take him in her arms and tell him they'd made a baby together.

Maybe then, knowing that, Ian would fall in love with her.

She leaned her forehead against the cool glass of the window and felt tears gather in her eyes. Hormones, she thought, smiling even as she cried, and she took herself back to bed.

Deep in the night Chris awakened, crying and calling plaintively for his dad.

Jacy went to sit on the side of the child's bed and gather him into her arms. "Shhh, baby, it's all right," she whispered. "Mama's here. Mama's here."

Chris clung to her, trembling, and after a while his sobs turned to noisy small-boy sniffles. "Dad'll be safe without us, won't he? Mrs. Wigget and Collie and Tom Sr. will look after him?''

Jacy hugged her stepson and kissed the top of his head. "Yes, darling," she promised, feeling an overwhelming tenderness and thinking she could get to like this mothering business. "And your dad is pretty good at looking after himself, too."

It was true; Ian was strong. Still, long after Jacy had kissed Chris goodnight, long after he'd gone back to sleep, she lay awake thinking of all the singular dangers of the outback.

Take care, my darling, she told him, telegraphing the words from her heart to his.

Ian lay alone in his bed, aching with loneliness and too proud to admit, even to himself, that he wished he'd gone to the city with Jacy and Chris. The muscles in his back and arms ached from a day of working with the horses, and he missed the comfort of his wife's strong, pliant body.

He closed his eyes, and somewhere deep inside he heard her voice. Take care, my darling, she said.

Ian spoke to the darkness and hoped somehow she would hear him. "I love you, Jacy," he told her.

18

JACY'S THOUGHTS TURNED OFTEN TO IAN, AND SHE MISSED him with a poignancy that frightened her. Oh, but it was dangerous to love so deeply, she thought, so fully, without restraint or reservation.

She spent most of her first day in Adelaide closeted away with a banker and attorney, since moving a trust fund like hers from one country to another was no simple process. While Jacy was doing business Regina and Chris explored the city.

Late that afternoon, when she returned to her hotel, her mother and stepson were still out. Jacy took off the prim suit she'd worn, splashed cool water on her face, and lay down for a nap.

She was awakened when Chris burst into the room like a torpedo, crying, "We saw Gog and Magog!"

Regina came in behind the child, giving Jacy a discerning look. "Statues," she explained. "They're in the shopping arcade. Put on your robe, darling—there's a bellman coming right behind us with some of the loot."

Jacy snatched up the hotel robe that lay across the foot of her bed and put it on. "What do you mean, 'the loot'?"

Chris's face was bright, and his freckles seemed to stand out from his skin. "Mrs. Walsh bought us presents, you and me!" he announced just as the bellman knocked. He rushed to admit him.

Jacy gave her mother a look. "Mom—"

Regina interrupted with a wave of one hand and an impatient whisper. "Oh, for heaven's sake, Jacy, let me have a *little* fun, won't you?"

The bellman brought in a cart loaded with bags and boxes, and Regina directed him to put everything on the nearest bed, which happened to be Chris's. Jacy stared at the small mountain in amazement while her mother thanked the hotel employee and took care of the tip.

"Is there anything left in Adelaide to buy?" Jacy asked in a tone of marvel. "Or did the two of you scarf it all up?"

Chris was happily plundering the sacks. While Ian had always provided well for him, life was simple in the bush, and there were many things a young and harried father would not think to purchase.

Chris brought out a beautiful pair of riding boots made of buttery brown leather, and stacks of jeans and T-shirts, socks and underwear for Jacy to admire. Regina had also bought him toys—a Viewmaster and plenty of reels, several hand-held video games, a cassette player and tapes, and a soccer ball.

Jacy felt a stab of plain, old-fashioned jealousy. She'd wanted to give Chris some of those very things, but Regina had beaten her to the punch. When she met her mother's gaze, however, she could not be angry.

Regina had been generous; there was nothing wrong in that. The expression in the older woman's eyes was at once mischievous and pleading.

"It's all very lovely," Jacy said, ruffling Chris's hair. She knew Ian would be irritated, his formidable pride being what it was, but he'd get over it soon enough. After all, none of them loved Chris more than he did.

"There're things here for you, too," Chris went on, arranging his own booty neatly at one end of the bed lest there be any confusion and Jacy should claim the soccer ball or some other treasure by accident.

She hid a smile at that, looked at her mother, and shook her head in good-natured consternation. "What am I going to do with you, Mom?" she demanded, throwing up her hands in mock frustration.

"I haven't seen you wear anything decent or stylish since I arrived in this godfor—" Regina paused, remembering Chris. "Since I got here. Naturally I took matters into my own hands. You're still a size eight, aren't you?" She went over to the bed and started rustling bags. "Sizes are different here, but in the good boutiques the salespeople translate them well enough."

Regina pulled a silky lavender jumpsuit from one of the sacks and held it up.

Jacy adored the outfit on sight; her mother had excellent—and of course costly—taste. "Ian will love it," she said, just to nettle Regina a little.

Regina grimaced prettily. "It would look awful on him," she retorted, and all three of them broke up laughing. When that had subsided Regina, ever the queen bee, clapped her hands and ordered, "Come now, the both of you. Get yourselves bathed and changed. We'll take in a movie tonight, I think—and I have theater seats for tomorrow night."

Jacy sighed. Even if she'd wanted to resist Regina—which in this instance, at least, she didn't—it would have been like swimming upstream in a river of wet concrete.

When Regina had gone to her own room and Chris was in the tub, Jacy went through the gifts her mother had bought for her that day. Tailored trousers and blouses, jeans and T-shirts, lovely lingerie, a sleek little black dress of silk crepe and sexy shoes and stockings to compliment it. Makeup and perfume—in exactly the shades and fragrances Jacy would have chosen for herself.

After Chris was out of the bathroom and dressed in his Sunday clothes, Jacy went in and did a transformation of her own. She felt renewed and glamorous, wearing her new makeup, a pair of black slacks, a soft white blouse with a scoop neckline, and sandals. In the morning she would get a haircut and a manicure for good measure.

While she and Regina and Chris were eating in a restaurant just down the street from the hotel Jacy got a surprise. Andrew Carruthers, the American manager of Merimbula, approached their table. He was elegantly dressed, for an evening at the symphony or ballet, perhaps, and a stunningly beautiful red-haired woman walked beside him wearing an exquisite bejeweled evening gown with a medieval look about it.

"Mrs. Yarbro," Carruthers said warmly, as though he and Jacy were well acquainted. He looked around, feigning an expression of confusion. "I don't see your husband about."

"He's at home," Jacy replied politely. She hardly knew the man and had no reason to dislike him, but knowing how Ian felt about him, how Jake had felt, made her cautious. "This is my mother, Regina Walsh, and my stepson, Christopher."

Chris was glaring up at Mr. Carruthers, his small fists knotted in his lap.

More to this than meets the eye, Jacy thought, interested. What with all the excitement back at the property, she and Ian had never gotten around to continuing their discussion about his antipathy for their neighbor.

Carruthers's smile was like something varnished, hard and shiny. He nodded to Regina and Chris and put an arm around the woman. "My wife, Carol," he said.

Jacy shook hands with Carol and remembered a mission she'd intended to carry out. "I understand you have children," she said. "We would love for them to join us at Yolanda School."

Carol Carruthers laughed; it was a rigid, high-pitched sound. "We have a governess," she replied.

Jacy was undaunted. The forays into the Dog and Goose and her confrontations with Redley Shifflet had engendered a certain sense of derring-do. "That's lovely," she answered. "However, you might want to send your girls to school at least some of the time—it's important for kids to interact with others. That's how they learn to share, and to take care of themselves."

Carol's varnish didn't crack; her smile was blinding. "We'll consider it," she lied.

Mr. Carruthers said a few more things but, being preoccupied, Jacy forgot them five seconds after he and his wife walked away from the table.

"Pretty good bonding job," Regina remarked once the Carrutherses were out of earshot. "You could buy a racehorse with the money that woman has put into her mouth."

Chris had been flushed with some private fury, probably loyalty to his father, but now his skin was its normal golden shade again. "Mrs. Carruthers put money in her mouth?" he marveled, making a disgusted face.

Regina patted his shoulder. "Children are such literalists," she said to Jacy before looking the boy in the eyes and answering his question. "No, darling. It was a figure of speech meaning that she's had a lot of dental work."

Chris still looked a little confused. "Oh," he said, his gaze following Mr. and Mrs. Carruthers as they left the restaurant. "He's a no-gooder, that one."

"Why do you say that?" Jacy asked gently, pushing away her plate. Her appetite had been fluctuating wildly since she'd left the property; sometimes she was ravenously hungry, but sometimes the sight or smell of food nauseated her.

Chris leaned forward in his chair and lowered his voice, even though there was no danger of anyone overhearing him, since the tables were set far apart from one another. "Dad thinks he's had fires started, and even arranged to get blokes killed, though it always looked like an accident. Jake thought the same thing."

Jacy set her napkin aside. "Chris, those are very serious accusations. I hope you haven't been talking about them to just anybody."

Regina was leaning forward, an expression of intense interest on her face, her eyes narrowed. She loved drama, on stage or off. "Fascinating," she said.

Chris was looking earnestly at Jacy. "They want to drive all the small graziers out, those Merimbula people," he said with utter conviction. "Linus Tate says they'll bulldoze Yolanda to the ground and put wheat in its place if they get the chance."

"Still," Jacy began, feeling uneasy. If she could have gotten on a train, bus, or plane and headed straight back to the property at that moment, she would have done it. "Still, Christopher—to say they'd *kill* people—"

Chris was resolute. "They have," he insisted. "Ask my dad."

Jacy laid her hand over his. "I believe you, love," she said, frowning. "That's what frightens me." After that she deliberately turned the conversation in another direction.

Soon the three of them left the restaurant and took a taxi to a movie theater. They saw a Disney feature, though Chris argued strenuously for a bloody-looking action/adventure film, and while she watched the colorful figures moving and cavorting on the screen Jacy found her mind wandering.

To Ian.

Was he all right?

Was the weather good?

Did he miss her?

After the movie Regina and Chris shared a massive chocolate sundae while Jacy sat across from them, sipping tea and wishing she could telephone her husband. She felt an aching, urgent need to hear his voice.

When they'd returned to the hotel and Chris was tucked up in bed watching his beloved television, Jacy put a call through to Nancy at the Yolanda Café.

Her friend answered on the fourth ring, sounding, as always, as though she were singing instead of talking. "Yolanda Café. Nancy here."

"Nancy," Jacy said. She was crouched over the phone almost furtively, her hand cupped around the receiver. It was a silly reaction, but she couldn't seem to help herself. "It's Jacy Yarbro."

Nancy laughed, not with amusement, but with joy. "Jacy! How're things in the big smoke?"

"Fine," Jacy replied a little abruptly. She took a deep breath, let it out slowly. "I guess I'm just a bit homesick."

"Well, now, you'll be back soon, won't you? Have a good time while you can, love, and don't be spending your holiday moping about."

Jacy smiled. Just talking to Nancy was making her feel better, though she would have given a large part of her soul to speak to Ian. "How goes the revolution?"

Nancy chuckled. "Swimmingly. The males of Yolanda are starting to come 'round—it looks like you'll be running the show, with twice as many students to teach, when school takes up again."

Jacy's smile faded. "Has—has Redley come back?"

"No sign of that rotter," Nancy chimed cheerfully. "Darlis is as well as can be expected, and my aunt's called twice from Darwin to say how well little Gladys is getting on. Auntie took the child to a doctor straightaway and has found a children's therapist so that Gladys can get some counseling if it's needed."

"That's wonderful," Jacy said, her eyes filling with tears. She would remember, when her fears got to her, that Gladys, at least, had come out of the situation as a winner. Scarred and bruised, for certain, but a winner nonetheless.

271

At last Jacy had worked around to the real reason for her call. "Have you seen Ian?"

Nancy answered without hesitation. "Not hide nor hair. Guess he's busy with those brumbies of his, not to mention the sheep. Only reason he'd have to come to town would be to sit in the Dog and Goose and swill beer, and I guess he can do that at home."

"You're being diplomatic," Jacy said, smiling a little. "He's probably gotten himself banned from the pub for having such a renegade wife."

"Probably," Nancy agreed readily. "No worries, though. These blighters 'round here, they've known Ian all his life. They'll come 'round one of these days."

Nancy was probably right, but Jacy still felt a sting to know she'd made a rift between Ian and his scruffy mates. "I didn't mean to cause him so much trouble," she confided, half to herself.

Despite the questionable connection, Nancy heard her clearly. "Ian needed a bit of trouble," she said staunchly. "The whole lot of them did. If it hadn't been for you, they might have gone along in the same old track for *another* hundred years."

Jacy laughed, but there were tears in her eyes. "If you see Ian, will you give him my—regards, please?"

"Your *regards?*" Nancy countered wryly.

"For now," Jacy answered, laying a hand on her lower abdomen, where Ian's baby, her baby, was taking shape cell by cell.

Jacy could see Nancy rolling her eyes as clearly as if she'd been standing in the Yolanda Café looking at the woman. "Oh, *hell!*" Nancy laughed, probably shoving a hand through her short, glossy hair. "I'm going to tell him you're mad for him, that you can barely control your passion—"

Jacy flushed. She wasn't sure Ian knew she loved him— he was just obtuse enough not to have guessed—but he was definitely aware that she could "barely control her passion." He'd experienced the fact often enough.

She changed the subject out of self-defense.

"Is there anything I could bring you, Nancy? Books, clothes, makeup—anything like that?"

"Bring me a man," Nancy said brightly. "Mel Gibson would do."

"Mel Gibson is married," Jacy felt duty-bound to point out, though she was smiling as she spoke.

"Oh, hell," Nancy repeated. "Just use your imagination, then. And don't forget a single thing you see or buy or eat or do. I want to hear about it all!"

"You will," Jacy promised, thankful that she'd made such a good friend in such a short time. She hadn't another one like Nancy, even back in the States—Paul had been the last person she could talk to so freely.

The two women said good-bye and then rang off.

Jacy turned her attention to Chris as she was hanging up the receiver and saw that he was sleeping. Tenderly she kissed his forehead, tucked him in, and then went over to turn off the television set. She hoped she wouldn't be creating a monster, so to speak, by buying the promised satellite dish and TV; she certainly didn't want to see Chris's lively mind sucked into the screen.

Perhaps because of her nap, and because she was missing Ian so sorely, Jacy made double sure Chris was asleep, then got her key and crept out. A moment later she was knocking on her mother's door across the hallway.

After a brief interval the door swung open, and Regina stood in the opening, her hair up in foam curlers, her face covered with thick, sticky white cream.

"Come in," she commanded impatiently.

Jacy leaned back against the woodwork, her mouth twitching. She failed in her valiant effort not to smile, and that opened the way for a giggle.

Regina scowled at her. "Your day will come, my dear. Especially if you're silly enough to stay out there in the bush for the next forty years and let that wretched sun turn your complexion to leather!"

"It's the same sun that shines on Manhattan, Mother," Jacy pointed out, still smiling. "And let's not scrap. I came to thank you for giving Chris such a wonderful day and for sitting through that animated movie. I know you wanted to see the romantic comedy."

Regina sniffled. "Nonsense. I love Disney features."

Before Jacy could reply she heard a cry from outside in the hallway. Alarmed, thinking there might be a fire or some other disaster, she flung open the door.

Chris was standing in the center of the hall, his face pale, his eyes wild with panic. He was obviously still more asleep than awake. "I thought you'd gone and left me!" he wailed when he found Jacy.

She went to him immediately and dropped to her knees on the carpeted floor because he was small for nine, and she wanted to look straight into his frantic little face. "Sweetheart," she said, putting her arms around him and drawing him close, "I'll never leave you—never! And neither will your dad."

He was sobbing, his thin body shivering against Jacy's. She got to her feet and, casting one meaningful look in Regina's direction, led Chris into their room and put him back to bed.

"Why are you so afraid of being left?" she asked softly when he was settled. She was sitting on the side of his bed, holding his hand. "Or is it just that you miss your dad and Mrs. Wigget?"

"My mum went away," he said in a very small voice. "There was something bad about me."

Jacy's heart broke right in two. She smoothed his rumpled, sweat-dampened hair back with a gentle hand. "Oh, sweetheart, that just isn't true. I've known a lot of little boys in my time, and you're the best one ever. Honestly."

"Why didn't she want us, my dad and me?"

Jacy bit her lower lip, taking a moment to frame her

274

answer. "I don't know, honey," she finally replied, curving one hand around his sweet face. "But I'll tell you what— *I* want you—both of you. And I won't be going anywhere."

Chris nodded and settled deeper into the pillows. "I guess I acted like a baby," he confided. "You won't tell Thomas Jr., will you?"

"I won't tell anybody," Jacy said, kissing him on the forehead.

"Do you suppose my dad's all right? And Mrs. Wigget and Blue?"

Jacy smiled at Mrs. Wigget's being lumped in with Blue, Ian's favorite sheepdog. "I'm sure they're fine," she said, and that part, God forgive her, was an act. She was uneasy about Ian's safety and wanted to go home as much as or more than Chris did.

One thing was clear to her, at least, and that was the fact that she didn't miss city living. Adelaide was a beautiful, gracious place with every amenity, but Ian's property was home.

The strange sense of anxiety spinning in the pit of Ian's stomach grew stronger and more insistent with every passing day. The weather was hotter than ever, and there was an incendiary feeling to the heat, a sort of explosive portent.

The third day of Jacy's absence, as Ian and Tom Sr. were taking down the fence between his land and Jake's, because it was all one property now, Ian felt the hair rise on the back of his neck. He raised his head, pushed off his hat, and assessed the ferociously blue sky.

"Not a cloud to be seen," Tom commented, as though he'd read Ian's mind. Like Ian himself, the other man was dirty from head to foot, and his shirt was soaked with sweat. A wry twist to his mouth, he gestured toward the unrelenting sun. "Take a rest, you bastard," he muttered to that blazing star, so big and so close it almost seemed a man could touch it.

Ian scanned the dry land around them. Just his horse, and the dog, Blue, and Tom Sr.'s old truck. Except for those things the two men might have been alone on some arid planet in another part of the universe.

"Looking for somebody?" Tom Sr. asked. He didn't seem to expect an answer, which was a good thing, because there wasn't one forthcoming.

Ian shrugged and took hold of another fence post with his gloved hands, struggling to uproot it. He was missing his wife and boy, that was all, he told himself. He'd never really been separated from Chris before, and as for Jacy— well, she'd made a place for herself in his heart and mind as well as his home, and he felt dismembered without her.

The two men worked in concert for another hour without speaking a word, pulling up weathered fence posts, cutting the barbed wire stretched between, loading both in the bed of Tom Sr.'s truck.

Tom Sr. broke the silence, grinning. "The wife's got cold beer in the fridge," he said. "Let's get over to Corroboree Springs and have a drop."

Ian thought of the Dog and Goose, where he'd been welcome ever since he'd come of age, and felt a certain defiant sorrow. "She won't be wanting the pair of us underfoot, now, will she?" he countered. "Let's go to town instead."

Tom Sr. nodded, affable to the bone, and got into his truck. "I'll meet you at your hay shed," he said, watching as Ian swung up onto the back of his horse.

Ian touched the brim of his hat in acknowledgment.

Half an hour later he stepped over the threshold of the Dog and Goose, with Tom McAllister right behind him. And found Redley Shifflet sitting at the bar, big as life.

"You're not coming home with me, are you?" Regina asked as she and Jacy left the beauty salon the next morning, their hair freshly cut and styled and their nails manicured. Chris was with them, but he was wearing the earphones of his cassette player, listening to one of the tapes Regina had bought for him the first day.

Jacy shook her head. "Not only that," she said gently, "I can't wait to get back home. I miss Ian so much, sometimes I think I'm not going to be able to stand it."

Regina sighed. "Hormones," she said.

Jacy looked at Chris, who was humming loudly to the music no one else could hear, and whispered, "What I feel for Ian aside, you saw what happened last night. Do you think I could leave this little boy?"

There was a distinct softening in Regina's impeccably made-up face. "All right," she whispered back, "I admit that would be hard—very hard. But you can't sacrifice everything—"

"I'm not sacrificing anything," Jacy interrupted in a polite but firm tone. "In fact, sometimes it amazes me that I could be so blessed."

Regina linked her arm with Jacy's and patted her hand. She was silent, but there was no need to speak. Her sigh said volumes.

They spent the rest of the day shopping, ordering the satellite dish, the TV, and a lot of furniture and other household items as well, and returned to the hotel for an early dinner. Jacy was alone at the table, Chris and Regina having gone into the gift shop to buy postcards, when Andrew Carruthers appeared again.

Jacy jumped, startled.

"I'm sorry if I frightened you," Carruthers said quickly, smoothly, with a hint of a bow.

Jacy had the feeling he'd been watching her, waiting for her to be alone, and it made her nervous. In the next instant, though, she put the idea down to homesickness and sore feet.

"May I?" he asked, pulling back a chair.

Jacy nodded. "Sit down," she said.

"I suppose your husband has told you that we at Merimbula want to buy his land, as well as that which belonged to your father.''

Jacy took a sip from her water glass. What was it about this elegant, educated man that made her want to leap to her feet and run?

She reminded herself that her running days were over and stayed put.

"Yes," she answered. "And I know Ian's told you that we don't want to sell."

Carruthers arched one eyebrow and smiled benignly. "We're prepared to pay a price that would surprise you," he said.

"I have all the money I need, Mr. Carruthers," Jacy said.

At that moment she saw Chris entering the restaurant with Regina. Catching sight of Carruthers sitting at his stepmother's table, the little boy looked so fierce, so like Ian, that Jacy had to grin.

Carruthers followed her gaze and smiled indulgently. "I'm afraid the Yarbro men tend to dislike me," he said. "I'm not sure why."

"Maybe it's because you won't take no for an answer," Jacy replied, watching as Chris zeroed in on them, looking for all the world as if he planned to challenge the manager of Merimbula to a fistfight.

"I didn't get where I am, Mrs. Yarbro," Carruthers said moderately, "by giving up on the things I want."

Something in his tone, something ominous, brought Jacy's gaze to his face again. He slid his chair back and rose.

"When I go after something," he said, tugging at the sleeves of his perfectly tailored jacket, "I never fail."

Jacy refused to flinch. "You've met your match in Ian Yarbro, Mr. Carruthers," she said calmly just as Chris reached her side. "And in me."

Carruthers bowed again, gave the angry little boy an amused look, and walked away.

"What did he want?" Chris demanded.

Jacy gave her stepson an admiring glance. "To buy our land," she said, seeing no reason to be dishonest. "And I told him the same thing your father would have—no."

Chris watched Carruthers until he was out of the dining room, his eyes narrowed. "He's just lucky I didn't give him a knuckle sandwich," he said.

Regina's and Jacy's gazes met and just as quickly skirted each other. No one commented on the fact that Mr. Carruthers was bigger, older, and far stronger than Chris.

They spent the evening at the theater watching a road company perform *Les Misérables*. Jacy had seen the play half a dozen times, but it was one of her favorites, and she enjoyed every moment. Regina wept at the sad parts, dabbing delicately at her eyes so she wouldn't ruin her makeup, and Chris was on the edge of his seat the whole time.

When they returned to the hotel, physically and emotionally drained, the red message light on Jacy's phone was blinking, and even before she called the switchboard she knew the news wasn't good.

19

THE DOG AND GOOSE WAS A QUIET PLACE MOST OF THE time. The jukebox was set on low volume, and the clientele—mostly station hands, truck drivers, and graziers—talked in moderate voices, their words punctuated by the click of pool balls.

That afternoon, when Ian walked in with McAllister, the whole place went dead silent.

Ian felt exaltation and relief seeing Redley Shifflet leaning indolently against the bar, but not fear. He would be dealing with this no-gooder, not Jacy—that was enough, considering the unpredictability of fate.

He grinned, took off his hat, and flung it onto an empty table. Ignoring Redley for the moment, he shifted his attention to Bram McCulley, who stood with a glass in one hand and a dish towel in the other, still as a tombstone set in hard ground.

"You going to throw me out, Bram?" Ian asked.

Bram's ugly mug shaped itself into a nervous smile. "No, mate—never that. That wife of yours, though, she's another matter altogether. I make no promises there."

Ian laughed. "Good enough," he said. Out of the corner of his eye he saw Redley move away from the bar and draw the knife he wore in his belt.

Ian was ready; he had been for days.

"Here, now," Bram protested, reaching for his handy rifle. "Put that blade down, Shifflet—"

Holding up one hand to silence his mate, Ian stared straight into Redley's mean, rum-fevered eyes. He looked half mad, Redley did, like a wild boar cornered in a thicket, and he was so filthy that the dirt was ground into his skin.

"Where's me girl?" Shifflet demanded, holding up the knife for everyone to see. He was good with a blade, being an idle man, for the most part, with plenty of time to practice such things.

Ian put his hands on his hips, keeping his body loose. Adrenaline made his blood race, but he was still, and he wore his cockiest grin. "Which girl is that?"

The muscles in Shifflet's skinny neck corded, and he looked as though he'd choke on his own Adam's apple. "Damn you, Ian, you know I'm talkin' about me own Gladys!"

"She's in a safe place," Ian said. "For now, that's all you need to know."

Shifflet paled beneath the thick layer of dirt. "I'll have the law on you, you bastard—you stole me daughter away!"

Ian eyed the blade—it was grungy and stained, like its owner, and, again like Redley, inherently dangerous. "The law, is it? I'd welcome that—give me a chance to explain to the police what a son of a bitch you really are, it would."

Shifflet's gray-as-grave-dust pallor turned to a crimson flush in an instant. If the blighter didn't watch himself, Ian thought, he was liable to have a heart attack on the spot and save Ian the trouble of taking his knife away and cutting out his rotten gizzard. "I'll kill you if you don't tell me where she is!"

Ian made a beckoning gesture, curving the fingers of both hands. "Give it a try," he said. "But why don't we go outside first? It wouldn't be right to slop your blood all over Bram's floor.''

The other men in the pub, including McAllister, were silent. Ian couldn't see them—it seemed there was a haze forming a ring around him and Redley—but he felt their presence. Knew they were with him, even if they still bore a common grudge over the trouble Jacy had stirred up.

Redley stood glaring at Ian, a mad and cunning creature, devoid of the scruples other men held. "It's that sheila— that Yank bitch—who brought this on. I'll see her suffer once I've carved out a piece of you, Ian Yarbro.''

A murderous rage came over Ian; he clamped his jaw down hard in the effort to control his temper. It wouldn't do to lose his head now, wouldn't do at all. Anger made a man reckless. He stepped aside and gestured toward the door, inviting Redley to precede him into the dry, dusty street beyond.

"You like hurting women, don't you, Redley?'' Ian drawled when the other man stood stiff-legged, staring at him with those beady, too-bright eyes. "That's because you're a coward. A weakling.''

Everything in Redley strained to sunder and tear and kill; the hatred was visible in his bearing, and on him like a smell, too, dank and sour.

"Afraid to turn your back on me, mate?'' Redley drawled in a mock-cordial voice.

"I'd sooner let a crocodile get behind me,'' Ian said, smiling again. He'd reached the door and opened it, holding it wide. "Come along now,'' he added. "I'm a thirsty man wanting me beer, and I can't have it until I'm done with you.''

Redley hesitated, then strolled past Ian, over the sidewalk, and into the street.

"Let it lie, Ian,'' Bram said from somewhere in the pounding fog that edged Ian's vision. "The man's crazy as a ship rat—he'll kill you if he can.''

Ian didn't reply. He followed Redley outside, and they

stood facing each other under the brutal, late-day sun like two gunslingers in an American movie. The difference was that Shifflet was armed, and Ian wasn't.

And he didn't give a damn.

"All right, Redley," he said, squinting against the afternoon glare because he'd left his hat inside. "You've proven you can beat the snot out of women and little girls, but you didn't do so well against me the other night, now did you?"

Redley made a soft hissing sound, peculiar and somehow inhuman, and held up the knife. Parts of the blade glittered in the daylight, showing through the crud, and Ian noted with satisfaction that the other man's face was still faintly marked from their last encounter.

Shifflet's only reply was to spit in the dirt.

Ian waited. He knew he looked outwardly calm, but his blood was up, and he was eager for a fight.

In the same moment that Redley took a step toward Ian, brandishing the blade, Nancy appeared out of nowhere and hurled herself between the two men. Even before she spoke Ian caught the scent of disaster in the air and knew, right down to the marrow of his bones, why he'd been so uneasy for the past week or so.

"Bushfire!" she screamed, pointing wildly in the direction of Corroboree Springs and Merimbula.

Smoke was rolling on the horizon, the black plumes rimmed with crimson.

"Jesus," Ian whispered as panic swelled inside him. "My sheep!" He forgot Redley entirely and ran for Tom Sr.'s truck. McAllister was there ahead of him and had the engine started before Ian slammed the door on the passenger side.

"Good God," McAllister rasped, "I hope me wife's got the good sense to get herself and the boy down to the water!"

During the next few moments pandemonium reigned in the normally quiet streets of Yolanda. Men shouted curses and vows as they got into trucks and cars to head for their own land.

Tom Sr. dropped Ian off at home and then sped off for Corroboree Springs, promising to return as soon as he'd made sure his family was safe.

The smoke was thick and acrid, and even though he couldn't see the flames, Ian felt their heat and knew the fire was close by. Alice rushed out of the house, wringing her hands, and followed him into the stables.

He was busy opening the stall gates, driving the animals out. Instinct would carry them to safety, if the fates were kind; he'd gather the creatures later, when the danger was past, and bring them home.

"My cats!" Alice wailed, tears rolling down her leathery cheeks. "God in heaven, Ian, what about my cats? I've got to go to them!"

Ian proceeded to the yards, opening the gate, whistling shrilly to drive six more frightened horses out. They thundered off after the others, whinnying in terror.

He didn't need to look to know Alice's little caravan would be gone by now, eaten up by the voracious fire. For the moment, though, he couldn't spare the time for sentiment. "It's too late!" he bellowed over the frantic screams of the horses and the rising roar of the blaze. "Get out of here, Alice—get in your car and don't stop driving until you get to Yolanda!"

"My cats!" Alice sobbed. "My photographs, and all my cowboy books, and the letters my brother Willie wrote me during the Great War—"

"It's gone!" Ian yelled, shoving the woman toward her odd little car. "It's all gone, Alice—just get going!"

She chose then, of all times, to argue with him. "No!" she yelled back, standing her ground. She was a sturdy woman, was Alice, weighing as much or more than Ian himself, and immovable. "If I can't save my own place, at least I can help save this one!"

Ian could see the fire now, a moving line of crimson and

orange with black smoke roiling above it. He thought with despair of the sheep, and the men and dogs who looked after them. Then he grasped Alice's shoulders. "Never mind the goddamned homestead!" he roared. "Save yourself!"

She pulled away from him, coughing now from the dense smoke, weeping, and went to the side of the house to turn on the garden hose. Moments later she was spraying the walls and what she could reach of the roof.

Sparks flew through the air, catching here and there in the dry grass when they landed, catching on Ian's clothes while he checked the stables once more in case he'd overlooked any of the animals.

It was empty, and it was a good thing, because firebrands landed on the weathered old roof, and it went up in the space of a heartbeat.

Ian shouted at Alice again to flee for her life, and she ignored him again and went round to the front of the homestead, probably to turn on another hose.

There was no time to stand and argue with the woman, but Ian made a mental note to strangle her with his bare hands if the two of them were lucky enough to survive the ordeal that lay ahead.

Getting into his truck, Ian raced off to do what he could for his sheep, heading straight for the low line of fire bearing down on the only home he'd ever known. There were gaps in the blaze, and Ian wove through them, driving at top speed, knowing that at any moment he and the truck might go up like a torch.

He thanked God, choking and coughing, barely able to see for the smoke, that Jacy and Chris were far away in Adelaide.

Soon enough he crossed through the fire line and found himself in a blackened wasteland where nothing remained but a scattering of charred sheep carcasses. Here and there spirals of smoke twisted in the still, hot air.

Ian felt a sheen of tears in his eyes and drew his arm

across his face. He pressed on, assessing the damage, finding more dead sheep, and still more.

He turned the wheel violently, nearly overturning the truck, when he spied the series of hills and gullies off to the west. There the land was singed and smoky, but the fire had passed it by.

Ian found a sizable mob huddled in one of the gullies bleating their beautiful, brainless heads off, and he jumped out of the truck only a split second after bringing it to a stop. He struck the ground running, his clothes wet with sweat and black with soot. They were scared, the woollies were, but these few, at least, had been spared.

Ian dropped to his knees in the grass. Not knowing whether to celebrate or to mourn, he did both.

After a few moments of quiet hysteria he felt it again— the prickling at his nape, the lifting of the small hairs there. He got up and turned, only to see Redley Shifflet standing on the low knoll above the gully, sighting in his dog rifle.

With a smile Shifflet pulled the trigger.

Ian felt the bullet rip into his flesh, felt the inside of his chest catch fire, and rolled forward onto the ground, aware of nothing.

Jacy trembled as she pushed the button that would connect her with the hotel's front desk. Chris, sensing her fear, perched on the edge of his bed, watching her with wide eyes.

The telephone rang once, twice, three times. Finally someone picked up, and Jacy introduced herself in a tremulous voice and asked for her messages.

There was only one. *Call Nancy. It's urgent.*

It took forever to get through to the Yolanda Café; the line was old, and crackling static fairly obliterated Nancy's voice.

"We've got a bad connection because of the fire!" Nancy shouted over the terrible noise. "Listen carefully, love— Ian's been shot. Collie brought him to Adelaide in his plane—Mercy Hospital in Queen Charlotte Street—do you know it?''

Jacy closed her eyes, sick with shock and yet not truly surprised at all. "Yes," she replied in a strong voice, not because she felt strong, but because strength was what was required of her. Jake had been at Mercy Hospital, too. "How bad is it, do you know?" she yelled, opening her eyes, forcing herself to meet Chris's fearful gaze.

"No!" Nancy shouted. "All I can tell you is that McAllister fellow found him lying on the ground and bleeding—"

At that, the connection was broken.

Jacy hung the receiver up carefully.

"My dad's been hurt," Chris said. "He's dead." He bolted from his seat on the bed with sudden, violent energy, his voice rising. "He's dead, he's dead!"

Jacy clasped her stepson's wiry little wrists and held him. He was strong in his fear and grief and writhed ferociously in her grasp.

"Stop it!" she cried at last. "I don't know how bad it is, and we can't go to Mercy Hospital and find out until you get hold of yourself!"

Chris went still. His eyes remained wild and glazed, though, and he was pale as death. He sniffled and made a manful effort to pull himself together. "Redley Shifflet shot him," he said, sounding more like an old, old man than a nine-year-old. "Or those bloody bastards at Merimbula."

"That's not important now," Jacy said, snatching up her purse and room key, along with a light wrap to protect her from the evening chill. "Hurry, Chris—your dad will need us."

Pausing only to collect Regina, who nearly fainted when her daughter blurted out the news of Ian's shooting, Jacy set out for the elevators. They caught a taxi in front of the hotel, with the help of the doorman, and sped off toward Mercy Hospital.

On arrival Jacy ran inside the modern building and all but collided with the admittance desk. She was told that

Ian had just arrived by ambulance from an outlying airfield. He had been taken upstairs to surgery straightaway, and his condition was critical.

He was alive. Jacy clung to that, repeated it to herself like a litany. Ian was alive, he was breathing, his heart was beating.

A nurse took the three of them to the surgical floor and showed them to one of the waiting rooms. She brought Jacy a blanket and ordered her to lie down, saying she looked as though she might go into shock at any moment, but Jacy refused. She and Chris sat huddled together in the corner of a sofa while Regina paced up and down in front of a row of vending machines, still clad in the blue sequined dress she'd worn to the theater.

Jacy, too, was still wearing the sleek black crepe.

They'd been waiting about fifteen minutes, according to the large clock on the wall, when Collie came in. He looked like a shrunken version of himself; his clothes were dirty and rumpled, and his expression was bleak.

Jacy stood, went to him on trembling legs.

"What happened?" she asked, almost in a whisper.

Collie was overwhelmed; he plainly wanted to bolt and run. He was a hero when it came to flying that asthmatic old plane of his, but emotionally he was out of his depth. "I—there was a bushfire—that McAllister bloke went lookin' for Ian—and found him shot."

Jacy envisioned the scene only too clearly—she had seen it many times before in her nightmares, and in those unguarded conscious moments when her fears had sneaked up on her, caught her off guard. She closed her eyes for a moment, and the vision, instead of lessening, remained cruelly vivid.

Chris had come to stand beside her, and she held him close with one arm. "The fire—do you know how bad it was?"

Collie looked intently at one of the vending machines, as though he expected it to prompt him, tell him what to say.

When he met Jacy's gaze again his eyes were glazed with some troubling memory. "It got a lot of sheep and grass, that fire," he said. "Burned itself out, though."

Jacy thought briefly of Corroboree Springs and Ian's house, but she wouldn't spare the effort to worry about them. For the moment she was only concerned with Ian's well-being.

"It was Redley Shifflet that shot my dad," Chris said with absolute conviction, sounding like a miniature grown-up. "Did they catch him? Is he in jail?"

Collie reached out and lightly ruffled Chris's hair. Jacy's throat tightened painfully because she'd seen Ian make the same gesture so many times, because he might never do it again.

She swayed, squeezing her eyes shut in a fruitless effort to brace herself against a swell of emotional pain. Dear God, Ian might never know he was going to be a father, let alone see the baby and hold it in his arms.

A hoarse sound, incoherent and animallike, rose in Jacy's throat. Collie took one of her arms, Regina the other, and they led her back to the sofa and made her sit down.

Collie stayed as long as he could bear to, then made his excuses and left. Jacy didn't blame him; she knew it was his nature to light somewhere for a short time, then fly away and come in for a landing in yet another place.

The night wore on.

Chris fell asleep, slumped in a chair—he'd have a crick in his neck when morning came, Jacy was sure, but she didn't have the heart to wake him. Regina nodded off over a magazine, snoring softly.

It wasn't yet dawn when a doctor awakened Jacy—she'd slept a cramped and fitful sleep on the short sofa—by gently grasping her shoulder. "Mrs. Yarbro?"

Jacy's heart went into maximum overdrive. She sat up, blinking and dazed, her lips moving with a silent prayer. Let him be alive. Oh, God, please let Ian be alive!

"How is my husband?" Her voice was a whisper, raspy and thick.

"Mr. Yarbro is holding his own," the physician said. He was a short, middle-aged man with a kindly face and compassionate gray eyes. "There was considerable damage to the chest wall, along with some serious internal injuries."

"Is he conscious?"

"He's been in Recovery an hour or so. He's probably at least partially aware of his surroundings."

"I want to see him," Jacy and Chris said in chorus.

The doctor smiled and patted the boy's shoulder. "One at a time," he agreed. "And only for a little while."

Regina had awakened, and for once in her life she seemed unconcerned with her smudged makeup and sleep-mussed hair. She put an arm around Chris's shoulders and said softly, "I'll keep Christopher company while you're gone."

Chris didn't protest, though his longing to be with his father was etched plainly in his small face. "Tell Dad I'm here, please," he said.

Jacy nodded, touched his hair gently, and followed the doctor out of the waiting room and down a long hallway lined with curtained windows and closed doors. Except for the *ching-ching* of the elevator bell the place was almost completely silent.

Finally they entered a spacious ward filled with morning light, and at first all Jacy saw were hospital beds and machines with cords trailing across the floor. Then she found Ian.

He was wan and gaunt, and there were tubes going into both his arms as well as his nose. He opened his eyes and looked at her, and her hand trembled as she reached out to touch the closest part of him—his foot.

Ian's toes wriggled against her palm, then his eyelids dropped, and he drifted off into sleep or unconsciousness.

Jacy squeezed his toes, her own eyes hot with tears, and silently begged him not to leave her.

"You can speak to him," the doctor said gently. "We're not sure whether or not patients can hear when they're not conscious, but in some part of his mind he'll know you're with him. That can make all the difference."

Jacy nodded, let go of Ian's foot, and moved to stand at the head of the bed. Looking down at her husband, lying there that way, immobilized, she saw the vulnerability he'd hidden so well ever since she'd known him. She wanted to touch his face, to smooth his hair back the way she'd done with Chris in that age-old effort to give comfort.

She bent close to him, forgetting the doctor's presence, the hovering nurses, the other patients. "I love you, Ian Yarbro," she said clearly. "Do you hear me? *I love you.*"

He opened his eyes, and she thought she saw the merest flicker of mirth in their violet depths, but he was asleep again just as quickly. Jacy didn't know if he'd really understood or if the action had been a physical reflex or some subliminal reaction to her presence.

She kissed his muscled forearm, lingered a few more minutes, and then slipped out because she knew Chris wanted to come in.

After the little boy had had his turn to visit—Ian didn't open his eyes again while Chris was there—Regina insisted that they all get some breakfast in the hospital cafeteria. Once they'd eaten, Jacy's mother went back to the hotel.

When she returned a little over an hour later Regina was wearing slacks and a crisp blouse. Her hair and makeup were perfect, and she was a veritable whirlwind of efficient energy. She'd brought fresh clothes for Jacy and Chris, and she arranged for them to have showers.

Jacy was grateful for Regina's thoughtfulness, glad she was there to make a difficult vigil a little easier.

"I've arranged to have our things moved to a quaint hotel just down the street from here," Regina announced when Jacy returned to the waiting room after taking her shower.

She felt stronger and braver now that she'd eaten and washed, and she gave her mother a grateful hug.

The day wore on, and Ian's condition didn't change. He didn't get worse, but he wasn't getting better, either. He seemed to be hovering on the brink, undecided.

When he was moved into a private room at long last, Jacy sat on one side of his bed and Chris sat on the other. Regina was in and out, bringing sandwiches and coffee and milk, chatting with the nurses, looking in on patients in nearby rooms.

At around six o'clock that evening Ian began to stir. After an hour or so he opened his eyes again, focusing on Chris's face for a long moment. A shadow of a grin touched his lips before he tumbled back into deep sleep.

Regina persuaded Chris to go to their new hotel for dinner and some television, now that Ian was plainly on the mend, but Jacy wouldn't leave her husband's side. She sat there stubbornly, shaking her head when first one nurse and then another tried to make her go.

She ate part of the pizza Regina had sent over and finally fell asleep with her forehead resting on Ian's arm. His voice awakened her, though it was barely more than a hoarse whisper, sometime in the depths of the night.

"Go home, sheila," he said, laboring over each word. "Go home to America—there's nothing left for you here."

Jacy sat bolt upright. Every muscle in her body throbbed, she felt like she was going to throw up at any moment, and yet she'd never been more determined. "What's the deal here, Yarbro?" she asked with a shaky, defiant smile. The room was dark except for thin light coming in from the hallway, and his face was craggy with shadows. "Are you trying to get rid of me so you can take up with another woman?"

Ian closed his eyes for a moment, visibly gathering his strength. God in heaven, but he was magnificent, even then, lying in a hospital bed with tubes and needles stuck into him, his chest swathed in surgical bandages.

He looked at her directly. Fiercely. "I don't love you anymore," he said.

The words struck Jacy like a steamroller going downhill, smashed her, but she didn't let her pain show. For the time being Ian had a corner on suffering; she would set her own aside no matter what it cost her to do so. "I didn't know you ever did," she responded. "But it doesn't really matter. You don't have to love me. You're a good husband in spite of that, and a good father to Chris." She leaned in close and lowered her voice. "Not to mention that you're great in bed. We can build on those things."

Ian stared at her for a long time, as if memorizing her features, and the misery in his gaze stemmed from more than just his physical condition. "It's gone. Corroboree Springs. The sheep. All of it," he said at long last.

Once more Jacy steeled herself not to react. Later, when Ian wasn't looking, she could find some private place to cry and beat her fists against the wall. For now she managed a watery smile. "I guess we'll just have to start over, then," she said. "We're young. We can do it."

A sheen of tears glistened in Ian's eyes, pooled along his lower lashes. "No," he said, shaking his head once. "No."

Jacy felt his agony keenly. She bent and kissed his forehead, silently thanking God for sparing his life. Everything beyond that, as far as she was concerned, was an embarrassment of riches. She considered telling him about the baby, but she wasn't absolutely certain she was pregnant because she hadn't had a test. Besides, Ian was hurting now. He might see the child as a burden instead of a reason to hold on, to hope.

"Rest," she said, and she sank back into her chair again, her fingers spread over his.

Ian watched her for a long time, his soul plainly visible in his eyes, but finally he drifted off.

Chris and Regina arrived bright and early, and Regina ordered Jacy to go and get some rest at the hotel, reminding her of the baby in an effort to reinforce her point.

"Baby?" Chris said, looking up from his portable video game.

Jacy shushed him, glancing nervously in Ian's direction. He was still sleeping, fortunately.

"We'll talk about it later," she promised her stepson.

Chris smiled for the first time since they'd learned Ian had been injured. "A baby," he marveled, with wonder shining in his face.

That time Ian awakened. There was no hope that he hadn't heard and understood; his eyes were sad as they searched Jacy's face. She leaned close to him, touching her forehead to his, and only she heard what he said.

"No. Oh, God, no."

20

HE PAIN WAS LIKE A GREAT IRON BOOT PRESSING DOWN
on Ian's chest, overflowing into his arms and his legs and
his head. The despair was even more crushing.

Lying in his hospital bed, Ian watched Jacy through his
eyelashes for long periods of time when she thought he was
sleeping. God help him, he loved her, and he cherished
their unborn baby, too, even though he'd managed to hide
his jubilation when she'd had herself tested and reported
the results as positive.

He had nothing to give her now, with most of his sheep
gone and probably the homestead as well, and certainly
nothing to offer another child. No, it was better for Jacy,
and for their baby, if she did what her mother wanted and
took herself back to the States.

Life was too hard in the bush, too treacherous and unpredictable. Especially for an infant.

Slanting his gaze toward the window, Ian studied his
young son. Chris was thriving, in spite of recent hard times.
Jacy's going would be a wrenching thing to him; the boy

was bound to see it as a betrayal, and there was no guarantee that he'd ever get over the loss. Still, it had been just the two of them before, and somehow they'd get on.

Chris's video game made an electronic blipping sound that got under Ian's right temple and pounded there. The lad must have felt his dad's eyes on him, because he met Ian's look straight on and smiled.

Ian's heart twisted. He couldn't afford to love another child the way he did this one—it was just too dangerous.

He looked away toward Jacy, who was perched on the wide sill of the window wearing slim jeans and an orange T-shirt, fair hair tousled, completely absorbed in a paperback book.

Ian felt a stab of irritation. Here he was, trying his best to get rid of the woman, to send her packing, and she was so unmoved by his decision that she could read some silly novel.

If he couldn't get her to go by asking politely, he thought, he'd have to be mean about it. He didn't care for that idea, for even though he enjoyed a good brawl now and then, with his mates down at the Dog and Goose, there was none of the bully in him.

Ian bit his lower lip, wondering if the old pub still stood. For all he knew, the bushfire might have wiped out the whole of Yolanda as well as his own holdings and those Jake had left to Jacy.

An abysmal depression settled over him, as heavy as his injuries.

"Why don't you get out of here," he growled at Jacy, who looked up at him in pleasant bewilderment, "and give a man a chance to rest!"

Jacy smiled. "I'm not sure whether it's rest you need," she replied in dulcet tones, "or an enema."

Ian felt color surge up his neck and into his face. Damn it, she'd bested him, and in front of his son, too. Never mind that he'd asked for it.

To make matters worse, Chris laughed. They exchanged

a look, the pair of them, like conspirators, and Ian was that much more furious. "Go on, the lot of you," he barked. "I'm tired of looking at your faces."

Jacy winked at Chris, then turned her sunny smile on Ian again. "Then don't look," she said. "We're not going anywhere."

And they didn't.

Ian was outraged at such flagrant disobedience, but then, he couldn't think why he'd expected anything else. A part of him, tucked away under layers of sorrow and emotional scar tissue, rejoiced because Jacy refused to leave him.

"Let me try that," he rasped, reaching out a hand toward Chris.

The boy handed him the video game, beaming.

"You're not going home with me, are you?" Regina asked glumly on the fifth day of the vigil as she and Jacy sat drinking coffee in the hospital cafeteria. Chris was upstairs with his grumpy father.

Jacy shook her head and smiled sadly.

Regina leaned forward, her voice lowered to a raspy whisper. "Ian's rejected you, Jacy," she pointed out. "He said so, and now he won't even speak to you!"

It was true. Ian laughed and chatted with Chris, but he'd stopped talking to Jacy at all. Once in a while she caught him looking at her, and each time the bemused expression in his eyes had soured into a scowl.

"Ian thinks he's saving me and our baby from a grim life on the charred and barren frontier," Jacy said. "He'll get over it."

She hoped to high heaven she was right in her suspicion, because if it turned out that her husband really didn't want her anymore, she was going to be devastated. For the present, she was taking things one crisis at a time.

Jacy saw the worry in her mother's eyes and understood it. She reached out to pat Regina's hand. "Go home to

Michael, Mother," she said gently. "I'm a big girl now. I can look after myself."

Regina smiled. "Yes, I suppose you can," she said. "Still, to just leave you here with that grouchy bear of a husband—God knows if you even have a home to go back to—"

"We'll manage," Jacy said quietly.

Regina drew a deep, resolute breath and let it out slowly. "Very well, then. I guess I'll get over to the hotel and start packing." She pushed back her chair, stood, and then abruptly sat down again, studying Jacy's face imploringly. "Are you *sure* you don't want to come back to New York?"

"Positive," Jacy said. "Just like my pregnancy test."

Regina made a sound of elegant and affectionate disgust and left the cafeteria.

Jacy lingered over her coffee for a while, then gathered all her emotional forces and went upstairs to beard the lion in his den. This was one standoff Ian Yarbro wasn't going to win.

When she reached the doorway of his room she stopped on the threshold, stunned to find Andrew Carruthers there, seated next to Ian's bed, with an open briefcase in his lap.

Ian looked at her with an expression of mingled defiance and desolation, and she felt the color drain from her face.

"What are you doing here?" she demanded of Carruthers, even though she knew.

"Leave it alone, Jacy," Ian warned. "It's none of your concern."

"The hell it isn't!" she cried, her voice rising a little with each word. "You're trying to sell my land out from under me!" She gestured toward Carruthers. "And this lowdown, sorry-looking weasel is trying to buy it!"

A grin twitched at the corner of Ian's mouth, and he subdued it, but not before Jacy saw. "Your property is worthless without the springs, sheila—and the water hole is mine. I can sell it if I wish."

Jacy stormed into the room, grabbed a stack of suspicious-looking papers out of Carruthers's open briefcase, and waved them over her head. "You just try it, Ian Yarbro!" she challenged, dodging the unwelcome visitor from Merimbula when he tried to grab for the documents. "I'll have you tied up in court for the rest of your natural life!"

It was then that she remembered Chris, who had been sitting on the windowsill, taking in the whole scene. He was grinning in admiration and encouragement.

At least *somebody* was on her side, Jacy thought as she ripped the contract to bits and threw it up in the air. It descended like snow.

Carruthers was muttering, and Ian's face was unreadable.

"I'll have another agreement drawn up," the American said, looking warily at Jacy, as if she'd lost her mind, and she supposed she had. Temporarily, at least.

"Don't bother," she said.

"You've lost all but a few head of your sheep," Carruthers argued, red-faced now, snapping his briefcase shut with a vengeance. "The house and barn at Corroboree Springs are completely gone, and so are every last one of the outbuildings at your husband's place—the stables, the shearing shed, all of it."

Jacy hadn't known the damage was so bad as that; she guessed she'd consoled herself with the fantasy that the bush had been satisfied with Ian's blood. Instead it had spat fire, like some dragon, and consumed her legacy as well.

"Get out," she said to Carruthers, but her voice was small, and her knees shook.

She collapsed into a chair.

"What the hell did you think you were doing just now?" Ian growled through his teeth. "Maybe the kind of money Carruthers was throwing about means nothing to you—a spoiled rich girl—but it would mean a new start for Chris and me!"

"Just us?" Chris interrupted tremulously. His smile had

faded, and his freckles seemed to stand out from his skin the way they always did when he was upset. "What about Mum, and the nipper?"

Ian closed his eyes for a moment, and his face was granite-hard when he looked at Jacy again. His words, though, were directed to Chris. "We don't need them," he said coldly. "We got along just fine before."

Jacy had been through a great deal in recent days. She was pregnant and exhausted, and her nerves were strained to the snapping point. She'd been eating only enough to keep going, and most of what she forced herself to swallow didn't stay down.

On top of everything else, Ian's words were too much.

She burst into tears with a wailing cry, but instead of fleeing from the room she snatched an extra pillow from the closet shelf and clubbed Ian with it. She struck him again and again until two nurses rushed in and stopped her.

Ian wasn't hurt—she'd never intended that—but he was pale as he stared at her, amazed by her outburst. Chris was hunched over his video game, his small shoulders trembling, and Jacy couldn't guess whether the child was laughing or crying.

"Here now," clucked one of the nurses, pulling Jacy gently toward the door, "she's at the end of her tether, poor thing, and needs a rest."

"Out on her feet," agreed the other woman, hurling a tart glance at Ian. "It's no wonder, either, with this one ignoring her half the time and bellowing at her the other." She made a huffing sound. "Ungrateful, I call it."

Jacy lay down in an empty bed, for she had no strength left to resist—Ian had taken it all. She slept soundly straight through dinner and didn't so much as stir until morning.

After a visit to the hotel, where she'd showered, put on fresh clothes, and looked in on a still-sleeping Chris, she returned to Ian's room. He was alone, and he didn't look any friendlier than he had the night before.

"It won't help, your acting like a bastard," Jacy announced crisply, "though I must say you've refined the technique. If you want me out of your life, you'll have to get a lawyer—excuse me, a solicitor—in here and start divorce proceedings. And even that will be pretty futile, because you'll have to throw me out of our house bodily to get me to leave. And it looks like it'll be a while before you have the strength to do that." She paused to take a breath, half enjoying the furious bewilderment in Ian's eyes. "Of course, if you do give me the boot, I'll just find a place in Yolanda and plague you from there. You'll be the talk of the Dog and Goose, letting your poor, helpless, pregnant wife fend for herself that way. Maybe I'll have twins and go around with bare feet—that would *really* make you look bad."

Ian's jaw tightened. He engaged in some internal struggle for a few moments, then muttered, "Why, Jacy? Why would you want to stay when you know I don't care for you, don't care for our baby?"

It was hard to keep from crying in the face of such coldness, but Jacy managed it. She'd learned a lot about courage in recent weeks. "I don't believe you, that's why," she answered. "I think you do love me, though God knows you probably wish you didn't, and you'll love our baby, too. That's the kind of man you are—you couldn't turn your back on Chris, and it'll be the same with this child. Personally, I hope we have a little girl, with your blue eyes and dark hair—"

"There's no point in all this, Jacy," he broke in grimly. "I'm selling out to Merimbula. It's only a matter of time before Carruthers comes back with another sheaf of legal papers."

"You idiot!" Jacy whispered, closing the door to the hospital room. "Are you out of your mind? Don't you think it was awfully convenient for the folks at Merimbula that you got shot when you did?"

Ian frowned. "It was Redley Shifflet—I saw him pull the trigger."

Jacy took a moment to react to the image, to struggle against the emotional reverberations of it. Then she went to stand beside the bed. "Who better? He wanted to kill you, and everybody knew it. And a little cash from Merimbula would have made the deal that much sweeter for scum like Shifflet."

"You've been watching too much television," Ian said, but he spoke slowly, thoughtfully, and with a lot of uncertainty.

"We'll never prove it, of course," Jacy rushed on, undaunted. "It's the perfect crime. Nobody on the face of the earth would believe Redley had been paid to do you in—everybody knows he's a mad dog, and that he hates your guts in the bargain." She jabbed at Ian's bandaged chest with an index finger for emphasis. "And you know you've been suspicious of Carruthers's methods of dealing with competition—so was Jake."

Ian narrowed his eyes, pondering the case. Then he glared at Jacy again; he'd done it often, and the hostility in his expression was expert.

"You're right—we'll never prove it. Either way, I'm finished as a grazier."

Jacy folded her arms. "I never guessed you could be such a wimp," she said. "One little fire and you're *finished?*"

Ian's face was downright stormy. In fact, Jacy figured if he could have gotten out of bed—he still had an IV needle in his right arm—he might have throttled her. "One—little—fire," he repeated very slowly. "Add to that a near-fatal gunshot wound, a global recession, and the fact that I was barely scraping by in the first place, and yes, I'm through."

She held her tongue for a few seconds, pondering the enormity of what he'd said, and gave the area immediately surrounding Ian a quick glance just to make sure there was nothing he could throw at her.

"Have you forgotten, Ian? You married a rich woman."

His free hand knotted into a fist, and he glowered up at the ceiling, but he said nothing for a long time. When he finally looked at Jacy again his aspect was bleak. "I won't take your money," he said.

Jacy felt it all slipping away, everything she held dear, everything she'd dreamed about since her marriage to Ian. "Why not?" she demanded. "That's why you married me, isn't it?"

A quiet, savage rage flickered in his eyes, and his skin was pallorous. "No," he answered, his voice as relentless and cold as a New England winter. "I married you for the water."

She stood at the foot of his bed, gripping the iron rails in both hands. "Liar," she said. "Jake gave you the springs outright, remember? No wedding required."

He was silent, angry, broken. Jacy longed to put her arms around him, to soothe and comfort and reassure him in much the same way she'd done with Chris, but it wasn't the time for that. Not yet.

"If it wasn't my money, what was it?" she persisted.

Ian's determination to drive her away was formidable; Jacy had a terrible, desperate feeling that she was losing the battle. "Sex," he said. "You were a good lay. But then there are plenty of those about, aren't there?"

"That was a lousy thing to say!"

He was absolutely obdurate. "True nonetheless," he said, looking out through the window instead of at Jacy.

She was crying by then, there was no hiding it. "Don't do this, Ian. Don't drive me away just when you need me most. And think about Chris! His life is in upheaval as it is. Does he have to lose the stepmother who promised never to leave him, on top of everything else?"

"I don't love you," he said, still not meeting her eyes.

Jacy left the room with her shoulders straight, her chin high, and her heart in splinters.

She almost collided with Nancy and Alice Wigget, who were just coming down the hall.

Nancy immediately took Jacy into her arms for a quick hug. "Oh, Lord, look at you. Ian's been a bear, I see."

Jacy sniffled and tried to smile, and it didn't matter that the effort failed miserably, because these two women were her friends. She didn't have to keep up a front for them.

Alice was actually wearing a dress, her infamous tattoo covered by a long sleeve, and she had on a straw hat that had probably gone out of style sometime in the sixties. She rolled her eyes. "He can be that impossible, our Ian. Don't worry your head about it, though. I'll sort him out soon enough."

Jacy's smile came more easily that time.

"I'm going to throw the first punch," Nancy said with narrowed eyes, and she turned on her heel to march into Ian's room.

Alice, for her part, took Jacy's arm and tugged her along to the waiting area. They sat facing each other across a round table next to the vending machines.

"I've come to see Ian all right," Alice said, looking reluctant, guilty, and determined all at once. When she went on, it was in a rush of words. "But there's more. It's taken the heart right out of me, that fire. I found my cats, thank the Lord, but my photographs are gone, and my books, everything I had that mattered. I've given the cats to Sara McCulley—she's a good sort and can be trusted to look after them proper—and I'm off to America to look for a cowboy."

Jacy took Alice's work-worn hand, full of sympathy and respect. "I'm so sorry—about your things, I mean. The fire must have been terrible."

Alice shuddered. "I've never been so frightened in all my life. Saved the main homestead, I did, but everything else is gone. Ian's horses are scattered from here to hell's front parlor by this time, and he lost all but a handful of the sheep. Not many were burned to death—that's a mercy, isn't it?—but the smoke finished them off just the same."

"Were any—any people killed?" Jacy held her breath.

Alice shook her head. "No—not so they'd have to lie down from it, anyway. But a lot of the graziers lost stock and buildings the way Ian did, and it will be the end of them." She gazed at Jacy for a few moments, as though gauging her ability to take more bad news. "Corroboree Springs is gone, too—the sheds and the homestead itself, I mean."

"I know," Jacy said. She supposed the tragedy wouldn't be real to her until she saw the charred remains of her father's house.

Alice was rummaging in her large canvas traveling purse. "Ellie McAllister managed to save these, though. I thought you might want them, since they're so cheery to look at and all."

Jacy accepted a shoe box, lifted the lid, and found her shell collection inside. For just a moment all was beautiful and right with the world again.

"Thank you," Jacy murmured.

Alice stood, smoothing her crumpled dress awkwardly. "Well, I'll go in and say my farewells to Ian now. I'm catching a plane to Los Angeles soon enough."

"You'll want to see Chris before you go," Jacy said, holding the shoe box carefully. She could smell and hear the sea, and the patterns on the shells reminded her that there was a order in the universe. "He's over at our hotel right now. I'll go and get him."

Alice had had years of experience at giving orders, and the skill didn't fail her then. "Nonsense. You're on the verge of dropping over, you're that tuckered out. I'll find the place and the boy on my own after I'm through with that father of his."

Jacy smiled. "I'm going to miss you, Alice."

The housekeeper returned her smile. "You're the best thing that ever happened to Ian Yarbro," she said. "He's nothing but a fool if he ever lets you go."

Jacy didn't answer; she couldn't. She watched Alice walk away to join Nancy and Ian in the hospital room, then went to the elevator, the shoe box of memories and reassurances tucked under one arm.

After an hour or so Nancy and Alice came to the hotel. Alice and Chris went to have Devonshire tea together in the tiny restaurant downstairs, and Nancy occupied herself chatting with Regina. Like Alice, Jacy's mother had a seat reserved on a departing plane.

Following a brief nap, Jacy felt better. Almost strong again. She had spread the colorful seashells, gathered years ago on the beach at Queensland, and was admiring them when there was a knock at the door.

The visitor was Nancy.

"Well, then, you look a little better," she announced in her chiming voice.

"Tell me about Yolanda," Jacy said. "Did the fire get that far? Was anyone hurt?"

Nancy looked bone-weary. And reluctant. "The fire didn't actually reach us, no. But there was a shower of sparks—you can imagine it—and the buildings are all so old, and they all had tarpaper on the roofs . . ."

"Nancy," Jacy insisted.

"The schoolhouse is gutted, Jacy," Nancy admitted. "So is the church."

Jacy sank into a chair. The schoolhouse. Now, if Ian truly didn't relent, there would be no place, no place at all, for her to go back to.

Nancy rushed into the bathroom and returned shortly with a glass of water, which she shoved into her friend's hand. "You look awful, Jacy. What's the matter with you?"

Jacy made a sound that was half laughter, half sobbing. "I'm pregnant."

Nancy's response was a low whoop of joy. "But that's wonderful—why do you look as though tomorrow's been cancelled?"

Tears trickled down Jacy's face. In the presence of her friend she could weep without restraint, and she needed the release desperately. "Ian's decided he doesn't want us—the baby and me, I mean."

"That idiot," Nancy said in cheerful dismissal. "He's off his head from the fire, and being shot and everything. He doesn't mean a bit of what he's been saying."

"I know," Jacy sobbed, hugging herself now, and rocking back and forth. "But it still hurts!"

"Sure it does," Nancy agreed sympathetically. She went back to the bathroom, this time for a box of tissues. "Just cry to your heart's content, love," she said. "It'll do you good."

The storm passed quickly, but there was a small mountain of wadded tissues in Jacy's lap by the time it had blown over.

Nancy sat there in accepting silence, listening when Jacy wanted to talk, making no judgments, offering no solutions. Presently, when they'd been sitting in comfortable silence for some time, Nancy spoke again. "I thought it would be a good idea if I took Chris home with me," she said quietly. "I'll look after him until you and that hardheaded husband of yours come back."

Jacy nodded. "Has Ian agreed?"

"Yes," Nancy said.

A fearful thought occurred to Jacy. "What about Redley? Is he still running around on the loose?"

"Nobody's seen him," Nancy replied, frowning slightly. "For all I know, he's dead. The police have been over from Willoughby, though, looking for him. They mean to arrest him, of course, for what he did to Ian."

Jacy's mind was racing. "What if he tries to hurt Chris?" she asked, murmuring the words, believing, until she'd heard them herself, that she'd only thought them.

Nancy looked determined. And ferocious. "He won't," she said. "If Redley Shifflet comes near that child, I'll shoot him in the kneecaps. And if he doesn't already know that, he'll find it out soon enough!"

Jacy winced, but she knew she could trust Nancy to look

after Chris and keep him safe. Not that her opinion really mattered—Ian had all the say-so where his child was concerned.

It was a day for good-byes.

First Regina left, lovely and tearful, kissing Chris, commanding Jacy to call and write more often than she had so far. Then Alice went, having said her farewells to all of them, heading for America and the Golden West. And after that, Chris and Nancy departed for Yolanda with Collie.

Jacy, having had a nap, a good meal, and a shower, was better prepared to face Ian again that night.

He seemed subdued when she entered his room. His supper tray was sitting nearby, untouched, and he was staring out the window. If he heard her come in, he didn't look around.

She approached the bed, took his free hand in both of hers. "Everything's going to be okay," she said gently. "Trust me."

Ian turned his head and looked up into her eyes. The hostility was gone, but Jacy found herself regretting that. In its place was the sort of hopelessness she'd seen in Paul's face when he knew his life was over.

Tears gathered along Ian's lower lashes. "God, Jacy," he murmured. "You should have seen them lying there, all twisted and black."

Jacy knew he was talking about his beloved sheep, and she didn't flinch, didn't look away. Neither did she speak, because she sensed Ian needed for her to listen.

He swallowed convulsively, and one tear slipped down his right cheek. "And the land. Oh, Jesus, Jacy, the land— it's nothing but soot now."

The land would heal, but Jacy didn't say so. She held Ian's hand a little tighter, though, and raised it to her lips to brush the knuckles with a kiss.

The anguish in his eyes almost brought Jacy to her knees. Ian was no weakling; he'd been through a lot of grief and trouble in his twenty-eight years and withstood it all. He must have been suffering terribly to say such things now, she thought.

"I'll go to Queensland, like Jake was going to do. Chris would like it there if we were somewhere close to the water—"

Jacy knew these plans didn't include her, or the child growing under her heart, and the pain was fathomless. She hid it well. Her voice trembled only a little when she spoke.

"Don't be too hasty about this, darling," she said softly. "Wait until you're on your feet again before you make any drastic decisions. You've got to go back after you get well. When you do that you'll know the right thing to do."

Ian's only response was a glum nod. He went to sleep soon after, and Jacy sat with him until the doctor came and sent her back to the hotel with stern orders to rest.

Instead she held the seashells one by one, turning them in her hands, remembering, reflecting that life, with all its infinite variety of patterns and shapes, goes on. A quiet, determined sort of joy filled Jacy's heart; she had a great deal to be grateful for.

Jacy smiled and sat back in her chair, spreading one hand over her still-flat stomach, thinking of Ian and how much she loved him, and of Chris, and of her good friend Nancy.

Oh, yes. There was a great deal to be thankful for.

21

IAN HAD BEEN IN THE HOSPITAL FOR THREE WEEKS WHEN the doctor finally released him. He'd spent most of that time staring out the window, looking at Jacy as seldom as possible and speaking to her even less.

"Go home," he told her bluntly on the last morning.

"That's just what I intend to do," Jacy answered. She'd bought a few clothes for him, along with shaving gear and toiletries. Now she tossed the items into a satchel; they were all a-jumble, like her emotions. "Since the homestead at Corroboree Springs is gone, I'll have to see about getting a trailer—a caravan—for the McAllisters to live in until the place can be rebuilt. And then there's the school—all those books and things I ordered have probably arrived, and they'll need sorting—"

Ian was standing beside the bed, looking stiff and a little gaunt in his brand-new jeans and a cotton shirt that still had creases in it from being folded into a package. His knuckles went white where he gripped the steel railing with one hand. "Damn it, Jacy, that isn't what I meant by telling you to go home."

Jacy set her jaw. She'd been extraordinarily patient with Ian, but his sullen attitude was beginning to get on her nerves. "I know that perfectly well," she said. "You want me to fly back to the States, just like I did ten years ago, so you can *really* feel sorry for poor old Ian. No doubt you'd tell yourself, and a few trusted mates, that you were right about me all along—that I was a quitter and you were better rid of me." She paused, took a breath, met Ian's glare, and held it. "Well, I'm not going to make it that easy for you, Yarbro. I'm going back home, all right—to Yolanda. To our house, if it's still standing. I'm going to look around and see what needs to be done and then push up my sleeves and get started."

Ian was silent for a long time, just staring at her. His expression was unreadable. "You're a fool," he finally said, in a low tone laced with wonder as well as irritation.

Collie Kilbride chose exactly then to make his entrance. "Here, now," he said with nervous good cheer, "that's no way to talk to a lady, now, is it?" He looked around and then shuddered. "This place gives me the quivery-crawlies," he said, grabbing up Jacy's suitcases, packed earlier at the hotel, as well as Ian's satchel. "Let's get out of here."

"Go ahead, Collie," Jacy said quietly. "We'll meet you downstairs."

The pilot glanced anxiously from Jacy to Ian, then went out. No words passed between husband and wife, just a silent battle that neither won.

A nurse whisked in with a wheelchair, and Ian settled into it, his face grim, knowing a protest would only delay his escape from a place he plainly hated. Jacy walked alongside, chin high, shoulders straight, heart tremulous and fragile, ever-so-ready to break.

Collie had hired a minibus, and Ian insisted on riding in the front with his mate. Jacy climbed into the back and snapped on her seat belt without comment. She didn't give a damn where she sat as long as she could go home to the property she loved and all the dreams waiting there. Ian, on the other hand, would probably have made an issue of it, in the die-hard hope that he could still drive her off.

Collie whistled through his teeth while they drove out of the city and made their way over a bumpy road to a small private airfield. Collie's plane was there waiting, and while he was loading the baggage and making his routine engine check, Ian and Jacy waited in the minibus.

The air was thick with silence, with things that needed to be said and things better left unspoken. Finally Ian turned in the seat and looked back at her with bleak annoyance in his eyes.

"You don't have any idea what it's like to start over from nothing in the bush," he warned. "It'll be ten times worse than the hardest thing you've ever done."

Jacy was well aware of the challenges that faced her, faced all of them, and she was nervous and scared, but she wasn't about to reveal that. She'd write about it someday, she thought whimsically, in her memoirs.

"You're right," she agreed tautly. "I don't know what it's like to start over from nothing in the bush. And neither do you, if you'll excuse me for pointing it out. But we're sure as hell going to find out, aren't we?"

Ian muttered a swear word, wrenched open the door, and climbed shakily out of the vehicle.

Within fifteen minutes the ancient bomber was airborne. Nobody tried to talk—Ian was sulking, and Collie was caught up in the pure joy of flying, as always. Jacy sat rigidly in her seat, praying she wasn't making the mistake of a lifetime by going back to Yolanda, willing her stomach back down out of her throat every time the plane banked steeply to one side or the other.

After a little more than an hour they put down on the familiar, rutted landing strip outside of Yolanda. Jake's truck, now Jacy's property, was parked nearby, where Collie had probably left it when he departed for Adelaide.

Well, baby, Jacy thought, laying one hand on her lower

abdomen in a gesture of communion with her unborn child, we're home.

Ian opened the plane's door and climbed down over the wing. Although he was waiting to help Jacy to the ground, he didn't meet her eyes. Everything seemed hopeless just then, and Jacy's throat tightened painfully.

Maybe Ian meant it. Maybe he truly didn't want her around, didn't want their baby either.

She sniffled and silently reminded herself that this was the man who had gone to Adelaide at the age of nineteen to claim his infant son. This was the man who had raised that child with love and patience in the face of almost insurmountable difficulties. He'd wanted Chris, Ian had, and he wanted the new baby, too, though he was probably telling himself that the little one would be better off without him.

Not so, Jacy's heart insisted.

They got into the waiting truck, Collie driving, and set off toward the land Ian's grandfather had settled. Neither Jacy nor Ian knew exactly what they would find, and Collie wasn't volunteering anything. He just drove, whistling through his teeth again, and occasionally pounding out a beat on the steering wheel with one palm.

They bypassed Yolanda—Jacy intended to drive in on her own later, after Ian had had a chance to absorb whatever awaited him, to reclaim Chris, stop by Jake's grave, and view the remains of the schoolhouse.

At first everything seemed the same. The grass was dry and brown, the dirt red, the trees few and far between, straggly and twisted from lack of water. Then, abruptly, the landscape changed to a black and barren expanse where it seemed nothing could possibly live.

Sitting in the backseat, Jacy reached forward and laid a hand on Ian's shoulder when they turned onto his property. He didn't shrug away, to her great relief, but instead covered her fingers with his own.

The sheds were gone, just as Nancy had said, and so were the fences. Jacy felt Ian's muscles convulse under her palm, and she squeezed his shoulder, trying to offer some reassurance.

Nothing could have prepared either of them, Jacy thought, for the reality of seeing those blackened ruins.

Jacy squeezed her eyes shut for a moment, then swung her gaze to the homestead. Alice had said she'd saved it, but that didn't mean there was no damage.

Relief swept through Jacy. The once-white walls were charred and stained with soot, and part of the roof had burned through, but the structure itself stood strong and valiant under the blazing sun.

Ian pushed open the door of the truck and got out without saying a word. Collie turned to look questioningly at Jacy, and she managed a smile.

"It'll be okay," she said hoarsely, hoping God would back her up and make her brave words true.

She could insist on staying on the property, living in the house, but what if Ian barred her from his innermost self? What if he never let her in?

Ian didn't seem to notice the homestead. He wandered like a sleepwalker, slow-moving and dazed, between the twisted ebony skeletons of his beloved sheds.

Jacy got out, meaning to go to her husband and lead him away, but Collie stopped her, taking a light grip on her arm.

"Let him have a minute, love," he said.

Jacy swallowed hard, then nodded. Collie was right; Ian needed a little time to face the brunt of his grief. She got some of her baggage out of the back of the truck and went into the scarred but triumphant house. Collie followed, bringing in the rest of the baggage.

Moving slowly, tears slipping down her cheeks, Jacy walked along the hallway to Chris's room. After taking a moment to gather her courage, she opened the door and looked in.

Everything was the same except for a faint odor of smoke, and the whole house smelled of that.

She moved along, finally, to the bedroom she and Ian had shared. She stood in the doorway, her heart full of love and fear and memories. This room, too, had been spared—this precious room where she and Ian had joined themselves together in passion and conceived the child nestled inside her now.

Jacy hadn't heard Ian approaching, and she was startled when she turned to leave and found him standing directly behind her. He didn't speak, but his eyes said everything as they searched Jacy's face.

She gave a soft cry and put her arms around him, laying her cheek to his chest, careful not to press against the healing wound. It was hard and warm, Ian's chest, and she felt his heart beating.

"Oh, Ian," she whispered raggedly, clinging to him. "Let me love you. Please, please—don't turn your back on everything we could have and do and be together—"

He stood stiffly for the longest time, but then she felt him relent a little, and she gave a strangled sob of pure, joyous relief. Ian's arms tightened around her, drawing her close, and she felt his breath in her hair.

"God help me," he murmured, "I've tried not to need you, Jacy, not to love you. But I can't stop the feelings— they're as elemental as the bushfire that ravaged this place."

She pulled back, stared up into his face, afraid to believe she'd heard him correctly. "You *love* me? You did say that—in a roundabout way—didn't you?"

Ian smiled, that slow, slanted smile that always made her heart do a little leaping pirouette, but in the next instant his expression turned solemn again. "Yes," he said gravely. "I love you. But such fine sentiments aren't always enough out here. This is hard country, Jacy—"

Jacy stood on tiptoes and kissed his chin. He needed a shave, and his skin felt rough against her lips. "We'll nurture our love, Ian," she said, "and it will grow and grow until it's bigger than anything this land can do to us."

He touched her nose, his mouth still tilted at one side, but there were shadows in his blue eyes. "It's going to be hard work rebuilding this place, love."

She stepped back and pushed up her sleeves. "Let's get started," she said with a toss of her head and a watery smile.

Ian laughed and caught her face in his hands. "Crazy little Yank," he murmured, and then he bent his head and kissed her with such thoroughness that she sagged against the doorjamb when it was over, dazed.

"I'd better go to town and get Chris," she said when she caught her breath.

Ian took her hand and pulled her over the threshold, into the cool, spacious room with its simple furniture and its silent echoes of passion and promises.

"Not just yet," he said, pushing the door closed behind them.

Jacy leaned back against it, closing her eyes, surrendering as Ian opened her blouse button by button. They hadn't made love in weeks, and their need was desperate. Within a few minutes they were on the bed, both of them naked, flinging themselves at each other in the lush violence of their love.

Jacy came first, crying out and arching high off the bedcovers. While her body bucked and strained beneath him Ian groaned and stiffened, the muscles in his neck cording as he plunged deep into her warmth and spilled himself there.

Afterward they lay entwined in each other's arms. Ian soon tumbled into an exhausted sleep, and Jacy held him, smiling and crying, promising herself and all the angels in heaven that she would make this marriage work no matter what she had to do.

Perhaps an hour had passed when Jacy slipped from Ian's embrace and put her clothes back on. He stirred but didn't awaken, and she bent to kiss his forehead, and the scar where Redley's bullet had entered his chest, before covering him with a lightweight blanket.

Ian opened his eyes, looked at her without recognition, and sank into sleep again.

Jacy loved him so much in that moment that she ached with the emotion, wondered if she could endure the depth and purity and sharpness of it.

She went into the kitchen and found Collie at the table, drinking beer and working a crossword puzzle in an old newspaper. She hoped he hadn't been inside long enough to hear her and Ian making love—it hadn't occurred to either of them, in the wildness of their wanting, to try to be quiet—and then put the idea out of her mind.

She invited her father's old friend to stay for tea, picked up the truck keys from the counter, and left the house before he could accept or decline.

During the drive to Yolanda she kept the window rolled down, despite the dust and the smell of burned grass, and tried to prepare herself for the trauma she still had to face—the burned-out school building.

It was a quietly horrible sight, and Jacy stood at the burned and crumbling gate ten minutes later, weeping. Then she proceeded to the Yolanda Café.

Chris ran to her when she stepped into the restaurant and flung himself into her arms, and just holding him tightly was a consolation.

After a long time he drew back and looked up at her. "Is my dad all right?"

Jacy smiled and ruffled his silky hair. "Sleeping like a baby," she said as Nancy came out of the back to join them. Her smile, while welcoming, was rather tentative, too.

"The police came out from Willoughby yesterday," Chris burst out before Jacy could question her friend's subdued manner. "They took Darlis away."

Jacy stiffened. "Darlis?" she asked, looking from the child to Nancy and back again. "Why?"

317

"She killed Redley," Chris replied.

Jacy's knees threatened to give way. She groped for a chair and sagged into it. "She—"

"Killed Redley," Nancy confirmed, bringing two diet colas to the table and sitting down across from Jacy. "He came home from dogging, full of rum and hate, and proceeded to beat her. She picked up his rifle and shot him between the eyes."

Jacy felt sick. She'd despised Redley Shifflet, but even at his most dangerous she'd never wished him dead. "Poor Darlis," she whispered, reaching for her bottle of cola with a shaky hand. "What will happen to her?"

"Nothing, I hope," Nancy answered. "We're all set to testify, Sara and me and a lot of others, that Darlis was off her head when she did it. Besides, she was only defending herself, now, wasn't she?" She paused, looking at Jacy with affection and concern. "How's Ian?"

Jacy answered only after Chris had lost interest and gone off to play with one of the portable video games Regina had bought for him. "Almost his old self," she said with a small grin.

Nancy laughed. "Lucky girl," she said. She sat back in her chair and studied Jacy for an interval before speaking again. "I guess you've seen the schoolhouse—or what remains of it."

Jacy nodded, feeling choked up all over again. She wondered what she was going to do with all the books, supplies, and equipment she'd ordered in Adelaide before Ian's shooting. The stuff would begin arriving any day.

Nancy grinned somewhat mischievously. "No worries, love—we've taken over the old institute—the women of Yolanda, I mean—and cleaned it from top to bottom. It'll do just fine until the government helps us get another school built, won't it?"

Jacy gave a burst of laughter, then a sob, and covered her mouth with one hand. "Yes—oh, yes!"

Nancy leaned forward and whispered in a confidential

tone, "The men are still a little unsure about you, Mrs. Yarbro, but the fire and what happened to Ian got them all to thinking about what's really important. They've troubles enough of their own, God bless them, but they're that set on helping Ian get a new hay shed put up. With Tom McAllister's help they've been gathering up those dratted brumbies of Ian's, too."

Jacy was overcome. She folded her arms on the table, laid her head down on them, and wailed.

"What's wrong with her?" she heard Chris ask.

"She's happy," Nancy replied, sounding surprised at the question.

The next few weeks were busy ones.

The supplies Jacy had ordered in Adelaide began arriving by mail, and the satellite dish and television set came by truck. She called a man in Willoughby—Bram gave her the name—and bought a caravan, sight unseen, for the McAllisters to live in over at Corroboree Springs. The men of Yolanda repaired the hole in the roof of the Yarbros' house and, with the help of crews called in from all over the bush, erected new outbuildings.

Darlis Shifflet was released from jail, after a hearing, on the grounds that she'd acted in self-defense. She didn't return to Yolanda but instead went to Darwin to be with Gladys.

There was a long letter from Margaret Wynne, Jake's lady friend in Queensland, full of love and grief and funny stories about the times she and Jake had shared. Jacy liked the woman even without meeting her.

One by one those brumbies that hadn't already been brought home by neighbors wandered back to the property and stood watching while the new sheds and fences went up. Jacy and Ellie McAllister spent most of their time cooking for the workmen who swarmed over both the Yarbro place and Corroboree Springs, but when they could they sneaked into the living room and watched soap operas on the television set.

A full month had passed before Jacy could bring herself to drive over to Corroboree and face the destruction there. She cried when she saw the rubble that had once been her father's home, and hers as well, and went down to the spring to crouch beside the water.

The grass that had thrived there before had been burned away, but when Jacy took a closer look at the ground she saw tiny specks of green poking up through the soot. She smiled at the reminder that life is born of catastrophe, that joy comes from trouble and hope from despair.

Only then did Jacy truly believe her own prophecies. Everything really *was* going to be all right.

She lingered there for a time beside the bubbling spring until it restored her. Then she walked back to the truck, parked where Jake's front yard had been, started the engine, and headed for home.

The workmen and neighbors were gone by the time she arrived, and she found Ian leaning against the new raw-wood rails of the fence, watching his beloved brumbies. He turned and watched Jacy walk toward him, stuffing the truck keys into the pocket of her worn jeans as she moved.

"You again?" he asked, but he was grinning under the brim of his hat. It was a new one, since the other had been lost the day Redley Shifflet shot him, but it had already been thrown down and stomped on enough to look properly disreputable.

Jacy linked her arm through his. "Me again," she said. "And always."

He turned her to face him and, hooking his index fingers in the belt loops of her jeans, tugged her against him. He was just bending his head to kiss her when they heard an engine in the distance and broke apart.

The fancy Land Rover from Merimbula swung into the yard and came to a stop a few yards away.

Ian cursed under his breath and prepared himself for another bout with Andrew Carruthers. Wilson Tate was driving, but the man who got out on the passenger side was nobody Jacy recognized.

A tall man with glossy brown hair and friendly amber-gold eyes came toward them, smiling. Even before he opened his mouth Jacy knew by the visitor's cowboy-style clothes that he was an American. Maybe, she reflected, Alice had left Australia too soon.

"Jack's the name," he said. "Jack Keegan."

Ian frowned at the Land Rover and then at the cowboy. "We don't want to sell, if that's what you've come round for," he said.

Jacy gave her husband a nudge for being so rude and opened her mouth to offer Mr. Keegan a cold drink, but he cut her off before she could say a word.

"Didn't come about that," he told them cheerfully. "No, sir, I figure I'm going to have my hands full straightening out Merimbula. This is no time to think about expanding."

A silence fell. Jacy figured Ian was probably as stunned as she was.

It was Wilson Tate who explained. Getting out of the Land Rover, he came to stand beside Mr. Keegan, smiling around the matchstick he was chewing. "Mr. Keegan here just bought Merimbula from the corporation. Sent old Andy Carruthers packing straightaway."

Ian was confounded—Jacy heard it in the sigh he gave, saw it in the way he fiddled with his hat brim. "Well, then," he said at last, a grin breaking over his face as he extended a hand to Jack Keegan, "welcome to the back end of nowhere."

Keegan laughed, and the two men shook hands. It was another beginning, Jacy thought. She wondered if Jack had a wife, then remembered Nancy and hoped he didn't.

Maybe she'd try her hand at matchmaking.

She invited the American to stay for dinner, along with Wilson Tate, of course, and he accepted, as Collie had earlier. Throughout the meal Ian kept glancing at her, and she pretended not to notice.

Late that night, though, after she and Ian had made love, he asked her, none to subtly, what she thought of Jack Keegan.

Jacy smiled and snuggled close to her husband. "I think he'd be perfect for Nancy," she said. "As a matter of fact, I plan to introduce them first chance I get."

Ian laughed, and Jacy heard relief in the sound, and she loved her husband that much more for being a little jealous and insecure. "I thought you'd learned your lesson about meddling in other people's business," he said, pinning her gently beneath him, entwining his fingers with hers and pressing her hands into the pillow on either side of her head.

She knew her eyes were sparkling. "Whatever made you think that?" she asked.

He kissed her, and that was another new beginning.

With June came the winter, and Jacy's belly was round as a basketball. She'd had tests in Willoughby that day, and her doctor had told her the baby was a little girl, but she hadn't relayed the news to Ian yet. She was lying in their bed savoring the news, letting it shine warmly in her heart.

Ian came in, fresh from the shower, naked except for the towel around his waist, and walked over to stand next to the bed, looking down at her.

"Still there, then?" he teased with a half grin. He said the same thing every night; it was a game they played, one of those silly rituals that mean so little and yet so much in a marriage.

Jacy grinned back, spreading her hands over her protruding belly. "Still here," she confirmed, as she always did. "And I'm not alone, either."

Ian bent to kiss her bare, mountainous stomach, and she

322

blushed because the gesture aroused her immediately. Fiercely.

He lifted his head, saw the flush under her skin and the blaze of passion in her eyes, and gave a great, heaving sigh full of drama. "Nothing for it," he said, with airy resignation. "You'll be wanting my lovemaking now, won't you?"

"Yes," she said, trembling as he drew down the sheet to admire her. To possess her with his eyes. "Yes," she said again, with just the faintest note of urgency in her voice.

Ian took her gently by the hips and turned her so that she lay crosswise on the bed. Then he knelt between her legs, stroking her inner thighs lightly with the tips of his fingers.

"Ian."

"Shhh," he said, caressing her stomach now, lifting her right leg over his shoulder, then her left. Then he bent to her, and took her into his mouth. She arched her back and cried out, but the winter wind absorbed the sound—or was it the other way around?

Jacy heaved under Ian's mouth, her fingers tangled in his hair, moaning as he pleasured her. He was invariably gentle, especially now that she was big with their child, and yet he insisted on her satisfaction every time they made love and drove her mercilessly until she achieved at least one shattering climax. That night was no exception.

She was still gasping when he mounted her and slid into her receiving warmth. As she welcomed him a light, rhythmic rain began to fall, the kind that nurtures the earth and prepares it for spring.

BW